Alyssa Astray

SAGE MALLORY®

THE *Alyssa* SERIES

Published by Cardinal Wellingham

ISBN: 979-8-9909085-4-3

ALSO BY SAGE MALLORY

Alyssa Awakens

Alyssa Arrives

For Baby, who indulges my whims with love

ALYSSA ASTRAY

vii

Author's note: This story occurs after the events of *Alyssa Awakens* and *Alyssa Arrives*. While this story can stand alone in conjunction with *Alyssa Atones*, you will understand the backstory, motivations, and interpersonal interaction better if you have read those two books first. Either way, enjoy!

1

SUNDAY, MAY 2, HOME

"Hold right there, Babe. Let me get used to you." Alyssa put her hand behind her ass to touch Robert's hip, letting him know not to push forward. *He fills my ass so well.*

"I'm about halfway in, Baby. Let me know when you're ready for more."

She purred. "You feel so good, I want you to just ram me, but let's go slower than what I want."

"I won't hurt your ass. Besides, you haven't moved slowly on what you want since February."

Alyssa raised her face from the mattress to look over her shoulder at her husband. "I don't know about that. I let you catch up after I got home from that trip." She relaxed her hand and returned her chest to the mattress. "Go ahead. Give me some more."

Robert pushed forward until Alyssa moaned and touched

his hip again. "A couple of inches left, Baby. And I disagree that you waited. You promised to sleep with Jessica so she would help bring me along, remember? And after I caught up, you went fast and hard for a while."

"True. I jumped into the deep end of the pool and stayed there for two months. I've been more deliberate with my partners since then, right?"

"You mean in the last month? Perhaps, though you were vague about what you did at the cybersecurity conference in DC last week."

Alyssa raised her head to glare at him. A spark of anger kindled in her belly. She let it seep into her tone. "You know I needed multiple opinions to verify what the first surveillance specialist showed me. They were actual spies, after all."

"Spies? They were techno geeks from the NSA. Don't make it sound like you were playing Jane Bond, sleeping with the enemy for queen and country." Robert patted her ass and smiled at her. "I said you were vague; I didn't accuse you of lying to me."

The anger diminished, and she winked before lowering her head. "I'll talk as soon as you torture me with that big tool in my ass." She braced against the mattress. "Give me the rest. I'm ready."

Robert eased farther into Alyssa's ass until his abs touched her cheeks. "That's all of it, Baby."

"Mm. I know. You feel so good in there." She reached under her pillow and pulled out a familiar dildo. "I want this in me at the same time." She handed it backward while keeping her chest on the mattress.

Robert laughed. "You want me in two places at once. When Jessica and I made those, I underestimated how often you would use yours."

"It keeps me company when I can't have you. And I love

getting the real thing at the same time. Let me put it in, then fuck my ass, Babe." Alyssa brought the tip of the custom dildo to her pussy, still wet and open where Robert had pulled out before entering her ass. Her walls rippled as she filled herself in one long shove, making her gasp. *So full. I love this.* "Okay, Babe. Ride me."

Robert pulled back until just the head of his cock remained inside her sphincter, then shoved into her. He gave her all his cock and ground his hips against hers, brushing his balls against her hand holding the silicone replica of the cock in her ass.

Alyssa moaned into the mattress and pushed back against him. They built speed as Alyssa's ass relaxed. Robert pounded into her as she used her hand to move the rubber cock against her cervix. Her breasts rubbed against the sheet as her body moved. Her hard nipples screamed at her as the friction burned an electric path between them and her clit, starting a fire in her belly. The pressure in her ass acted like a bellows for that fire every time Robert pushed forward. She raced to orgasm.

"I'm close, Babe. Don't stop!" She ground against him on every stroke, using one hand to move the dildo and the other to strum her clit. *Oh god. So good. Him in both holes is amazing. If only he could come in both at the same time.*

Robert pounded her ass. "I'm close, Baby. Where do you want my cum?"

"In me. Deep. Don't stop." She pinched her clit hard and pulled it when she jammed the dildo into herself as far as it would go. She pushed back against Robert. She wailed as her climax burst from her pussy. Fluid ran down her thighs and over her hand. She arched her back, changing the angle of Robert's cock inside her, and she felt like he would burst through her back as he kept fucking her hard, pulling her hips with both hands. Her pelvic muscles spasmed, clenching Robert's cock in her ass and its silicone replica in her pussy at the same time, driving her pleasure higher.

Alyssa's wail faded as her lungs emptied, but she didn't inhale. Instead, her mind overloaded on the fullness, the touch of one cock beside her cervix, stretching her pussy while it gripped at it, the other swelling, stretching her ass open and pressing deep in her guts. Her eyes locked open, unseeing. Robert's cum filled her ass, providing the last stimulation driving her orgasm. Her legs extended, and her belly moved to the mattress, Robert following his cock down with her to lie on her back. When he settled gently on top of her, she gasped and closed her eyes. She mumbled "more" as her breathing slowed.

Alyssa snuggled against Robert after she regained her senses. "That was so good, Babe. Having you in my ass and Little Robert in my pussy? I loved it."

Robert laughed. "I know. And Clay knows it, for sure. Maybe the neighbors too."

"Was I that loud?"

"Like a jet engine."

The flash of embarrassment rolled her stomach like a sudden drop, and vanished just as quickly. "Oh well. He and Susan have heard us for years. It shouldn't be a surprise to him tonight."

"Hearing his mom yell 'fuck my ass' is new."

"Probably. I won't apologize; I loved it too much. If it bothers him, we'll talk. He is comfortable with uncomfortable subjects lately." She kissed his shoulder and looked at his face. "Are you ready for tomorrow night? You have the toughest job."

"I'm not excited about it. I don't want to watch those guys use you, but I need to repay them for what they did. I wish there were another way. And your job won't be easy either. Three of them at once? You remember what happened last time."

"This time, you'll be there to collect me before it gets ugly."

"I will, but our plan starts at ugly. A lot can go wrong. Are you sure what those NSA people told you still works?"

"It can't go worse than last time. We have tested that process time and again, and it worked every time. It had better work, given how much I fucked them for it. You would have liked the girl. She was hot."

"You never said. How much did you do?"

She had not wanted to tell him the full extent of what she did at the conference, but she would not lie. She did what she had to do and a bit more, even knowing he would find it excessive. His practical side would outweigh his disappointment at her actions.

"The first guy just once, plus a blow job in the stairwell, all on the first day. The second guy kept me up most of the first night in his room. Every orifice, multiple times. He was good with his dick and made me come a ton. He must have come six or seven times. Young guys." She smiled. "I spent the second night with the woman. She kissed my sore pussy and made it better before I came home to you the next morning. I liked her best."

"How did you have time to learn the technique? I only reclaimed you three times that day. Do I still need to do some work?"

"Oh, Babe, you had me from the first time. And you have given me such good loving since then. We are good. You are still first in my mind, and you are always first in my heart." She patted his chest. "Those assholes tomorrow, they are first on my shit list. I can't wait to get even. Even if I fuck them all night to make this happen, they need to pay."

"They do."

"And you will reclaim me after? No matter how much it hurts?"

"We have been through this before. If you are sore, we can wait."

"Robert, I'll endure anything to come back to you. Besides, Keegan will be at the hotel. I might have to reclaim you from her that night too."

"More likely I'll have to reclaim you from her."

She smiled. "Maybe. If so, can we reclaim each other together?"

"Double duty? Sounds very efficient."

Alyssa laughed. "We don't want efficiency. We want the most pleasure. Maybe we'll just take each other twice. One for me, one for you."

"Deal." Robert sighed. "We have to get through the night first."

"We will, Baby. Then they will pay."

2

MONDAY, MAY 3, EMBASSY SUITES

Alyssa readied her thoughts when she felt Robert take a deep breath. His next words would be about tonight, and she knew most of her answers would hurt him. She had thought about what to say and what not to say for a week. She had her mental lists ready, one to discuss and one to bury. She didn't want to hurt him, but she knew that hiding her thoughts and feelings would hurt him more than being honest. At least tactfully honest. Brutally honest would be cruel.

"Are you sure you want to do this?" Robert held his wife as she leaned back against him on the hotel bed.

"I do. Are you sure you can do this?"

"I don't know. Watching you with these three assholes, knowing what happened last time, will be almost impossible. Can I just bring a big hammer?"

Alyssa laughed. "No, Babe. I want to hurt them too. You

bring your brilliant mind, and we will hurt them more than we could with a hammer.”

“I swing pretty hard, you know.”

“I know, Babe. Let’s stick to the plan though.” She lifted his hand to kiss his fingertips. “It will be over soon, and we can celebrate.”

“Revenge isn’t something to celebrate. They will get what they deserve, but I doubt we will feel good doing it.”

First honesty point. Tell him what you think, but help him stay on board. She lowered her voice like low volume made it less true. “Well…I might feel good.”

“What?”

She sighed and looked over her shoulder at her husband. Keeping her voice low, she spoke, trying to keep any excitement buried. “I am, after all, going to get fucked senseless. I will like it. I’ll feel slimy afterward, but if it is anything like last time, you will have to forcibly stop me when you’re done. I’m sorry, Babe. My body doesn’t know everything my brain knows.”

Robert’s face flushed red. “Jesus, Alyssa. This is hard enough without that kind of commentary. Maybe I can’t do this after all.”

Her guts knotted, as she was afraid he would back out. “Sorry, Babe. I want to be honest with you. If it makes you feel better, my brain wants you to pull me out as soon as everything is complete, not a second later. To hell with what my body wants.” *Now he’ll be angry enough to leave his qualms at the door. As if he won’t be when he watches the show.*

“I didn’t need to think about that.”

She stroked his cheek. “I’m sorry, really. I’ll make it up to you later.” Her phone dinged with a text. “They’re here. I’d better get dressed. I love you, Babe.”

“Love you too.”

❧

Alyssa felt, more than saw, eyes shift to her when she entered the hotel bar. She had chosen the short skirt and four-inch heels to emphasize her lean legs, and the sheer blouse revealed a hint of nipple. She stood in the doorway, knowing the backlighting from the lobby would show the outer swell of her breasts. She scanned the crowd with her eyes but kept her head still, searing her silhouette into the minds of those inside.

Ninety seconds later, Robert approached her from behind, and Alyssa led him to the seats she had selected. Her long exhale through her nose belied her calm smile. *Stay calm. Don't look too eager.* She waved at the bartender. "Gin and tonic, please."

"Alyssa—"

"Just one, Babe, for courage."

"Okay. It's going to be a long night. Be careful." He looked at the bartender. "Maker's and water for me."

The tall redhead brought their drinks. "You certainly made an entrance." She nodded her head toward the end of the bar. "Those three stopped talking to me midsentence. You got their attention. They didn't talk again until Robert walked up. They are targeting me, it seems. Pretty empty tonight."

"Thanks, Keegan." Alyssa took a long slug from her drink. "After a couple more rounds, send them a round on me."

"Will do." Keegan looked at Robert. "You okay with this?"

"No. And yes. Thanks for your help."

An hour later, Robert ducked out to the restroom, and the tallest of the three men led his group to Alyssa's seat. "Thank you for the drink, beautiful lady. The last time we saw you, you were a little more disheveled, but perhaps a bit more satisfied?"

Alyssa forced the corners of her mouth up like she was fighting a smile, but it covered the anger burning in her chest. *Sexually satisfied. Psychologically abused, you piece of shit.* "I remember. 'Satisfied' might not be the right term. 'Devastated' sounds more like it."

The men laughed. The tall man spoke for his colleagues. "We gave you what you asked for. And you kept asking for it."

Alyssa smirked and nodded. She wanted revenge for what they did, but she remembered the pleasure. He needed to see that she liked it. "I did. And you three delivered. It was a hot night."

"One we won't forget." He looked up. "Your husband is coming back. Before we leave you two alone, I wanted to ask your name."

"No names."

"All right, then. You two have a good night."

"You don't have to leave because my husband is coming. Why do you think I bought your drinks? Have a seat."

The three men looked at one another, then the tall one sat beside Alyssa. The other two stood behind them.

Robert sat in the empty seat on Alyssa's other side. "Are these your friends, hon?"

Alyssa spoke without turning away from the tall man. "Yes. These men gave us that great night a couple of months ago. Say thank you."

"Thank you, gentlemen. It was an experience I'll never forget."

The three men looked quizzically at one another.

Alyssa leaned between the three men. "My husband knows that sometimes I am, shall we say, uninhibited. Knowing the three of you had me while he waited drove him wild. This is the third time we have come here looking to encounter you again. I'm glad we caught you tonight."

"You are? Interesting." The tall man smiled and placed his hand on Alyssa's thigh.

Those perfect teeth. She smiled at him and placed her hand on his thigh. "Yes. We were thinking of a repeat performance with my husband watching."

"You want your husband to watch?"

"I want to get obliterated, like before. He wants to watch, which is his decision, at least until I decide he can't."

The blond man standing finally spoke. "That's a weird arrangement."

Alyssa frowned at him. "No more unusual than your hanging around with your giant-dicked friend here, getting scraps of the action he generates. Don't judge what excites us, remora."

She turned back to the tall man. "Your friend's cognitive dissonance could stop a train." She eased her hand up his thigh over the tip of his cock. "It's a work night. We can't stay too late, which means we need to get started if we are going to play. I'm offering to let you three have a wild time with my body. You interested?"

The tall man ran his hand far under her skirt. Disgust didn't stop the shocks running along the skin of her thigh where his fingertips grazed her. She knew where this would lead and how it would feel, and her pussy was preparing.

He smiled at learning she wore no panties. Alyssa gasped when his finger opened her and the shocks he had released on her thighs congregated on her lips. He trailed his hand out and sucked his glistening finger. "I don't know. I thought we would finally get together with the redhead. She's new territory, and on her own. Why don't you leave your husband down here?"

"No dice. We're a package deal. He's willing to share me with you three, but he gets to be there." Alyssa nodded at Keegan behind the bar. "If you want, bring her along. We want to start now; she can tag in after her shift when I leave, I don't care. I want you guys again. I've never come so much in my life." *Come on, jerk. Bite. I've made my whole play. Take the bait.* She squeezed the end of his cock. "This is saying yes. You ready?"

He turned to Keegan, who had been nearby. "You've been listening, Red. What do you say? Are you still interested, even with this kink?"

The tall redhead leaned over the bar. "I was already willing to fuck your henchmen to get that log of yours. If I have to let him watch, I'll do that too. I like beautiful girls like her, if you need a show while you recover. Can you keep it up for both of us?"

"With both of you? Yeah. I'll be a steel bar all night. So will these two. Are you in?"

"I would feel bad saying I want that big cock of yours, if you didn't proposition me with it in the first place. It's impressive enough to entice me to join this orgy. I'm in. I'll come up."

The tall man handed her a key card. "Room 1236, a couple of hours. I can't wait to feel you and fill you." He turned back to Alyssa. "I'm hard for you, too, even with your husband watching. You are already wet. Let's go."

Alyssa stood. The tall man palmed her ass and held it as the five of them walked to the elevator. When the door closed, Alyssa embraced Robert, kissing his cheek. "Thank you for letting me do what I need to do tonight. Watch me. Watch over me, hon."

He kissed her cheek and patted her hip, the final signal that they should proceed. "I will."

She released him and moved in front of the two accompanying the tall man. She cupped their dicks through their pants. "You boys ready? You going to fill all my holes? You going to come on me? In me?"

The blond man answered. "Oh yeah. We are going to make

you pass out again and paint you with cum. You won't walk straight for a week."

Robert turned to the tall man. "She can't stop talking about you. I am looking forward to seeing you make her come. Do you mind if I get a little video? We will enjoy it for a long time."

The tall man shook his head. "You are a weird dude, but if you want proof that your wife climaxes better for me than for you, go ahead."

The doors opened, and the five of them walked down the hall and around the corner to the men's suite. The door closed, and everyone paused. Alyssa pointed to a chair across the room. "Hon, you sit there. You can watch everything that happens in here, but when we go to the bedroom, you only get to listen. Understand?"

Robert moved to the chair. "Yes, hon."

She moved in front of the tall man, cupping his cock. "Let's start. I want this inside me." She kissed him while she unbuckled his belt.

He pushed her back and grabbed the center of her blouse with both hands. He yanked, tearing the thin fabric down the middle. He jerked it off her shoulders and down her arms. Alyssa gasped and let the fabric fall to the floor. "God, yes." She leered at the tall man, who gripped the waist of her skirt, jerked it to pop the flimsy clasp and zipper, and dropped it on the shredded blouse. Standing in only stockings and high heels, she smirked. "That makes me wet, big man." The three men stood still, and she knelt. "Give me some cock."

The tall man stepped to her face, freeing a stiff cock almost the size of a can of tennis balls from his pants. Alyssa licked her lips and opened her mouth. *That's what I want.* She stretched to get the head inside her mouth while the other two men stripped naked beside their friend. Alyssa pulled down the tall man's pants and briefs, letting them pool at his ankles, before sliding one hand to her pussy to alternate between strumming her clit and fingering herself. *I'm dripping wet, but I need to loosen up. I want this cock in me soon.*

Alyssa worked the large cock in her mouth, letting her drool run down the shaft to slicken it. She let the head pop from her mouth and licked from the tip, down the shaft, to the balls, which she took, one by one, into her mouth, sucking them. She licked back up one side of the length and down the other, spreading more spit on it. She returned to the head and dove her mouth onto it, not stopping until the tip tickled the back of her throat, gagging her and bringing up a load of thick slobber that oozed from her mouth over the intruder. His cock grew in her mouth, reaching full hardness. Alyssa stood and moved to the couch, kneeling on all fours. She looked at the tall man, who was stepping out of his shoes and pants. "I'm ready. Fill me with that monster."

The tall man moved behind Alyssa and rubbed the head of his cock along her slit, spreading her open and smearing her juices on his head. He tapped her clit from below, making her ass clench. When he moved the tip back over her opening, he pressed forward as she pushed back. After a momentary catch, the head slid inside, and Alyssa gasped at the pain in her lips as they stretched. *So big. Tearing me apart.* She rocked forward, then back, meeting his next slow advance. Her eyes closed, and her head dipped. When she raised her head, she pushed back again.

"That's about half." The tall man patted her ass. "Keep going. You know you can take it all, slut. That is what you are tonight, a slut?"

"Yes. Tonight I'm a slut. I want your cock in me, and another one too." She looked at the two other men who were close by, watching, and at full hardness. "Come on, guys. Give me something to scream around."

The dark-haired man moved faster than his companion and stood with one foot on the couch in front of Alyssa while the blond man moved beside her to cup her breast and pinch her nipple. The dark-haired man tapped her cheek with his cock, and she engulfed him. When she pulled back, she took more of the huge cock into her pussy. It tapped her cervix, and she moaned. She rocked back and forth a minute, taking all of one cock into her throat and more of the large cock into her crackling pussy. *Here I go.*

A guttural noise came from her throat, her muscles flexed, her back arched, her arms tensed, and she came, sending more lubrication over the last inch of the cock stretching her vagina in every direction. The man in her mouth gripped her hair with both hands and thrust in her mouth as she shook. This pushed her back, finally touching her ass cheeks to the tall man's hips. She moaned and spasmed again.

Several seconds passed with the cock in her pussy still and the one in her mouth pounding her throat. Alyssa gagged and drooled, then felt the cock swell on her tongue. The first jet hit the back of her throat, then she pulled back enough to catch the rest in her mouth before swallowing it. When the dark-haired man pulled out to swap places with the blond man, Alyssa looked at her husband in the chair across the room. "Is this what you wanted to see, hon? To see me as the slut I am? Take a good look. Get some video if you want it for later. After the other two come, you only get to listen and imagine." *Get some video, Baby. I'll hide my face.*

⁂

"It is what I want, honey. You look so hot." Robert stood and took out his phone.

As Alyssa swallowed the cock in front of her, the tall man pulled back and began fucking her, driving her forward and keeping her face in the abdomen of the blond man.

Robert raised his phone and moved closer. The camera over the blond man's shoulder showed Alyssa's sexy back and firm ass rocking between the two men on the screen. The tall man leered at Robert's camera and slapped Alyssa's ass. She jumped, but the men used their hands on her head and hips to restore a steady rhythm.

"This is so hot, and you guys don't even break stride." Robert started his video. "Do you share women a lot?"

The dark-haired man turned to Robert. "Every city we're in, man. Women find out what Dave is packing, and they do anything to get it. They take two at a time, three at a time, bring a friend or two. They just want that huge dick, and we make them pay for it, any way we like."

The tall man, Dave, looked at Robert's camera. "Few of them are like this one. She couldn't move, almost passed out from sex, she was covered in cum so she couldn't even see, and all she said was 'more.' This slut wanted it bad."

Robert moved beside Dave, capturing the blond man driving his cock forward, with his hands entwined in Alyssa's hair. He laughed, waved, then returned his hand to her head. "Yeah. I can't wait to use her ass again. It was so tight, and she loved it when I spanked her hard. She is some slut."

He stopped his video. "She is amazing," Robert replied, then started filming again, moving closer to her stretched pussy and the froth-covered cock pounding it. He backed up to capture the red handprint on her jiggling ass and the sweat on her back. He moved around, filming her nipple being stretched away from her body by the dark-haired man, then close to her mouth, careful to keep the rest of her face out of the frame. He wanted to show her taking all of it, and he stayed close to capture the audio of her moans and breathing as she neared another climax.

She pushed back, fucking Dave just as much as he was fucking her. A low whine began in her chest and continued until she gasped in a quick breath, then it resumed. Her neck flushed red. The veins and tendons stood out. She gasped one more breath between thrusts and groaned loudly while her body shook. The men didn't stop driving their cocks into her from both ends, and her sensitive body extended its release. Her arms gave out, but the dark-haired man switched from fondling her tits to supporting her by them as his buddies kept fucking her.

The blond man stiffened. Robert moved his camera closer to Alyssa's mouth. The thrusting stopped, followed by a grunt. The camera caught the small portion of his cock outside Alyssa's mouth throbbing, then the waterfall of semen and saliva that fell from Alyssa's lip to the cushion below. She sputtered and coughed when he pulled out.

The dark-haired man lowered her chest to the couch, leaving her at an obscene angle with her ass in the air and her face in the puddle of cum and drool. Dave stood taller to pound down into her, driving her chest and face into the cushions. He stiffened and went deep into her, yelling as he came inside her.

Alyssa slid forward on the couch, pulling off the giant cock as she did. She kept her eyes closed and said, "More. Fuck me more."

Robert stopped his video and moved back to the chair. The three men sat in silence, staring at Alyssa. Dave stood and looked at Robert. "She said after we came she wanted to go to the bedroom and fuck some more. I'm going to carry her in there and do just that when she wakes up a little. You can come watch, but I think she wanted you to just listen. Your call."

"I'm awake, just enjoying the feeling. He stays out here." She opened her eyes to look at Robert. "I'm going to fuck all of them at once. You stay here and be a good husband."

Dave lifted her off the couch and slung her over his shoulder. Alyssa yelped, giggled, and kicked her feet a little. She looked at the other two men, smiled, and said, "Come on, boys, we're just getting started." The three of them walked naked into the bedroom. Robert followed to the doorway.

Alyssa giggled again when Dave flopped her onto the bed. "Close the door. No peeking, hon!"

The door latched. Alyssa rose to her knees on the bed. "Gentlemen, here is what I want. You"—she pointed to Dave—"cannot go in my ass. I love that cock, but it's more than I want there. You two"—she pointed to the other two—"can go anywhere, but after you go in my ass, you wash. Understand? I want all three of you at once first, then go at me as you please, just keep a dick in me one way or another. I want to fuck from now until I leave, and I expect to be dripping in your cum and mine. I'm asking you to remember all this because, well, you remember how I was before. Does that sound good to you?"

Dave grinned and wagged his hardening cock at her. "That sounds fine. Are you sure you want us to keep going nonstop? We will, if you want to be that sore in the morning."

The blond man cupped his large balls. "And it's a lot of cum."

The dark-haired man looked at his partners. "I want her ass first. You had it first last time, Joe."

"Boys, there is no need to argue. I'll take you both back there while I'm here. We'll all love it." She pointed at Dave. "Lie on your back. Let me get you hard so I can ride you."

He lay on the bed. Alyssa lowered her face over his semi-hard cock and licked it up one side and down the other. She held it straight up in her hand and sucked the head, then looked in his face. "Hold it up for me."

He did, and she wrapped her tits on either side of it and began jacking the big cock in her cleavage. Titty-fucking usually did not excite her, but the size of the cock and the afterglow of her orgasm tingled her nipples. She rewarded them with a flick of her fingers.

As she moved, she looked back at the dark-haired man. "You want my ass first, so lick it and get it ready for your cock."

He did one better. He stepped to the dresser and produced a bottle of lube. He pulled her cheeks apart and dipped his face to lick her pussy. She squeezed her pussy muscles to expel some of the combined cum, and he licked it up her slit to her asshole. He repeated the trip several times, getting her lubricated. When she was ready, he licked her ass and shoved his tongue into her rear opening. He hardened the muscle and rotated his head to stretch her while putting some moisture inside.

Alyssa stopped bouncing when the cock between her tits poked her mouth. It was hard, and she was ready to have it inside her again. She smiled and rose, moving to squat above the wide head. She rubbed it on her slit, adding to its wetness, then lowered herself. *So big. So good.* She squatted deeper, taking about half the big cock inside. *It feels like I didn't just have this all the way in just a few minutes ago. He will break me again tonight. And I will love it.*

Alyssa rose until just the head remained inside. She looked over her shoulder at the dark-haired man. "Not yet. Let me get all the way on." She lowered herself with a long grunt, then rose and eased down again. Her thighs quivered with the exertion of holding herself in the air. She inhaled as her legs failed, dropping her body down to Dave's hips. The sudden fullness forced a wail from her lips. His head bumped her cervix, and she reflexively leaned forward, taking some of her weight off the pole inside her and slipping it out a bit.

Her nipples rubbed Dave's hard chest, shooting sparks from them to her straining pussy, building the orgasm accumulating there. Leaning forward, she ground her hips, stretching and filling her pussy in every direction, and pressing her clit onto his pelvic bone. Alyssa hung on the edge of an orgasm after only one full thrust. She ground harder. She heard someone yelling, "Yes! Yes! Yes!" over and over again without realizing the words were coming from her own mouth. Her head rose as her back arched when the wave of pleasure swept from her pussy up her body. She stilled, her entire body flexing, until she inhaled with a gasp.

She breathed again, then began sliding forward and back, getting some full strokes on the huge cock. Her sensitive chest missed the hair that had been tickling it when she lifted and looked over her shoulder at the dark-haired man. "Put it in there. Go slow."

She jerked when the dollop of cold lube landed on her ass. After smearing it, he inserted a finger, spreading some inside, then touched the head of his cock to her anus. He pressed forward, gently at first, then harder. The head popped inside her sphincter. Alyssa yelped, and he stopped to let her adjust.

"Okay, go deeper."

He pressed forward steadily, then pulled back before pressing forward again. More lube dribbled onto her ass, which no doubt smeared the slickness on his dick. He repeated the process several times before pressing her ass cheeks with his abs.

Alyssa exhaled the breath she didn't realize she had been

holding. "Now go, guys. Fuck me." She ground her hips a bit to line things up, then remained still as the two men inside her alternated thrusting into her. *God, I'm always full. So good.*

The blond man, Joe, moved in front of Alyssa and tapped her cheek with his hard cock. She inhaled it to the root before bobbing back and forth on it. He grabbed a fistful of hair and moved her head as he pounded her throat. She moaned deep in her chest.

The men inside her changed their rhythm. They went from alternating to stuffing her at the same time. Alyssa's belly clenched as the huge cock below her battered the end of her vagina somewhere about the height of her navel, and her ass stretched. Dave's hands pulled her nipples far from her body. Alyssa's senses overloaded, and she screamed onto the cock in her mouth as yet another climax hammered her.

The three men kept up their pace as she came. Another orgasm burst on the heels of the first as the stimulation continued. She didn't notice the cocks swelling inside her, but when her ass emptied, she whimpered. When the hot cum rained down, she arched her back, pressing her belly into Dave's abs as her hips and head were both impaled on cocks. *I'm getting dirty. I'm a dirty slut.*

Joe gripped her hair with both hands as he swelled and jammed his cock fully into her, pressing his abs onto her nose. Alyssa gagged, but he held her as he fired his first spurt directly into her throat. Between the first and second spurts, he jerked his cock out of her mouth and aimed at her eyes, filling first one then the other with cum before finishing in her hair. *Oh so dirty.*

When he released her hair, Alyssa matched the long strokes from beneath her. She lifted and dropped onto the huge cock as he thrust up and dropped to the bed. Dave moved his hands to her hips as his cock swelled even larger. He held her in place as he thrust into her and pulled her against him as he splashed directly on her cervix until the cum ran out of her, around his cock, and onto his belly.

The sensation forced another peak onto Alyssa, who flexed, then collapsed onto his chest, repeating the word *fuck* until she ran out of breath. When her breathing slowed, she slid forward off the huge cock deflating in her cunt, then rolled onto the bed. The dark-haired man went to the bathroom, and Alyssa heard the shower start.

Dave rolled onto his side and cupped her pussy with his hand. He squeezed gently across all of it, the warmth and pressure sending hot ropes inside her to begin her next orgasm. Joe moved to her other side and sucked one nipple while cupping her other breast with his hand. Alyssa let them grope her while she rested, but when Dave's fingers entered her, she moaned. He wiggled his fingers, then lifted them to her mouth, glistening with their combined cum. She licked and sucked them clean, and he returned his fingers for another helping. After she swallowed that one, he used his first and ring fingers to spread her lips, then tapped her erect clit with his middle finger. Alyssa humped her hips forward to increase the pressure.

Joe lifted her thigh off the bed, then slid his hand up the back of her leg to cup her ass. He wiggled his fingers toward her anus, then smeared some of the cum dripping from her pussy over her pucker. She gasped when his finger poked inside. She reached for his cock and found it hard in her hand.

"You recover well. Ready to fuck?"

"Yeah. I want that ass. Roll over."

Alyssa sighed as she moved Dave's hand from her pussy. She rolled onto her belly, and Joe pulled her hips until she was on her knees. He lubed his cock from the bottle on the bed and pressed all the way into her. "Oh fuck yeah, baby. You have a great ass."

"You fill me so perfectly. And don't call me baby. Just fuck me."

He sneered. "All right, slut. Take this." He rammed into her hard and fast, jiggling her body. He slapped her ass hard several times on each cheek. The pain shot through her, making her wince even as it tingled her clit. "How's that, slut? Sure you don't want me to treat you like my baby?"

She glared over her shoulder. "Fuck me as hard as you want, spank me hard, but don't call me baby."

He grabbed a handful of her hair and yanked, pulling her head up and arching her back. "Then here it comes, slut. How's this for a remora?" He rammed his cock into her ass, swiveling to stretch her straining opening. He spanked her again and again with his free hand, the slaps and her yowls filling the room. When her hot, sore cheeks were thrilling her clit and pussy, and her climax was straining to break free, he shoved her face into the mattress and lifted her thighs, putting all her weight on her face and chest. He kept fucking hard, bouncing her face across the bedding.

Alyssa cried out when he leaned back, pressing his cock against the back of her anus, opening her more than she had been. She felt the sweat run up her back from the crack of her ass to pool in the gaps between her muscles. The breath flew out of her when he dropped her legs and followed her ass down to pound her into the mattress. His entire body rested on hers.

She couldn't regain her breath, and his weight on her back made it harder to even try. Her eyes watered as she gaped without inhaling. Panic moved into her brain, but so did the strong pleasure of her nipples rubbing on the sheet and her ass being ravaged by the man pinning her down. Her vision clouded as her orgasm built to an apex she had not reached before. Her ass screamed at her, but her orgasm exploded from her brain as her vision went black.

As her climax peaked, she caught her breath in a quick inhale followed by a low purr from deep in her throat. She struggled for her next breath as Joe kept crashing into her ass. Her body spasmed and shook, but he maintained his rhythm. He pulled out and straddled her back near her shoulders. Seconds later, warm cum splashed into her hair.

"Now you look like a slut, slut." He dropped his hand between her legs to pat her pussy. "I didn't even fuck this, but look at that wet spot. You come like a slut too." He got off her back and went to the bathroom to start the shower.

Alyssa felt hands on her ankles, and she was spun across the bed. A body climbed on top of her, and a cock plunged into her soaking pussy. The dark-haired man had replaced his partner. "Take a deep breath, slut. You are going to need it."

He pounded into her pussy, keeping her body close to orgasm. He reached under her with one hand and pinched her nipple. He fucked her fast and kept pressure on her back, but she could breathe. She heard a chuckle, and Dave's giant cock tapped her lips.

Alyssa opened her mouth wide, expecting just the tip. He worked the head inside, then pinched her earlobes and shoved the thick meat into her mouth, hitting the back of her throat. Alyssa gagged around the cock and sputtered through her nose. He rammed the cock in again and held it there. Alyssa couldn't breathe until he pulled back a moment later. He shoved to the back of her throat again, picking up the pace but making her gag and only allowing bites of air between thrusts.

The cock in her pussy was working wonders. It jabbed her G-spot on every stroke, and Alyssa grunted with every impact. She felt juices dripping down her onto the bed, no doubt creating another wet spot as small orgasms racked her every minute or two. *God, this feels good. Just keep fucking me.* The cock in her pussy swelled and then withdrew from her hungry opening. Hot cum landed on her ass. With the weight off her body, she curled her knees under her belly as she came yet again.

The large cock had remained in her mouth, but the pinching fingers left her ears as she spasmed. Alyssa pressed her hands against Dave's abs, and he stepped back. She rolled onto her back, spinning to point her sloppy pussy toward him, the wet sheets cold on her back. She spread her legs wide, holding them with her hands. "Fuck me missionary. Climb on."

The tall man smiled. "I'm going in deep, you know."

"I'm counting on it." Alyssa inhaled and rolled her hips upward, giving the big dick access to her pussy and making the angle conducive to the deepest penetration. He climbed between her legs and lined up his tip with her opening. He shoved forward, putting almost all of the impressive tool inside her on the first thrust. He tapped her cervix, then backed up to thrust again. Alyssa gasped, "Fuck me," with the breath she could draw.

He sped up his assault on her pussy, stretching her mercilessly and leaving her empty on each backstroke. Alyssa clutched at his back, pulling him forward and thrusting her hips at him, seeking that full feeling again. Sweat dripped onto her chest and face as he grunted above her.

She remained in a state of orgasm or near-orgasm while her pussy crackled with the action. When the other two men joined them on the bed and pinched her nipples, she roared and came. Her vision blurred, and as her body fell from its tension, her head lolled to one side. "More," she murmured.

Dave continued fucking for a few strokes, then pulled out and moved beside her chest. As he jacked his dick, giant globs of cum shot from the tip, painting her tits and nipples, and rolling up her chest to her neck. "A pearl necklace for our guest to show Hubby." The three friends cackled.

Joe moved between her legs next and guided all of his cock into her gaping pussy. He fucked her hard, fully seating his hips inside her legs, stretching the muscles and jarring her joints. Alyssa remained still on her back with her legs splayed limply to each side as he fucked her, her abs clenching and a low moan coming from her lips every couple of minutes as another orgasm rolled out of her overstimulated pussy. He pulled out and shot his cum across her tits and belly, then gave way to his dark-haired friend.

The three of them fucked her in turns for the next hour, each adding to the cum on her body. Alyssa mumbled "more" and beckoned to a bystander each time her pussy emptied. When Dave came on her again, a voice from the door disturbed them.

"That's the hottest thing I've ever seen. She's covered and asking for more."

⁓

The door to the bedroom clicked shut. Robert held his head in his hands and counted to a hundred. His breathing slowed as he heard Alyssa talking to the men through the door. He sat, breathing and listening, until Alyssa wailed. He swallowed the bile that had collected in the back of his throat, sighed, and got out of the chair.

"Just like we planned," he muttered to himself as he moved toward the three men's pants. He picked them up and extracted the phone from each one before laying them on the couch. He sat at the desk. He pulled his phone and a second one from his jacket pockets, texted the first video he made of Alyssa to the burner phone, then opened the notes app on his phone. He looked up when he heard Alyssa yelling yes repeatedly and saw his bright-red face in the mirror. He frowned and returned to his work, picking up the tall man's phone and turning off the ringer.

"Hey Siri, what time is it?" Robert smiled as the iPhone opened to the clock screen. He tapped the world clock button and hit the plus sign to add a clock. He typed "Moscow" and then clicked Select All, then Share. He exhaled when the phone opened the sharing window and pressed the message button. When the new message opened, he typed "Raguel" in the "To" field and muttered, "The angel of justice will see you now, Dave."

Robert tapped to create a new contact, then to choose a photo. A drop of sweat splashed on the screen. Robert touched the screen to his shirt and wiped his brow. He touched the home button, relieved that the phone was now open to him.

From Settings, he retrieved the phone's number, then opened the photos to look for any that may have been taken of the last time these men were with Alyssa. Finding none, he browsed through the text strands to find Dave's wife and parents, and three women with whom he had sexts. Robert took screenshots of these text strands and added them to the replies he was building. He checked the emails to find Dave's boss and coworkers, and smirked upon finding the group email for the parents of his daughter's soccer team.

Robert put in an earbud and reviewed the first brief video he took of Alyssa and the three men. There were no ways to identify her. Her face was hidden in Joe's abs. She had no tattoos or identifying marks, she wore no jewelry, and her hair was different from her normal style and disheveled in the blond man's hands. Robert listened for his own voice. He had kept his voice quiet, speaking away from the camera when he asked his question, and he had adopted an accent and a lower pitch. It didn't matter. The video commenced when the dark-haired man spoke. Alyssa was completely silent while the three men bragged about their conquests. He watched it again, to be sure. He was certain that he and Alyssa would not be identified from the video. He gritted his teeth and sent the video from the burner phone to Dave's.

He put that phone down and opened the blond man's phone as he had the first, returning to touch the first phone occasionally to keep it active. Again relieved to find no evidence of the earlier encounter, he scrolled texts and emails, finding the wife and boss but no parents or girlfriends. He did find a neighborhood group email and smiled. "You are the one being spanked, Joe."

Robert opened the dark-haired man's phone last. He saw no photos and proceeded into the communication. Chuck was getting divorced, so there were emails and texts from the wife and her attorney. A couple of sexting partners appeared to be girlfriends. Robert took some screenshots of their texts and included those in what he prepared, like he had for Dave. Chuck's sister and parents were both in communication, and his boss, who was not the same person that the other two men reported to. The email included two different church groups and a young professionals association. Robert set down the phone. "This is the way we make you pay, Chuck. Fuck you."

All three phones had the video. He pasted it into the Reply All emails on each one. "Are you sure you want to do this?" he said aloud. Through the bedroom wall, he heard a smack and Alyssa scream. He clenched his fists before returning to his work. He hit send on each one. He opened the texts and noted the eleven o'clock hour. He sent the texts to family next, then girlfriends and sext partners, and finally the wives. He hadn't finished sending the last one before one of the phones buzzed. He smiled and powered each phone off. He saw it was 11:28. "An early witching hour for you three." He leaned back in the chair and rubbed his eyes.

A few minutes later, Keegan opened the door and came to his side. "Are you finished?"

"Yes. I just need to return them to the right pants."

"You should do that if you want to finish without being seen. Those grunts sound pretty muted. They might be finishing up."

"It's about time." He picked up the phones.

"I can't imagine how hard that was to hear, and see, but at least you are getting even." She hugged him. "Thank you for letting me help a little. Now get those put away so I can rescue your wife."

Robert put the phones in the proper pants pockets. He folded the pants neatly on the couch, along with the rest of the men's clothes, just like a good cuckold would. He left Alyssa's shredded clothing on the floor and returned to his chair. He nodded to Keegan. The tall redhead removed her clothes and opened the bedroom door. Her hand moved to her pussy. "That's the hottest thing I've ever seen. She's covered and asking for more."

Keegan posed in the doorway. The three men leered at her nude before them. The two shorter men sported full erections, and the tall man kept jacking his huge cock, no doubt in an attempt to keep it hard despite what was clearly a fresh load on Alyssa.

Keegan stepped closer to hold the big tip in her hand. "I want this first." She looked at the other two. "No offense, fellas; you will get your turns, but this is why I came." She turned back to the tall man. "Why don't I give you a little show to harden you up, then you slide into me when you are ready?"

"If you think you are ready for that, fine."

"I will be when you are." She pulled him out from between Alyssa's legs by his cock and knelt. She kissed the insides of Alyssa's thighs, working up from her knees to her pussy, alternating sides.

She licked off some of the cum deposited on them on the way, then licked Alyssa's outer lips from bottom to top, swallowing more cum. "Delicious, guys. You saved some for me, right?"

The blond man wagged his dick at her. "Oh, we have plenty for you, if you will be as good a slut as this one is."

Keegan smiled and kissed Alyssa's clit with the lightest of touches while firmly rubbing the older woman's hamstrings with her palms. Alyssa's hips jerked forward toward her touch, and Keegan backed away. Keegan rubbed the lax thighs up and down, giving them a hard massage, and dipped her tongue to lightly lick the sloppy pussy between them, always pulling her head back when Alyssa moved toward more contact. She lingered longer when Alyssa's hips were still, licking along the slit and rubbing the joints between the tops of Alyssa's thighs and her hips. Keegan increased her tongue's pressure on the battered lips but stayed below the clit. She didn't want Alyssa to climax yet, and she didn't want to remove more of the white cum gelling on her pussy than needed.

Alyssa began to stir more deliberately, waking from her orgasmic haze. Her hand moved to Keegan's head and entwined in her hair, but Keegan moved as she pleased, bringing Alyssa's hand along.

Keegan slid one hand down her body, caressing a breast on the way to putting a finger inside herself. She followed with another, spreading them as she moved inside her wet slit, preparing it for the monster to come. She added a third finger and slid her hand in and out, then rotated it, pulling at the sides of her opening. She jumped when she heard a voice.

"Put it in." The tall man was nestling behind her, whispering in her ear between Alyssa's thighs. He gripped her breast and pulled her nipple.

Keegan pulled her fingers from her pussy. Reaching beneath

herself, she found the thick cock. She caressed it before rubbing the tip on her open, wet lips, preparing it to enter her. She notched it into her opening, then grasped it to control the movement to come. "Go slow," she whispered as she pulled the cock forward.

The tip stretched her open, and the tall man maintained his pressure on her until the tip was inside. Keegan moaned into Alyssa's pussy and gripped the cock harder, signaling to stop moving. She remained still, letting her pussy stretch around the large head, enjoying the pressure as it separated her walls even while they gripped at it. Keegan realized she had stopped licking Alyssa's pussy and resumed. Alyssa sighed.

Keegan pulled on the cock. The tall man pushed forward some more, and electric shocks radiated from Keegan's pussy as it accommodated his size. Her belly clenched, and her thighs strained to move together, blocked by the weight of her body. She groaned into Alyssa's pussy and pressed forward onto her lips, driving her tongue farther inside. The tall man pulled back until only the head was inside, then inched forward until almost half filled her. Keegan again was pressed into Alyssa's lips, and Keegan's scalp tightened as Alyssa's fingers found their strength. She exhaled on Alyssa's clit, causing her thighs to jerk.

The three repeated this process five more times, until the giant cock was fully inside Keegan and Alyssa was holding on to her hair. Keegan lifted Alyssa's hands with her own to look over her shoulder. "It's all the way in?"

He nodded.

"Then fuck me. I'm about to come already." She lowered her mouth to Alyssa's pussy and lapped at her opening, up to her clit. She returned Alyssa's hands to her red curls, letting the older woman guide her mouth where she wanted her pleasure.

The tall man pulled out until just splitting her lips with the tip of his cock, then rammed forward. Keegan wailed as her orgasm burst from the sudden sensations. She clenched her ass, and her vaginal walls tightened around the cock, but the tall man continued his assault on her pussy with long, hard strokes, fighting her grip. Keegan's mouth slammed into Alyssa's pussy with every thrust, and the women grunted in unison as they absorbed the impacts.

Alyssa whined as if edging toward climax. Keegan slid two fingers into her and curled them upward to rub Alyssa's G-spot, and Alyssa's whine became a scream. Her rejuvenated thighs clamped against Keegan's ears, but Keegan still heard her cry of pleasure. When Alyssa relaxed her thighs and pulled her hands from Keegan's hair, Keegan looked over her shoulder at the stud railing her from behind. "Let me ride you."

The tall man pulled out and lay beside Alyssa. Keegan scrambled to fill her empty pussy, climbing on top and shoving down, fully engulfing his rod. She put her hands on his chest to hold herself up and ground her hips against his. When he grabbed her tits and pinched her nipples, she started bouncing. She wanted to give him a good show, so she put her hands behind her head and arched her back. His hands fell to her hips, and her full breasts bounced in time with her squats.

She quickened her pace, keeping her cervix in contact with his cockhead as much as possible to keep the electric pleasure building in her belly as her release mounted. Some women found that contact uncomfortable—not Keegan. It drove her to orgasm fast and hard. She grunted with each descent. Heat flushed through her neck, down into her chest and breasts, to her nipples. She struggled for breath. Her orgasm began as the tall man's cock swelled inside her.

He grabbed her hips and thrust up from below, hammering her cervix, the pain exploding her orgasm. She felt the cock swell even more inside her, astounded it could get any larger but pleased with the final stretch as she came. As her cunt gripped his cock, he jabbed upward while pulling her down, seating his tip on her cervix and his cum directly on it, the force of it greater than any man she had ever had. Their combined cries echoed off the stucco walls. Keegan fell forward to his chest as her body relaxed.

"Fuck, that was good. Stay here. I want to feel you inside me a minute."

"My boys want their turn with you."

"They will have it. I need a minute to recoup." She looked at Alyssa, who was wiping the cum from her face. "Can you guys do that to me tonight?"

The tall man patted her ass cheek. "Maybe. We fucked her hard for the past couple of hours. We still need a little sleep tonight."

The blond man spoke up. "Oh, we can cover you. Just get ready. My balls are still full, even after that slut."

"I mean that dazed from pleasure. Can you leave me fucked out?"

Robert knocked on the doorframe. "It's after midnight. She wanted me to make sure she got home early." He crossed to the bed and took his wife's hands. "Come on, hon. It's time to go home."

"Do I have to? This feels so good. Just one more for the road?"

"No, honey. You asked me to be firm on quitting time. Let's go."

The dark-haired man put his hand on Robert's shoulder. "She said she wants one more. You do what she says, right?"

Robert brushed the hand away without turning. "I am doing what she says. Just like I was earlier. Don't misunderstand your position in our relationship. I'm her husband. You're a toy. When I say she goes, she goes."

The blond man laughed. "Not last time. You remember that, big husband?"

The tall man raised his hand. "Guys, we have had a good time, and we may want to play with this couple again. And we have a lovely guest who is fresh and ready to go. Mind your manners." He looked at Robert. "I don't understand your kink, but if it gets you off, so be it. I do love fucking your wife. If you two want another round, we will be here tomorrow night."

Robert smirked. "We'll see." He pulled Alyssa up and held her hands until she steadied her legs and smiled at him. "Come on, hon. Let's go."

They walked to the door, Alyssa wearing only heels and cum.

The blond man held up her torn clothes. "Do you want to cover up?"

Alyssa turned. "You kept my underwear last time as a souvenir, remember? Keep those rags this time."

He tossed the skirt to the dark-haired man. "You are walking to your car like that?"

"I'm proud of this body and what I did tonight. My husband likes showing me off. I love him and trust him completely. I'll walk wherever he wants, however he wants. Tonight, I walk through the hotel, naked and well fucked, because he wants people to see the gift he gave me. And I'm proud to do it."

She opened the door. They strode down the short hall while the three men and Keegan watched from the open door. They closed it when the pair turned into the elevator lobby and they heard the ding of a car arriving.

Keegan grasped the two hard cocks at her sides. "It's time you two had a turn."

3

TUESDAY, MAY 4, EMBASSY SUITES

Alyssa and Robert rode down, thankful the hall and elevator were empty. They got out on the eleventh floor and hustled to the room immediately below the one they had just left. Before the door even finished closing, Alyssa ran to the bathroom and started the shower. She removed her heels, amazed they had remained on her feet during her adventure. She peeled the ratty remnants of her stockings from her legs and tossed them in the trash can. The shower still ran cold, but she stepped in to rinse the cum from her face and body. She dug two fingers inside her pussy to scoop what had not yet run out.

She used more shampoo than usual, and she washed her hair twice before lathering up a washcloth. Her skin was bright pink when she stopped scrubbing. She let the hot water soothe her aching back, ass, and thighs for only a minute before getting out and drying off, then donned a robe and joined Robert in front of the TV.

Alyssa wrapped her arms around his neck and kissed his head, lingering while she rubbed his cheek. "You okay, Babe?"

"That was terrible. Don't ever ask me to do that again. Pretending to like that is too hard."

"I know, Babe. I won't ask you again. We won't need to do it again. Thank you for doing it tonight." She turned his face to hers and kissed him. She held his face in her hands after she broke the kiss, panting. "God, I love you. You are the best man I've ever met."

"Are you sure? Those three sure made you happy tonight."

Alyssa hung her head. "They did. I won't deny it. I came so much and felt so good. But I felt bad for you."

Robert cocked an eyebrow. "You did, huh?"

She shook her head. "That's fair. I couldn't think at all except to ask for more cock. Do you understand how I got that way last time? How I lost track of my reason? Tonight I was rested and sober, and still couldn't think at all. That's why I need to call you before I use our arrangement. You keep me thinking." She looked at her hands. "When you helped me up, I felt bad for what you had been through." A tear escaped her eye. "You had the hardest job. I'm sorry that you saw and heard, and then saw me covered like that."

"You liked it though. Enough that you would still be there if I hadn't pulled you out, even understanding these three scumbags. Is that what you want from our open arrangement?"

"I can't lie. Being pleasured by so many men is thrilling, dirty, and naughty. I feel sexy and desired. Clearly, it makes me come a lot. But I want what we have. I want it much more than I want to be the center of several men, even if that many men feels so good. That's why I need you to help me. So I don't lose it."

"You talk like you forgot why you were there to begin with. Are you interested in how our plan went?"

"I am, but I am interested in us first. Are we still okay? Do you still want me after what I just did?"

Robert frowned. "I still love you. I still want you. But this can't happen again. Open within the rules we established is one thing. Tonight is entirely different."

Alyssa's smile dipped a little in the corners. "I understand, Babe. Oh, it's good to call you Babe again. That 'hon' thing drove me nuts, but I'm happy we kept that part of our relationship away from those three."

"Yeah, but when you told one of them not to call you Baby, it sounded like he took offense. He took it out on you."

"You heard that?"

"Hotel walls, Baby. I heard every slap."

She looked down. "I'm sorry, Babe. Nobody calls me Baby but you. Ever. Even if I get spanked for it." She clasped her hands together between her breasts. "Did we succeed?"

"I think so, but let's see."

They both turned to the TV. The screen was split into four blocks. In the upper left, Keegan was on the bed being fucked by the tall man while sucking the blond. The dark-haired man sat on the other bed, stroking a limp dick and watching.

Alyssa pointed the remote at the TV. "I want to hear." The gagging sound from Keegan's throat filled the room as the blond fucked her face.

Robert looked at her with his eyebrows raised. "Those things have sound too?"

"Only the best for us, Babe. I want to hear when it all falls down on them. Did you have any trouble?"

"No. It worked just like your spies said it would. I finished up just before Keegan got there."

Right then, Keegan growled as she came on the screen. The tall man grunted and shot his load onto her back.

Alyssa straddled her husband's lap. "Damn, that sound makes me horny. You want to reclaim me right now, Babe?"

The sound of a phone ringing precluded Robert's answer. They both turned to the TV, noting that the action on the screen had stopped. The four on the screen were all looking at the room's phone as it rang again. The blond man resumed fucking Keegan's face. "I'm close. Don't answer."

The tall man answered the phone as the blond man pulled Keegan's face deep onto his cock, grunting as he shot his load in her mouth.

"Hello?"

…

"Whoa, Sweetheart. Wait. What? My phone hasn't rung."

…

"No. I was sleeping." He covered the mouthpiece and nodded to the dark-haired man. "Get my phone!"

…

"Sweetheart, wait…" He pulled the phone from his ear. "She hung up. She was screaming about some text I sent."

Keegan stood in the background, sidling toward the bedroom door as the dark-haired man walked in and handed the phone to the tall man.

"Our clothes were all folded on the couch. That guy must have been told to clean up after us."

"Oh shit. My phone is off. I never turn my phone off."

Alyssa squeezed Robert's hand with both of hers. They watched the TV as the tall man waited for his phone to boot up. The sound of his phone dinging came through the TV. He tapped the screen.

"Shit! Oh shit. She received a video of us fucking that slut tonight."

"How?" the dark-haired man asked.

"Does it matter? My wife got that video. I'll be divorced in the morning. The cuckold husband had to send it."

"Shit. Me too," the blond added. "My wife told me not to come home."

"Um, guys," the dark-haired man said, "better check your email. It got sent to work. Shit. And my wife's attorney."

"Son of a bitch!" The tall man knocked the phone off the desk and across the bed to the far wall. "How could that bastard open our phones?"

The door to Robert and Alyssa's room opened, and Keegan squirted through and locked it behind her.

Alyssa raised an eyebrow. "Were you in such a hurry to leave that you forgot your clothes?"

Keegan laughed and flashed the bundle in her hands. "Your strut down the hall beside Robert inspired me. I couldn't strut though. A door opened behind me, and I ran. Have they figured it out yet?"

"They know I sent the video. They don't know how."

Alyssa muted the TV. "Who did you send it to?"

"Their wives, sexting partners, parents, siblings, bosses, coworkers, and a couple of neighborhood group emails."

"Jesus, Robert," Keegan laughed, "do you want to post it to a revenge porn site too?"

"Absolutely not. We wanted to damage their lives for what they did to Alyssa and me, and we've done that. Unfortunately, Alyssa's role left her too exposed. Nobody could identify her, but that is still the love of my life in that video. I won't expose her more than is needed to accomplish what we wanted. I love her more than I want to ruin these men across a wider audience."

"God, I love you, Babe."

"God, I do too, and you're not even my husband. You make me swoon every time you talk about Alyssa." Keegan moved to sit beside him.

Robert raised his hand. "Sorry, Keegan. Go wash off all the residue from those slugs, then you can snuggle up with us. We love you, and we want to celebrate a successful end to this, but we've had all of them we can stand."

"Oh. Sure. I completely understand." She rubbed her hand on her ass cheek, scrunching up her nose at the cum she smeared. "And agree. Back in a few."

"Babe, can you reclaim me twice?"

"I'll reclaim you as many times as you like. Why do you ask?"

"Because." Alyssa leaned over her husband, pressing her body to his, kissing him, and holding his head still until she released him, panting. "Keegan won't be in the shower long, but I can't live with the stain of those three any longer. Reclaim me fast now, before she comes back, but I want you to reclaim me with slow, beautiful lovemaking later. Wash away any part of what happened tonight so it can never stand between us, even if that takes a hundred nights. But I want to take the first step right now. Will you do that for me?"

"I understand, Baby. Yes, I will make you mine, right now and again later. You have the right idea." He reached between them to untie her robe and pull it open.

Alyssa pulled open his pants, pushing them down when he raised his hips. She grasped his cock, which was hot and throbbing in her hand. "Perfect, Babe." She spread her legs and slid up the couch to notch his cock into her open and wet pussy. She descended, taking all of him in one move. She nestled his cock into her, rubbing the tip against the spot beside her cervix. "Oh, there it is. God, I love this cock."

Robert pulled her face to his for another toe-curling kiss, then pushed her upright by her shoulders. He gripped her breasts, squeezing until Alyssa gasped, then pulled them up, bringing her body with them. "There we go. Ride me, Baby."

Alyssa bit her lower lip and let her head roll back as she began to bounce with his guidance. *Fuck, that hurts.* She winced, her pussy already sore from the pounding it received earlier, then lowered her gaze to Robert's face. She slammed down, ignoring the tug at her tits as she ground her cervix across his cockhead before resuming her energetic ride. *That's good though.* The burn in her thighs started within a few thrusts, Keegan's earlier massage insufficient to overcome the abuse she took, and she grunted with every move.

Robert's face flashed a recognition of the discomfort in his wife's voice. He sat up, then leaned forward to deposit her back on the couch. He lined up to slip back inside her, then pistoned in and out, touching her cervix and her G-spot on every trip inside, building yet another orgasm inside her racked body. She loved him for what he could do to her. She lifted her legs up beside his head, getting his cockhead deep into her, and she squeezed her exhausted pussy around him, coaxing him to come, willing to endure any pain in her pussy until he did.

"That's it, Babe. Come in me. Fill me. Make me yours again." *Hurry. This hurts. But it's so good. He loves me so much.*

Robert kissed her ankles before leaning forward, stretching Alyssa's hamstrings and burying his cock as deep into her as he could reach. A low groan came from deep in Alyssa's stomach when her orgasm burst upon her just as his burst inside her. The splashing of his cum on her cervix closed Alyssa's eyes until she inhaled a minute later.

Robert moved one leg at a time down to the couch before pressing his chest onto hers and kissing her. "I love you, Alyssa. You are mine again."

With her arms, she pulled his neck down to her. "I have always been yours. I love you, Baby."

"See? This is why I can't find a boyfriend. Nobody does to me what Robert does to you."

Alyssa cocked one eyebrow at Keegan, who stood nude in the bedroom doorway. "Only because of what he does to me? Or maybe because of what he does to you?"

Keegan laughed. "Well, there is that. But I compare every guy I date to Robert, and they just can't cut it."

"You will find your Robert. Take your time. A great husband makes everything better."

Keegan knelt beside them on the floor. "I'm clean. Can I join you now, or do you still need a few minutes?"

Robert and Alyssa each reached one arm around her and pulled her head to theirs, each giving her a soft kiss.

"Joining us sounds great, Keegan, if Alyssa is ready." Robert nodded toward the door. "Let's go to the bed. The couch may get a little small with three of us." He stood and removed the rest of his clothes while they watched.

The two beauties took his hands and snuggled close on either side of him. Alyssa slid her robe off, letting it pool behind her. With a chuckle, he bent his knees, wrapped an arm under each woman's ass, and lifted them, one on each hip. They squealed and cackled as he carried them sideways through the bedroom door.

Keegan waited until Alyssa's breath slowed as she drifted off to sleep, then propped her body up on her elbow to talk with Robert over Alyssa. "You went through the worst tonight, and not a complaint. How are you, really?"

Robert matched Keegan's pose. "I'll be fine. We did what we had to do. Thank you for your help with it. I'm glad they got what was coming to them. I wish she hadn't had to play a part."

"You know she didn't have to participate. I offered to let you pretend to be my boyfriend. She insisted that she be the one." She stammered as she realized this might be news to him. "I think…no."

"What? As close as we are, you can say it. What do you think?"

"I think she wanted them to know she burned them, that she got her revenge." She twisted her hair with her free hand and looked down at Alyssa's body.

"And?"

Keegan closed her eyes. She didn't like what she thought, but she cared too much about Robert to hide her fear from him.

"I think she wanted another gang bang. When we set this up, she talked about how horrible they were to you, but more about how good the sex felt. As angry as she was, she might have wanted one more taste as she destroyed them. I'm sorry for rambling. I shouldn't have said anything. I'm probably wrong."

"It's okay, Keegan. Thank you for telling me. That must have been hard for you. If it helps, you aren't betraying her trust. She told me about your offer, and we both agreed on her answer. Beyond that, before we came downstairs, she warned me that she planned on enjoying it. We are honest and open with each other, even if the truth hurts. Wallowing in lies hurts worse."

Relief washed over her in waves. "I'll never, ever find a man who measures up to you."

Robert laughed. "You will. You are just as beautiful on the inside as you are on the outside. You deserve someone as wonderful as you are, and he's out there. You might not find one while you are sleeping with old married couples though."

She leered at him. "That's where the best ones are, you know. I already found a good man in bed with you guys."

"You can't have him, Keegan. He's mine."

"Baby, you were supposed to be asleep." He patted Alyssa's chest.

Alyssa opened her eyes. "Who can sleep with you two telling secrets and talking about relationships?"

"Alyssa, I am only kidding about Robert. I would never try to take him. I was just joking with him."

"Oh, I know, sweetie. You aren't the type to steal someone away. Of course, I let you have one of his best parts inside you tonight."

It was Robert's turn to feign offense. "You two are treating me like a piece of meat."

"We love your piece of meat, Babe."

"Really love it, Robert."

They laughed, then Alyssa took Keegan's cheeks in her hands. "Thank you for telling Robert your concerns. Sometimes I need help with my impulses, and he helps me with them. When you talk with him, you help him help me." She brushed a wisp of red hair back over Keegan's ear. "Thank you for being a trusted friend."

She pulled Keegan in for a hug, then looked at Robert. "And you, Babe. I'm not letting anyone take you from me. Nobody breaks our love. Not even this tall, beautiful firecracker here."

"Nobody, Baby. Sorry, Keegan."

Keegan smiled. "Now that we have stated the obvious, you ready for me to turn out the light so we can sleep?"

Robert paused as he exited the bedroom door. Keegan sat sideways on the couch with her feet tucked under her, watching the TV. He pondered how important she had become to them. In the month they had known her, she had proven to be smart, bold, and levelheaded for a bartender in her midtwenties. He wondered how many people never saw past her beauty, and shook his head.

"Robert, you are just in time."

He sat beside Keegan. "Just in time for what?"

"Our boys are getting evicted from the hotel. It seems their corporate cards got canceled this morning."

"Their bosses must not have appreciated the recruiting video I sent."

"Should I get Alyssa for this?"

"No. Let her sleep. I'll record it on the laptop if she wants to see it later." He hit record on the video feed and turned up the TV volume so they could hear it.

Dave was on the screen, dressed in a suit and talking on his cell phone. "I tried that too. She canceled all our personal cards. I don't have one to cover tonight. They said they would take cash at the desk, but I don't have enough for tonight. What about you?"

. . .

"Maybe we can hit an ATM. Maybe one of our cards still works."

. . .

"Motel 6 by the airport? I guess we have enough. We just need a place to stay until our flight tomorrow."

. . .

"I don't know. She said she'd have the locks changed today. My sister lives in Louisville. Maybe there. She hasn't sent me a 'go to hell' email yet."

. . .

"Yeah, but I don't have a credit card to change the flight. I'll have to drive."

…

"Yeah. And I've been getting replies from everybody else too. They are all upset that I sent that to them."

…

"I know that, you idiot, but they don't. And with my smiling face telling them how hot that bitch was, that doesn't matter. I even got one from my best friend, Nick, and it didn't go to him."

…

"Yeah, Diane sent it to him last night. My best fucking friend."

…

"Yep. Best divorce attorney in the state. He let me know he'd be representing her, and your wives too, if they want. Three for one deal on the fees to boot. He always looked down on cheaters; he was none too kind when he told me we are through as friends."

…

"Yep. Fucked."

…

"Yeah. Downstairs in fifteen."

Dave stood. In a burst, he kicked the mattress, then stomped its side with his heel five or six times until it slid off the other side of the bed, upended. Robert and Keegan didn't need the TV audio to hear the yell in the room above them. The sound stopped. He hung his head. "Fuck it," he said as he crossed the room to the minibar. He pulled the door, but it didn't open. "They even locked the minibar remotely. Damn it!" He grabbed his suitcase and walked out of the bedroom. Robert and Keegan watched him go into the living area and out the main door to the room.

Keegan pulled Robert's face to kiss him lightly on the cheek. "They got what was coming to them. I'm glad."

"Yeah, probably."

"Remember what they did to you, and to Alyssa. Both times. Doesn't that make you mad?"

"Oh, it does. And what we did was nothing more than telling the truth to people they had deceived. There's a big part of me that hopes they end up unemployed and homeless. But that little part wishes I didn't have to be the one to do it."

"I know. But you were the only one who could."

"And a big part of me wishes Alyssa didn't have to be involved. That video will eventually live on the internet forever, and probably in the phones of some of the people who received it, and it will be used in those divorce trials. Alyssa can't be identified, but we know she will have a sex video on the web forever."

"Nobody will ever know. I can't tell it's her, and I know it is. You did the right thing, and you protected yourselves while you did it. You are a good man, Robert."

"Thanks. Some days I wonder."

The sexy redhead pulled his head to her shoulder and leaned back into the corner of the couch. She stroked his hair while they stared at the unmoving image on the TV. After the laptop went to sleep, and the TV went black, Keegan kissed his head and nudged him off her. She swiped the touch pad on the laptop, bringing the image from the spy cams back up. "I need to go collect those, then head home. Are you okay?"

"Yes. Thank you for the calm moments."

"Glad to do it. Anytime you want to cuddle against me, I'm game." She stood and pulled him up with her. "Can you watch those until I get out? Just in case he comes back?"

"Sure. I'll call you if he does."

"Thanks. Give Alyssa my best. Tell her to call me later." She cupped his cheek, then walked out.

Robert sat to monitor Keegan's recovery of the cameras. He saw the door open. Keegan winked at the camera and removed her shirt. She cupped her braless tits, offering them to the camera in the outlet. "To keep you watching, Robert."

She walked to the kitchen area, turned, bent at the waist, and pushed her jeans down her long, straight legs. Her almost bare ass looked delectable on the screen, stretched and flashing the green thong covering her cleft. She looked upside down beside her legs at the camera and winked again. "You recording this, Robert? You should be."

"Oops!" He looked at the laptop. "Good. Didn't stop recording before."

Wearing only her thong, Keegan showed up on the bathroom camera mounted in the plug facing the mirror. She stood so Robert could see her front in the mirror and her back directly in the camera. She gripped the bow strings in the waistband of her thong in her fingers and pulled them away from her hips, moving the strings up and down before stretching them out and pulling them to untie the bows on her hips, then releasing them to let the thong fall to the floor. She winked at the camera again. "All the clothes are off. What can I do to make camera number four interesting?"

Keegan strutted nude into the bedroom, not stopping until only her shins were visible. Her legs bent to the side, and her pussy lowered into the frame, followed by two fingers of her left hand. They slid along her glistening lips. "I guess I have to jill myself off for camera four. I hope you two like it." The two fingers dipped into her wet slit, the back of her hand filling most of the screen.

Keegan backed up to sit on the bed closest to the camera. She spread her legs wide and plunged the fingers back where they had just been. Her head rolled back, and her back arched, thrusting her lightly freckled tits at the ceiling as she pleasured herself. Her ever-more-ragged breathing came through the microphone as if she were sitting beside Robert. Her hips humped against her hand, and her free hand pinched and pulled her nipple. She grunted deep in her belly and curled forward, clutching her spasming pussy. She released as her breathing returned to normal, still with her fingers embedded inside herself. She spread her legs wide, smirked, and pulled the fingers out of her pussy to lick them clean. "Mmm, tasty."

She blew a kiss to the camera and pulled it out of the wall, ending that feed. She showed up in the bathroom, making a show of tying each side of her thong before removing the camera from the wall. In the kitchen, she wriggled into her jeans, taking much longer than needed to pull them up her slender legs and never breaking her sultry eye contact until she disconnected that one as well. She knelt in front of the living room camera and caressed her breasts before slipping her T-shirt over her head. She waved to the camera and said, "Hope you enjoyed the show. Love you guys," before the feed went dead. Robert laughed and turned off the electronics.

After taking four Advil, Alyssa stepped into the tub. "This is nice, Babe. Thanks for running me a bath."

Robert cupped her breasts as she leaned back against him in the water. "Glad to do it, Baby. Thought you could soak the soreness away."

"Mm-hmm. And you thought you'd get your hands on my soapy tits, too, right?"

"I'm making sure you're clean. I'll cover the rest of you eventually." He kissed her neck below her ear.

I love that. "You know what that does to me."

"I'm counting on it. You did ask me to make love to you again this morning. Reclaiming you a second time, I believe?"

Her abs fluttered where he trailed his fingers over them under the water. "Yes. That feels good. Don't stop."

"I don't intend to." His hand slid lower on the next down-stroke. Alyssa spread and bent her legs, letting her knees rise through the foam. Robert traced down her inner thighs to her knees and back up to her hips, using his strength to massage her muscles.

Her knees bumped the sides of the tub. "Mm, yes, Babe." She leaned her head back on his shoulder and let him massage her under the water, the heat and his hands arousing her without leaving her belly and legs.

She relaxed until she melted into his body. With her eyes closed, the rippling of the water seemed to fill the room while his hands soothed her. As the water cooled, he hugged her from behind and kissed her ear.

"That was heavenly. Thank you, Babe."

"That's just the warm-up, you know."

"I'm counting on it." She giggled, kissed his cheek, and stepped out of the tub, letting the suds fall off her body onto the floor. "Come on, Babe. Reclaim me properly. Make love to me." She grabbed a towel and wiped the remaining suds off before walking to the bed.

When Robert arrived in the bedroom, Alyssa was reclined on the bed, reaching for him with both hands. He crawled above her, kissing her and stroking her hair with one hand. He pulled her earlobe between his lips before dipping to suck her neck and kiss down to her collarbone.

Yes. Love me. Remind me why I always come home. She put both hands in his hair and guided his mouth lower, staying engaged as he kissed around the underside of her breasts and up the valley between them before licking sideways to her nipple and sucking it behind his teeth. His free hand traced her firm belly, down to her upper thigh, and back up to her breasts, barely touching the fine hairs enough to tingle.

"Stop teasing and touch me."

He laughed and switched hands but provided no more direct contact except for his sucking mouth, just on the other side of her body.

"Aah, come on. I'm already warmed up for you. You don't have to take your time."

"I am. You wanted slow, and all the anticipation that comes with it. Here it is."

Alyssa gripped the sheet to keep from grabbing his hands and pulling them to her body. *God, he's right. I'll come so hard.* Her legs straightened and flicked across the sheet as she struggled to contain her desire.

When Robert trailed kisses down the side of her belly, Alyssa sighed. He licked back up the center of her abs, all the way to her breasts, then kissed back down the other side before licking to her mound. He dropped open-mouthed kisses across it and down to her clit, each one getting a little flick of his tongue before he lifted off her for the next one.

Robert stopped teasing Alyssa with his hands. He gripped her knees to still her legs, then planted sloppy kisses up the inside of her thigh. The warm wetness as he moved farther up for the next one quickened Alyssa's breathing. His eyes narrowed in the corners, and she knew he was smiling at her over her undulating belly.

Robert nibbled to the top of her thigh. Alyssa held her

breath. *Kiss it. Kiss my pussy like you did my leg.* "Ugh, Robert." Her leg pushed against his hand as he blew on the wet kisses he'd left on his way up her thigh, the chill making her squirm. He switched legs and resumed on the inside of her knee, the trail of wet kisses on all her sensitive spots shooting sparks up her legs to accumulate behind her clit. Just as the next kiss should land on her engorged lips, he blew on the wet spots and retreated to her knee.

She huffed and reached for his hair, but he smiled and dodged her.

"What do you want, Alyssa?"

"Stop teasing me. Eat me. Make me come."

"You want me to make you come? Only me?"

"Yes. In the end, only you. Reclaim me."

He held her legs open and blew across her open pussy. A flash of cool followed by a wave of heat surged up her vagina, making it clench the emptiness it wanted to fill. Her thighs pushed against Robert's palms as she tried to press her hips to his mouth.

"You want to be mine again?"

"Yes, Babe. More than anything. Make me yours."

Robert licked her pussy from bottom to top, spreading her and covering her open lips from side to side. She was mentally begging him to flick her clit when he reached it. He left it quivering in the air like a hair trigger needing one tiny touch to fire.

Alyssa cackled and gripped her husband's hair while he licked her open lips, sometimes pulling the inner labia with his lips, sometimes nipping the outer labia with his teeth. Finally he sucked her swollen clit into his mouth, holding the hood back with his front teeth and pressing the exposed nub against them with his tongue. The electric storm inside her exploded. Alyssa clamped her thighs to his ears as she came.

Alyssa released her husband's head from her thighs and

stretched her arms out to him. "Now make love to me, Babe. Get up here."

Robert climbed up her body, placing a couple of kisses on her undulating belly and sucking each of her nipples along the way. He sucked her neck below her ear while he positioned his cock at her soaking slit and slid inside.

Alyssa bit her lower lip and closed her eyes as the curved cock crawled along the front wall of her vagina, crossing her G-spot and not stopping until it touched the sensitive area beside her cervix. *Right there. That's my husband.* "Mm, yeah, Babe." She held him inside by his sides as she ground her hips, rubbing his perfect cockhead back and forth over her cervix. "It's good to have you inside me, Babe. You're perfect for me."

"Then it's time I took you back." He inched his hips back until his cock almost left her, then reversed course, returning to her depths as slowly as he had pulled out. The slow movement tugged at her lips despite the lubrication of her recent orgasm, making her pussy feel stretched beyond the fabulous job his thick cock actually did. The slow pace let their eyes connect as they moved.

"That's good, Babe. Keep going." *He loves me. He's watching my eyes for what feels good, and what hurts. He knows I'm sore from last night. I love him too. That's what makes this better than all the others. God, this is good. He does exactly the right things, every time.*

Alyssa felt her chest flush hot. Robert smiled and pinched her nipple. *He knows I'm close.*

She broke their eye contact by forcing her head back, and she started to pant. "So close. Keep going." Robert maintained the slow pace that thrilled and tormented his bride. With a cry, she stopped breathing and lurched her hips upward while pulling his sides, impaling herself as far as she could on his cock. Robert returned her force but didn't thrust while she came.

Alyssa raised her head and palmed his cheek as she recovered her breath. "That was wonderful. Now take me and make me yours again." She pressed his chest, and he pulled out of her. She put her ass in the air and laid her chest on the bed.

"You want me to take you, huh? Okay. I'll take you back, Baby."

Her lips tingled as he lined up his cock and shoved into her with one motion. The tip of his cock molded the back wall of her vagina differently than it just had from the front. He tapped her cervix when he bottomed out, then thrust back in to do it again. He sped up and left her feeling more full than empty.

He squeezed her ass cheeks, spreading them open. Alyssa's ass ached from the pain, but her clit tingled at the same time. *Ow. That bastard spanked me hard last night. And it feels good.*

"You all right, Baby?"

"Mm-hmm. I got spanked hard last night."

"That prick." Robert moved his hands from Alyssa's cheeks to the front of her hips and slowed his pace.

"No, Robert. Don't slow down. Pound me. Fuck me hard. I'm yours to use as you see fit. I mean it, no matter how much it hurts, you reclaim me afterward and I'll bear it. Grab my ass. Remind me whose I am. Fuck me hard and come inside me, Babe. Do it."

Robert sighed, then clamped onto his wife's cheeks with both hands and pulled her back onto his cock as he pounded forward. Alyssa's grunts became tinged with whimpers as he continued, but when he slowed, she growled at him to go harder.

The spongy tip of his cock hammered across the nub of her cervix. Alyssa squeezed her vaginal walls, trying to feel all of him and let him feel all of her. His cock swelled inside her, fighting her and signaling his coming eruption. He shoved forward even harder, faster, holding her cheeks tight in his fingers, and she felt the hot jet hit her cervix before she heard his bellow.

When she felt the last drips fill her, she spoke. "Keep fucking me. I'm close." *The pain amplifies the pleasure.* "Hard, Babe."

Robert resumed his pace, pulling her cheeks roughly and slamming forward, still tickling her cervix with every plunge.

Alyssa arched her back farther as her pussy clenched his cock in waves. She pushed back and writhed her hips, rubbing her cervix against his cock to prolong her release. "Yes, Babe. Yes."

She slid forward, pulling off his cock. She shuddered as the cool air touched the insides of her lips and a warm dribble of cum rolled out and over her clit. Robert lay beside her and stroked her back and ass.

"You are mine again, Alyssa."

"I am, Babe. I love you so much."

"I love you too. Remember that, Baby."

⁓

Dressed and packed, Alyssa sat on the rumpled bed while Robert tied his shoes beside her. "You saw them this morning? We succeeded?"

"Yes, their punishment has commenced. It sounded like they got fired, their wives are divorcing them, and the other people who received the video are mad at them too. Do you want to see it?"

"Not now. Maybe later. Can you send the videos to me?"

"I can. It's Dave talking with his buddies this morning. Keegan added a surprise at the end that I think you'll enjoy."

"Can you send me the videos from last night too?"

Robert finished tying his shoe, then retied it. "You want to see that? You want to hear what they said about you? You want a souvenir of those three assholes?"

Alyssa looked at the ceiling. "Maybe. I don't know. It's just a thought."

"Wait, Alyssa. You asked intentionally, knowing what is on the videos from last night. I'll send you the videos if you want. Can you please tell me why you want them?"

"I want to see them pay."

"That happened this morning. You want last night's videos too."

"Yes." She sighed and hung her head before looking at him. *Be honest. Don't keep this a secret.* "I want to remember the feeling. You don't want me to be with multiple men at once, so I won't do it again. Sometimes, though, I might want to remember how it felt. Seeing, hearing…well, it might help me scratch that itch."

"Baby, I haven't put any limits—"

"You haven't, I know. But you said that last night was different from our open relationship. I know that means you don't want me to…well…participate in an orgy again. I know I get too aroused by it, and I can't control myself. You don't like it, so I won't do it."

"Baby—"

Alyssa held up her hand. "No, Robert. I know how this affects me, and I know how it affects us. I won't do it again. I won't hurt you with it."

She stared out the window at nothing. Envisioning a pile of bricks, she began walling off the last eighteen hours, both saving them unspoiled for later and removing them from her consciousness to reduce the temptation. "But…"

"But what?"

"But I might want to remember how amazing it felt, even if it was with those assholes. When I feel slutty, I could watch the video. I'm sorry if this hurts you, but I think I may want to remember."

"Alyssa…Baby… We have no limits beyond those already established. Our marriage is open. We can have sex with others, but we are discreet, we don't stay overnight, and family obligations always come first. You added that you call me before you play, so I can slow you down and come help you when you get discombobulated like you did last night." He took both her hands in his. "I admit I don't like the thought of men using you like a piece of meat to be discarded. If you want that from time to time, it isn't my place to forbid it. I'll even come get you out of it if you need me to. I'll never watch again though."

"It never needs to cross your mind again. I know you'll let me because you love me and want me to be happy. But I love you and want you to be happy. I won't do it again. Please let me ease your mind."

"I won't argue. You control what you do, so long as you keep our agreement." He thumbed his phone. "There you go. I'd love to watch them with you, especially Keegan's part, except for the first two. I won't watch those again. The rest could be fun together."

"Can we play them this afternoon, lying in bed?"

"Sounds great. Let's go."

"Robert?"

"Hmm?"

"Thank you for accepting and loving me for who I am. I love you, Babe."

4

THURSDAY, MAY 6, HOME

Alyssa turned off her hair dryer and brushed her wavy brown mane a few times. She watched Robert shave a stroke before picking up her eye liner. "Babe, I've been thinking."

"Oh no. When you start a conversation while we are getting ready in the morning, I worry. What have you been thinking?"

"Nothing bad. I've been thinking how to spend that raise Doug gave me."

"The twenty percent buying your silence after he sexually harassed you?"

"You make it sound so bad. Remember, I didn't ask for that. He did it out of the goodness of his heart. Anyway, yes, that twenty percent raise."

"Okay."

"I thought we could buy some rental property."

"That would take a lot more than your raise."

"We use the raise to supplement the rent in paying the mortgage. We end up with income property for retirement."

"I like it, Baby. You beat your banker husband to that one. What did you have in mind?"

"Maybe a house or two, depending on the cost. I don't want to deal with a commercial building. I'll call Lauren today and see what she recommends."

"Okay. See what she says, and tell her I said hello."

❧

Robert raised his glass to his wife. "Dinner was excellent, Babe, as always."

"Thank you."

"What did Lauren say about rental property?"

"She handed me off. She's about to have another baby and stopped showing property. They have a rental housing specialist who can help us on Saturday morning."

"I have golf then. I'll back out."

"Don't do that, Babe. I can narrow the list down, then we can make the decision from the finalists together. Go enjoy golf."

"You know I used to evaluate these things for the bank, right?"

"That's why you will make the final call. I can cull the herd. Besides, I want to do this on my own because I got this raise by standing up to Doug. You play golf. I promise, I'll get your expert opinion before choosing."

5

SATURDAY MORNING, MAY 8, REALTY OFFICE

ALYSSA WAS REPLYING to an email when a tall man walked into the conference room carrying a cup of coffee.

"Mrs. Davis? I'm Hayden Robinson." He shook her hand and smiled.

She tried to hide her surprise with a quick smile. *A man? A gorgeous, sexy man? Every woman at Queen must want him. I do. God, how will I think about houses?* "Nice to meet you. No offense, but Lauren always told me Queen was a women-only office."

He laughed, shook his head, and continued holding her hand. "I get that question every time. It used to be. I joined about a year ago on a trial basis. If you prefer, you can switch out for another agent. Some women use Queen because they are uncomfortable seeing houses with men."

Alyssa smiled and pulled her hand back, disappointed that the subtle electricity flowing from his hand to her nipples stopped but not wanting to look awestruck. She wanted more of that feeling. *Not a chance.* "No need to switch. Lauren spoke highly of you, and she has been our realtor for years. She neglected to disclose that Hayden was a man."

"All right then. Let's discuss what you are looking for. I'll pull houses that fit your parameters so we have an efficient day."

An hour later, they pulled into the driveway of the first house, a plain ranch with puke-green shutters and a red door. Hayden turned to Alyssa in the passenger seat. "It's a little above your price range, and it needs new colors, but the neighborhood is good. A lot of young families live here, and fewer than half the houses are rentals, which keeps the rents higher. I haven't shown it before, but it's worth assessing as a rental."

Alyssa grinned. "Let's go in. Maybe I can convince my husband to pay up for a good one." *That dark hair and blue eyes... Even if the house is ugly, you aren't.*

They walked toward the front door. "Will your husband be joining us later?"

"Not today. He's golfing."

"I see. If you don't mind me saying, if my wife were as beautiful as you, I would stay close to her around other men."

Her stomach fluttered at the compliment. *He probably does that to every woman he's trying to sell. But I won't complain. In fact, let's play with your words.* "That is a bit forward, but thank you for the compliment. Honestly, we expected you to be a woman, not a handsome man, if you don't mind me saying."

He chuckled. "That is a bit forward, but thank you for the compliment. Shall we go in?" He walked in the front door and yelled, "Hello. Realtor showing the house." He turned to Alyssa. "In case someone is here."

"I see."

They moved through the house room by room. Alyssa and Robert had moved several times when they were first married, so she looked for what she liked in a house. The interior colors showed that the owner only displayed poor taste on the outside. She led the way. Hayden trailed behind, answering questions and pointing out features.

Alyssa led them to the basement. She opened a door to the right of the stairs and flipped on the light.

Holy shit! Her hand covered her mouth as she took in the room. Large black-and-white photos of people having sex adorned the red walls. She jumped when she saw a woman in the room to her left, then realized it was her own reflection in the wall-to-wall mirror. She stepped into the room toward the king-size bed covered only in burgundy sheets and four large pillows. She lifted a black leather cuff from the corner, rubbing its padded surface. Her nipples hardened. She felt a tingle in her pussy. *God, now I'm wet.*

"This looks scary," Hayden said from across the room.

Alyssa spun to her right to see Hayden resting his hand on a rack of feathers, whips, and paddles. "Oh my. I didn't expect this."

"Me neither. There was nothing about this in the listing. You never know what you will find in a house."

"It's fine. I'm a little curious." Alyssa looked at the photos. *It's the same woman. This is her room. She's tied up, but she is the one in charge; it shows in her eyes.* Alyssa strolled around the room, caressing the implements she found and picking up a few. The fuzzy, warm feathers and smooth, cool leather crossed her palm, both making her imagine how they would feel teasing her body. And punishing it. Her ass tingled as if anticipating a spank.

She stopped in the corner, where a mannequin wore a leather

bustier, leather thong, and thigh-high boots. She touched the domino mask on its face, rubbing the lace. *The contradiction is sexy.*

She lingered, taking in the room as she pivoted toward the door. She noted Hayden watching her in the mirror. His erection tented the leg of his khakis lower than most she had seen. Her nipples tingled. *That cock says he likes watching me. I wanted this guy when I saw him, and now coming here made me horny.* "Interesting room, but we've probably seen enough. Ready to head out?"

"Sure. This is interesting. I'll message the listing agent to post a warning. I'd hate for a family with kids to walk in expecting a playroom."

Alyssa cackled. "Oh my. Yes, that would be uncomfortable." *Maybe you want to play with me though.*

He laughed and followed her out of the room. Alyssa put a little more wiggle in her hips as she went up the stairs.

❧

Six houses later, Alyssa wondered why he pulled into a small parking lot. "I didn't know there was a restaurant out here."

"They have been here a couple of months, and it's fantastic. It sits off the beaten path, so only a few people come. I like to help them out by introducing my clients to it."

Alyssa cocked her head and smiled. "That's so sweet of you. Wait, do you own a piece of it?"

He laughed. "No, no. I wasn't even their realtor. I met George, the owner, one day volunteering with a housing charity. He's a nice man with a good heart, so I try to help by bringing people here."

"Aw, you are such a sweetheart."

A short man with salt-and-pepper hair greeted them.

"Hayden, thank you for coming, and for bringing such a pretty lady. Hello, pretty lady. I'm George. We will take good care of you today."

She took his offered hand. He kissed the back of hers, and heat ran up her neck into her cheeks. "Thank you, George. I'm Alyssa. I'm already glad we met."

"He brings the best people here to see us." He winked at her and led them to a corner booth.

"I can see why you want to help him out. He's charming."

"And has a heart of gold. I told you I met him at a charity house. He closes the restaurant one day a month and pays the staff to work on a build. He can't afford it, but he believes in it."

"What about you? Do you believe in it, or are you scoping out new construction?"

"No, I've volunteered in construction since college. I love that people get an opportunity to help themselves, and people like me can help them help themselves. You should try it."

Good-looking and with a kind heart. Mm. "I haven't swung a hammer in years, but I grew up helping my dad around the house a lot. Maybe I will." She picked up her menu. *Could be fun. It would be a good thing to do. And if he's sweaty with his shirt off...*

"If you want to own rentals, you might want to get back in practice. Contractors are expensive."

She laughed. "You sound like a salesman. What are you, a realtor?"

Hayden laughed and picked up his menu. He looked at Alyssa after they put their menus down. "So what have you seen that you like?"

You, but I won't say that yet. "The houses look fine as rentals. Nothing really got me excited." She leaned forward and lowered her voice. A low-grade throb pulsed between her legs. "Except the sex dungeon."

His eyes gleamed, and the corners of his mouth twitched up. "You liked that? We can arrange a second showing. Did you envision yourself being whipped or doing the whipping?"

The low-grade throb blazed hotter. No vanilla realtor would be so bold. She liked it. She wanted more. *Let's play.* "Maybe not whipped so much, more restrained. I want the power."

His smirk stretched just a bit farther up his cheek. He leaned closer. "How does being restrained give you power? Regardless of whether you like it, the man can do whatever he wants to you." He let his eyes wander to her tits. She knew he wanted her to see his interest. He renewed their eye contact. "Absolutely anything."

A vision of this man standing over her, leering, pondering how to use her, flashed in her mind and flowed down through her body, igniting every cell between her head and her toes. She recrossed her legs to change the pressure on her needy pussy. "That's the power. I'm restrained. Powerless. He can do anything, use me for his pleasure. But it's me he wants. That's my power."

The realtor leaned closer. His pupils dilated into large spots in his blue eyes. His mouth opened just enough to show a hint of white teeth above the tip of his tongue. The salty cedar smell of his cologne mixed with the breath mints he'd popped all morning, the unique blend burning into her memory, forever associated with the infernal need between her legs. "Even if he whips you until you cry?"

Alyssa leaned forward to match his pose. "Whips me or caresses me, it's all foreplay. In the end he wants to fuck me. Not someone else. Me. The power comes in allowing it. And if I let him tie me, rest assured I want him to fuck me."

The waitress sputtered as she put the drinks on the table. "I'll give you a minute."

Alyssa laughed as the moment disappeared, taking the tension with it. She sat back, the fire between her legs still smoldering. "That was poor timing."

Hayden looked in her eyes. "Yes. We should have had the discussion in the room itself."

She wanted to let the mood cool a bit more. "I thought those kinds of places only existed in bad movies. Truth really is stranger than fiction." *Like people in open marriages. And hot realtors who seduce women in empty houses. Alyssa! You've been horny all morning. Calm down. You don't even know this guy. But you want to.*

"It is that. What else would get you excited?" His hungry look told Alyssa that he wasn't ready to abandon the topic.

"Me? Or in a rental?"

He smirked. "Whatever you want to share."

Ease this back. "For a rental, low maintenance excites me. I want to rent it and leave it. Something solid the renters can't break." She moved her hand to her chin and looked at his blue eyes, narrowed to the point that she knew he liked what he saw. *A hot guy with a kind heart excites me.* "For me, I want a little privacy, some space so the neighbors can't see or hear everything. And a little something unique."

Keep him interested. "Maybe not a sex dungeon, but something special to feed my every—" She dragged her tongue across her upper lip slow enough to take a breath while he waited. "—fucking…desire."

The waitress put down their food. "Y'all keep talking about a sex dungeon, and I'm gonna break my husband's back when I get off work." She smiled. "This is the best conversation I've overheard in months." She walked away.

Hayden followed her with his eyes. "She just might break his back. She's no waif."

"Her legs are strong. Look at them. They'll squeeze him in

half." Alyssa chuckled and looked away from the waitress's firm ass. "He'll be lucky if she does."

"He would be at that."

The waitress brought the bill, and Alyssa and Hayden stood to pay at the front. Alyssa caught the waitress's hand and whispered to her. "Tell your husband why you're so horny tonight. Tell him two hot customers kept talking about a sex dungeon. Then, when he's inside you, imagine the two of us tying you up, then spanking and loving your sexy body." She patted the young woman's rump, then pulled back. "You were great. Have a delightful evening!"

They went to the register and paid. Hayden opened the car door for Alyssa and held her hand as she got in.

"My, my. Quite a gentleman." She leaned so he got a glimpse of her cleavage as she sat. *Enjoy your reward.*

"For the right lady. What did you say to her?"

"I shared an idea for tonight with her husband."

"Oh boy." He closed his door and smirked at her. "I have an idea based on what you said at lunch."

Alyssa again fashioned an image of Hayden standing over her looking hungry. Her nipples tingled. "Excuse me?"

"About a house. Not about the other stuff." He pulled out his phone and opened his navigation app. "Would you be interested in buying a house to flip instead of rent? There is one that isn't on the market yet, but it's a steal. It has privacy and a unique feature as well. It's being sold furnished. It needs some work, and you could sell it in about a month. Would you like to try that?"

"Would I have to do the work? I'm not up for that." Alyssa's excitement ebbed. A niggle of doubt lodged in her brain as she decided that she was being sold something problematic. *It's less work to sell one big house than three small ones. He's trying to make this easy on himself.*

"I can coordinate our contractors for you."

I don't want a money pit. "I'm really looking for long-term retirement income."

"I understand. You could roll the profits on this one into more rentals."

She decided one look couldn't hurt, even if he was trying to boost his commission. *Go see it, pass, and look at more potential rentals.* "Okay. I'll look. I don't intend to take any risk here."

"I understand. We'll look, and you can decide."

The long driveway wove through dense woods, ending at a two-story house with brown siding. The front porch and the steps were broken. The roof above it sagged where a support had been.

Alyssa let Hayden come around to open her door and help her out of the low car. He kept her hand in his. "Let me help you up the steps. You can see the work that needs to be done."

"Great first impression." She stepped onto the less damaged side of the steps.

Hayden held her hand from behind and placed his other hand on her waist as he followed. "Don't want you to fall."

His hand on her waist was comfortable, like it had been designed to fit there, just above her jeans. *Right, big boy. I'm not that dumb. I'm also not protesting.* "No, we don't. Thank you for taking care of me." She stepped away from the damaged portion of porch while he opened the door. "What happened here?"

"The couple is divorcing. The husband caught his wife with another man, so all she receives is half the sale price of the house. He's angry and intends to sell cheap, only two fifty."

"What about this damage?"

"After the divorce decree, she got drunk and rammed her car into the porch. Ugly situation, and the damage lets him sell it for even less. Bad for her. Good for you, though, if you want to buy. The porch, front steps, and porch roof need work, but everything else is solid. After about forty thousand of work, it should sell for four fifty."

"Sounds too good to be true, but let's see it."

He placed his hand in the small of her back as she walked in, sending a little spark through her body. She hissed a small breath when it lodged low in her belly. Every touch found the uneasy titillation from the last few hours lingering and fluttering in her belly, then joined to it, making her shudder.

"I like the great room. The built-in shelves are nice." *You want to flirt with your hands? I can too.* She pulled his hand to the right. "Show me the kitchen."

"The kitchen was redone a couple of years ago. New appliances, open plan, new ventilation. Go through to the dining area."

He again steered her at the small of her back. She again had a tingle travel through her body to join its predecessor in her belly. It was time to turn the tables and make him tingle. And maybe more.

"I love the windows. The view of the woods is lovely." Alyssa turned toward him before hopping with excitement. *That's right. Watch the girls bounce.*

"Then come upstairs. You will love this."

"Give me a minute. I need to call my husband."

⁂

Alyssa stepped onto the deck overlooking a back yard surrounded by woods. She could see no other houses, nor hear any traffic. She opened her phone and leaned over the deck railing. She hoped Hayden was watching from inside.

Alyssa spun her rings while she opened her phone. The plan

this morning had morphed into something very different this afternoon. She woke wanting only to find some rentals, but now she wanted Hayden. She intended to keep her agreement with Robert and get his agreement to change their strategy. She rehashed the talking points in her mind while it rang. Robert answered, and she forced herself to smile, knowing it would come across in her voice.

"I think I found one."

"The finalist you want me to see?"

"Yes, but we're going to flip it."

"That's more risk than we talked about. What is going on?"

"We can get this house and six acres for two fifty. We have to fix the front porch, and Hayden thinks the market value is more like four fifty. We could almost double our money in about a month."

"Sounds fishy. What is the story?"

Alyssa paced, the movement siphoning the emotion as she verbally fenced with Robert. "Divorce. The husband is lowballing the price to get back at a cheating wife. It isn't on the market yet, but we can buy it. Hayden will only take half commission now and take a full one when we sell it. We can roll the proceeds into more rental property. I haven't finished looking at all of it, but if it checks out, I think we should do this."

"You haven't finished looking?"

She again bent over the rail, leaning on her elbows, hoping the casual pose relayed in her voice. He asked a reasonable question, and he needed to be comfortable with the house before moving to the real reason she called early. "I need to see the upstairs. The downstairs looks great, so I stepped outside so we could talk in private before I go up. If it looks good, I want to make an offer. We have to be fast before it goes on the market this week."

"So Hayden says we can sell it for four fifty, and she's willing to only take a half commission now?"

"He will only take a half commission now, and he'll coordinate the repair work through the realty company."

"He? When did Queen start hiring men?"

Alyssa chuckled. "I asked that too. About a year ago. He's done a good job today, and if he's right on this house, we can make a great profit." *Come on, Babe. You can trust me.*

"I see. It might be okay. Slow down a bit though. Take a good look at everything. Look for any reasons that you are being pushed to act fast."

Good advice. I hadn't thought of that. "I will, Babe. I don't want to get stuck either. I tell you, the lot is beautiful and wooded, and the house looks great so far."

"Slow down. We should talk about spending that much money, but this is your project, and I trust you to make the right call."

She smiled. His faith in her always warmed her heart, and it did now. *Now the real reason for the call. Just jump in.* "Plus… he's hot."

"Are you having a hot realtor fantasy?"

"I am, Babe. I want to seal the deal for the house we decide to buy right there on the spot. I think it's this one, but if not, one later today. Can I?"

"Jeez, Alyssa. What happened to being more deliberate with who you sleep with? You just took three men at once on Monday. Now you want to nail the hot realtor you just met. Does that sound deliberate to you?"

His reference to Monday changed the warmth in her chest to anger. He had agreed to do what they did, knowing everything it entailed. *But he didn't like it. And watching me hurt him so much. Be gentle. Your best answer is honesty.* "Babe, we did what we did

Monday for revenge, and I know it was hard on you. Please don't compare the two. This is different. It's a fantasy. This house deal makes me horny."

"Then come home."

Alyssa frowned and leaned on the railing of the back deck, dropping her head. "I want to live out the fantasy. Please?" *This hot fantasy with a hot realtor has tortured me all day. Please give me permission.* "You get to reclaim me when I get home…"

Alyssa envisioned Robert shaking his head when he sighed. "Go ahead. Calling isn't supposed to stop you, just keep you safe. Send me the address before you do anything, and text me when you are done so I know you are safe. Enjoy your fantasy, and remember that when you get home, you have to convince your banker husband to let you spend this much money. That's my part of the fantasy."

Alyssa squealed. "Yippee! Two fantasies in one afternoon. I can't wait. And, I promise, I'll convince you so well, Babe. On the house, are you fine with the change to flipping this one?"

"If it's as sure as he says. Well, if it is half as sure; real estate is never a sure thing."

She squealed again. "Yay! Thank you, Babe. This is going to be great. Love you! See you at home."

Alyssa hung up and bounced into the kitchen. "Let's see the rest."

She headed up the stairs in front of Hayden, then stopped at the top.

Hayden put his hand on her hip, nudging her left. "Master bedroom. This way."

He kept his hand on her as they walked down the hallway and into the high-ceilinged room. More tingles. Her belly quivered with the electricity amassing inside it. Her pussy throbbed.

"Oh. The big windows!" She moved to the bathroom. "And in here too!" Again, she turned to hop in front of Hayden, who made no attempt to look at anything beyond her bouncing breasts. *You like this, don't you?*

"They are great, but this is what I wanted to show you." He pushed a panel in the wall, revealing a narrow stairway. "Follow me."

Alyssa stared at his ass the entire way up the steps. She palmed it when he stopped suddenly. "Oops. Sorry."

"It's fine with me." He opened the trapdoor above his head. "You go ahead. You should experience it alone first."

He pressed his back against the wall, and she turned to slide by. The narrow stair left no room between them, and she felt his belt buckle against her belly and rubbed her breasts against his firm pecs. She placed one hand on his chest and the other on his hip, letting it trail across his erection as she scooted by and into the cupola above.

"Oh my god! The cupola is an actual room! Windows everywhere, even in the dome! I can see everything! It's gorgeous!" She spun, looking out and thinking about people looking in. Her breasts ached to be touched. Her pussy needed to be filled. The setting, the simmering tension between her and the sexy realtor all day, the conversation with the waitress all pushed her to a decision. *I'm in an open marriage for a reason. Stop waiting and get what you want.*

He climbed into the room. "It's high enough to get some great views, but still away from the neighbors' eyes. Is this the kind of unique feature you are looking for?"

"I never knew a room this perfect existed. And I love the two chaises. What a great place to make love." *Here is your chance.* She looked him square in the eye, letting him know that what came next was to keep up appearances. "I shouldn't have said that."

"You are right. It is a great place to make love." He closed the small distance between them and wrapped his arms around her waist.

Alyssa reached behind his head and pulled him down for a kiss. She dropped her hand to his ass, pulling his crotch against her belly. His hands cupped her ass, squeezing the cheeks over her jeans.

Alyssa broke their kiss to lift Hayden's shirt over his head. With her hands, she explored the contours of his muscular arms and shoulders as she slowed to appreciate what she uncovered. *His arms are so hard. Big, hairless chest. And a six-pack. God, he is a wet dream.* She traced her fingers down his chest and rubbed his nipples, then ran them across his washboard stomach a couple of times before working on his belt.

He unbuttoned her jeans and peeled her T-shirt over her head, letting his fingers graze her skin as he inched it upward. The fingertips generated tingles that danced across her skin until they reached her nipples, which hardened and sparked when he reached between her tits to unclasp her bra. "You are so beautiful. You deserve a beautiful spot like this."

"Do it now, before I change my mind." She let the bra slide down her arms while she stepped out of her tennis shoes, then slithered out of her jeans and panties. Her legs quivered as she stood naked in front of him, wanting him to want her. Wanting him to take her.

He stepped out of his loafers and unfastened his pants slowly, smirking at Alyssa. "You have been thinking about this since that first house, haven't you?"

Her eyes stayed glued to the bulge running down his leg. She held a breast in each hand, lightly strumming her nipples.

"Answer me. You have thought about this all day, haven't you?"

Alyssa's throat could only manage a whisper. "Yes."

"Now you are going to get it." He dropped his pants and stepped out of them.

Alyssa gasped at his cock. Veiny and thick, with a curve toward his belly, it almost reached his navel. The shape reminded her of Robert; the size reminded her of Paul. Her pussy gripped against itself, wanting to be filled. *It's perfect.*

He whisked her up and laid her on a chaise. He climbed on top of her, putting his knees inside hers as she opened to receive him. He sucked and bit her breasts as he climbed up her body, then continued up her neck to her mouth, each touch igniting coils of warm delight that flailed inside her body until they latched onto the top of her vagina, adding fuel to the coming explosion. He moved his hand to her slit and spread her. One, then two fingers slid into her slippery opening, and he curled them forward, rubbing her G-spot.

Alyssa gasped into his mouth and ground her hips, wanting him deeper inside and harder against her clit. *He's good at that.*

When she began humping against him, he pulled his fingers out. She whined at the emptiness, then groaned as the head of his cock rubbed her lips. Alyssa stilled, fighting to give him a stationary target.

He looked down at her. "Put it in."

She did. He shoved forward. Her soaked pussy stretched around his girth as he worked about half his cock inside her. Hayden pulled back and forward again, stretching her wider. He did it again and touched the sensitive spot beside her cervix.

She quivered. *Only Robert has the curve and the size to hit that spot. This one is bigger. Yes.*

Hayden drove forward one last time. He touched that sensitive spot again and stretched it deeper into her belly as he pushed until his hips touched the back of her splayed legs, and the knot of pleasure perched atop her vagina erupted, spilling down her walls in waves.

Alyssa cried out as her first orgasm washed out of her pelvis and up to her nipples. She gripped his hips to hold him in place until she rode out her climax. "Now fuck me."

Hayden gave her long strokes, pulling back until her lips began to close, then driving in until his hips rammed into hers. He started slowly. As he accelerated, Alyssa's tits bounced in time with him, which pulled them, stretching the connections to her chest the way she liked. He leaned his body back. His head pressed harder against her G-spot and beside her cervix.

Oh god. His cock touches me just like Robert's but more. Her muscles tensed, widening her eyes and gaping her mouth as another orgasm built. A flush of heat rose above her breasts and spread up her neck and down her boobs, and she saw her faint tan lines glow pink. She locked her legs around his back, pulling him into her as she thrust against him, seating his tip against her cervix. She wailed.

Hayden ground his hips, unable to thrust while she clutched him. His thumb found her clit and pressed it hard before flicking across it, driving her climax higher. The tip of his cock skipped across the small, hard point of her cervix as he moved, each flick an aftershock rattling her body. Her cries had stopped, but she had not inhaled.

He sneered. "There it is. Come hard for me."

Alyssa didn't respond. She hadn't even heard. Her ears buzzed from pleasure. Her body became desperate for air, and she inhaled while pulling his hand away from her electric clit. "Too much. Too sensitive." Alyssa's legs collapsed from his back to the chaise.

He pulled out, leaving Alyssa empty and rousing her to grab for his arm, wanting to pull him back into her. He was already standing, leering down at her. He offered his hand, and she let him help her off the chaise.

He walked her to the glass overlooking the back yard. As she faced it, he pushed her face and chest against the glass and stepped behind her. He tapped her feet with his, spreading her legs. He pulled her hips back, making her lean harder against the glass.

"Won't this break?"

"It's laminated glass. We can't break it." He dipped his hips and slid inside her.

Alyssa moaned deep in her chest as he pushed forward, filling and stretching her pussy while pressing her breasts against the warm glass. Once his abs pressed against her ass, he stopped.

"Look out over the woods. You can see rooftops around us. Someone in the upper floors of those houses could see us." He pulled back and drove back into her. "They could see us with binoculars or a telescope, maybe a telephoto lens on a camera." He slammed into her again. "Does that excite you? Knowing that people could see if they tried?"

Alyssa pictured herself, cheek and tits pressed flat against the glass, hands pushing against it beside her face. Even if someone couldn't see detail, her pose made it clear what she was doing. Her pussy clenched at the thought. "Yes."

"Do you want to be seen?" He gave her another thrust. "Seen taking my cock? Seen coming with closed eyes and an open mouth, silently screaming for a voyeur? Seen with my cum running down your legs because your pussy can't hold it all?"

"Yes." *Just like Houston. So hot. I'm gonna come again.* Her pussy clenched around his cock, and her juice ran down her lips to her thighs. *Shit, a little one. A big one's coming.*

"Oh, you do like that. You like fucking in this room, don't

you?" Hayden stroked into her at a steady pace, pushing against the front wall of her vagina with the curved underside of his cock.

"Yes." *His cock hits my G-spot like this too. Fuck, I need more of this.*

"Are you going to fuck me again in this room?" He wiped his thumb over her anus, making her shiver. All her erogenous zones were collaborating toward her next orgasm.

"Yes."

"This will be our room, won't it? You won't tell anyone about our secret place, will you?" He dipped his thumb to her pussy, collecting some of the frothy cum working its way out, then smeared it on her anus, again sending a shiver up her spine despite the heat.

"No. It's our secret." *As long as you fuck me this good, anything.*

"Only I get to fuck you here."

"Yes. Only you." Alyssa's body started to shake as a much larger orgasm built within her. Her breath came in fast gasps, matching the strokes Hayden was giving her pussy. Her warm nipples pinched as they stretched along the warm glass, the pain becoming pleasure when it reached her cunt. The warm cum on her asshole felt good, but she spasmed when he stuck his thumb all the way inside. She screamed and quivered as her release rolled through her entire body.

Hayden moved one arm across her ribs, supporting her against the glass as her legs lost their strength. He continued to fuck her through her climax, the thumb in her ass compressing her tissues against the tip of his cock as it went in and out. Her body went limp, only remaining upright because he wedged her in place against the window. Her ass clenched against the emptiness when he used both arms to hold her up, cupping beneath her compressed breasts.

She muttered something unintelligible into the window as

her legs stiffened. His cock swelled inside her. He quickened his pace, and she began to bear her own weight as her legs strengthened. With a large, firm hand between her shoulder blades, he pressed her chest hard into the window as he slammed deep inside and erupted directly on her cervix.

"Yes! Come in me! So good!" Alyssa's orgasm squeezed her walls against the large cock separating them. *It's almost hot. I love how it fills me, squishing as I move.* Hayden leaned forward to kiss her neck and press her body against the window with his. She stroked his hair with one hand and held his hip to hers with the other.

He's softening. It's going to slip out. Oh god, there it goes. Alyssa moaned and lurched as the tip of Hayden's cock slid out of her stretched opening, followed by a large glob of their hot cum. *Fuck, I came a little from that.* She sighed. "Thank you. That was so good."

She slid down the window and sat on the hardwood floor. She looked at his deflating cock as he sat open-legged on the chaise across from her. *That cock is perfect. I will have it again. Often.*

He leaned back, using his hands to hold his body up at an angle. His body glistened with sweat, and his abs flexed as he panted to recover his breath. *He is so beautiful.*

While they panted, she made eye contact and held it until he let his eyes wander. She watched as he looked over her body, lingering at her neck and belly as he appraised every inch from head to toe. She knew he had seen the veins in her neck pulse and her belly pump. *Not a good look, but he made my heart race and breathe hard. Maybe he will be proud of it.* Her chest fluttered; she hoped he liked what he saw. *Maybe he'll want to make me this way again.*

He smiled at her. "Thank you, beautiful. It was better than good. You are awe-inspiring."

"I bet you say that to all the women you sell houses to."

"Did I sell you a house?"

"After what we just did, how could I not buy this house? I can double my money in a month, and during that month, I can come here. I love this room."

"You really are buying this?"

"Yes. I'll talk my husband into it. I'll call him when we go downstairs." A guilty ache crept into a dark corner of her chest, tainting the powerful afterglow of her orgasms and restoring more logical thought. *I should have called him again before agreeing to buy in the afterglow of great sex.*

"You want to call him now?"

"No. I should get dressed first. We won't FaceTime, but still." *He'll be upset, but he did say he trusted me. He will be okay with it.*

⌁

Alyssa leaned over the deck railing and spun her rings as she waited for Robert to answer his phone.

"Did you buy it, Baby?"

He's happy. No need to worry. "I'm going to make an offer. It's a great house." *Oops. Was I too enthusiastic?*

Robert chuckled. "I hear that in your voice. Is there anything unusual in the house that might make it hard to sell?"

"No. It's just a great vanilla house on a great lot." Her stomach tightened. She had lied to Robert for no reason. *Except Hayden wanted me to keep a secret. Technically, I didn't lie. The cupola won't make it hard to sell. It makes it wonderful.* "You said you trusted me on this. I'm telling you it's a great deal."

"Are you so excited to buy the house or to have your hot realtor fantasy?"

She turned to lean her back against the railing. Through the giant kitchen windows, she watched Hayden talk on his phone, noting his perfect teeth when he laughed. He towered over the table and chairs as he paced in a three-step circuit beside them. His clothes were arrayed perfectly, but dark spots on his shirt revealed their sweaty fuck minutes before. Her memory of the sunlight glistening on his abs reawakened her pussy. It clenched at itself, opening the path for pleasure to build at its top. A tiny ache followed. She would be sore tomorrow. *Gloriously sore.*

"Both of those, Babe, but I'm most excited about talking you into financing my real estate venture. Be ready when I come home. You're getting the hard sell."

He chuckled again. "Okay. See you soon?"

Hayden made eye contact with her through the window. He looked down her body and up again. When their eyes met, his hungry leer matched the fire growing between her legs. *Maybe we stay a little longer.*

"It may still be a while."

"He's resisting? Interesting. Maybe he's gay. That would fit for the only man in Queen's offices."

"I don't think that's it." She slipped her hand under the hem of her shirt to tease her belly with her fingertips while maintaining eye contact with the hunky realtor. Tiny shocks skimmed from her fingertips, along her skin, to her nipples, congregating there and building the tingle she wanted. "I'm being thorough with this house." *And the realtor. No need to rub it in though.*

"Okay, you must be serious. You have been inspecting it for an hour already. If you still intend to have your fantasy, will you send the address?"

Alyssa had not heard the question. Her mind had traded her fingertips to Hayden's, and they traced along the seams in her ab muscles, tingling as they crept higher. She noticed the pause and responded. "Uh-huh."

"And text after?"

"Sure." Her finger brushed the bottom of her bra, and she traced along it from side to side, imagining it was the man inside touching her. She needed to get inside. "Need to go. See you at home. Love you." She disconnected before he could respond.

∽

Alyssa strode through the kitchen door without taking her eyes off Hayden.

He smiled. "Let's go to the office and fill out the paperwork."

"Not yet. We need to seal the deal." She sank to her knees and unbuckled his belt. She opened his pants, dropping them and his underwear to his ankles. She pulled his hardening cock into her mouth, licking and sucking the head before bobbing and taking all of the curved shaft into her mouth.

She bobbed some more. *I love a cock getting hard in my mouth, especially one that tastes like pussy. My pussy.* Alyssa opened her jeans as she shoved her face all the way to his abdomen. She dipped her hand inside and rubbed her clit.

Hayden moaned while he wove his fingers into her hair, guiding her head back and forth as she fellated him. He didn't grip her head, but his hands moved with her as she bobbed. She felt the strength that could put her wherever he wanted her.

She gagged as he reached full hardness in her throat. *Big and curved. Fuck, this is good. I'm going to need practice.* She pulled off. "Can you come again?"

"With you? Yeah. Easy."

She dove back onto his cock, swallowing it all. She gagged. Tears dripped down her cheek, falling hot on her T-shirt. Wetness on the back of her hand as she lowered her hand to insert two fingers into her pussy made her smile around his cock. *I leaked everywhere. More to come.* She moved her other hand to his ass, pulling it toward her face, letting him shift to fucking her face rather than accepting her blow job.

"Yeah, take it." He tightened his grip in her hair and thrust forward into her mouth. The gagging noises she had made occasionally before became louder and occurred on every thrust. He sped up, and she opened her mouth so the contact with her only occurred along her tongue and in her throat.

Alyssa surrendered the pace to Hayden. *Fuck my face. Fuck me hard.* Her fingers slipped up from her slit, dragging cum to lubricate her clit as she swiped and pulled it, enjoying the sparks rising through her belly. Her gagging streamed drool from her mouth down the front of her shirt enough to feel the wetness on her breasts as it soaked through. She squeezed her clit as her ass clenched. She squeezed her thighs around her own hand as she came. Her pussy flowed into the crotch of her jeans. *So good. Use my throat.*

Hayden sped up as his cock swelled in Alyssa's mouth. As much as she wanted him to come in her mouth, she needed him in her again. She pulled off his cock. "Fuck me again." She pointed to a kitchen chair. "Sit there."

He pulled out a chair and sat, pants still around his ankles. Alyssa stood to remove her jeans and panties. She ran her fingers over her wet lips. She used two fingers to spread herself open, showing him her moisture. She inserted her middle finger and moved it around before pulling it out and lifting it above her face.

"You see this cum? You put it there. Your cum came from you. My cum came because of you. I'm sloppy with it." She tilted her head back and dipped the wet finger into her mouth, slurping the juice off it as she raised her hand.

"Delicious. I want more. Can you make me come again, right

here?" She watched his eyes follow her hand down her body and graze her lips. They followed as she brought another wet finger to her mouth. She sucked it, pulling her finger in and out like she would suck a cock.

Her eyes met his. *You're hungry for me again, but I'm in control.* She let him watch her look at his cock. It had softened a bit, but it glistened with her spit. His cock jumped. *Excellent.*

"Can you come more, right here?" She dipped her finger into her slit and thrust her hips, fucking herself. She broke their eye contact and lolled her head back to growl. When she raised her head again, his cock lurched again. *You like that look.* She added a second finger inside herself, pulled it out, and took three strides to join him at the kitchen table. She gripped his hardening cock with her wet hand and stroked it.

"You feel that? That's our cum getting you ready for me. You'll be hard in a minute, and I'll climb on and let your cock stir up the cum inside me. I'll come again and again while you build up, and then you'll fill me full." She tugged him harder. "You want that? Do you?"

"Yes."

She tugged him more. "You sure? When you whisper, I'm not sure you mean it."

"Yes. I want it. I want to make you come."

"Will you give me yours?"

"Yes. I'll come wherever you want it."

She smiled. "You're ready." She climbed on his lap and lined up his tip with her dripping slit. She dropped down hard, screaming when her ass hit his thighs. Her head lolled back again, and when she raised it, she put her hands on his shoulders and started bouncing on his cock with short strokes. *Stay full. Feels so good.*

He lifted her shirt above her breasts and opened the front clasp of her bra. He gripped both her tits as she bounced. He kept his hands still, stretching them as she raised and dropped her body. When he shifted his grip to pinching her nipples, her breasts elongated as she lengthened her strokes.

"Yes. Pull my tits. The hurt feels so good. Pinch them." Her legs quivered as they lifted her almost to the tip of his cock, then gave out as she crashed back down on him. *Here I come.* A hot flush began above her breasts, spreading to combine with stinging finger marks around her nipples. Her stomach rolled where the pain from her breasts and the pleasure from her pussy collided. She gasped, then slammed her forehead onto the meaty part of his shoulder as her release exploded.

He moved his hands from her breasts. They glided down her sides and thighs to her knees, then back to her hips. He moved them to the tops of her cheeks, then slid them down, forcing them between her ass and his thighs. Still inside her, he stood. She gripped his neck with her arms and wrapped her legs around his hip bones.

Her pussy pressed down onto his cock until her still-orgasming clit was wedged into the joint of his abdomen and his cock. *Wonderful pressure forcing him deeper.*

His strong hands dug into her cheeks as he lifted her, spreading them apart and pulling her back door open a little. He lowered her until she hit bottom, then lifted her again. He lifted her again and again. All she could do was hang on.

Alyssa mewled from the pinching her clit was getting. His thick, long, curved cock rubbed her G-spot and tapped beside her cervix on every stroke. Having her ass pulled open lit the match to another impending orgasm. *He hits all the ways Robert does but bigger and harder. So fucking strong too. Amazing.*

He stopped lifting her and slid one hand up her back to hold her between her shoulder blades. He pulled her close to him. "You like being taken? I'll take you."

He bent at the waist. Alyssa tensed her arms around his neck, then relaxed as his hand on her back held her weight. As they bent, his hand moved from her ass cheek to her arm. He gripped her just above the elbow.

"Release my neck."

She did. He held her up with his hands and his cock, lowering her neck and shoulders to the floor while her pussy remained impaled on him. Her ass cheeks pressed against his thighs, and the head of his cock created a bump in her stomach where it levered against the front wall of her vagina.

Once her weight was on her shoulders, his hands unwrapped her legs from his waist and pushed them down so her toes touched the floor above her head. He again gripped her ass cheeks with his hands, digging in to hold her steady.

"This is how I take you."

He pulled up until just the tip of his cock remained inside, pressing hard on her G-spot on the way. He dropped into her until his balls mashed on her asshole. Her vagina stretched even farther than it had before as his head pushed her cervix into her guts. She cried out and came, the juices flowing out of her and down her stomach.

Hayden fucked into her at a steady pace, not hard, but using the angle to both penetrate deeper than he had been and apply firm pressure against her front wall and G-spot. Every time he descended, his warm, heavy balls rested on her asshole, teasing it and driving Alyssa mad with lust.

"Oh god. Just like that. Fuck me. Take me." *Never this good. Not by anybody. Ever.*

Alyssa's body bounced between orgasm and almost-orgasm, staying on a plateau of stimulation that left her mouth only capable of drooling and moaning. The stimulation from her entire pelvis crackled inside her. The blood rushed to her head, making her lightheaded. Every downstroke forced the breath from her lungs. Her tits rode up her chest to rest against the bunched T-shirt above them. Every sensation doubled in her engorged brain.

He sped up, powering into her without hammering her into the floor. His cock swelled inside her, pinching her lips as they strained to contain him at this angle. He pressed her thighs down with his hands, dropped his cock fully into her, and held it. She felt her face flush, and her eyes welled with tears as she struggled to breathe.

"Where do you want it?"

Alyssa recovered from her orgasm enough to touch her forehead and smile as much as she could given the manic fucking she was getting. *I want to be dirty.*

"Oh yeah." He pulled out of her pussy, gripping her thigh with one hand. He jerked his cock above her, raining jizz on her tits and face as her ass pressed back against his thighs and she gasped. Everywhere it landed, heat radiated into her skin, from her forehead down to her nose and mouth, her eye, and the undersides of her tits. Their cries echoed in the empty house.

Hayden eased her legs up and shuffled sideways to lay Alyssa's hip on the floor. He rolled forward to lie beside her. He softly stroked her side as her breathing slowed. "Don't get up yet. You will be dizzy."

"Mmmm. I love it." Alyssa smiled and looked up at him with her open eye. "You really took me. I like that."

"I'll take you anytime. You are amazing. You even look beautiful covered in cum."

"Is that because you put it there?"

"Probably. It's true nonetheless."

Alyssa pulled the collar of her shirt over her face and wiped the cum off. The fabric stuck to her chest.

He made eye contact and hinted at a smile. "I want to do it again."

"Now?" She reached to his soft, slippery cock. "You aren't ready."

He laughed and tapped her hip with his fingers. "Not now. Another time. Another day. This has been too marvelous to be a one-time thing."

Alyssa grinned, her stomach fluttering because he felt the same way she did. "Marvelous isn't the word. Breathtaking. Earth-shattering, perhaps. Yes, we need to get together again." She caressed his chest. "How did you learn to do that? Wait, I don't want to know. That felt so good. And it was a little scary when I struggled to breathe. Thank you for teaching me that."

"If you are going to try it with someone else, don't let your partner drop too hard. He could hurt your neck."

"I think I'll just keep this between us for now. Something special to look forward to." She sat up and repeated the T-shirt wipe of her face before fastening her bra and pulling her shirt into place. She pressed it, sticking it to her skin. "This makes me feel so dirty. I love it."

Hayden rose. "I'm glad, my dirty girl." He pointed to his dick, covered with their cum. "You like being dirty? Clean this for me, baby."

The name caught her in the gut. She hadn't betrayed Robert, but only he called her Baby. She didn't want to ruin the mood, but he couldn't call her that. She spoke sharper than she intended. "Don't call me baby. Nobody calls me that."

Hayden recoiled slightly. His eyes widened, then narrowed. "Sorry. I didn't know that was off-limits."

She nodded. "It is. Nobody calls me Baby but my husband." She smiled. "You didn't know, so I'm not mad. I think there was something you needed me to do?"

He smiled. "Oh yeah. Clean me."

Alyssa smirked as she moved to her knees and sucked the head of his cock into her mouth. She sucked more of it in before dropping it out, holding the soft tip in her hand, and licking the sides all the way down to the base. When it was clean and shining with her saliva, she sucked one ball into her mouth, swirling her tongue around it, and then repeated herself on the other. "I didn't want to miss anything."

He chuckled. "You didn't."

§

Hayden pulled his car in front of hers in the realty parking lot.

"I'll send the documents electronically. I don't think you want to go in the office looking like you spent all afternoon in bed."

"Thanks for the compliment. You're a little disheveled yourself, by the way." She laughed. "No, thanks for the consideration. I'll just head home. We don't need to shock that pretty little receptionist of yours."

"She might not be as shocked as you think."

"You do this with all your clients?"

"No. She's the one who taught me that butter churner position."

"That little girl? You could crush her. Is she your girlfriend?"

"No. There are advantages in being the only man in an office of women."

"I bet." She stroked his cock through his pants, smiling when it hardened, confident they would get together again. She wanted more from him. "That's so you can properly entice her to help with the paperwork. Send it to me when it's ready." She got out of the car before he could respond, but looked back to see him shaking his head and chuckling.

6

SATURDAY, MAY 8, HOME

ALYSSA LOOKED AT herself in the visor mirror. Her hair hung in uneven strands around her face, and the top stood up before falling to the side. Her lipstick was smeared, and mascara streaked her cheeks. Her white T-shirt stuck to her chest, outlining her bra cups. The cum had begun to dry into yellow splotches.

This will be so much fun. He'll know he needs to reclaim me. I'll let him decide if he wants me to clean up or if he takes me dirty. I'll walk in wearing cum-soaked clothes, my hair a mess, and tell Robert I need to buy that house. He can reclaim me and have a "bargaining wife" fantasy all at once. Or he can force me to wait and make me go clean up before he takes me back. God, it makes me horny either way.

Alyssa walked through the laundry room door into the great room and stopped. Clay and Sawyer stood gaping at her.

"I didn't expect you to be home, honey. Where's Dad? Hello, Sawyer."

90

Before Clay or his girlfriend could respond, Robert entered from the back bedroom hallway. "I found it, Clay." He noted his son's face and turned to the kitchen portion of the great room, seeing the laundry room entrance from the garage. He flashed a frown before it slid from his face.

"Hey, Baby. It looks like that fixer-upper you saw was worse than you said on the phone. Why don't you go clean up while we work on supper?"

"Um, yes. It was a mess. Quite a story. I guess I'm a mess too. I'll go clean up and join you for supper." She moved through the room, facing away from her family, accelerating as she hit the hallway. She shut the bedroom door behind her and ran to the bathroom. She turned on the shower and faced her mirror.

"Damn. I don't look like I was in a dirty house." She picked at some of the cum in her hair. *Discreet? Not so much. You did it again, Alyssa. You caused problems at home because you fucked outside of it.* "Might as well clean up."

Alyssa showered, cleaning the cum and sweat out of her hair, off her body, and out of her well-used pussy. She stood in the water, letting it run on the back of her head before turning it off and drying off. Being in for the night, she would normally let her hair air-dry, but she didn't want to sit at dinner reminding her family, and Sawyer (*even worse*), of what she had clearly done. She dried her hair and put on shorts. She was choosing a polo shirt when Robert walked into their closet.

"I appreciate the effort." He gave a wan smile. "I'm guessing you had different plans for your big entrance?"

"Oh, Babe, I thought Clay was out rowing with Sawyer this afternoon. You were going to choose between reclaiming me wild and dirty and making me go clean up before I 'persuaded' you to buy the house. I thought we could have a good time. I didn't mean to be indiscreet. I'm so sorry."

"I know, Baby. Thanks for trying to spice things up. Maybe you should notice Clay's car in the garage next time. He's embarrassed. Sawyer asked him why you looked like you had sex when she thought I couldn't hear. You'll need to apologize to him. You might need to talk with her, though he may want to do that himself. We don't want her telling the story." He hugged her.

"I only wanted some excitement with you, and I blew it, didn't I?"

"Well, you also wanted some excitement with the realtor, didn't you? To play out a fantasy? It appears you succeeded."

She felt the smile on her face before she could stifle it. "I did. It was so good. You will have to reclaim me well, Baby."

Robert's head flushed red.

She leaned back from him while remaining in his arms. "We tell each other everything afterward. We've never shied away from telling when it was good. Why are you upset?"

"I don't know. Maybe I haven't gotten over Monday night yet."

"That's not fair, Robert. You agreed to that plan."

"Emotions aren't fair, and my emotions are still raw from watching my wife screw three men and ask me for the video of it to relive the experience later."

Alyssa counted to ten. She had asked why he was upset. He'd responded with honesty. *More honest than I was about the house today.* "Fair enough. Any reason beyond an emotional hangover?"

"Perhaps one you will accept. You were in such a hurry to have your realtor fantasy that you didn't text me the address." He let her go. Her back and sides missed his warmth.

Goddamn. You blew it in every way, Alyssa. She looked down, then back up while her stomach roiled inside her. "I'm sorry I forgot to text. I was so excited."

"You need to honor our deal, Baby. I can't help you if you don't."

"I know. I'm sorry. I'll do better." She pulled the shirt on before painting on a smile for Robert. "The house is great too. If we can make a lot on it, we can pick up two more rentals than we planned."

"We can talk about it over dinner. I came back to tell you it's ready." He glanced down her body and flushed red again. "Change into jeans. Your knees are red. Let's avoid repeating your earlier entrance."

She looked down at her red knees. The nausea that had begun to take hold grew, fueled by the shame of flaunting her actions to Robert not once but twice and being called on it. "Okay. I'll be there in a minute."

Alyssa finished the dishes and fixed her hair using the microwave as a mirror. She turned off the kitchen light and stood beside her husband, who sat watching TV.

She lowered her voice. "Babe, how can I persuade you to buy that house? I know it's more money, but we'll make a profit, and I really, really want it."

"Baby, we already decided to—"

She put a finger to his lips. "I'll do anything you want if you buy that house for me. Anything."

He nodded with a smile, then frowned. "I see. It's a lot of money. I need to think about it."

"I can sell my clothes." She pulled her shirt over her head and threw it into a nearby chair. "Some people buy used clothes." She unclasped her bra and let it fall to the floor. "Mine are nice."

"It's a lot of money, Baby. I don't know if that will be enough."

She opened her jeans and pushed them to her ankles before

stepping out of them. "Some guys want them dirty. I could wear them first, and we could charge more."

Robert stifled a laugh. "Really?"

She nodded and broke the pleading wife character she was playing. "Really. There are online stores for used women's clothes, especially panties. I don't get it, but…" She returned to character, softening her voice and barely flirting with eye contact as if she were asking too much of him. "With no clothes, I could stay here naked, all day, every day, just to take care of you."

He smiled and nodded, apparently getting into character himself. "I don't know. It's still a lot of money."

She knelt in front of him. "You always said my blow jobs were worth a million dollars." She unbuckled his pants, and he raised his hips to let her pull them down his legs. "Even if you exaggerated, what if I gave you one?" She pulled him by his hard cock to the edge of the seat while she smiled at him.

"What about two?"

"Ooh! Yes! Let's start!" She took the head of his cock in her mouth. She sucked it and swirled her tongue around the head, then flicked the frenulum.

Robert groaned.

She drove his cock into her throat and swallowed, letting the muscles ripple around his head. She stayed there, swallowing, until she needed to breathe. She pulled off with a pop. "Does that feel good, Babe? Are you going to paint my face with your cum? Will that buy me that house?"

"Make me come and that house is yours."

"Deal! You're going to love this!" She took him into her throat again, staying until she needed to breathe, getting a breath and returning, until his head swelled in her throat. She acceler-ated, bobbing her head, taking his cock into her throat twice per second. *Getting dizzy.* She didn't stop sucking, just cupped his balls and squeezed them with both hands. She pulled them out from his body, then applied enough pressure for them to compress in her hands. Robert roared and exploded in her throat.

Alyssa pulled off his cock to direct the rest of his load onto her face. She giggled when every spurt landed on her. "Oh yes. Paint me!" The last of Robert's orgasm trickled down her hand. She milked the rest out of him, then licked her hand clean.

"That was good, Baby. Did it tickle when I came on your face?"

"I felt like a giddy little girl when you came. I giggled because I was so happy."

"Because you get to flip that house?"

"No." *Because I'm going to fuck Hayden in that house.* "I mean, I'm happy about that too, but it elated me to make you come. Is that weird?"

Robert chuckled. "I guess not. I'm glad my orgasms make you so happy." He pulled her onto the couch beside him and snuggled her close. The heat of his body warmed her as the thin sheen of sweat she had worked up began to evaporate. "Tell me about today, before I reclaim you."

"I didn't think you wanted to hear." *I'm not sure I want to tell all of it.*

"It's our agreement. Maybe hearing will remind me that everything is normal again. Well, as normal as two people in an open marriage who just revealed that to their son's girlfriend can be."

"Babe—"

"I know. It was an accident, and you were trying to have fun with me. It's okay." He kissed her head. "I love you, and we will always be okay, as long as we are together. So tell me."

"About the house hunting, or just the sex?"

"Start with the house hunting. Finish with the sex. I need to recover a bit."

"We looked at six or seven houses before lunch. They were all fine as rentals, but nothing special. We talked at lunch, and he asked what I wanted. I mentioned a little privacy, and he mentioned that he knew of one being sold cheap. He said we could flip it quickly because it didn't need much work."

"And he gets a commission on the higher sales price and the other rentals we buy."

She hadn't thought about his benefit but reasoned it out. "Yes, but he would anyway."

"True. As long as we benefit, I don't mind him being an opportunist."

"We turned down this long, narrow driveway through the woods. We pull up, and the front porch looks like a car had run into it, because it had. That's what we need to fix. The rest of the house appears to be in good shape. The wife got mad and plowed her car into the porch, and the husband decided to sell it for even less than it's worth. We can make a bundle, and we could end up with four rentals instead of two."

"You sold me on that. I assume I get to look at it before we buy?"

"I can have Hayden set up a visit, if you want. The papers will be in my email tonight."

"Isn't that convenient? I guess I'll see it after we make the offer. What will the repairs cost?"

"Hayden estimated about forty thousand."

"We would still make, theoretically, one hundred and sixty thousand, of which he will get twenty-seven. Less taxes and closing costs. All right. That's worth doing. We can sign tonight. We can use our line of credit and make it a cash offer to close fast. Now—" Robert sighed. "—tell me your realtor fantasy."

"It started at the first house."

"The first house? You didn't call until—"

"Easy, Baby. I got turned on at the first house." *He's on edge. Better not tell him we had two sessions.* "We didn't have sex until I called you, just like our agreement."

"Okay. It sounded like—"

"I know. I should have said it better. I'm keeping our agreement, Babe." *Almost.* She kissed his cheek. "The first house had a sex dungeon in the basement. It turned me on. There was a big bed with restraints, racks of paddles and whips, and a leather outfit on a mannequin with a mask. There were big pictures on the walls of a woman with different men using the stuff in the room. I was wet and he was hard before we left. It roiled me. When we went to lunch, the waitress overheard us talking about the power of it, and I told her to imagine us using her in it when she made love to her husband tonight." She gripped Robert's cock but didn't move her hand. She wanted to feel it swell as she talked.

"Imagine you and the realtor?"

"Yes. She was fit, and it made me hotter to imagine myself with her." She rubbed her thumb along the ridge of his cockhead.

"And him?"

"Yes, and him. He is tall and good-looking, and I had been thinking of sex ever since that basement. Add in the muscular waitress…I was like a firecracker with a lit fuse."

"I see. Go on."

"Well, we saw the house. It was in good shape, I realized that we could profit from it, and the thought of the money made me hornier. That's when I called you." She pulled his almost hard cock. "After you agreed, I blew him and fucked him in the kitchen."

"You blew him and fucked him? That's all? I thought it was so good?"

"Oh, it was. I just didn't go into detail. You didn't seem to be in the mood for it." *Why didn't I mention the cupola again?*

"I wanted a sexy story. It's all right. It's time to remind you why you come home every night."

"Yes it is, Babe. Let me get this ready. I'll do anything to get you rock-hard, Baby." She cupped her breasts and rolled her nipples between her finger and thumb. She licked her lip.

"Why don't I fuck your tits while you jill off?"

"Ooh, Babe. I like that. You're getting creative." She rose, getting her tits around his semihard cock. She slid them up and down with her hands, slowly at first, then speeding up and using her legs to move her entire body rather than just moving her boobs.

He replaced her hands with his and gripped her breasts with his strong fingers. Alyssa dipped her mouth to lick his tip when it emerged from her cleavage, then dipped her hands to her wet pussy. With one hand, she pinched and pulled her clit, while with the other, she jammed two fingers inside to press her G-spot. Her head rocked back, and she moaned before resuming her movements in time with bouncing her body.

Alyssa drooled onto his cock in her cleavage, keeping it slick as she pleasured him. "Are you going to make me come on this big cock, Babe?"

"Yes, Baby. Why don't you climb on?"

"Uh-huh."

She straddled him, facing out into the room. She lined up his cock with her slit and slid down to rest on his thighs. "That feel so good, Babe." *But not as good as usual. He isn't hitting my cervix.*

She leaned back to him and squeezed her muscles to grip him tighter. His hands cupped her breasts. He pinched her nipples, stretching them as she bounced on his cock. He moved her hair and kissed her neck just below her ear. *Oh, I love that.* She turned her head and kissed him on the mouth, then leaned forward to rest her hands on his knees. *Look at my sexy ass and put that cock in me deep.*

Robert's hands slid along her belly as she leaned forward. He let his fingers brush the seam between her abs and obliques as she rode him, bouncing on the ridges in the muscles beneath as she worked, sparking along her skin to congregate at her clit. His hands slid back to her ass cheeks. She popped up before slamming down, but he matched her rhythm and pulled her cheeks open with his thumbs, spreading and guiding her. One thumb moved to rub her pink pucker, resting on it as it opened and closed slightly with her movements.

"Oh yes. Rub it." *That feels good. Now shove it in. Just take my ass. Don't ask if I'm ready, don't look for lube, just fill me with your fingers.* Alyssa slowed her pace to let him do what he wanted.

"You tired, Baby? Let me work for a while." Robert lifted her ass and spun her to the couch, flipping her to her back. His strength made her pussy throb. He kissed her pussy and flicked her clit with his tongue a few times before straightening and lining his cock up and shoving it in to the hilt. He groaned as he tapped beside her cervix.

Alyssa wrapped her legs around him and tilted her hips. *Go deeper. Hit my cervix harder. Please, make me come like you always do. Come on, reclaim me.*

Robert pounded into Alyssa, leaning back every time he withdrew. His cockhead kneaded her G-spot on the backstroke, then as he shoved it in, his curved cock found that spot beside her cervix that always made Alyssa climax hard.

But her body resisted.

He pounded away, and she humped against him and squeezed

her walls on his cock, seeking a release. She held her breath, applying pressure inside her body to force the climax that eluded her. He was touching the right places inside her. She wanted him, was happy to be with him, wanted to let him release her love in one giant gush, but her body remained steady, even as she sweated and urged him on with her voice.

"Oh god, Babe. That's it. Right there. Come in me." *Please. Let that cum hit my cervix and set me off. Please.* Alyssa felt his cock swell inside her. She pulled her nipples as far as she ever had and twisted them. The pain fluttered her stomach, and she groaned. The first shot of cum splashed her cervix. Alyssa relished the sensation as spurt after spurt followed. She felt deep pleasure. *Maybe if I squeeze him a little.* She tightened her pelvic muscles. *Better, but no climax.*

Robert's orgasm stopped, but he kept fucking Alyssa. "You close, Baby?"

"Oh yeah. Almost there." She looked him in the eye. She held his gaze for a few strokes before closing her eyes and rolling her head backward. She held her breath and tensed her body. She clenched her legs around Robert, holding him fully inside her while she ground against him.

She rolled her head forward and looked up at her husband, then out into the room. "Oh, that was wonderful, Baby. Thank you for reclaiming me. I'm yours again, and always. I love you." *Not as wonderful as usual. I haven't faked an orgasm in a long time. And I'm still thinking about Hayden, not Robert. What are you thinking, Alyssa? Talk with him.*

"Love you, too, Baby. I'm glad I could bring you back to me." He pulled out of her. He sat beside her and pulled her against him, letting her head rest on his chest. They sat unmoving and quiet until the clock on the mantel chimed.

Alyssa rose off his chest and kissed Robert's mouth. She

embraced his neck, pulling herself tight against him before kissing him again. "I love you, Babe." She looked from his left eye to his right and back again. "It's late. I'm headed to bed. You coming?"

"I'll be there in a minute. Just need to recover my legs a bit longer."

"Okay. I'll have the bed warmed up for you."

She left the room quietly. Looking back, she saw Robert staring at the wall.

7

SUNDAY, MAY 9, HOME

"Clay, honey, would you please hand me the tongs? The bacon is ready."

"Sure." Clay handed her the tongs. "Mom, before Dad gets up, can we talk about yesterday?"

Alyssa blushed. "I'm sorry I embarrassed you. I didn't know Sawyer was here. I didn't even realize you were here."

"I know. But when you and Dad told me about this arrangement of yours, you promised that you would keep it secret."

"I did. I promised that I wouldn't let it hurt you. You and Sawyer are close enough that she won't tell anyone, will she?"

"She won't. But she asked me why you looked like you were having an affair. I couldn't lie to her. She got quiet, then asked me if I wanted an open arrangement with her."

"Oh. I see. What did you say?"

"No! Mom! She's my girlfriend. I don't want her with any other guys."

"Good. You told her that, right?"

"Yes. But I could tell she kept thinking about it. I can't determine if she wants to try other guys, or if she's worried that I think cheating on her is okay because my parents do it."

"Oh, sweetie. Surely she won't think that you two have to be like your dad and me."

"I don't know. She was incredibly quiet when I took her home."

Alyssa nodded. "She seemed okay after dinner. You two had fun in the basement before you left."

"Mom, you know that's different. Please?"

"I wanted to point out that, one, she didn't seem worried about your intentions toward her, and two, you have some pretty cool parents to stay out of your way when she's here. Part of that attitude is because we have the arrangement we have. Does that make sense, sweetie?"

"Yes. You guys are way cooler than my friends' parents, so thank you for that. I worry that she won't trust me, or that she thinks you two will encourage me to cheat on her."

"I can talk with her about that."

"No, Mom. Thanks, but, just, no. She's still weirded out by what she saw."

"Okay. If you change your mind, let me know. She's a smart girl. She'll think about how you treat her, about how good you two are together, and she'll figure it out. Trust her to know you."

"I will. Can I ask a favor?"

"Sure, honey. Always."

"Can you please clean up before you come home from one of your, um, what do you want to call them? Affairs? Trysts?"

"Why don't we go with 'adventures'? That way other people won't know what we are referring to."

"That's fine. And will you clean up, just in case?"

"Sometimes it is fun to not clean up. What about this? I'll clean up unless I am certain you are away from home. Then it's between your dad and me. Will that work?"

"So if you aren't sure, like yesterday?"

"I'll clean up."

"That works." He shook his head. "Jesus. The conversations we have in this kitchen."

❧

"Here is the email from Hayden, Babe." Alyssa double-clicked and began opening attachments. "Here is the contract…property info sheet…here is the inspection report they got in preparation for listing…oh, look. Here is an estimate to repair the porch. Forty thousand. If we get these signed in the next"—she looked at the clock—"forty-five minutes, he can deliver them to the seller today."

Robert leaned over his wife's shoulder to see her screen. "Let's see the contract. Two fifty, like we agreed…sold as is…all personal property as well…close in five days…looks right to me. Let's see the inspection."

Alyssa opened the file as Robert rubbed the length of her back with one hand. "Mm. That feels good, Babe. Keep going."

"Roof only five years old…HVAC too…no plumbing issues…or electrical…no mold in the basement…no radon… structural damage to front porch; we knew that. No other issues identified. Okay, let's see that estimate."

Robert moved a second hand to Alyssa's back as she opened the last document. "Fifteen days' work, forty thousand, we cover changes in cost of materials and plans. And these guys work for

Queen?" He slid his hands up her sides, brushing the sides of her breasts under her arms.

"You bad boy. You're trying to distract me."

"Yes, I am."

She pinned his hands under her arms. "They do work for Queen's property management division. They repair the rentals Queen manages. Hayden says they are reliable and do good work."

"All right. We'd better hurry if we want to do this today."

"We still have thirty minutes. We should be fine."

"Then you'd better hurry. You promised me two blow jobs for this house, and one is yet to be delivered." He spun Alyssa in her office chair. She started, then laughed when she saw him standing with no pants and a full erection.

"Robert! Clay's home!"

He laughed. "No, Baby. He went down the street to play basketball. You had better get started if you want this house today. I don't sign until I get what you promised. The clock is ticking."

Alyssa grinned and gripped his shaft, gobbling the head in her mouth and swirling her tongue over the head while she stroked him. She took more into her mouth, looking up at his eyes and smiling around his cock. She dropped her hand and dove her head down, swallowing his cock as it reached her throat. She gagged but held still and kept swallowing until the feeling passed, then rose off him to breathe.

"That's pretty good, Baby, but you need to go fast. I might come quicker with a little visual stimulation."

She released his cock and gripped the hem of her shirt.

"You know, I think I want to see how excited you are about this house. Instead of showing me your world-class tits this time, why don't you pull off your shorts and make yourself come when I do?"

"Mm, Robert, that is so hot. Yes, I'll show you how much I want this house." She leaned back and raised her hips to pull her shorts off.

"No panties? You dirty girl."

"I hoped we might end up naked somehow." She opened her pussy for him with one hand, then stroked her clit with the other. "This is how horny this house makes me, Babe." She plunged two fingers from her spreading hand into her wet slit. She pulled the fingers forward and moaned. "And this is how horny you make me, Babe. Now let me make you feel good."

She leaned forward, never breaking eye contact, and took his entire cock into her mouth with one motion. She bobbed her head slowly, sucking until she could feel her cheeks between her teeth.

Robert held her long brown hair in a ponytail with one hand and cupped Alyssa's breast through the fabric with the other.

Alyssa rubbed and fingered herself faster, bobbing her head in time with her fingers. Her pussy clenched at them, satisfied with the resistance her knuckles provided, and empty beyond her fingertips. *God, this is like taking two at once. So good. I'm about to come.* She ground her hips against her hands, which were beginning to cramp from her efforts. She moaned around Robert's cock as she kept up her oral assault, maintaining eye contact as her orgasm began to boil in her belly. Alyssa's hair pulled tight on each change in direction, as Robert's hand moved slightly after her body did. *I like that. Pull my hair. Oh yes. Yes.*

Alyssa slammed her throat over the end of Robert's cock, driving her nose into his abs as her eyes closed and she spasmed in her climax. Robert's cock swelled inside her as she swallowed but didn't breathe. The first spurt of cum went straight into her throat, then he pulled her head off him and shot the rest of his significant load onto her, leaving white streaks on the dark-blue shirt.

Alyssa smiled up at her husband. "Jesus, that was hot, Baby." She dipped her finger into a glob of cum and sucked it off. "I'll give you a hundred of those if we can come together like that."

"Yes, it was. I'll take all of those you want to give me, as long as you get off too. Your throat tightened on me when you came."

"It felt so good when you swelled in my throat. It made me come harder." She brought another glob of cum to her mouth. "Any reason you wanted to come on my shirt?"

"I want you to have a good memory when you do the laundry. Besides, it looks good on you."

"I'll never look at laundry the same again." She laughed and hugged her face into his stomach. "I love you, Babe. I love how you make things fun, and I love how you love me. Thank you."

"I love you, too, Baby. Now, we only have ten minutes. I'm going to keep my side of the bargain. Let's sign these docs and buy that house."

Alyssa kissed his belly and squeezed his ass cheeks before letting go. "Let's do it, Babe. Let's make some money." She spun and clicked in the electronic signatures. "Now the ones in your email. There. Sure you are ready to send?"

"Yep. Send them."

She hit send, stood up, and grabbed Robert's wet cock. "That's done. If you come to the bedroom, I'll negotiate getting it painted." She wiggled her bare ass and laughed over her shoulder as she walked out of the room, Robert hustling behind her.

8

WEDNESDAY, MAY 12, OFFICE

Alyssa jumped when her phone dinged with an incoming text.

She was composing an email for the tenth time to the exclusion of any other thought. Coordinating a famous Michelin-rated chef to teach a seminar for Martin Restaurants' top chefs had been a nightmare. The chef's calendar was tight, and his personal assistant had the personal touch of a rabid wolverine. The initial October date had morphed into next April. The issue was that the best hotel in town was booked for a trade show, and the chef in question had immutable standards. At least, his assistant did.

All her calls to the hotel manager had gone unanswered. She only needed one room but had had no luck snagging a cancellation or offering to pay double the already exorbitant rates. She had called Robert, thinking the bank might have a room or two reserved for important guests, but he shut her down. He never pulled business strings for personal reasons. She had known asking would waste her breath, but she was desperate. Sometimes his moral compass was a serious problem.

With no ability to get the hotel, Alyssa had to persuade the personal assistant from hell to accept another hotel or change the date yet again, neither of which had gone well so far.

She picked up her phone with a sigh. *Train of thought lost, anyway.*

The message from Hayden surprised her, and a warm tingle fluttered in her chest.

"There are some last-minute questions about the offer. I'm nearby. Can you step outside?"

The negotiations had finalized yesterday. *Great. Another problem I don't have time to address today.* She texted back. "What kind of questions? No patience for problems today."

"Rough day?"

"Yes."

"I know the perfect spot for a quick and relaxing lunch. Cover the questions while we eat."

The clock in her computer showed eleven forty-three. *Maybe a break would help.* "Okay. Where?"

"I'm in the parking lot. Come out when you are ready."

One minute later, she slid into the passenger seat of his car. "What a pleasant surprise. Where are we going? I really don't have a lot of time today."

Hayden smiled at her. "You will be in your office in forty-five minutes, I promise. Fast enough?"

"Fast enough."

He zipped out of the parking lot and through one of the more industrial areas of town while they discussed a couple of changes to the closing meeting and the fact that the sellers would not be present. By the time he pulled up to a roadside stand in a gravel lot, the real estate business was complete.

The wooden walls had once been red, and the faded white sign above the door read "Junior's Roadside." Beside the small structure were a couple of tents covering produce in crates and a couple of coolers overseen by a middle-aged woman in a lawn chair.

"Is this place safe, Hayden?"

He grinned. "You are going to love it."

She followed him inside to a small floor area in front of a counter.

The old man behind the register smiled and waved at Hayden. "Hayden, welcome back."

Hayden waved back. "Good to see you, Junior. We are in a hurry today. Can we get two BLTs and two Cokes, please?"

"Yep," the old man replied, then turned to an old woman behind the counter. "Two BLTs, Mabel, my dear." He turned back to Hayden. "Did you see the Braves last night?"

While the two men talked baseball, Alyssa peeked over the counter as Mabel sliced into a large loaf of bread, placing four slices on two sheets of deli paper and smearing mayonnaise on them. The crunching sound as she cut the lettuce drowned out the conversation. When Mabel sliced the tomato, Alyssa's mouth watered. "Did you grow that yourself?"

Mabel smiled with yellow teeth. "No. Our first batch will be ready in a month or so. But these are good."

"And the bread? It looks delicious."

"I bake every evening. Today it's sourdough. My mama's recipe."

She handed the wrapped sandwiches over the counter and turned to her husband. "Junior, stop gabbing. They are in a hurry."

Alyssa looked around for somewhere to sit as Hayden led her out the door. He chuckled. "This way. We will have great seats."

He placed his hand in the small of her back and led her on a gravel path through a small stand of trees. Before they emerged from the shade, he steered her left to some picnic tables. He seemed to know most of the people there and said hello as they moved toward the only open one. She looked over the city below.

"What a great view. I've lived here for years and never knew this place existed." She opened her sandwich and stretched her mouth to take a bite. "And how can a sandwich this good come from a roadside shack? This is delicious."

Hayden shook his head. "I thought you would like it. Junior's is an institution. Look around. See all the workmen? They know the lunch spots with good food and low prices. On sunny days, this place is packed."

"I'll come back here a lot."

He smiled. His perfect teeth sparkled as much as his eyes. Butterflies fluttered inside her stomach. *And I'll remember that smile.*

"It's a beautiful spot to ease the tension. What has made your day so rough?"

She had wanted to avoid thinking about work, but his eyes softened around the edges like he wanted to know instead of making noise to fill the silence. *Surely he isn't genuinely interested in my day. Oh well, he asked.*

"I have this VIP coming in during the April trade show, and I can't get him a room at the Estate. Per his PA, it is the only suitable hotel for fifty miles. If I can't get that hotel then, he won't come, and scheduling this guy is a nightmare. It's eating me up today."

"Is that all you need? A room?"

"Yeah, during the city's biggest annual influx of people. Those rooms have been booked since last year's show ended."

Hayden smiled and pulled out his phone. "I might be able to help. Please excuse my rude texting."

He typed out a text. "Which dates do you need?"

"April second and third. Those are the first two days. The whole city is booked. Some people even rent out their houses."

Good luck. The hotel is a lost cause. Alyssa watched him and savored her sandwich. *Even if he gets nowhere, this lunch has brightened my day.*

He set his phone on the table. They chatted and ate between the few intermittent texts he responded to. Initially skeptical of each new text, Alyssa let the tiny smile he tried to hide when each one arrived give her hope until her stomach fluttered between replies. By the time they finished eating, she was laughing at his jokes and happier than she had been all day.

His phone dinged as they were standing. "I have a room for you."

Her heart leaped into her throat on a wave of joy. The frustration of spending three weeks trying to do what he had done in ten minutes quashed her optimism. There was no way he had finagled a room at the Estate that week. "Really? You are teasing me. I've talked to everyone about it for three weeks. No dice."

"I would never tease about helping you. Of course I'm serious. Do you want the room?"

"Yes, yes, of course. How did you do that?"

He grinned and texted before putting his phone in his pocket. "I called in a couple of favors from some friends coming to the trade show. They are going to use my house that week for free. I'll stay with another friend."

She knew she should feel guilty that he was moving out of his house for her, but the tremble growing in her belly was joy and relief. Someone had come through for her when she needed it. Trying to provide the socially correct answer, she shook her head. "Hayden, you shouldn't have. That's too much."

He put up his palm toward her. "That's not all. The waitlist at the hotel is long. I traded a favor from the GM of the Estate. If you call her this afternoon, she will change his reservation to your name without canceling it. I'll text her contact. Call her cell."

"Traded a favor?"

"She gets Columbus Day weekend for free in a mountain cabin we manage."

"That's peak leaf season."

"It won't be a problem. The owner likes me."

She fought the elated giggle struggling to escape her throat. She had needed help. The chef's PA had refused her. The hotel had refused her. Even Robert had refused to help her. But with a few texts over the course of a quick lunch, Hayden had engineered the perfect solution.

Just like the house, it was perfect. Hayden always had the right option at the right time. He had connections everywhere and knowledge others didn't. Everyone seemed to like him, and he was willing to share those connections with others.

With her.

She released the giggle with a squeal and wrapped him in a quick hug, releasing and stepping back after only a second.

"Thank you, Hayden. You are a life saver. What do I owe you?"

"Just pay for the room in April."

"Of course. But you inconvenienced yourself for this favor. How can I repay you?"

He smiled. "The look on your face right now is all I need."

Alyssa felt her face flush hot. The relief that he solved her problem and the giddiness that he had done it just to make her happy fanned the tingle in her stomach until it tickled around her heart. She grinned while looking into his eyes.

"Then take a long look. You put it there."

"Even that little blush?"

He just solved my biggest problem in the last month just to make me happy, and he's playful. He likes me. Her cheeks grew hotter.

"Especially the little blush." She smiled and headed to the car.

⸙

Alyssa called Tasha, the GM of the Estate, as soon as she returned to the office. She wanted to lock in the room. The lady answered on the first ring.

"This is Tasha."

"Good afternoon, Tasha. My name is Alyssa Davis. Hayden Robinson told me to call you about a room on April second and third."

The GM cackled in her ear. "I have been waiting for your call. I owe you a big thank-you for whatever you did to Hayden."

"What I did to Hayden? What do you mean?"

"I hoped you could tell me. I have asked for five years straight to use that cabin for my anniversary. He always said no because the owner uses it over Columbus Day. Today he offers it up front if I do you a favor. Tell me, how did you get him to do that?"

That bubbling elation returned to her belly. *He went the extra mile for me. Everything I learn about him is good, no, great.* "I don't know. I told him my problem, and he said he could fix it. He did."

Alyssa stopped to process what Tasha had said. Her stomach knotted tight. His story didn't fit. "Did you say five years?"

"Yes. Why?"

"Hayden told me he's been with Queen a year. You couldn't have asked him for five years if he wasn't there."

"The cabin is part of a managed portfolio that he brings to whatever realty firm he joins. It must be big. They hire him away from each other every few years."

Happy bubbles relaxed Alyssa's stomach. He had been honest, and Tasha had apparently worked with him for years. "I see. That makes sense. About the room…"

They worked out the change in the reservation. The price was hefty but in range for a great room in the best hotel in the city during the hottest event. It was a business expense. After the details were settled, Alyssa learned that Tasha wanted the cabin as a getaway from the stress of raising her young grandchildren. She and her husband had raised the ten- and eight-year-old boys since her daughter and son-in-law were killed in a car crash five years before.

"He must really like you. That cabin is always booked. He has never been willing to let us have it until today. I offered him more free days at the Estate than you needed, but he never even nibbled until today. I'm not complaining; I'm thrilled. Thank you, whatever you did."

Alyssa remembered Saturday. *I'm sure that isn't it. He's too experienced to be won over by a little sex. Maybe she knows something.* "He doesn't even know me that well. It seems helping people is his nature. Is he as kind as he seems?"

"He is an absolute prince. Every woman I know adores him. So do most of the men. I think the ones that don't might be jealous, but I can't say for sure. He loves to connect people. He passes out favors like candy. There is a point where he stops, like everyone, I guess, but his is further out. I thought the cabin was past that point. If he offered it, he must think you're special."

Alyssa giggled. "I caught him on a good day, maybe. Anyway, I'm thankful he put us together and helped us both get something we want very much."

After the call, Alyssa stared at her calendar. She noted the reservation for April, then grinned the entire time she composed the email confirming the important visit. *The personal assistant can bitch at somebody else now. I got this done.*

She remembered the little smile Hayden had cracked when he described getting the room. He'd looked happy to do it. *And he's an amazing lover. I'm going to like buying this house.*

9

WEDNESDAY, MAY 12, HOME

Alyssa rinsed the pan and handed it to Robert to dry. Tonight's dinner had been complicated, but she wanted to celebrate a great day. The price was more dishes than usual, and there were several stubborn pans yet to wash.

She appreciated that she and Robert cooked and cleaned together. They could talk, and if sensitive topics came up, they didn't have to wait until they went to bed because Clay was excused to do homework. They loved connecting over the dishes.

She looked at Robert, unable to contain her grin. "I got my hotel problem solved."

He smiled back. "Wonderful. How did you manage that? I knew you were out of ideas when you called me for help."

"Yes. You and your rigid ethics were my last hope, but then I had lunch with Hayden."

Robert's brow furrowed the tiniest bit before returning to neutral. "Why did you have lunch with Hayden?"

A sticky spot on her pan claimed her attention as she scrubbed, then answered. "There were a couple of details about the closing meeting that changed a little. The sellers won't be there. Nothing serious."

"You told me in two sentences. How did that lead to lunch?"

"He was close by, and I was having a bad morning. I needed a break, and he offered. While we ate, I described my morning, and by the end of lunch, the room was mine. It was like a miracle."

Robert turned away to put a pan in the cabinet. "Just like that, he magically produced one of the most in-demand rooms in town?"

"He had to trade a few favors. But he got it for me."

"What did these favors cost you?"

The niggle of irritation Robert's questions had fostered in her chest slipped into her voice. "Robert, just because you refuse to trade business favors doesn't mean it's evil. He traded for the room without my asking. He did it while we ate, and when he told me, I'm sure I smiled a mile wide. He said that smile was payment enough."

His voice hardened in response, and a red flush crept up his face. "Those rooms are booked a year in advance with a long waitlist. He must have traded some big favors. And all he really wanted was a smile?"

He's upset. Be playful. She faced her husband, adopting an exaggerated pout. "You love my smile. You do everything you can to see it, right, Babe? Maybe Hayden thinks it's worth a favor or two as well? And aren't I better company at home when I'm smiling?"

The red flush left Robert's face, but the corners of his mouth tightened. "You're right. I love to see you smile. Other people do too. Promise me you will be careful. He didn't call in favors for free."

Always a warning. "Oh, Robert, can't you be happy that I got what I needed, even though you didn't provide it?"

Before he could respond, her phone dinged, announcing an incoming text.

Saved by the bell.

She leaned toward the end of the island where it lay out of the splash area. The notification showed "Hayden." Her heart leaped into her throat. The same person who provided the best part of her day was saving her from the tense conversation about that very event.

Then she remembered she had not thanked him for connecting her with Tasha. She handed the dirty pot in her hand to Robert and began to dry her hands on his towel.

"Babe, I never let Hayden know I worked out the room. I'll be back after I thank him."

Without waiting for his response, she picked up her phone and walked away from the kitchen island and into the great room before opening Hayden's text: "Did you get everything worked out?"

"I did. Tasha is great. Thank you for putting us together."

She stared at the three dots flickering on the screen while he typed, eager for his reply.

"I was glad to do it."

"Tasha said she wanted that house from you for five years. Why now?" Her chest tightened. She didn't know why she asked him that, but now she wanted to know. She held her breath watching his three dots.

"I wanted to make you smile."

Her heart skipped a beat. This man she barely knew, this

good man everybody liked, had called in big favors for her. And he had done it on an impossible task.

Even Robert wouldn't help me, but Hayden did.

"You did. I owe you big time. How can I return the favor?" A tingle swept through her pussy as she remembered the fullness of him driving into her. She shifted in her seat to fan the heat.

"Not at all. I liked doing it for you. Just flash that big smile at the walk-through tomorrow. I'll know what you mean."

The kitchen light flicked off behind her as Robert had finished the dishes. Now in the light, she saw her reflection in the window, smiling and twirling a lock of her hair in her fingers.

"I'm smiling now. I'll think of another way to repay you." *And I won't be wearing this many clothes.*

"I can't wait to see what you can imagine."

Robert passed behind Alyssa and trailed his hand along her shoulders. "I'm done in the kitchen. Come to the porch if you want when you are done saying thank you."

Alyssa winced because she had left him the worst of the cleanup to text with Hayden. She nodded, hoping he had not seen her face in the window. She turned her phone face down and looked over her shoulder. "Almost done. I'll be there in a minute."

After Robert walked off, she returned to the strand. "I'll think of something good. Got to go now. See you tomorrow."

She looked at her reflection again in the window. Her thousand-watt smile had dimmed. She held the phone with both hands. She wondered why, then decided not to think about it. With a violent shake of her head, she stood and headed to the back porch.

10

THURSDAY, MAY 13, CUPOLA HOUSE

"Wait until you see the master, Babe." Alyssa skipped up the steps ahead of Robert and Hayden.

"You act like you want to move in here instead of flipping it," Robert replied.

"No. I couldn't leave our house. I just love the unique feature in the master. Come on. You two are so slow."

"It's a walk-through. We are checking the house over before we buy it tomorrow."

"The house is fine. Come see the fun part." Alyssa missed the top step when Hayden coughed. She turned, the smile on her mouth forced in an attempt to cover the guilt of the secret he wanted her to keep from her husband.

She had already been a little too friendly when they arrived.

She had hopped out of the car as soon as Robert turned it off and bounced too quickly up the porch steps where Hayden was waiting to let them in. She had given him a quick hug, and the huge smile he'd wanted to see was real. She had just released the hug and told him thank you when Robert took her hand with a gentle tug. She had forgotten he was there for a moment, and knew she had flaunted to him that not only had Hayden helped her when Robert didn't but he had fucked her in the very house they were about to tour.

She stayed close to Robert as they went through the house, but her gut tightened when she looked at Hayden, and her pussy tingled. She didn't know how to handle her husband and a lover in the same room, even in an open marriage. She focused on showing the house to Robert.

Regaining her footing at the top of the steps, she pointed to the left and smiled at Robert. "This way."

Robert stopped inside the bedroom door. "It certainly has big windows. Glad the acreage comes with it, or the blinds would take all our profit."

Alyssa leaned to Robert's ear. "Let the neighbors watch. And get jealous." She squeezed his rump and moved into the bathroom. "Come see this."

Hayden stood blocking the access panel to the cupola. "Yes. The windows are even more revealing in here."

The cold knot of guilt in her stomach loosened as she rationalized. *I won't show the cupola because I didn't tell Robert about it already, and he's still sensitive. You aren't a complete secret, Hayden.* She decided that they could discover the cupola together later, and they could use it the way it was intended—for making love. Her stomach relaxed a bit more. "They are even part of the shower wall."

Robert grinned. "Makes backyard barbecues a little more exciting, don't you think?"

Hayden chuckled and hit a button beside the light switches, and the bottom six feet of glass frosted. "So Grandma and the kids don't get an eyeful on Memorial Day."

Robert turned to Hayden. "That is an expensive upgrade. The attorneys won't come after the seller for selling too cheap?"

Hayden shook his head. "The wife and her attorneys have agreed to the sales price. We are clear to close."

"I can see why you like the place, Baby. It does look to be in good shape, once you get past the porch. Is there more to see?"

Hayden rubbed his hands together. "You've seen it all. Sounds like you are ready to close."

Alyssa nodded when Robert caught her eye, then she looked out the window, struggling with lying to him even as he spoke with Hayden.

"I think we are. And, by the way, thank you for cutting your commission on this."

"Glad to help out. I hope you will remember me when you sell and when you buy the next ones."

"We will." Robert chuckled. "Lauren will regret she is out when we do this. And the work is slated to start tomorrow?"

"Right after we close."

Alyssa barely heard her phone ding over the radio in Robert's car on the way home. The conversation about the house had lasted a few minutes, then lapsed, so he had turned up the volume.

She pulled it from her purse, then turned the screen away from Robert when she saw the name. Hayden. Her nipples tingled even as her stomach knotted. Unable to wait, she opened the text.

"Good girl."

She knew what he meant, but she wanted to play a little. "Uh-huh. To what do I owe such high praise?"

"You kept our place just for us. I can't wait to visit it with you again."

Her pussy flexed against itself, aching to be filled. She couldn't wait either. "I didn't intend to. I expect a reward the next time we're there together."

"I can slip a reward in, I'm sure."

That thing is too big to just slip in, but once it's in, slip it in again and again, please. She smiled at her own double entendre as she readied her fingers to type her thought.

"What's so amusing, Baby?" Robert asked from the driver's seat, breaking her reverie.

She turned her phone over. "Nothing's amusing. Why?"

He turned to her while they sat at a light. "You were a zombie. You get a text, and you are grinning like a cat. Who improved your mood?"

"Oh, it's just Amelia from work. You know how sarcastic she can be once she crushes a problem for me. Sometimes you have to laugh to keep from crying." *I can't believe he noticed that.*

"Tell her thank you for waking you up." He pulled the car forward as the light changed.

"I will." She returned to her phone, careful to keep it angled away from Robert.

"Got to go. See you at closing."

She closed the phone without waiting for a reply.

11

FRIDAY, MAY 14, CUPOLA HOUSE

Alyssa followed Hayden's car to the house. He met her at the porch steps. "Congratulations. It's yours."

"Quite the gentleman again." *And still gorgeous. I like him better every time I see him.*

"Always for you, milady."

"Where is the contractor, um…?"

"Joey."

"Joey. At the closing, you said he would meet us here so we could make any final decisions and get off on the right foot. I need to get back to work. He needs to provide a good first impression as well."

"He will be here. Why don't we wait inside?"

His hands on her hip and elbow as they mounted the broken porch steps started a tingle low in her belly. She fought it, knowing the contractor would soon arrive.

"Still want to make sure I don't fall?"

"Very much so." He grinned and squeezed her ass cheek. "It's a chance to feel you against me again."

It does feel good. Alyssa's nipples stiffened. "Careful. We don't want the construction crew to see anything."

"They won't be here for another hour. I thought you might want to celebrate." He unlocked the front door and guided her inside.

"Even though I need to get back to work?" She turned, annoyed that he had made such a delicious but inconvenient presumption. He pulled her against him, his arms too strong for her weak attempt to step backward. His hardness pressed against her belly. And down her hip. Her vagina pulsed, remembering how it felt inside. Alyssa stopped trying to step backward.

"If you need to go, I'll handle Joey and his crew. In that blouse, your cleavage distracted me the entire time you signed papers. My invitation was a crazy impulse at the closing table."

One arm held Alyssa firmly against his body. The other hand floated across her back, lowering as it went, almost like a skier glissading down a hill, electrifying her skin and sending tingling pulses around her body from his fingers. Alyssa shuddered a breath when he switched to small circles where the curve of her ass began. The light touch sent a chill up her spine that his strong other arm countered at the middle of her back. The combination of firm control and feathery teasing stirred a storm in her belly.

"Yes, crazy."

He had pinned her hands between them when he caught her. Now, instead of pushing him back, she caressed his chiseled pecs. They were hard on the underside, squared off on the outside where his nipples hardened under her touch, and between them her fingers rippled over the ridges where the muscles attached to his sternum. Her nipples ached as she remembered how his chest had crushed against them only five days before.

The light finger circles lowered and firmed until he was caressing her ass cheeks. Her body sent waves of pleasure from everywhere he touched her to battle her weakening obligation to return to work in her mind. She fought kissing him, knowing that would signal surrender to what her body wanted.

After only a few passes, he dipped lower and inward, pressing the fabric against her craving lips. They spread under his touch, and lightning shot through her body from inside them. She groaned, and her legs quivered. His arm tightened around her back and supported her as she recovered.

"Still need to go?"

"No…" Alyssa's breathing quickened. *I need to call Robert. Now.*

Hayden bent to meet her lips with his, opening them to accept her frantic tongue. Maintaining a tight grip, he slid his hands up her sides to grip her breasts, thumbing her hard nipples through her shirt before unbuttoning it.

Alyssa worked at his belt and pants, getting them open and shoving them down with his briefs to release his cock to spring upward. *Got to have this now. Robert already told me I could fuck Hayden. I'll just tell him later.*

She pulled the hem of Hayden's shirt up, making him raise his arms just as he opened the front clasp of her bra. She dropped the shirt behind him, and he flicked her bra straps and shirt off her shoulders. Alyssa stepped out of her shoes as he unbuckled her slacks, dropping them once they passed her hips. She pulled her panties down, dropped them, and leaned over the arm of the small settee on one wall of the foyer.

"Do it now. I'm so ready."

Hayden moved behind her and positioned the head of his

curved prick against her wet opening. He slid across it twice, then lined up and pushed in, spreading her canal and stretching her lips with a sting that went directly to her clit. *Shaped like Robert's but bigger. I can't believe how good it is.* Alyssa looked over her shoulder at him. "Oh yeah. Just like that."

Only a few plunges had his cock wet with her juices and her channel stretched around the girth of him and the length as he pushed the top of her pussy into her belly. The stretching and the pressure hurt and pleased, and her orgasm began to boil just beyond her cervix. Again she looked over her shoulder.

"Now fuck me hard."

As she turned her head forward again, she caught sight of the wide mirror hanging on the opposite wall in the foyer. *Porn with all the sensation. My tits look so good, bouncing like that. God, his cock looks even longer like this, and my ass ripples every time he rams me. His arms are so big and perfect. His body is like a sculpture.* As if the way Hayden's cock filled her, stretched her, and hit her cervix wasn't enough, the visual stimulation worked her building orgasm like a bellows.

"Keep going. Harder. I'm close." Her body tensed, and she panted as she built toward her climax. *It's a big one.*

Alyssa had spoken to his reflection. When Hayden looked over to watch their image, they made eye contact.

"Watch that, Alyssa. Look at my cock fill you and bounce your whole body. God, look at your boobs sway. They're hypnotic. Look at your face, the way your mouth hangs open and your eyes burn. You look hotter than any woman ever has. Where do you want me to come?"

"Inside me." *No, you can't bring that home to Robert.* "No, wait—"

The hot, powerful splash against her cervix exploded Alyssa's orgasm. She stiffened and pressed against Hayden as he emptied into her. Her arms flexed, pushing her backward onto quivering legs. She saw her reflection—wide eyes, gaping mouth, neck muscles and veins straining against flushed skin—and surrendered to the ferocity of her completion, collapsing when her body released her. *Unbelievable. So good. And the cum inside me, amazing… Shit, cum inside me. I'll have to clean up.*

He remained inside her, minute twitches of his cock triggering her own orgasmic aftershocks, making her jerk. She lay still, loving the diminishing stretch of her lips and tunnel as he softened and the pooling of warm cum inside her. When he slipped out, he helped her stand.

"Welcome to your new house, Alyssa. I hope we can break it in well before you sell it."

"I agree with you. Let's get cleaned up. I don't want to look like this when the workers arrive."

He put his hand on the small of her back, eliciting a final small shiver up her spine. He gestured toward the stairs. "Shower?"

"Oh no, big boy. If we get in the shower together, we will do this all morning. I'll rinse off upstairs, you get cleaned up in the back. Meet you in the cupola in fifteen minutes?"

❧

Alyssa got a towel off the wall rack and rinsed herself in the shower, keeping her hair dry and spending most of her time cleaning her pussy and trying to push the cum out. She dried off, dressed, and used the stuff in her purse to repair her hair and makeup. She ascended to the cupola to sit in a chaise staring out across the woods.

I love this view. Maybe we keep this place. No, this is a fling of a house. I'll use it for the short time we have it, then flip it and move on to something better.

"What has you so captivated?" Hayden asked when he tapped her shoulder.

"Oh, I was watching all the blue jays in the trees. I love blue jays."

"You know they eat other birds' hatchlings and destroy their families. They aren't nice birds."

"They are so beautiful that it doesn't matter." Alyssa turned to Hayden for the first time. "They make this place even better."

"You belong up here, in the center of all this sunlight. You're more beautiful than everything as far as the eye can see." Hayden kissed her cheek.

"Thank you. If I belong here, then you do too, as beautiful as you are. I couldn't believe how you looked in the mirror downstairs." She pushed his shoulder. "Sit over there, or we'll start up again, you beautiful man."

"I will, but I want to make love to you again up here soon. You know, you should probably come by to check on everything frequently, even every day. I could meet you to help out."

"To help out? Or to help me out of my clothes?" *I wouldn't complain.*

"Both, if that's what you wanted." He winked at her. "I would help you with the crew and making any decisions."

She sat at the opposite end of the other chaise, out of his reach. "Out of the goodness of your heart?"

"Of course. I know rental property, and I like you."

"Noticed that."

"I enjoy doing nice things for people I like. I try to be a good person."

"Like taking people to George's restaurant? Or building charity houses?"

He moved to the end of his chaise. The spot where their knees touched kindled warm tendrils that reached up her thigh toward her lips. She didn't pull away.

"Or helping you with a hotel room and showing you this steal of a house. Yes. Doing nice things."

"You sure make me feel nice. Well, naughty too."

He caressed inside her knee past the first knot of muscle in the sensitive hollow. Her nipple tingled, and a warm glow radiated through her chest to her waist.

"Especially up here, where you belong?"

Mmm. He makes me wet with every touch. "Especially up here."

"And this is just for us, right?"

Alyssa cleared her head with a shake and leaned back. "Why is that important to you?"

"I guess it's because I brought you here to show you something special, like you asked, and then it was the first place we made love. In a month, you'll flip it and we won't meet here again, and I'd like to have a good memory that is just ours."

"So you're a romantic about it?" *How sweet. More sensitive than I expected from a young stud.*

"I guess so, when you put it that way."

"And a little possessive too?"

He laughed. "I guess. As much as I can be with another man's wife."

"Don't go there. We can enjoy ourselves, but leave Robert out of it." *I need to talk with him.*

"Fair enough, as long as this room remains ours alone. Let me have my memories, please?"

"I can't promise. He owns this house too. If he wants to come up here, he will."

"You don't have to show him. And he won't need to come here if you and I handle everything."

"Probably not." *We'll see.* She stood. "If this is our secret, then let's meet the contractor downstairs."

Hayden put his palm on her belly as she walked by, stopping her. He stood, wrapped her in his arms, and placed a whisper of a kiss on her lips. "You're right. Let's go."

❧

"What do you mean, the cost just went up eight thousand?" Alyssa stared at the burly construction foreman with her hands in a shrug.

"Like I said, ma'am. Our lumber supplier increased our costs on Monday. That is about eight grand on the lumber for this job. This COVID lockdown stuff is driving lumber demand and prices up because people are doing home projects. I'm not trying to pull anything over on you, I'm just telling you what the costs are doing."

"And we bear the increases."

"Yes, ma'am."

"Can we lock in our prices with your supplier now?"

"No, ma'am. They charge us at delivery every week, and we don't want a lot of extra lying around. People are stealing from job sites like crazy."

Alyssa walked in a small circle, spinning her rings. Robert would not have closed if he knew the prices could increase so quickly. Neither would she. *Where was this information three hours ago?* She faced Joey. "The price could go up two more times?"

"Maybe three. Some of my guys are quarantined after testing positive, so I'm short men."

"Another, what, fifteen thousand?"

"Maybe not that much, 'cause the amount gets less each week, but maybe. This is crazy."

"You have to be kidding me. This is robbery." Alyssa put her hands on her hips.

The large older man stiffened, then relaxed his shoulders. "Don't insult me, ma'am. I'm only passing on the costs. I'm not increasing the fifteen percent profit portion of the job, even though I could. I'm being honest and fair with you. You should have already been told." He glanced at Hayden.

"Can I offer a thought, guys?" Hayden spoke for the first time since introducing the two. He received two frustrated glances but kept going. "Joey, you want to space out the deliveries so nothing gets stolen, right?"

"Just like I said."

"Alyssa, you want to lock in the costs?"

"Yes, so I don't get ripped off." She held up her hands. "Sorry. Not by you, Joey. By the lumber supplier. I don't mean to offend; I'm a bit taken aback by all this."

"I am too. I didn't accuse him of robbing me though."

Alyssa shrank back. "Again, I'm sorry for that."

Hayden pointed to the gravel drive beside the house. "Guys, we are hidden by woods on all sides. Joey, if we stored the materials behind the house, nobody would know they were here. You think we could get everything delivered Monday and lock in the costs?"

"We could. They could still be stolen, but it's less likely."

"Alyssa, are you willing to risk that, knowing that you have to replace anything that is stolen?"

"Is there any way to lock it up?"

Joey laughed. "No, ma'am. It's bundles of lumber and pallets of shingles. Over a thousand pounds each. His idea of hiding it in the back is as good as it gets."

Hayden pointed to a curve in the driveway. "You see that curve, how the trees are close beside the driveway there? Could we park a car there to make it impossible to get a truck back here?"

Joey shook his head. "I'm not leaving a truck here to get stolen."

"I have an old one we can use," Hayden replied. "Your guys can move it out of the way in the morning and block the driveway at night. Would that work?"

"That works." The older man nodded.

Hayden looked at Alyssa. He cocked his head, and the corners of his mouth hinted at a smile. "Does that make you feel better? Costs locked in and materials protected as best we can?"

The costs won't increase further. Robert would appreciate that. The location lets us keep the materials a secret. Another secret. She smiled to cover the flip of her stomach.

"That works perfectly. Thank you for the solution." *Another solution from Hayden. He likes me. And I like him.* She offered Joey her hand. "I'm sorry for my reaction. Please forgive me for not putting my best foot forward."

He smiled, and they shook hands. "I think we will be fine. You remember I'm not trying to swindle you, and I'll remember you are nice when you aren't surprised."

They all laughed. Alyssa put her hand on Hayden's arm. "We'll call Hayden to sort it out if we can't."

12

FRIDAY, MAY 14, HOME

"Is Clay home?" Alyssa called into the great room as she burst through the laundry room door. "I don't see his car."

"Just me, Baby. He's hanging out with his buddies. You're running late."

She adjusted her path toward Robert's office in the front of the house. "I had to stay longer because I got hung up at the new house before lunch." She spun her husband's chair to face her and kissed him deeply while unbuttoning his pants. "I need you right now. I've been horny all afternoon."

Robert smiled and unzipped her slacks as he kissed her back. He pulled them down to her knees and let them drop. Before he could bend to untie his shoes, Alyssa pushed his chest back, stepped out of her shoes and slacks, and straddled him. "I can't wait any longer." She pulled her panties aside and slid his

135

hardening cock inside her. "Oh yes. I need that so bad." *Swell inside there. Stretch me out. Make me come.*

As Alyssa rode her husband, her knees wedged against the arms of the chair, preventing her from taking all of him. "I need all of it, Baby."

The chair's squeaking filled the room as she rose, turned her back to Robert, and impaled herself again, not stopping her descent until her ass rested on his abs. "Oh, that's it." She bounced as fast as her spread legs could go, keeping the strokes short so she never felt empty.

She jerked when she saw someone in the foyer. The bright lights in the office made the glass in the sliding door reflective, and Alyssa watched her dim image ride her husband. She lifted her front shirttail to see her pussy stretch around Robert's thick cock. *Twice in one day. I love watching this. So hot.*

Robert pulled his head beside hers and bit the top of her shoulder through her blouse.

Alyssa caught his head. "Look at us, Babe. We're so sexy. Fuck me harder. I'm almost there."

"Ooh, I like that. I'm close too." Bracing against the arms of the chair, Robert drove upward into Alyssa hard, bouncing her forward. Even the dim reflection showed her breasts jiggling under her shirt.

She dropped her hand from his head and stroked across her clit fast and hard, hitting it more than stroking it to release the knot of anticipation that had tightened between her legs all after-noon. Her back arched and she moaned deep in her chest as her climax hit. Her pussy tightened on Robert's cock, and it swelled. He pulled her hips down until his cock rammed her cervix, then spurt after spurt drenched it. Her legs squeezed against his as her orgasm grew. She ground her pelvis on him, rubbing his cock against her walls and tripping it across her cervix. *Yes. Replace any of Hayden's remnants.*

Her body jerked twice more when aftershocks racked her abdomen, then she relaxed her legs and leaned her back onto Robert's chest. With her hand behind his head, she kissed his cheek and whispered, "Thank you for reclaiming me, Baby. I'm yours, and I love you."

Robert took a deep breath and sighed it out. "I didn't know I needed to. You didn't call. What do you want to tell me?"

Alyssa took a deep breath of her own. "I'm sorry. Everything happened so fast, I didn't have time."

"That rule is there to keep you safe, Alyssa. You are taking a risk when you don't follow it."

"I know. I was at the house with Hayden waiting on the construction crew, and you gave permission before to have him, so I didn't feel at risk, or that you would mind, and it really did happen fast. It was just a touch and a word because I was so hyped up after the closing."

"Hold it there. I don't give you permission. *You* added the provision that you call me beforehand. It protects you physically and reputationally. You do it in the guise of asking permission. That said, if I 'give permission' once, it doesn't extend to that person forever, whenever you want. There may be circumstances when you need me to do the thinking for you, as you put it, so if you still want me to do that, then you need to call. I expect it. Anyway, this was a safe partner in a situation where you needed to act quickly, so the risk of a meltdown was low. Okay. What then?"

"We didn't get through the foyer before I was bent over that little sofa getting reamed. Watching us do it in the mirror was a hot way to celebrate the closing." She leaned forward and turned to look at his face. "Is that okay? I am sorry I didn't call."

"It's disappointing that you didn't call, but now I have a

question. Do you plan to flip this house or use it as a love nest? Whether that's with Hayden or anyone else."

Damn. He always knew the ulterior motives that lurked beneath her conscious thoughts. Her momentary feeling of falling passed, and she shook her head with a smile.

"Flip it, one hundred percent. When the porch is fixed, it goes on the market. And I don't need a love nest when I can come home and get all the loving I need from you."

"Which explains today's rendezvous."

His sarcasm twisted a knot in Alyssa's belly. *Sarcasm to soften how he shows the anger. I messed up. Again.*

"That hurts, Babe, but I understand. I promise, this was a spur-of-the-moment thing, not part of a plan to sleep with the realtor for the next month."

I can joke to soften my message too. She smiled and winked. "Besides, the construction crew will be there. I like a little public exposure, but not that much."

"I should hope not. Please remember the rules we agreed to. They protect our family and us. Your impulsiveness puts us at risk."

He hugged her back into his chest. The combination of his strong arms around her and the warm glow still radiating from between her legs relaxed the knot in her stomach. She sighed and rested her head on his shoulder. Alyssa luxuriated inside his protective, loving arms while she waited for him to speak.

"Is there anything else you need to tell me?"

"Just a second." Alyssa folded her arms over his and squeezed. "Mmm. Thank you for this, Babe. I love everything about making love with you." She spun to sit across his lap and wrapped her arms around his neck. "Good news and bad news. The bad news is that the porch will cost more money."

"How much more?"

"Eight thousand."

"Eight thousand? That's twenty percent of the repair cost. I wish we had known that before we closed this morning."

"Me too. Joey mentioned that I should have known already. Anyway, the lumber costs are shooting up because of the COVID lockdowns."

"That part is true. And the good news is?"

"It will only be eight thousand more. All the materials will be delivered Monday, and we lock in our price."

"Forty-eight thousand is more than we discussed. I think you should talk me into spending more."

"Robert, we are in it now. We might as well finish."

"I said it was a lot of money that you should convince me to spend. Or do I need to sell your clothes?"

Alyssa smiled in recognition as she knelt in front of his chair. "I guess we're up to three?"

"I think so. You are one short."

She gripped his hardening cock with one hand and his balls in the other. "Well, I'd better get on it, then." She took his cock into her mouth, savoring their combined taste.

13

SATURDAY, MAY 15, HOME

"Wow, Baby. It's a good thing Frank is speaking tonight. You look too stunning for anyone to hear what you say."

"Does that include my darling husband?" Alyssa grinned at Robert as she straightened the short skirt on the black dress.

"Of course not, my dear. I hang on your every word. But…" He ran his finger across the top hem of the dress, starting on her bare shoulder, low across her chest, and into the narrow plunge that revealed her deep cleavage, digging his finger in to rub between her breasts. "I also hang on these beauties. They are delectably distracting and scandalously displayed. You look beautiful."

"Thank you, Babe. Beautiful is what I was going for. You deserve a beautiful woman on your arm tonight and every night." She put her hand flat on his chest. "Besides, you look so good in that suit, I had to do something to keep up. I'll struggle to sit beside you through the concert without sneaking out to jump your bones. You make me want to misbehave."

Robert chuckled. "Maybe we sneak out, then. I'm thinking about it. The symphony crowd wouldn't appreciate it though. Perhaps we build the anticipation for when we get home."

She stood on her toes to kiss him, moaning before pulling away. "That's for anticipation, then. Can't do that once my makeup is on." She returned to the bathroom with a giggle.

14

SATURDAY, MAY 15, PERFORMING ARTS CENTER

"THAT'S YOUR SIXTH one, Babe," Alyssa admonished her husband as he reached across her to get yet another oyster. "Leave some for everyone else."

The gray-haired man on her left leaned over. "Robert can have all he wants, Alyssa. It seems he and I are the only ones eating them. Besides, given how well you organized this year's fundraiser, Robert deserves some oysters to make up for your time away."

"Thank you, Frank. I was happy to do it. Of course, when the owner of the company asks you to head up a project…"

Frank laughed. "Yes, I own the company, and we are the principal symphony sponsor this year. But this was an outside charity project, and you could have turned it down because of your other duties. You didn't, and you have done a great job in a tough year. Thank you."

"It wasn't just me. Amelia and Jeff did so much work. I couldn't have done it without them." She raised her wine glass and tipped it at the petite blonde on Robert's right and the balding man across the table. They had not heard the conversation, but when she caught their eyes, they tipped their glasses back at her.

"That's why I like giving you projects, Alyssa. You inspire good people to work hard, and you give them the credit for it. I don't think you know how appreciated and rare that combination is. I wish you had been around when I got started in 1989. But you weren't even born then, were you?"

"I was twelve."

"Well, if you don't mind an old man saying so, your looks belie your years. I would not have guessed you were a day over thirty-five, even with your skills and maturity. My Patricia is the same way. Still looks ten years younger than she is." He patted his wife's hand on the table beside him. "Now, let me get another oyster before Robert eats them all."

⬦

"Gosh, Frank, you look awful. What happened?" Alyssa met Frank Martin in the lobby soon after they arrived from dinner.

He gave a wan smile. "Alyssa, I need your help. Something I ate doesn't agree with me. Patricia is taking me home. Would you give my little speech before the concert, please?"

"I'll be glad to. You sure you want me to do it? Doug is your VP."

"And you have headed up this project. Give the community the chance to thank you, to see a star in the making."

She shook her head. "I'll do this to help, Frank, not for any accolades. I hope you feel better soon. Please let me know if there is anything else I can do for you."

He handed her a folded piece of paper. "Here is my speech. Use it or parts of it as you see fit. Beverly at the side door over there will get you in the right place. Thank you for letting me be sick in private. Have a great evening."

As Frank left, Robert walked up, a sheen of sweat on his face. "The parking deck isn't far, but it is hot out tonight. You are welcome for the door-to-door service. What's that?" He pointed to the paper.

"Yes, thank you for delivering me, Babe. Frank is ill. He wants me to give his speech. I shouldn't have had two glasses of wine with dinner."

"I hope he's okay. He couldn't have a better stand-in, wine or no wine. Besides, you have worked hard on this. You deserve a little recognition. Enjoy it. You'll do great."

She pecked his cheek. "Thank you, Babe. I need to hit the ladies' room before I head backstage. I'll be back in a minute."

⋙

Amelia, Alyssa's young blonde fixer, walked up to Robert. "Is everything all right?"

"Frank is sick, apparently. He asked Alyssa to speak in his place."

"She will do great." She looked around and leaned closer to him. "Dinner wasn't the right place to tell you this, but I misled you the night you called looking for Alyssa. I thought I was protecting her, but she told me to be honest, even in situations like that. I apologize I didn't say anything that night."

"So you're the one. She told me someone saw her, but she didn't say who. It's okay. If I witnessed a friend walk into a hotel with someone, and then her spouse called me looking for her,

I would stay quiet as well. Thank you for the apology. It isn't necessary though."

"Yes, it is. I saw her when she came back to work. She had a rough time, and you tried to find her. She has been so good to me. She has opened her door as a confidante and mentor, and this fundraiser has been wonderful. I wish I had helped her then."

"It's all right. She got past it, and it sounds like you have earned her trust. I appreciate your talking with me about it."

"Thank you for saying that." Amelia's eyes went wide as she looked past Robert.

He turned to see a tall, beautiful blonde woman walking his way. Her golden-brown jumpsuit had two strips of fabric rising from her waist to meet behind her neck, a thin black string laced between them across her belly the only thing securing those strips over her pendulous breasts. The lightweight, gauzy fabric of the pants swished as she strode toward them, showing the slits up the sides almost to her waist. Her gold open-toed heels flashed almost as bright as her perfect white smile.

"Hey, neighbor." Jessica put her hand on Robert's shoulder as she walked up.

"Jessica, good evening. This is Amelia. She has been Alyssa's right hand at the office and on this fundraiser."

"Nice to meet you. If you don't mind, where did you get that outfit? It's breathtaking."

Jessica laughed as she spun to show her bare back. "A gift to myself after my divorce. A seamstress in town made it for me. I can send you her name."

"Please do. It looks gorgeous on you." Amelia gave Jessica her number, and Jessica tapped out a text.

Robert shook his head. "It's the model. Jessica looks good in everything she wears. Even baggy sweatshirts at the neighborhood fall chicken stew."

"Stop, Robert. It was only one time, and where I grew up, chicken stews were casual."

"I'm only playing with you, neighbor. All kidding aside, you look exceptionally beautiful tonight. Amelia is not the only one spellbound by your appearance."

Amelia scanned the room, and smiled when she looked at the door. "Speaking if which, my boyfriend is coming in now. If he sees you first, he'll never notice me. Nice to meet you, Jessica. Thanks for the tip on the outfit."

Jessica leaned toward Robert. "Is she one of your paramours, Robert? Or one of Alyssa's?"

Robert chuckled. "Neither, yet. I think Alyssa may have some plans for her down the road."

"I am scouting my competition. It's been too long since the three of us played. We should get together soon. I have big kisses for you two. Where is Alyssa, by the way?"

"Ladies' room, getting out some nerves. She has to make a speech. She'll be back before she heads backstage. What about you? In that outfit, you must have an escort."

"Yes. I'm using the company tickets, and I met one of our doctors here. He's married, but he can't keep his hands off my back, for starters. I told him I wasn't for his extramarital enjoyment, so he has retreated to the bar. It's a shame he's married. I was feeling horny.

"You always feel horny, Jessica," Alyssa said beside her ear while feathering her hand across the tall woman's lower back. "I walked up at an interesting time. You hitting on my husband?"

"A little. I told him I have big kisses for you two when we get together again."

Alyssa rolled her eyes, then leered at the tall blonde. "You're horny tonight, and you look hot enough to turn sand into glass."

"Thanks. So do you. Yes, I'm horny, but the doctor I met here is married. Not that it seems to hinder him."

Alyssa squeezed her hand on Jessica's bare side just above her hip. "I know it bothers you. I'm glad it doesn't bother you with us. We do need to get together again soon."

"It's different with you guys. Nobody's cheating, sneaking, or lying; we just enjoy each other."

Robert smirked. "Yes, we do. In fact, Alyssa offered to sneak away from the concert tonight for some fun. I think your revealing clothes are affecting you both."

Jessica cackled and lightly slapped Alyssa's shoulder. "You bad girl. I'll be watching. You'd better not sneak out of your own event."

"You never know what happens at these things." Alyssa lifted Robert's hand to see his watch. "I'd better go. See you in the seats, Babe."

"You'll do great, Baby. Love you." The lobby lights blinked. Robert turned to Jessica. "As your date isn't here, shall I escort you to your seat?"

Nerves fluttered Alyssa's stomach and she danced from foot to foot while she waited to be introduced. When her name was called, she walked to the microphone at center stage, leaving the nerves behind her.

"Hello, everyone. I'm clearly not Frank Martin, despite the name in your program. He got called away and sends his regards and thanks to all of you supporting the symphony. I'm Alyssa Davis from Martin Restaurants. Frank asked me to speak for him tonight. Here is his speech." She held up the paper, then began to read. After a few lines, she stopped. "He says some awfully nice things about me, which I won't bore you with."

"Read them!" a voice from the back called.

"Yes! Read them! You did the work!"

"Okay, I'll read them, but what he says about me, I'll say about the important people who helped me. First, to my husband, Robert, thank you for taking care of everything at home while I worked on this for the last few months. As with every other facet of my life, I could not have done this without you. Frank didn't say that, of course. I did." She blew a kiss in his direction while the audience chuckled.

"Second, this campaign would not have happened without the hard work and efforts of Amelia Foster and Jeff Smith, whom all of you have seen in your offices. Your work with each of the sponsors and donors here tonight, your coordination of the events and their changes because of COVID, your dedication and long hours made this fundraiser successful. You did it all while not letting your day jobs suffer, and I would have known it if they had. Despite the bumps in the road, your consistent positive attitudes and pluck made this endeavor fun and enjoyable. Would you two please stand for a round of applause?" Alyssa gestured toward her coworkers.

They stood for their applause, visibly a little embarrassed but grateful and smiling. They both waved and nodded to Alyssa.

When the applause died, Alyssa resumed. "Last of all, my heartiest thanks to each and every one of you who, despite the tough conditions of the year, continued to support the symphony so we can not only enjoy beautiful music like we will hear tonight but also so the symphony can continue its outreach programs, like performing in retirement homes and providing music lessons for underprivileged children in community centers. Thank you so much." She led the audience in another round of applause.

"Just in case any of you are feeling a little more generous, the team and I will be in the lobby during intermission and after the show to take any last pledges or donations before we close the campaign tonight. Please enjoy the show."

❧

Alyssa slid into her seat as the conductor entered the stage.

"Great speech, Baby," Robert whispered to his wife when she joined him in their seats. "You looked so good blowing me a kiss I almost carried you offstage."

Alyssa stifled a laugh. "The timing might not have been good, but maybe in a little bit." She squeezed his thigh.

As the first piece concluded, Robert whispered to Alyssa that he needed to step out, and he left the hall. Alyssa smirked and waited a moment before following him out. As she breached the lobby, she saw the door to the men's room close. A furtive glance in every direction, and she opened it. The sound of vomiting echoed off the tile walls in the bright room.

"Robert? Are you okay?" She followed the sound to the closest stall, where Robert knelt beside the toilet.

His sweaty, pale face showed a weak grin. "Not what you had in mind?"

"You look awful. Just like Frank did. Maybe it was the oysters. Oh, Babe, I'm sorry you're sick. Let's get you home. Think you can walk out of here?"

"I need a minute. Don't think I'm done." Robert vomited again.

Alyssa stroked Robert's hair between episodes for the next fifteen minutes. He looked up after a weak heave. "Maybe that's it. Let's go. I'm sorry to ruin your night, Baby."

"It's not ruined. You are more important than the fundraiser. Come on, let's get you up."

They ran into Jessica at the door. "You know this is the men's room, right?" Alyssa asked.

"I came to warn you that the piece before intermission is almost over, and you'd better get dressed. When you weren't in the ladies', I came this way. You two snuck out, but I thought you were having fun."

"He's sick. Probably bad oysters. I'm taking him home."

Jessica shook her head. "You can't leave. This is your big night, and you promised to collect donations at intermission. I'll take Robert home. You finish the event."

"Are you sure, Jessica? It's a shame to ruin your night." Alyssa nodded at her outfit. "You didn't wear that to take care of my sick husband."

"Trust me, when Doctor Handsy reached into the slit to feel my thigh two seconds after the lights went down, the night was shot. Leaving is better than sitting in there with him. You stay."

"Jessica, you don't need to take my husband home. I'm his wife. I should do it."

"Alyssa, I'm a nurse and quite equipped to take care of Robert. You take care of all these people, then meet me at your house." She gave Alyssa a hug, took Robert, and left.

Alyssa put another check in the case behind her, then looked up for anyone else wanting to donate. Hayden strode to the table where she, Amelia, and Jeff were taking donations during intermission. A tall pregnant blonde woman held his arm.

"Great speech, Alyssa," she said.

"Lauren! What are you doing out? You're almost due. If you are working and didn't show me houses, I'm taking it personally," Alyssa laughed. *Damn, that suit. Every girl crazy 'bout a sharp-dressed man. Jeez. ZZ Top lyrics are making me moist.*

"Hey, Alyssa. No, I'm not showing property right now, but Rosalyn wanted us to bring Queen Realty's donation in person, so I got dressed up and came with Hayden. Here you go." She handed Alyssa an envelope.

Alyssa looked at the check. "Wow. Thank you! Please tell Rosalyn that this is a most generous gift. It's even better that my two favorite realtors hand-delivered it. Thank you for coming, guys. We need to celebrate this soon."

"Why not after the show? My house is just two blocks down the street…" Hayden pointed behind him. "That way. We could have a nightcap. Water for you, Lauren."

Alyssa glanced down to notice the faintest outline of the bulge in his pants, and her nipples hardened inside her dress. *God, no bra in this dress. Everyone will see what the outline of his cock makes me think.* "Robert went home sick. I'll have to take a rain check." *Don't let me see your perfect smile.*

"Me too." Lauren patted her pregnant belly. "This baby makes me too tired to stay up that late."

Hayden flashed a brief smile. "Another time, then."

As the line thinned out, Alyssa tidied up behind the table. A woman with long black hair approached. "Alyssa, could I talk with you a moment? In private?"

Alyssa turned. *Who is she? Oh, Doug's wife! Shit, what is her name?* "Oh, hey. Um, Donna, right? Doug's wife?"

"Yes. Thank you for remembering."

"I can take a minute." She spotted an open corner. "Is over there good?"

She nodded. Once in the corner, she stood close and spoke in a low voice. "I was furious with you a couple of months ago."

"My goodness, why? I haven't seen you since the Christmas party. What did I do?"

"Doug came home on edge for weeks. I noticed it. The kids

noticed it. When I asked, he'd say, 'It's that bitch Alyssa.' It was awful. One day, he sat in the kitchen, silently watching me cook dinner. When I brought everything to the table, he stood, took me in his arms, and kissed me. We hadn't kissed like that in years. After I caught my breath, I asked him what brought that on. He said, 'It's that bitch Alyssa.'"

"I'm sorry he took it out on you. Did he tell you how I made him angry? I don't remember anything." *Except letting him jack off onto my tits and blackmailing him to stop harassing the women in the office.*

Donna blushed and looked around. "I won't tell him that you don't remember. It would crush his ego."

Alyssa felt her cheeks get warm.

Donna smirked. "He told me about what happened in your office. He told me about your husband's recorded line, and he told me you demanded he leave the women in the office alone."

"I don't know what to say."

"Say 'you're welcome.' After he told me what you did, he told me how much you scared him by not asking anything for yourself. He was afraid of losing his job, his family. And he admitted being angry at losing his opportunities to cheat on me."

"Donna, that's terrible."

"It hurt, but he was honest with me about that for the first time in years. He told me that after the anger faded, he thought about our marriage. He remembered how well it started before he got complacent. He laid another scorching kiss on me and said he didn't realize what he had until he almost lost it. He swore that he would be a good husband, if I would give him a chance." She blushed again. "He lifted me off my feet, and we reheated dinner for the kids later. We have had a sort of second honeymoon since."

"I didn't intend to meddle in your marriage. Only to calm the office. I'm glad it worked out both ways."

"I know you didn't. By the way, he said you have a selfie of the aftermath." She looked around again. "Could I see it?"

"That is a bit personal, even in this conversation."

"I know, but it is my husband's cock and sperm, if what he said is true. And what you did returned my loving and considerate husband to me. Plus, I bet it is so sexy. You are beautiful, and to see him there, in the aftermath…I really would love to see it."

Alyssa looked around. "A quick glance. Give me a minute to find it." She turned with her back to the corner and pulled Donna beside her so nobody could look from behind them. "Here it is."

Donna slapped her hand over her mouth as she saw the image of Alyssa with cum covering her tits. Alyssa didn't think Donna could blush deeper, but she reddened from chin to hairline. "My god, that is so hot," she said to herself before looking at Alyssa. "That is definitely him. No way you would share that with me, is there?"

"No, sorry. This is just for HR, if he revisits his despicable ways."

Donna laughed. "All right, keep it. He's been a new man, and that little threat may keep him in line." She touched her breast, rubbing a finger over the hard nipple that raised the satiny fabric. "But I think I'll make one of me, to remind him how good he has it. Maybe in the car before we leave." She looked back at Alyssa. "Thank you for bringing my husband back to me." She hugged Alyssa for a long moment before walking away.

Alyssa approached the young man and thirtysomething woman standing by the large window long after the concert ended. "You two have been such good sports to let Amelia and Jeff work on this tonight. Thank you for your patience." She gave each of them a side hug. "Now, let's get them out of here so you can enjoy the rest of your night." They approached the donation table and the last five people in line.

"Amelia, Jeff, get going. You've done enough, and your dates deserve a fun nightcap for their patience."

"We can stay. You need to go take care of your husband," Amelia responded while Jeff nodded.

"He's a big boy, and he's with a nurse to boot. Go. I'll finish up." She handed each of them a gift card for one of the better restaurants in town. "They are open late on Saturdays if you want to go now, or you can use these later. It's a small way for me to say thank you." She gave Jeff a hug and nudged him toward his wife. When she hugged Amelia, she whispered, "Have fun with your hot date. If you need to talk on Monday, my door closes behind you." *She has the hottest stories.*

"Thank you. I might need to stop by. I promised him a great night."

"Then go." Alyssa pulled Amelia to her date and placed Amelia's hand on his arm. "Thank you for letting me borrow Amelia tonight. You two go have some fun."

When the last people finished, Alyssa placed the donations in her bag and scanned the area before leaving. She jumped at a touch on her shoulder.

"I didn't mean to scare you."

"Hayden. I thought everyone had left."

"I waited. Do you want to celebrate?"

"It would be fun, but I need to check on Robert."

"Doesn't he have a nurse with him?"

"Yes." Alyssa noticed the usher hovering nearby, waiting for them to leave.

"Then one drink won't put him in danger, right? Come on, you have earned it."

"Is Lauren coming?"

"No. She went home after intermission."

"So this drink at your house is just the two of us?"

"Sounds like it."

"Seems inappropriate on a Saturday night." She nodded just enough for him to notice. *I need to be quick. I'm so horny tonight.*

"Understood. Shall I walk you to your car? You are carrying the donations alone."

"That would make me feel much safer. Thank you."

As Alyssa entered the brightly lit parking deck, a car slowed down and honked as it neared her. The passenger side window rolled down. Donna was smiling, her hair tousled and her makeup smeared with what appeared to be a large load of cum. "Thanks for the inspiration. We wanted a selfie!"

Alyssa laughed. "Glad I could help. Enjoy your night."

Donna cackled, and they drove off.

"Friends of yours?" Hayden asked.

"My boss and his wife."

Alyssa waited to speak again until they were in the elevator of the parking deck. "Which house is yours?"

"Four ninety-eight East Fifth Street. Right on the corner with Spruce Street."

"Which house is it?" *Why do want to keep the address out of my Waze history?*

"The one with the brick wall circling the back yard. It's the only actual house on that intersection."

The doors opened, and Alyssa found the car parked exactly where Robert had described. She put her bag in. "I'll drive around a minute to let you get there. I don't want to stand on your front porch waiting."

"I walked, so give me a few extra minutes."

"Oh. Then hop in. I'll give you a ride."

"I know you will." He leered at her as he got in the passenger seat.

"A quick one. I need to get home."

When Alyssa pulled out of the deck, Hayden slid his hand onto and up her thigh until he reached her thong, making her lips pulse with her heartbeat.

"Because you are in a hurry." He slid the tiny fabric aside and rubbed. Every movement of his fingertip around, over, and across her pussy compounded the writhing electric pleasure behind her clit.

"You're going to make me wreck." *That is so good.*

"Then you'd better get there fast." He increased the pace, circling her hard nub. "Right here. Pull forward by the door."

He was out of the car before she turned it off, opening the gate to his backyard as she got out. "Come through here." He held the gate as she passed through, then placed his hand on her ass to steer her to the left. "Go under the deck."

In the halogen light filtering under the deck, the white cushions on a large sectional sofa beckoned Alyssa. Touching the cushions with her shin, she turned just in time to meet Hayden's kiss. His fingertips found the hem of her dress and inched it to her waist, then he gripped her ass to pull her against his crotch.

She pushed his chest with both hands. "Back up a moment. You look so good in that suit. Let me watch you take it off."

He took off his jacket and stepped out of his loafers as he took two steps toward the other side of the sectional opening. He removed his tie while her gaze roamed from his face, to his crotch, and back.

He unbuttoned his collar.

"Slowly," Alyssa said. "I know I said to hurry, but I want to see you in this mood lighting." She circled her clit through the silky fabric of her thong, never taking her eyes off the tall man who was revealing his muscles to her button by button. "Very nice. The shadows make your muscles look even better."

The blue shirt discarded by the jacket, Hayden unbuckled his belt. "Still want me to go slow? You know you like what's inside here." He unbuttoned the button, then stopped, clearly waiting for her to answer.

"Go slow. Don't stop. Heat me up, don't shut me down."

He grinned and eased the zipper down. Over fifteen seconds, it moved the five inches from top to bottom before he pulled the waistband below his hips and dropped the pants to the floor, revealing his semi-hard, long, thick, curved cock and dangling balls in front of his muscular thighs.

"I didn't notice you had skipped socks this evening."

"You should have looked lower than my crotch."

She chuckled. "You look wonderful. Come here and let me reward you for the show."

He crossed to her, kissed her while pulling her dress below her tits, making it a wide belt. "No bra. Your tits don't need one anyway. They are perfect." He kissed around one of them, spiraling in on the nipple before sucking it between his teeth and biting.

The pain of the bite shot through her body. Her abs flinched, and she gasped. "Yeah, no bra in this dress. Don't stop."

He grabbed her bare ass cheeks, squeezing and running his fingers below to graze her lips through the thong before running one hand up her back to her shoulder blades and pushing her back with his forehead. He laid her on the cushion and moved his mouth to her other breast, giving it the same slow tease that the prior one received, sliding his hands to her waist as he bit down on her nipple.

Anticipation, the massage on the drive over, and the sharp bites on her nipples had Alyssa ready to explode. Patience be damned, she wanted him now. "Oh god, that's good. Don't wait. I want you inside me."

He yanked the thin waistband of her thong apart, stinging her back and the inside of her left thigh. He threw the remnants aside as Alyssa yelped in surprise, but her heart fluttered at his power.

She gripped his cock, barely able to wrap her hand around it as she guided it to her wet slit. "Slide it in."

Her breath caught as he entered her. Her lips stung, his girth stretching them to their limit as he inched forward. The curve placed his head against her G-spot, her wetness letting him push until he touched the sensitive spot beside her cervix. He continued his slow drive forward, stretching her channel far into her belly until his hips rested against the insides of her outstretched thighs. She clutched at his sides, holding him fully inside her as she panted. Her muscles gripped his cock even as they stretched around him. The pressure, pain, and fullness flowed out from her tunnel to fan her building orgasm. With a tiny spasm, her pussy relaxed, and she released his sides.

"Now fuck me."

He pulled back just as slowly as he'd entered her. Every vein and ridge rippled along her lips as they exited. His cockhead lingered, compressing her G-spot until he slid almost all the way out. The noise that exploded from her chest as he slammed forward into her echoed off the underside of the deck and the concrete of the patio, creating a metallic undertone to her high-pitched scream.

God, so good. Coming soon. Oh shit, give me more.

He repeated the slow-exit, slam-forward move three more times, and each time she screamed as he stretched her pussy. Her juices lubricated his thrusts, and she knew they had soaked the cushion. He sped up and established an even pace. Her breasts bounced and tugged on her chest as they resonated with every plunge inside.

Alyssa pulled a nipple with one hand and held on to the back of the sectional with the other, trying in vain to keep from being fucked farther up the cushion and away from Hayden's wonderful cock. When Hayden moved one of his hands to the cushion above her shoulder, he pinned her body in place between his arm and his cock. She pulled her other nipple, lightning from her breasts and pussy overwhelming conscious thought. She opened and shut her mouth while each thrust drove low, staccato grunts from her belly.

I'm coming now. God, so good.

"Come with me. Come in me. So close." She wailed as her orgasm overflowed into her body, tingling her abs and back.

"Here it comes." Hayden plunged a few last times deep inside her, pounding her back wall and stretching her opening before burying himself inside her to splash hot jets of cum directly on her cervix, the sensation driving her orgasm to explode.

She clamped her legs around his thighs, holding him captive inside her while her pussy clenched against his iron hardness. He lowered his hard chest onto her breasts, and the warm, secure feeling of being enveloped by a man filled her chest. He kissed her neck, making her pussy spasm yet again around his deflating cock.

This is why I need an open marriage. This feeling right here. Well fucked, euphoric, and worn out.

His cock slipped out of her pussy and down her ass crack, followed by a glob of their combined fluids. Alyssa shuddered again with a small orgasmic aftershock. "Mm. Thank you. That was the perfect way to top off the night."

"It was perfect to celebrate together. We need to do it again soon."

Alyssa laughed. "You say that like this is our first time. I agree, we need to do this again. I love the way you feel inside me. It's amazing."

"You are amazing. I've never had a woman respond as well as you do. It does wonders for my ego."

"We seem to fit perfectly, don't we?"

"We do indeed."

She let her legs fall open, and his hips pressed onto hers. His weight bore down onto her pussy, keeping it compressed and warm as her body continued to relax. "I planned to go by the new house on Monday to make sure we are off to a good start. Maybe you could meet me there?"

"Sure. Three thirty? Those guys start early and quit about four, and they return to their shop first. We can catch them before they leave, then I can make you come after they go."

"That should work. I would love to stay longer, but I need to go." She nudged him off her and stood. She picked up the remnants of her panties from across the patio and wiped the cum running down her leg. "These were my favorite panties, you animal." She tugged the skirt down and the top up, covering her nudity but not the dishevelment that proclaimed her activity of the past half hour.

"I'll buy you new ones, but only if you model them for me." He wagged his soft cock at her. "You sure you need to go?"

"Yes, but I'll see you on Monday." She kissed him and stroked his cock, then wiped her hand on the cushion. "Thanks for the celebration." She got into the car and drove home, humming.

15

SUNDAY, MAY 12, HOME

THE TWO EMPTY bottles of ginger ale and hand towel on the nightstand told the story of a tough night at the Davis household. Light escaping through the cracked bathroom door let Alyssa check Robert's returning color and kiss him on the head without waking him.

"He's only been asleep a few minutes."

Alyssa smiled at the whisper from the far corner of the room. She turned and opened her arms to her tall neighbor, now walking toward her. They hugged, and Alyssa whispered, "Would you like a drink?" Alyssa set down her shoes, and they padded to the great room. "Wine? Or coffee?"

"I think wine to cap off the night, thank you."

"Me too." Alyssa retrieved a bottle and set two glasses on the kitchen island in front of two tall chairs. Alyssa raised her glass to her friend and sipped with a smirk. "You're wearing my robe. Anything fun happen?"

"I wish. No, Robert had a rough night. He threw up on me as we drove home. He didn't even react when I stripped and put on your robe."

"You were naked and he didn't react? He did feel bad."

"By the way, I think I surprised Clay. I was getting another ginger ale from the fridge when he came home about midnight. I explained that Robert was sick and I had subbed in for you as his nurse until you got home. He offered to take over, but I told him to head on to bed. I am a nurse, after all. He's a good young man."

"Thank you for staying to take care of my boys. I hope your sexy outfit isn't ruined."

Jessica laughed. "My dry cleaner is quite experienced at removing bodily fluids from my clothes, both from work and play."

"I'm glad. But if it doesn't come out, we will buy you a replacement, okay?"

"Thanks, but he's really good. It looks like you might need his card."

"What?"

"Your hair is a mess, that vee in your neckline is skewed almost to your left nipple, and you showed me the big wet stain on your ass when you got the wine. Do you need my dry cleaner's name?"

Alyssa's chest ran cold like she had chugged ice water. *I didn't bother to check my appearance. I was so euphoric that I don't remember driving. This could have been much worse. Again.*

She realized her mouth was hanging open and closed it. *But it didn't go badly. Jessica knows our arrangement, and she's the only one who saw me. No consequences tonight.* The dread in her chest dissipated, driven out by a giddy relief that rose to her face. She felt herself smile. *I can talk with her about Hayden without camouflaging how much I like it.*

She focused to give a sheepish half smile instead of the beaming grin fighting to surface. "I've been horny all night, the concert and the fund drive went perfectly, and this guy I like was there. I had a nightcap at his place. Sorry if I kept you too late watching Robert."

"Not too late. It's not even one a.m. A guy you like? Is that part of your open marriage?"

"No. I mean, yes. I mean, wait. I didn't mean it that way. Yes, I like the guy, but no, emotional attachment isn't part of our arrangement. Yes, I have had him before, so he is a part of our arrangement, but no, he isn't aware Robert and I have an arrangement. Does that sound as confusing to you as it does to me?"

"No. I get it. Tell me about it."

"I met this guy last weekend when we went to look at houses. He's tall, muscular, and ripped but not like a muscle head, just strong with no fat. He looks like a model, and his teeth are perfect. You know how weak I am for good teeth."

"Sounds delicious. Have you gone past looking at him?"

"That's just it. It gets better. He's smart, he's got this quick, sarcastic sense of humor, and if that's not enough, he spends time volunteering, and he's thoughtful. Like, he takes people to a new restaurant on the edge of town because he wanted to help the owner get established. He's got connections everywhere. He even helped me with a problem at work last week that nobody else could solve."

"He's beautiful, a great guy, smart, and funny. There has to be something not perfect. Is he mediocre in bed?"

"Oh god, no. You noticed how I look? We only had a quickie on his patio, but it was so amazing that I rode the afterglow the whole way here. I didn't think to look in a mirror. Hell, I don't even remember driving. It's like I floated home."

Jessica's eyes narrowed, and the corners of her lips flashed downward before she smirked. "You sound like you have a crush."

"I don't have a crush. I'm enjoying an amazing new guy for a while. No emotional attachments means no crushes. I won't mess this up."

Jessica chuckled. "Uh-huh. You have a crush. And I thought I was your only crush."

Maybe I said too much. Change the subject. Alyssa placed her hand on Jessica's thigh, which had slipped through the front of the robe. "You are my only crush, my smoking hot neighbor. Mm, no wonder Doctor Handsy reached into your outfit. Your skin is so silky, I can't resist feeling it."

"Then don't." She pulled the robe off her other thigh and took a sip of wine.

Alyssa traced her hand up and down one thigh, then the other before she spoke again. "I owe you for taking care of Robert tonight."

"Not at all."

Alyssa continued to stroke Jessica's long legs, which had opened a bit. "Then I owe you for ruining your date."

"You feel better on my thighs than he did." Jessica grinned around the lip of her glass as she took another sip.

Alyssa took a sip. She feathered her fingertips along Jessica's thighs, which parted at the same tortuous pace that Alyssa reached higher. "Then I owe you for ruining your outfit."

"It will be fine. You let me borrow your robe." Jessica ran her hand down from her collarbone to her breast, circling it until the nipple stood hard and obvious under the pink satin.

"Then I owe you for getting some while you played nursemaid

to my husband." Alyssa stroked her thumb alongside one of Jessica's outer lips, flicking one of the hard tendons there.

Jessica's breath fluttered. "You might. So does Robert, I hope." She flopped her legs open wide.

Alyssa drew her thumb across the top of Jessica's mound, just above her clit, then down beside the other outer lip. Tightening her slow tease, she circled her thumb upward along the first lip.

"He owes you for helping him. I'm sure he wants to repay you in bed just as much as you want him to. But I owe you for taking extra time."

Jessica shuddered when Alyssa avoided her clit on the next pass of her thumb.

"I guess you do. How will you ever repay me?"

"Like this." Alyssa leaned in for a kiss. Both women put down their glasses and held each other's cheeks with both hands while their kiss grew deeper. Alyssa entwined her fingers in Jessica's blonde curls, cupping the back of her head.

Jessica moaned into the kiss and dragged the top of Alyssa's dress to her waist, then caressed her skin from her waist, between the valley of her breasts, up her neck, to her ears, then down over her shoulders. Every fingertip sent tingles rippling along Alyssa's skin in random patterns, colliding and strengthening, reigniting the euphoria from earlier. She gasped when Jessica brushed her armpits and continued down the outside of her tits, then traced the undersides with her fingertips before sliding up to the nipples. They hardened, giving the roaming tingles an exquisite place to gather and pulse between her breasts.

Alyssa untied the sash of Jessica's robe. Skimming her hands up the outsides of Jessica's thighs and inside her robe, Alyssa grazed her hands up Jessica's sides until she enjoyed the firm bottoms of Jessica's breasts.

Those nipples. So hard. Without lingering on the hard points pressing into her palms, Alyssa flicked her wrists apart until the robe opened to Jessica's shoulders.

Alyssa placed a small kiss between Jessica's lower lip and chin, then another on the cleft of her chin, then worked along her jaw-line to her neck while she continued to caress Jessica's body from shoulders to thighs. Each kiss down Jessica's neck and across her chest included a teasing lick, leaving small glistening wet spots on the blonde beauty, who had begun to pant.

Alyssa stood, took a sip of wine, and returned to the top of Jessica's right breast. She released the mouthful of wine, making Jessica flinch and bristling her skin with goose bumps. The wine rolled down the white breast and the tanned skin below it until soaking into the robe under Jessica's thigh.

"How's your cleaner with wine?" Alyssa nibbled, licked, and sucked all of Jessica's breast, enjoying the sweet wine with the salty skin.

"Not as good as you are with your mouth." Jessica rubbed along Alyssa's back and up to her neck to her wavy brown hair, then repeated the trip. The firm hands were warm on Alyssa's back, and she understood their message: "Don't stop what you are doing."

By the time Alyssa repeated the wine treatment on Jessica's left breast, Jessica was sliding her hips across the chair, clearly searching for relief. Alyssa kissed down her belly, following the trail of wine one tiny kiss at a time. Alyssa took a smaller sip of wine and released it low on Jessica's belly, letting it coat her pussy and puddle between her thighs. Jessica's abs fluttered as she shuddered a breath.

With Jessica's hands now entwined in her hair, Alyssa enjoyed the last few moments of teasing as she licked the outside of the puffy and open outer lips before wedging her tongue between the outer and inner lip. Up and down she licked their length, then repeated the trip on the other side.

When Alyssa reached the top of Jessica's opening for the fourth time, she planted her lips over the hard clit and sucked, letting a little air seep through to vibrate it until the spread thighs clamped against her ears.

Alyssa released the suction, and Jessica's thighs relaxed. Alyssa looked up over the heaving belly at the flushed breasts, pleased to see how close Jessica had come to release. "Slide your hips forward a little and put your leg on the bar so you don't fall."

Jessica did, and Alyssa slid two fingers into her wet opening, angling them down to press on the back wall. She smiled at Jessica's purr before reattaching to the hard clit and sucking while circling the nub with her tongue. She moved her fingers in and out, maintaining the pressure against Jessica's back wall.

Jessica made a low, throaty noise. She pressed Alyssa's head against her sex with both hands and humped her hips. Alyssa readied herself for the coming climax. Jessica grunted and clamped her thighs together again. Her hips slid forward. Alyssa pressed her shoulders into the backs of Jessica's thighs, preventing her from sliding off the chair, never breaking the rhythm of her fingers or her suction on Jessica's clit. Only when Jessica pulled Alyssa's hair back did Alyssa stop. She released, smiled at her panting neighbor, then planted a small kiss just below Jessica's navel, a sensitive spot she knew Jessica loved, before standing up.

"Damn, that was good." Jessica reached for Alyssa, pulling her close for a kiss. "You are always good, but I loved the wine trick."

"It was an impulsive thought. The first time, at least. When you liked it…"

"Now let me do you. Pull that skirt up and sit down."

Alyssa hiked her skirt up. *The second time tonight this dress has been just a belt. I like it.* She sat in the tall chair and placed her foot on the bar. "I hoped you would want to. You know how horny I get when you come on me. Just dive in. I don't need foreplay tonight."

Jessica pulled Alyssa's nipple. "Just a little." Jessica sucked the other nipple into her mouth and pressed it against her palate with her tongue several times in a milking action. Alyssa groaned as the currents ran from her nipple to her pussy.

"God. Eat me now." Alyssa pushed Jessica's head south until the blonde curls tickled the insides of her thighs, and Jessica's tongue licked from the bottom of her slit to the top, then back down. The light touches along her lips made her pussy throb. Inside, she clenched against the emptiness as her nerves concentrated warm pleasure behind her clit.

Jessica licked the full length of Alyssa's slit a few times before plunging her tongue deep inside. She wriggled it around and slurped at the fluid. "I normally like this straight from the tap, but getting it out of your pussy is so depraved. I like it."

Suck it out. I can't bring it to Robert. I didn't think about that at Hayden's. "Have some more."

She sucked some more, the feeling of fluid flowing out of her making Alyssa writhe against Jessica's face, craving more contact.

Jessica pulled back and stood.

Alyssa's pussy ached for more sucking, and she reached for the blonde hair, stopping when she recognized Jessica's smirk. The blonde leaned forward, and they met in an open-mouthed kiss. Alyssa moaned when she received the cum cocktail Jessica delivered. They pushed it back and forth, spilling some onto Alyssa's chin, before Alyssa swallowed it down.

Jessica returned to Alyssa's pussy, licking her slit one more time before inserting two fingers to rub her G-spot and licking around her clit. She kept a slow pace with her fingers, pressing hard against the rough front wall and making Alyssa grind her hips, making the pressure of two fingers on her G-spot feel like three.

"Keep it down or you'll wake Robert," Jessica admonished her, catching her eye through her breasts.

If I do, I want him to fuck me too. I can't get enough. Alyssa's hips shuddered as her upraised leg quivered. *I'm about to come. It's only been a minute or two. This is so good.* Alyssa held herself on the chair with one hand and moved the other to roll and pull her nipple.

"Just like that. I'm coming."

Jessica pressed Alyssa's G-spot and sucked her clit. Alyssa's quivering thighs found their strength and clamped Jessica's head into place. Her orgasm spilled out from low in her belly, waves rolling through her body, alternating flexing and relaxing her muscles. Her skin crackled with energy, the shocks that had accumulated behind her nipples releasing to fire every nerve they could touch. Only the leg flexing atop the bar prevented her from falling from the barstool. When the waves lessened enough so she could open her legs, Alyssa pushed Jessica's head away from her flaming pussy.

She kissed the insides of Alyssa's thighs before standing to hug her friend. "I hope you enjoyed that."

Alyssa cupped Jessica's cheek. "Mm. Yeah. Always. Come on. Let's go to bed."

"I'll just head home."

"Nonsense. You have nothing to wear, it's late, and I'm sure Robert will want to thank you in the morning."

"I'll just drive home naked. It's three houses down."

Alyssa grabbed Jessica's arm. "Come on. You are sleeping with us tonight."

In bed, Jessica pressed against Alyssa's back and kissed her neck. "Thank you."

Alyssa pulled Jessica's hand over her breast. "My pleasure."

❦

Alyssa stroked Robert's head as he slept. He had been the first one up this morning and had started a shower. Jessica and then Alyssa had joined him, riding his face and cock under the cascading water. They finished by washing him and putting him to bed before taking separate showers themselves. He had been exhausted this morning after last night's illness, but he gave every ounce of energy he had to pleasing two women this morning. No wonder she loved him so much.

A threesome for breakfast. Why am I not walking on air?

Because he didn't please me. I didn't feel him like I should have. I faked an orgasm. Again. Because he wasn't Hayden. Shit.

❦

Alyssa walked Jessica to the front door. "He looks so pale. Will he be okay?"

"He's still wiped out after last night and this morning. Let him sleep, eat whatever he feels like eating, and keep pumping the water into him. He'll be completely normal this afternoon." Jessica looked at herself in the mirror hanging in the foyer. "Thanks for the clothes. Glad I'm driving home. My tits are giving this shirt a workout that the neighborhood husbands wouldn't ignore."

Alyssa laughed. "True, but your boobs are bigger than mine. Sorry about the revealing neckline. I never wear it out of the house, but Robert loves it." Alyssa dragged her finger along Jessica's exposed cleavage to the scooped neck of the shirt, then tapped one of the obvious nipples poking out the thin fabric. "Thank you again."

"Glad to help." Jessica placed her hand on Alyssa's shoulder. "Listen, about what we discussed last night. It's none of my business, but be careful getting attached to this guy you like. It's impossible to have sex with someone a lot and have it not mean something. A crush could cause problems at home. I like you guys too much to see that happen."

Alyssa's stomach dipped, then settled. Jessica mentioned the one worry that had sparked in her brain when she again didn't feel Robert as well as she should this morning. *She's right about that. Hayden is too impressive to stop yet. But I'm not getting emotionally attached.* "I appreciate that. And it is your business; you have helped me with this entire change in our marriage. Don't worry. I know who my husband is and who my hot guy fuck partner is."

Jessica raised one eyebrow.

"I didn't say that right. I understand the difference between Robert and Hayden. Don't worry. I won't hurt Robert by getting attached to Hayden. Thanks for caring though."

"Mom, can we make breakfast?" The women looked up as Clay rounded the corner from the great room to where they were standing. "I'm—" He stopped when he saw his tall neighbor.

"Clay."

"Oh, um, sorry. Good morning, Ms. Hedgecock. I didn't realize we had company, Mom."

Jessica smiled. "Good morning, Clay. Good to see you this morning. Thank you for the compliment."

"Um, you're welcome? What compliment?"

"The one your stammering is still giving her. Go get the eggs and bacon out, and I'll be there in a minute."

"Okay, Mom. Um, bye, Ms. Hedgecock."

The two women burst into laughter when he left the foyer. "My apologies for that. I'll talk with him about his manners."

"Don't be too hard on him. It surprised him to see me here, again wearing your clothes when he came hunting breakfast. Besides, it's good to know I can still stop a man in his tracks."

"He's not a man. He's my little boy."

"You aren't paying attention. There's nothing little about the look he gave me, or the one he gave you. Let me know if Robert isn't feeling better after a nap." She kissed Alyssa's cheek as she left.

Alyssa rounded the corner into the great room and stopped still. Clay was scowling at her. A chill ran up her spine when he didn't speak. She took a deep breath and let it out as she continued toward the kitchen island.

"Mom, has Ms. Hedgecock been here all night?"

"Yes, sweetie. She brought Dad home sick from the concert and stayed because it was so late."

"I saw her last night. Was she in your bathroom this morning?"

"Oh. I see. Yes. She was.

"Mom, remember how you said that the house was just for you two, and you wouldn't have partners here? Is that changing?"

"No, sweetie. Last night was an exception because Dad was sick and I was out late. You can assume that there will be no other adults in the house being intimate with us."

"Being intimate? That's a nice way of describing this morning."

She looked down, not sure if the embarrassment at being overheard or the understanding that she again had violated their rules grew the lump in her throat until she could barely breathe. "I take it you heard?"

"The walls are thin, and you weren't quiet."

"Sorry we disturbed you."

"I wasn't bothered when I thought it was just you and Dad. What bothered me was her standing there in your shirt knowing she was wearing your robe last night."

"I see. Nonetheless, as you are becoming an adult, you need to be more polite about staring at people. I know you were surprised, but you need to be able to control your emotions quicker. She noticed the looks you gave the two of us."

"I will. I didn't expect anyone else to be here, especially wearing your clothes. I got upset." He cracked an egg into the bowl. "Tell me, you still plan on not having people over? I don't need to worry about some man being here in the middle of the night?"

"No, sweetie. We won't make you wonder who is in the house all the time."

"Good." He started whisking the eggs. "You two do whomever you want, but don't let your shit impact me."

"Clay!"

"What? I'm asking you to keep this stuff away from me. Is that unfair?"

"No, but you shouldn't butt into people's relationships that way."

"You brought me in when I had to explain last Saturday to Sawyer."

Shit. He's got me there. Alyssa swallowed hard, but the lump in her throat grew every time Clay spoke. "I apologized for that particular accident. Is Sawyer okay with what you told her about our open marriage?"

"She understands that what you guys do doesn't impact what she and I do. We are good with her looking at hot guys and me looking at hot girls, like we always have been, but we agree that anything beyond that is unacceptable." He looked up from the eggs and smiled. "Of course, she might revoke permission to look if she saw Ms. Hedgecock in your tight shirt."

Alyssa laughed, relieved that Clay had sufficiently accepted what he had seen to make a joke. He had made his point and given her an exit, the same way Robert would do. *Smart young man. He makes me proud even when he takes me to task. Take the exit.* "The conversations we have in this kitchen."

❧

"I brought you some water, Babe." Alyssa set the water on the back porch table and sat beside her husband.

"Thanks. I need it."

"You feel better?"

"Yeah, just tired."

"You weren't tired this morning."

"I was, but you two pinned me down and had your way with me."

"How did that happen? I got there late."

"I woke up and wanted to get a shower. After I stepped in, Jessica got in and just started to suck me, then she laid me down and hopped on my face. I think you came in right after."

"She didn't say anything?"

Robert chuckled. "Something like, 'I need to check your temperature. Would you stick your thermometer in me?' I was beat, but she was naked, so it didn't take much to get my thermometer hard enough to check her."

"That reminds me. She said I need to check your temperature frequently today, as long as you felt up to it."

"You will need to do the work. I'm exhausted."

"That's what a good wife does—pick up the slack when her husband is tired. Let me get those off." She unbuckled his shorts, and he raised his hips to let her pull them down. She stood and dropped her shorts to her feet before stepping out of them and mounting Robert's lap.

"Where's Clay?"

"Rowing with Sawyer. We're alone. I need you to take me, to reclaim me."

She gripped her husband's hard shaft and guided it to her wet lips. She rubbed the tip on her slit, teasing Robert and herself. With a sigh, she sank down on it. *Come on, hit the spot.* She rose again and plunged down onto his cock, letting the curve drag his head along her G-spot, feeling his thickness spread her lips and his length stretch her depth. *Not as full as usual.*

Alyssa bounced harder, dropping faster, letting the full force of her weight drive him into her and taking the time to grind her clit against his pubic bone while he was fully buried inside. *Come on. Make me come.* Her hands moved from his shoulders to the hem of her T-shirt, lifting it off and flinging it away before lifting her tits to Robert's mouth, one at a time. "Suck them, Babe. Make us both feel better." *Come on. Make me come.*

Sweat dripped from her face onto her tits, and beads combined to run down her belly onto Robert's. She felt it drip down her back to her ass. She panted and grunted with each pump of her thighs, which burned with the exertion. She grabbed his hand and moved it to her ass. "Rub my ass, Babe. Tease my opening. Make me come."

His finger teased across her pucker. It opened enough to let him bounce across both sides of the sphincter as he dragged his fingertip across it.

"Oh yes. Keep doing that." *Come on. Make up for not hitting my cervix.*

"Here it comes, Baby." Robert gripped her hips and held her down on him as his cum splashed into her. After several spurts, he raised her hips to bounce her again on his cock. "Let's get you to come too."

I love when he comes on my cervix. This wasn't it, but maybe it's good enough. Alyssa bounced faster than before, grinding in tighter circles, feeling the stretch in her lips and the bone press against her clit. Robert's renewed ass rubbing sent tingles through her body to her clit, and he bit down on a nipple before releasing it to let her bounce. *Close, but no cigar. He's tired. Give him a break.* Alyssa pounded down a couple more times, then laid her head on Robert's shoulder and growled while she ground onto him with a long grunt. "Oh god, that's good, Babe. Thank you for reclaiming me. I'm yours." She kissed him briefly before panting some more.

Robert hugged her tight, keeping her face over his shoulder. "Am I reclaiming you from Jessica, or was there someone else?"

Alyssa sagged against him. "Both. I had Jessica and someone else last night."

"Thanks for not calling. Who?"

"Hayden again."

Robert held his breath and noticed Alyssa was holding hers as well. "At the concert, or after?"

"After. I was discreet. We went to his place."

"Three times this week. You like this guy."

The unfulfilled orgasm still simmering inside her cooled at Robert's assessment. *He's not wrong.* "I can't lie. He's very good."

"Do you have feelings for him?"

Alyssa pulled back to look at his face, buying time to address the knot in her stomach. She didn't know and hadn't thought about it, even after her earlier discussion with Jessica. The most important thing was to avoid hurting Robert. "No. Yes. Well, sort of."

"Which means?"

"I like him. He's a good man, and he seems to have the right answer every time I need help. Every interaction shows me something else good about him, like there is nothing bad to find. He's not you though. He's just a friend. I like him, but I love you, and there is no comparison."

Robert didn't answer while a red flush came and went on his face, returning to the washed-out look. "Remember our rules."

"Don't worry. There is no emotional attachment here. I am very clear on who I love, both in my head and in my heart."

"That's all I need to hear." He drank three gulps of water and nudged her. "I'm going nap here a bit. Do you want to join me?"

"No, the porch sofa only accommodates one. You rest and I'll do a few things inside." She kissed him, gathered her clothes, and walked inside.

As she shut the door, her phone dinged. The screen showed "Hayden." Her belly fluttered, and she scurried to the bedroom to open it.

"Great speech last night. Too bad everyone in the room was too awed by your beauty to hear it."

"Thank you."

"And your performance after the show was even better."

She remembered how he'd taken her, the way he'd shredded her panties to get to her, the power that had driven her body up the cushions until he pinned her and used her for pleasure. But every ounce of satisfaction he'd taken, he gave back to her. He knew the precise balance between taking what he wanted and giving her what she needed. Her clit tingled, and she rewarded it with a flick before typing her response.

"Oh no. You took me for yourself. I was along for the magnificent ride."

"The entire night celebrated your hard work. You deserved to feel wonderful."

"Oh, I did." Alyssa looked at herself in the mirror across from the bed. One hand held her phone, and the other twirled a lock of hair. Her smile spread from ear to ear. *And I'm glad he knows I deserve it.*

She dressed and walked toward the kitchen. On the way, she looked out the window to the back porch. Robert had lain down, but his eyes were still open.

16

MONDAY, MAY 17, THE CUPOLA HOUSE

ALYSSA LIFTED THE cooler out of her trunk as four sweaty construction workers trotted toward her. "Here, ma'am, let me get that for you." The young man was barely taller than Alyssa but lifted the cooler easily from her hands. "Where would you like it?"

"The Gatorade inside it is for you guys. Would you like to bring it in the house and drink it in the air-conditioning?"

Joey came around the corner just as she asked. "No, ma'am. We only go inside the house when working in there. We are too dirty. We take our breaks in the garage."

"The garage it is, then." Alyssa walked beside Joey to the open garage doors. "We didn't get off on the right foot, and perhaps cool drinks on a hot day might let us start over?"

"That is mighty kind of you, Mrs. Davis, but not necessary. We sorted everything out last week."

"Nonetheless, I wanted to show my appreciation for what you are doing. Did the materials get delivered where we planned?"

"It worked out well. The truck was almost empty, and it's been so dry that we put everything all the way in the back. You can't see the lumber and shingles unless you walk around the house. We have to walk a little farther, but everything is there. When Hayden brings that truck, we should be set."

"Great. What flavor?"

Joey stammered when Alyssa bent over the open cooler. She looked down to see her thin blouse drooping forward, giving him a perfect view of her cleavage and lacy beige bra. *Oops. Better not do that again.*

"Um, um, yellow will be fine."

Alyssa handed a yellow Gatorade to the foreman. He downed it without stopping for breath. "Wow. How about another?" She held her blouse in place this time when she retrieved another bottle.

"Yes, thank you, ma'am. This was a nice way to end the day. Thank you for bringing it." The workers behind her echoed his thanks.

"I'm glad you guys liked it."

The rumble of a big engine disrupted the conversation. Hayden climbed out of the old pickup and threw the keys to Joey. "Here you go, Joey. Keep the keys so you can come and go as you need."

"Thank you. All right, fellas, let's head to the shop. Mrs. Davis, you will want to move your car also, unless you plan on staying until we get back in the morning."

"I'll pull out past where we park the truck, but I want to do a quick walk-through before I go." She walked to her car.

Joey opened his truck door. "All right. Hayden, do you need a ride?"

"You go the opposite direction from me. I'll Uber home." Hayden pulled out his phone.

Alyssa walked back into the garage after moving her car. "A gravel driveway is murder in high heels. Thanks for providing the truck."

Hayden finished sipping his Gatorade. "Glad to help. It's my dad's old work truck. I use it mainly at charity houses. What did you want to see inside?"

Alyssa's nostrils flared as she stepped to him. She cupped his crotch, smiling at his burgeoning hardness. "This fabulous cock…sliding inside me. Can you show me where it is?"

"I can, but you do something for me first. Will you trust me and do what I say?"

"Don't get too carried away. I need to be home about five thirty."

"That works." He kissed her and gripped her hips with both hands. Pushing her hips with his hands, he walked her backward. He moved one hand to the back of her head, dipping it forward, then urged her backward until the cold steel of the support pole pressed against her back. Alyssa gasped, then resumed kissing. One at a time, Hayden raised her hands above her head to let her grip the pole. He squeezed them there and broke the kiss.

"Okay. You aren't restrained, but you are to keep both hands on the pole at all times, as if you were tied to it. Can you do that?"

"Ooh, yes I can." Alyssa pressed her ass crack against the pole, splitting her cheeks ever so slightly. Her back arched as she pressed her shoulder blade against the pole, leaning her head on her arm, bent so her hands gripped the pole above her hair.

Hayden stepped back from her and made a show of looking from her feet to her hands. "Excellent. Now remember, your hands are tied to the pole." He pulled her blouse from the waistband of her skirt, raising it up her body as her back pulled away from the pole. He brought it higher, careful to keep the neckline from rubbing her face, until it was bunched at her wrists, held in place by her spread elbows. His hands drifted down her bare arms, torturing the sensitive spots inside her biceps and her armpits, making her skin tingle everywhere he touched. He teased down the remainder of her smooth sides until he reached her skirt, when he reversed course, tickling her as his fingers traced up her ab muscles to her bra.

"This would be easier if it were a front clasp." He reached behind her and released the clasp with one hand.

Impressive dexterity. I wonder what else he can do with those talented fingers.

Hayden lifted the bra strap with both hands, keeping it close to her body so it raised her tits before popping past them, tweaking her nipples. Pulses of electricity fired between them. Once the bra joined her blouse around her wrists, Hayden kissed both nipples and drew his fingers down her arms, again teasing her sensitive spots.

He wedged his fingers inside the waist of her skirt by her navel, then parted them, working them around each side and across her back until he reached the clasp. Unclasping it, he pulled the zipper down, letting the metallic purr echo against the concrete floor. Anticipation tightened inside her belly even as the waistband of her skirt loosened outside it.

Hayden gripped her ass cheeks inside the skirt and pulled it away from the pole, forcing Alyssa to step forward and take some of her weight on her arms to stay balanced. He skimmed his fingers and the tan skirt down her legs, raising one foot, then the other to help her step out of it.

As he turned to carry it to the steps, Alyssa caught her breath.

Such a great ass. And I'm on fire with his teasing. Alyssa looked down her body, breasts and belly rolling with each labored breath, her nipples rock-hard and protruding to their full length. Her hips thrust forward, and her legs were spread and taut to keep her balance against the pole pressed against her back. She watched him return. *There's that cock, hard and just begging to get out. I'm ready for it.*

"Do not rip my panties this time."

"Oh no. That's not the plan at all." He walked past her, trailing his fingers from her thigh, up her belly, and past the side of her breast. She shivered with the chill that followed his fingers up her body.

"Don't go."

She heard Hayden digging in the cooler. He leaned from her side and kissed her. An ice cube pressed against her lips, and she opened to receive it, then pushed it back to him. With it in his mouth, he moved to kiss her neck, running the cube against her straining muscle.

"Ah! That's cold!" Alyssa laughed and kept her hands on the pole. The ice melted, and Hayden returned to the cooler, making enough noise that Alyssa anticipated another icy kiss.

He reappeared beside her and held a large ice cube above her chest. The first drop of icy water landed beside her left nipple, making her yelp and giggle at the contrast to the hot garage air. After the first drop, Hayden moved his hand so the cold water landed between her breasts, on her smooth belly, and in her navel. His other hand moved to her thighs, teasing below her throbbing pussy. When the ice had melted onto her body, he ran his watery fingers across her lips, then inserted them.

"Suck them."

Oh, I like this. She did, enjoying his control over her more than the cold water she slurped down her throat. As the cool refreshed her, her arms tired and began to tremble. She pressed her back harder against the pole and pushed with her legs, relieving her arms but not lowering them.

After another trip to the cooler, he touched a cube below each ear and trailed them down to her breasts, spiraling them to her nipples before icing the seams between the abs and obliques down to her panties.

"Oh god, that's good. Go back to my tits."

Instead, he left the melting remnants inside her panties, trapped against her slit, before returning to the cooler. The cold froze the heat that had been building there, but the sensation of her lips tightening after beginning to open shot straight to her clit, making it hum and pulse.

"Fuck! That's so cold! Get them off!" Alyssa shook her hips like she hadn't since her dance club days, but the ice tormented her, chilling each new spot it touched.

Hayden knelt in front of her and grinned as she squirmed.

"Please." She groaned as he placed a cube on each of her ankles and pulled them up to paint the backs of her knees. She shivered her hips again as the cold migrated up the insides of her thighs, stopping just below the large tendon on each leg.

"Do you want the ice out of your panties?"

"Yes, please."

He hooked the gusset of her panties and pulled it away from her lips. The small slivers that remained clicked on the concrete below, and Alyssa exhaled as the cold diminished, leaving her lips and clit still tingling. Before she could inhale, he wedged one of the cubes between her cheeks, resting it perfectly on her anus. She screamed and tried to drop the cube, but the panties and the inability to relax her cheeks without falling conspired to hold it in place. If the first cubes had chilled her lips, the pressure of this cube froze her ass, the jumbled mass of desire and discomfort building an orgasm inside her belly.

"You bastard! Take it out!" Alyssa wailed but held fast to the pole, unwilling to move. Unwilling to relinquish the pleasure. Unwilling to break his hold on her.

Hayden put the other cube in his mouth and removed his clothes and shoes, laying them on the steps beside her skirt. When he turned, Alyssa stopped wriggling. *That is one perfect body. Come warm me up with it.*

Hayden leaned over her breast. The cold water trickled onto it, freezing her already straining nipple before his warm fingers pinched it. Alyssa moaned as the hot and cold collided in her chest. He kissed her mouth, then trailed kisses down her body, his lips shifting from cold to warm with each new nibble. He knelt and pulled her panties off only to wring a few icy drops onto her belly before tossing them toward the steps.

The ice between her cheeks stayed put as she shifted more weight onto her arms to stay upright in the awkward position. They groaned at her, but her thighs relaxed just enough to avoid quivering when he licked her lower lips. His warm tongue lapped away the cold, replacing it with a heat that radiated through her body to inflame the patchwork of hot, cold, pressure, and exhaustion building her orgasm.

Hayden wedged his shoulders against the insides of her knees, and as she came, she clamped his shoulders. His head was free to move as far as her hips did as she writhed under his chasing tongue. He continued to suck her hard button, then shifted to licking and nibbling her lips. When her climax left her with only the aftershocks, she relaxed her legs with a sigh.

"Oh, that was so good. Now please, fuck me."

Hayden smiled and stood. "Keep your hands on the pole."

He returned to the cooler. After an initial rumbling of ice, Alyssa didn't hear anything for a few seconds.

He stepped back between her legs, using his hand to rub the tip of his cock on her open slit before plunging inside.

"Ah, cold! And hot!" Alyssa's head flew backward, and her body shook as his iced cock sent chills and shocks inside her. The cold dissipated inside, but her lips tingled a while, stretched and cold. His girth stretched her even as her pussy gripped his hardness and his curve scrunched her G-spot.

So good. Not as deep, but so good. I'm coming again.

Her arms strained to hold her weight while spasms rolled through her abs. Her thighs again clamped against his body until they shook with the exertion.

He ground into her, his cockhead wedging between her walls and stretching them against her spasms, prolonging her ecstasy.

"Yeah. Come hard."

When the spasms stopped, Alyssa released the pole with one hand to push him back. "Too much. Wait."

Hayden pulled her outstretched hand until she stood upright.

Alyssa wrapped her arms around his waist until her legs strengthened. "Now you do what I ask." She dropped to all fours, presenting her ass to him, and looked over her shoulder. "Lube two fingers and fuck my ass with them while you fuck my cunt."

"Gladly." Hayden knelt behind her. Two fingers slid inside her pussy. They spread and rotated, stretching her lips and walls, fanning the coals of her recent orgasm. She writhed around them, seeking more pressure, and the sudden emptiness jolted her body.

He teased over her sphincter a few times, smearing the pussy juice, then blowing on it to chill the skin before refilling her pussy. The third time he did it, she opened her asshole, and his fingers stretched her open to dive in one knuckle at a time. Alyssa gasped as her anus stretched to accommodate his knuckles, then constricted around the meaty fingers between them. When the rest of his hand touched her cheek, his head spread her lips, and he rammed his cock inside her.

Braced for the assault, Alyssa pushed back against Hayden with every thrust. *Fuck, almost like getting two at once. I won't take long to come again.* She matched his pace and felt her breasts stretch and swing as she fucked him as much as he fucked her. The head of his cock rapped at the sensitive spot beside her cervix, and his fingers stretched her ass, pulling her with every thrust. She felt Hayden's cock swell after only a few minutes. Alyssa lowered her tits onto the cold floor, the cold and the pressure shooting tendrils of pain into her belly. She looked over her shoulder. "Now fuck my ass. Come in my ass."

Hayden stopped a moment, leaving Alyssa empty and aching to be filled. Before she could inhale, his cock shoved into Alyssa's ass. The speed of his insertion racked her, stretching her opening and the channel inside. Her breath wouldn't come as the pain fired down through her pussy and to her clit, making her jerk. He remained still while she adjusted to his size, the pain giving way to supreme fullness and a delectable stretch, guaranteed to make her come. Another moment and she inhaled before pushing back against him.

Fuck. He's stretching my ass. Every time he pumps, my tits stretch too. So good.

Alyssa felt every texture of his cock in the tightness of her ass. Her tits were cold and stretched. Her pussy clenched inside her, looking for something to grip as she prepared to come. That combined with the dirtiness of the act had her teetering on the brink in just two dozen strokes. When he swelled inside her, she relaxed, allowing her release to flow.

He gripped her hips and shoved himself deep into her,

touching his thighs on her cheeks, and yelled as he released his seed. Her breath shuddered, the spasms fluttering her belly and chest.

Alyssa slid forward, pulling her gaping ass off Hayden's cock. She lay on her stomach, legs apart, letting the cold floor help her relax and catch her breath. She was spent and didn't try to raise her head when she spoke to him. "That was so good. I loved the ice treatment. And the great fuck. And the double penetration. I'm stoned on pleasure."

"I'm glad. You lie there like that as long as you want. I'll enjoy the view." He moved beside her, lying on his side. "You like that, in the ass and pussy at the same time?"

Alyssa nodded. "Yes. Not all the time, but occasionally. I feel so full. Every little touch is heightened. God, I can't believe I'm telling you all this."

"It's fine. We have been quite intimate lately. You can open up to me. I would never betray any secret you tell me; I care for you too much to hurt you like that. Here, I'll tell you that I like two women at once. I don't get it often, but those couple of times have been great." He caressed her ass. "You said you like being double penetrated. By two men?"

"Oh no," she lied. "I use toys when I want that. I'm married, remember."

"I remember. That 'forbidden fruit' aspect makes you even sexier. Not that you aren't super sexy on your own."

"Glad I can fulfill one of your fantasies." She rose to her knees and looked at herself. "As good as this was, the ice and dust have made me quite the mess. I need a quick shower." She looked him over. "You might want one too. Stay downstairs and I'll drop you at your place on my way home. But stay downstairs, or I won't have time."

She walked to the cooler and bent over, making sure he had

a great view of her legs, her ass, and the sloppy cleft in between as she pulled a Gatorade out and chugged half of it. "I have to know. How did you cool your dick in the ice and stay hard?"

"I dipped it in the ice and watched your tits and belly heave as you panted, waiting for me, obediently holding the pole. You were so sexy, I was rock-hard the whole time."

"So your hard cock was in this ice, right here in my cooler?"

"Yes."

Alyssa dropped two ice cubes in her mouth, smiling and making exaggerated slurping noises. "Mm. Yes, it was." She walked into the house to the sound of his laughter.

17

MONDAY, MAY 17, HOME

ALYSSA DROPPED THE small, gauzy green nightgown over her head. She looked in the mirror and tousled her hair just enough to give it a wild look, then picked up the glass and headed to Robert's office. She tinkled the bourbon on the rocks, enticing him to look from his desk. His eyes narrowed, and he licked his lips.

"I brought you a present." *Then I'll let you reclaim me.*

"In that outfit, you are a present. Stand there a minute, you sexy thing."

She watched Robert let his eyes wander up from her high heels, along her bare legs. Her body was hidden by the nightie's hem, hanging just below her sex, the lace trim not quite revealing her shaved mound beneath. He hummed as his gaze crept over the shadow of her navel, then he leered as he saw her breasts,

190

clearly enticing him. He adjusted his crotch. As his eyes made contact with hers, Alyssa laughed.

"Took you long enough. Did you enjoy the sights?"

"Yes, I did. I always do. Come bring me my present."

She sauntered over, sat in his lap, and handed him the sweaty glass. He took a long sip.

"You have let this sit a while."

"I had a few sips while I let you finish working."

"Oh. Am I finished working?"

"You are for now. Give me a sip." She tipped her head back enough to get a good mouthful, then kissed her husband. She tickled his lips with her tongue, and when he opened to let it in, she pushed the bourbon from her mouth to his, letting some spill onto her chest.

Robert didn't sputter or cough as he broke the kiss and swallowed what she had given him. He smirked. *He knew that was coming.* "That's good. I need more." He dipped his mouth to her breast and sucked on the wet fabric and the nipple beneath.

"I like that, but here, have some more." She raised his chin with her hand and held the glass to his lips.

He swallowed, then returned his mouth to her nipple, sucking it in. The coolness of his lips electrified the space between her nipples, and pulses shot between them with every flick of his tongue. His hand feathered down her side to her ass, rubbing it and raising the hem of the nightie until he was caressing her bare skin.

"You are bad, Babe, distracting me from what I want to do." She set the glass on his desk and used both hands to open his pants. She slid off his lap to kneel on the floor. "Ass up, Babe."

He raised his hips, and she pulled his pants to his ankles.

Alyssa stroked his cock before taking the head in her mouth. She swirled her tongue over it and sucked as he hardened. *I love it when he hardens inside me. I'm making you hard, my love.* She retrieved the glass of bourbon from the desk, taking a small sip before plunging her mouth down, taking half his shaft past her lips. She let the bourbon trickle down to coat his cock and balls, then plunged her mouth down to the base, slurping and swallowing the alcohol along with his cock.

"Oh god, that tingles, Baby." He rested one hand on the back of her head and used the other to stroke her breast.

She bobbed, letting the tingle of the alcohol abate before pulling off to smile at Robert. She lifted the glass again, draining it and tilting her head back. When she returned to his cock, he jumped.

"Ah, cold. What are you doing?"

She smiled around his cock and kept bobbing her head, rubbing the ice in her mouth along his shaft. As it melted, she dipped her head to swallow the water and his tip before pulling back again to tease him with the hot and cold treatment.

"Yes, Baby, I'm close." He wound his fingers into her hair, moving his hand with her head rather than controlling it. After a few more strokes, he swelled to full size in her mouth.

Knowing what was to come, she smiled again, sucked hard, and drove her lips to his root, swallowing him into her throat yet again. She felt him spasm, and she pulled back, catching the rest of his salty cum in her mouth. When his climax ended, she sucked on the tip, extracting the lingering drops, then opened her mouth to show him the fluid inside. She winked, closed her mouth, and swallowed with a noisy gulp. She opened her mouth, showing that his load was gone, then stood for a chaste kiss on his lips.

"Wow, Baby. That was amazing. What did I do to deserve that?"

"Do I need a reason to give my husband a blow job?" *Tonight*

I have one. He won't think it's as delicious a reason as I do. Her stomach tightened before she said what she needed to say next.

"No, and please don't think I am complaining. Using the drink was new. The thought did cross my mind that you learned it today and needed to be reclaimed."

Alyssa laughed to cover the knot in her stomach consuming her heart, his intuition leaving an aching void in her chest. "No, nothing like that." *Not the time to ask you to reclaim me from Hayden today. You're still sensitive about him. We'll do a double later.* "I wanted to make you feel good. You had a rough weekend."

"Well, thank you. I do feel better. Is there something I can do to make you feel better, in say, ten minutes?" He raised his eyebrows at her.

"Oh no, Babe. This was entirely for your enjoyment. Plus, I love your taste." She took the empty glass off the desk. "Go back to your work, if you can focus. I'm going to bed. Don't stay up too late. Love you." She kissed his head and left the room, knowing she wouldn't sleep soon. She needed to understand why she'd lied to her husband.

Again.

18

WEDNESDAY, MAY 19, OFFICE

Alyssa smiled when her phone dinged. She had hoped it would. For the third Wednesday in a row, Hayden invited her to lunch. They were quick—about forty-five minutes from pickup to drop-off—but it boosted her attitude for the rest of the day. She replied on her way to the door.

She settled into his passenger seat. "This is becoming a regular thing. Every Wednesday you take me to lunch."

"Do you want me to stop?"

She shook her head. "No. I look forward to it. I'm just noting that it is becoming a habit."

He grinned. "A good habit, I hope. I like getting to know you beyond our physical connection."

"Is that why you text me every night too? To get to know me?"

He laughed. "You know my texts don't discuss world events. I text when you are on my mind."

"Several times a day?"

"You are quite an impressive lady."

A warm glow kindled in her chest. *A guy like this thinks I'm impressive? Wow.* "Thank you. You are impressive yourself."

He parked on the street across from a small storefront. About ten people stood in a line outside the door. "Have you been here before?"

She got out of the car. "Of course. Everyone loves Poppy's. Who would believe that people would line up down the street for hot dogs, but they are amazing."

In less than two minutes, Alyssa saw Nancy, Robert's assistant, walking down the street toward them. A cold knot gripped Alyssa's stomach. *Even though this is just a lunch between friends, she'll tell Robert we were together. He thinks I'm getting too close. I'll have to calm him down at dinner without reminding him we are in an open marriage.*

Nancy had made eye contact already. She couldn't say anything to warn Hayden. They smiled and waved, and Nancy got in line behind them.

"Hey, Nancy. You on your own for lunch?"

Alyssa watched her glance linger over Hayden. "No. I'm picking up lunch for Robert. He has a crazy day today. What about you?"

"My day is crazy too. That's why I'm doing a lunch meeting with our realtor. Hayden Robinson, please meet Nancy Hopper, Robert's personal assistant."

Hayden shook her hand. "Nice to meet you. You work at the bank? Alyssa and I were going to talk about some rentals to buy after they flip the house they just bought. Would you mind giving your opinion on a couple? You know, as investment properties? I bet you know all about them from working there."

He opened his phone to some photos, and they talked real estate until they ordered. *He's so smooth and natural. We weren't doing anything wrong, but he also made sure she knew that too. He did exactly what I needed him to do.*

Being open with this meeting will make Robert feel better. Alyssa paid for Robert's order with hers. As Nancy picked up the bag for Robert, Alyssa stopped her. *I'll remind him I love him, and we can have a good night tonight.*

"Could you wait just a second, Nancy? I'd like to add a little something to Robert's lunch."

Nancy nodded, and Alyssa pulled her lipstick from her purse and refreshed it on her lips. She pulled a napkin from the dispenser on the counter and folded it between her lips to blot the excess. The imprint on the napkin was a perfect kiss. She wrote "Love you, Babe!" underneath, then dropped it in the bag with his food.

"Please tell him I sent a kiss to brighten his day. Good to see you, Nancy."

Alyssa and Hayden talked real estate while they ate. She couldn't make things more personal in the tiny, packed restaurant. *Be discreet.* The delicious hot dogs seemed to gain flavor as they passed through the warm glow in her chest as she swallowed. When she finished eating, she reapplied her lipstick and blotted it on a napkin, leaving a perfect kiss. She folded it and put it in her purse.

When they were finally alone in the car, she turned to Hayden. "Thank you for understanding what to say with Nancy. By the time I saw her, she had seen me, and I couldn't warn you. Asking her opinion on the houses was perfect."

He shook his head. "Glad to do it. His assistant is pretty and wasn't wearing a ring. I assumed she would cause trouble for you if she could, so I showed her what she needed to see about our business lunch. I would never let someone hurt you like that."

He helped me again. Why me? Don't worry about it. Just enjoy it while it lasts. She caressed his forearm. Her fingertips bounced over the ridges of firm muscle, reminding her of the sculpted body underneath his clothes. *And a magnificent body to match his heart. Too good to be true, but it looks like it is.* She smiled at him. "My hero."

She pulled the folded napkin from her purse. As she opened the door to get out, she handed it to him. "Since I can't give you a real one here, have this." She closed the door before he could respond.

19

WEDNESDAY, MAY 19, HOME

Alyssa handed Robert a clean pan, then picked up the final pot that had been soaking. As she scrubbed, Robert finally mentioned what she had been waiting for since Clay went to his room.

"I hear you ate with Hayden today. Looking at rentals now is planning way ahead, even for you."

She took a breath to prevent the irritation sparking in her chest from creeping into her voice. *Straight to that. No mention of the note I sent.* "He mentioned that looking now will help him understand our criteria when the new house sells. We can avoid feeling rushed."

"I see. He didn't understand our criteria the first time you went shopping and found the house we bought?"

Always the questions. Her body tensed, and she took another deep breath. "He wanted to show some new listings to fine-tune his understanding." *Reassure him. Remind him you love him, not anyone else.* She gave him her best forced smile. "Did you get my note?"

He sighed. "I did, thank you. I appreciated your thinking of me. Or was it your way of warming me up to reclaim you tonight?"

She spun, flicking water across his shirt as she pointed her finger at him. "That's unfair, Robert. First of all, it was a business lunch to discuss how *we* spend *our* profits. Second, we both agreed to an open marriage, so if you had needed to reclaim me tonight, that is within our rules. How did my little love note become a problem?"

Robert looked down at her finger almost touching his chest. His head flushed red, and he didn't move until she put down her hand. He looked her in the eye as the flush faded from his skin. "Fair enough. First, if it was a business lunch to discuss how *we* spend *our* profits, why was I not aware of it? Second, we did agree to an open marriage, so a nooner with whomever is within our rules. Did you see anyone else we know? Poppy's is a popular spot downtown, and indiscretion violates our rules. So does emotional attachment, and you can see what lunch dates with your lovers might indicate."

A knot tightened her stomach, weakening the anger that flared in her chest seconds before, but not overtaking it. She counted to five to let her voice settle. "And how did my love note to you become a problem?"

"Because you felt the need to send it."

Her stomach dropped to the floor. The shock of his words extinguished her anger, leaving a vacuum that dread crept into. *It's like he was in my head at the time. I sent that note to make tonight easier, and he knew. Shit.*

Before she could respond, Clay rounded the corner from

his room. "Dad, could we play a little basketball? I finished my homework."

Robert held his gaze on Alyssa for another second.

She shrugged. "Go ahead. I'll finish here."

He smiled at Clay, and they headed outside.

She finished the dishes in a daze while the knot in her stomach grew. Her phone dinged. She dried her hands and opened it while watching her boys play in the dusk outside the kitchen window.

A picture of the kiss imprint she gave to Hayden appeared.

She typed, "Thinking of me tonight?"

Three dots flickered as he typed. Her stomach relaxed, and the tingle of anticipation grew in her chest. The next message popped in.

"Always. I want to trade this in for the real thing."

She reread the message four times before raising her phone to respond, each time building the warmth filling her chest. With the darkness outside, she saw her reflection in the window. Her smile, banished moments ago by Robert's accusations, had returned, and she was twirling a lock of hair in her fingers.

They can see me too. She flicked the outside light on, getting thankful waves from Clay and Robert as they rested between points. She walked to the back porch and sat in a chair facing the house before rereading the text again and responding.

"Me too. Soon."

20

MONDAY, MAY 24, CONSTRUCTION SITE

"When Hayden talked me into volunteering on this charity house, I was leery, but I'm glad to be here." Alyssa took the light fixture from the dark-haired, muscular woman helping her. "Thanks, Paige."

"I was the same way when George told me that the restaurant staff spent one day a month doing construction, but it is fun. Even if it is a million degrees." She lifted the hem of her shirt to wipe her brow yet again.

Alyssa hummed and nodded toward the door and down the hallway. "There are benefits to the heat." Paige turned to look at a shirtless Hayden attaching a sconce at the other end of the house.

"Jesus, the website should list that as a benefit to volunteering. My husband is in for it tonight."

I wonder if she remembers us. Alyssa stepped off the ladder to ogle Hayden beside Paige. "Paige, do you remember when we first met?"

The waitress lowered her voice. "The gorgeous sex dungeon couple? The woman who patted my ass and told me to fantasize about them tying me up? Honey, I remember you two at least once a week with my husband. Why do you think I volunteered to come with you when we broke into teams this morning?"

"I've thought about you too." Alyssa traced her fingers up the smooth skin of Paige's hamstring. "Did you think about being touched like this?"

"Yes."

Alyssa tickled the swell of Paige's cheek inside the loose jogging shorts. "Would you like to do more than fantasize?"

Paige turned her head to Alyssa. "Your fingers have me fantasizing right now. What do you mean?"

Alyssa. rubbed Paige's pussy through her panties, eliciting a moan. "He wants to fuck during the lunch break. Would you like to join us?"

"I've never cheated on my husband."

Alyssa worked a finger inside Paige's panties to stroke her bare lips. Paige shuddered a halting breath. "He has a threesome fantasy. I'd like to make it real for him. You are gorgeous and the perfect third person. But if you are uncomfortable with that, go to lunch with the others. No hard feelings."

"Let me think about it after you finish with your finger. But don't stop yet."

"Simply letting you know I'm serious." Alyssa pressed her fingertip between Paige's lips before removing it and climbing the ladder. "You don't need to say anything. Respond by choosing your lunch crew."

As they returned to hanging light fixtures, Paige looked up

at Alyssa. "You think I'm gorgeous? Most people think a woman with muscles is too masculine, but I love bodybuilding."

"Gorgeous is in the attitude, not the dress size. This morning, your attitude has enhanced how hot your body is. I want you regardless of some guy's threesome fantasy."

"You do? Are you into women?"

"I like both." Alyssa's stomach tightened as she realized Paige was close to joining them.

"I've never been with one."

"Would you like to try? Women are different from men. It's something to experience, but no pressure."

Paige wrung her hands. "Maybe. I don't know. Do you think Hayden would let me join you even if he didn't touch me? My husband probably wouldn't think being with a woman is cheating."

She wants to try me. I'm a safe option, not cheating. Once she sees his cock, she'll want it too. "He'll like whatever we do. I'm sure of it."

"I don't know if I can."

The foreman called from the front door, "That's lunch, everybody. Take ninety minutes. I'm going to the shop to get more supplies, but Hayden will stay here to watch our stuff. See you at one."

George stuck his head in the door before the women put down their tools. "Paige, are you joining us for lunch?"

Paige looked to Alyssa and back to George. She smiled and placed her tools on a nearby box. "Thanks, George, but I think I'll eat with my new friend here. See you after?"

The older man smiled. "Of course. Always good to make new friends. You two enjoy some girl time."

Jumping up and down in her mind, Alyssa took Paige's hand. "My car's out front."

Paige wrinkled her brow. "Where are we going?"

"Hayden told me the foreman won't go off-site until all of us leave. We are, ahem, getting lunch."

They drove down the street and around a few blocks to kill about ten minutes. Alyssa's pussy throbbed the entire time. She shifted in her seat, trying to get a little relief to no avail. As they drove, she turned to Paige. "I'm glad you came with us. Have you decided how much you want to participate when we get back?"

"I don't want to cheat on my husband, but I'd like to see what being with a woman is like."

Her nipples tingled at the good news. *That's how we will start.* "I can't wait to taste you. We'll give him a show to get warmed up and see what happens."

The two women walked into the back bedroom, where Hayden lay on a blanket, naked. "What a pleasant surprise, Alyssa. You brought a partner. A beautiful one at that. I can't wait to make her come."

"Hayden, Paige doesn't want to cheat on her husband with a man, so I'll be the only one making her come. You watch the show, then start on me when you are ready." She turned to Paige. "Are you ready? Once I kiss you, I won't stop."

Paige took Alyssa's cheeks in her hands and kissed her.

Alyssa returned the kiss and caressed Paige's belly under her shirt before removing it. She disposed of Paige's shorts just as quickly and snuck her hand inside the panties to cup her cheek. "Your ass is so strong. It's hard as a rock."

"Waitressing and working out keep me solid from the waist down."

Alyssa ran her free hand up Paige's ripped abs onto her small, hard breast. "And what keeps these beauties so firm you don't wear a bra?" Alyssa circled the breast with her fingers, teasing in ever smaller circles toward the nipple.

"Mother Nature made them small; benching one thirty-five keeps them hard. Your hands are making the nipples hard, but you knew that. May I?"

Paige lifted Alyssa's shirt off. "That's a sexy bra," she whispered while tracing her fingertips along the top edge, under Alyssa's arms to the back. "You had this planned." She unclasped the bra, and Alyssa let it fall to the floor. "They're perfect," Paige whispered as she cupped both breasts.

Alyssa pulled Paige's panties down past the muscular thighs until they dropped. She whispered between nibbles on Paige's cheek and neck. "Look at him. His beautiful face. Look at his body. His muscles. A cock that gorgeous, and it isn't even fully hard. I want him every second I'm near him. Yes, we planned this."

Paige opened Alyssa's shorts and edged them over her hips to fall to her feet. "Was I in your plan?"

Alyssa shook her head. "You are such a delightful surprise bonus. Let us admire you. Turn around." Alyssa removed her own panties while Paige turned.

When Paige again faced Alyssa, she returned the admiring stare. "You are even more beautiful naked." She held her arms open, inviting Alyssa closer with her hands and a smile.

Alyssa stepped into the embrace, kissing Paige and exploring her body. She squeezed one cheek and pulled one nipple. Paige moaned into their kiss, then Alyssa switched hands and earned the same moan.

Paige caressed Alyssa's breasts from below, hefting them as she ran her thumbs over and around the nipples. She kissed down Alyssa's neck to the orbs that fascinated her. She kissed around them, lingering on the bottom and outer side of each one before making her way to the nipple. She sucked each one into her mouth, then bit down with her teeth. Alyssa jerked each time as the pain flashed from the offended nipple to her pussy, somehow becoming hot pleasure by the time it arrived to tingle her lips. Paige ran a finger along Alyssa's slit before sliding inside.

While her pussy warmed and pulsed around Paige's finger, Alyssa pulled Paige upright and kissed down to her nipples. She let her fingers ripple across Paige's abs as she flicked each nipple with her tongue. She sucked almost the entire breast into her mouth, then pulled back until the suction broke with a pop. "Lie down. Let me taste you."

Paige lay on her back with her knees bent and spread. Alyssa crawled over her, kissing Paige's mouth, then working down her body, lifting off just as she reached the shaved mound. Placing a kiss inside each knee, Alyssa started working her way up. She hovered over Paige's open pussy, inhaling its aroma and watching the bodybuilder's stomach rise and fall with her panting. Alyssa winked at Hayden and flicked Paige's clit.

Alyssa licked as Paige's breathing accelerated. She lifted Paige's knees toward her chest. "Hold these. Open yourself for me."

Paige pulled her knees up and out, curling her hips up and exposing everything to Alyssa. She licked from anus to clit with a wide, flat tongue, then did it again while wiggling her tongue from side to side. When she pulled the outer lips open, she stroked them with her fingers up and down and sucked the inner lips one at a time. When she reached Paige's clit, she sucked it in and pushed two fingers inside her slippery pussy. Pressing down, Alyssa drew another moan from Paige.

"That feels like I'm being fucked. Don't stop."

Alyssa replaced her fingers with two from her other hand and slid a wet one to rub Paige's ass. It spread, and she pushed in until the second knuckle. As she continued to suck Paige's clit, she pumped her fingers in unison, using Paige's purring to guide her speed.

Alyssa's body moaned when Hayden's cock split her opening, stretching the lips with a pinch and parting the canal even as it gripped against his hardness. He paused when their skin caught, stopping his progress.

Not rising from the nub in her mouth, she nodded and pushed back slightly, letting him know to continue. Alyssa focused on the woman in her hands, knowing Hayden would soon rob her of her ability to make Paige come.

The thick cock spread her. He had slid inside her opening easily, but he took his time spreading her walls and stretching her depths with his large cock. Torturous minutes passed as he inched forward and back, pressing Alyssa into Paige's cunt and pulling her back from it. Her legs quivered when he finally tapped her cervix, sending tendrils of golden pleasure radiating from the top of her vagina through her body, sparking where they touched the skin from inside.

Hayden pulled all the way back until just the tip split her lips, then rammed home. For several strokes he repeated the process, before accelerating to match the rhythm of Alyssa's fingers inside Paige, who was humping against Alyssa's face and gripping her hair.

Paige's legs clamped onto Alyssa's head as she spasmed. Her body tensed, pulling Alyssa's face against her body. Alyssa couldn't breathe but continued sucking and fingering, drawing new spasms and new yelps as Hayden persisted in filling her from behind.

As her spasms subsided, Paige pushed Alyssa's forehead. "Please. Too sensitive."

Alyssa looked up, smiling over the heaving belly. "Did you like having a woman make love to you?"

Paige smiled. "Uh-huh. So good."

"Ready to taste me?" She winked over her shoulder and pulled off Hayden's cock.

Paige nodded, and Alyssa knee-walked to straddle Paige's face. She lowered her pussy onto Paige's face, and Paige licked her slit before their lips even met. Paige gripped Alyssa's ass cheeks, spreading them and pulling them to move Alyssa to nibble, lick, and suck her lips, her clit, and her ass.

Hayden stood in front of Alyssa. She took him into her throat. She bobbed on him as she ground on the tongue below her. She pulled off Hayden's cock and looked over her shoulder when one of the hands released her ass. Paige had three fingers buried in herself, stroking in time with her humping hips.

Alyssa winked at Hayden again and rose from Paige's face. "Do you want some more?"

"No. It's my turn to please you."

"We can please each other." She rose, turned, and descended into a sixty-nine. Alyssa dove into Paige's pussy, nibbling her lips as Paige licked hers. She looked over her shoulder. "Oh yeah. Now, Hayden, fuck me while she eats."

Hayden slid into Alyssa until he touched her cervix again. Alyssa moaned into the swollen, hot pussy below her. He worked his way back and forth, stretching her walls, then leaving them grasping at emptiness before stretching them apart again. He sped up.

Alyssa licked Paige's pussy and ass, loving its new size, its different taste, its different feel, as the other two rocketed her toward her own orgasm. *Eaten and fucked. This one will be huge.* Alyssa moved as her body tensed. The orgasm began in her belly, then flowed out, racking her muscles with spasms. Her breasts mashed against Paige's hard abs, adding pressure to the pleasure cycling through her cunt. When she arched her back, lifting her pussy off Paige's mouth, Hayden slipped out, and she felt juice drip down her lips. She collapsed onto Paige while the tremors ebbed and spread out.

Alyssa rolled off Paige, caught her breath, and turned. Hayden's motion thrust him forward along Paige's lips, dragging the underside along her tongue. He thrust twice more in the same spot, letting her gather Alyssa's juices from him before she pulled the head into her mouth and let him enter her throat with a moan.

Surprised that the married woman had Hayden's cock in her mouth, Alyssa moved between Paige's legs to resume her feast. Paige's legs writhed and straightened before Alyssa had thrust a dozen times in her two openings, and Paige pushed Hayden's thighs backward and his cock out of her mouth.

"I need this inside me. Fuck me."

Alyssa raised her head. "Paige, are you sure? You said you didn't want to cheat on your husband. Take a minute and don't get caught up in the moment."

"I'm sure. I want it. It's bigger than any dick I've had before. Just this once, I need it. My husband will never know, and I'll never do it again. Please, fuck me."

Hayden grinned at Alyssa and moved to take her place. "Last chance. Once I'm inside, I'm going to fuck until I say you are done. Is that what you want?"

"Yes. Do to me what you did to her."

Hayden drove into Paige. She wailed.

"God, so big. Hit that spot right there. Stretch me. Fuck me hard." She locked her ankles behind his hips and pushed against him as he thrust.

Facing Hayden, Alyssa crouched above Paige's face to grind her pussy as Paige licked and moved her head. The moans vibrated her clit, and she cupped her breasts, twisting her nipples in search of another orgasm. Alyssa watched Hayden watch the bodybuilder's breasts jiggle as he filled her. *If the tits are out, men like all shapes and sizes.* She watched Paige's stomach distend over the head of Hayden's cock as he filled her. *Speaking of all shapes and sizes, he's huge inside her.*

Motion outside the window to her left caught Alyssa's eye. Looking to the side, she made eye contact with the older Black man she had seen next door that morning. He stood in the shade of a tree less than ten feet from the window. He had his cock out, stroking it. *Watched again. Delicious.*

Alyssa said nothing. Instead, she stared at the neighbor and slowed her grinding on Paige's face. The younger woman's moans and gasps settled into a long purr, and her face pressed harder against Alyssa's pussy. There was no doubt Hayden was making her come, and he pumped into her faster. That orgasm was followed by another only moments later, with the same decadent hum and pressure buzzing and mashing Alyssa's lips, whipping tiny ropes of heat around and over her lips to lash at the very tip of her clit.

Alyssa moved her hands to her head, entwining her fingers in her hair and lifting her breasts, giving a better show to the neighbor. She watched Hayden's breathing hasten and his face tinge red. The muscles of his chest and abs flexed as he rammed harder and harder into Paige. *God, I love watching him fuck.* She tapped Paige's chin. "He's about to come. Do you want it inside?"

Paige shook her head between Alyssa's legs.

Alyssa smiled and nodded at the neighbor, then tapped Hayden's shoulder. "Don't come in her. Come on our tits." She leaned forward and cupped her breasts in her hands, offering them to him.

After two more strokes, he pulled out, launching three spurts onto Alyssa before the rest fell onto Paige's body. The hot splashes on her skin and watching the neighbor shoot spurt after spurt from his thick cock made Alyssa come. She pressed her pussy down on Paige's face and pulled her own tits, the pinch on her nipples and the pull of the breasts from the chest fanning her orgasm like a bellows. When the pulses between her pussy and tits slowed, then softened into flutters in her belly, she winked at the neighbor.

Alyssa dismounted Paige's face and licked the cum off her hard pecs and belly, careful to leave a clear line of sight to the window as she did. She pushed Hayden toward Paige's head. "Let her clean you. Let her taste how delicious she is."

Hayden knee-walked to the younger woman's face, still shiny with Alyssa's juices. Paige smiled at him and raised her head to suck his cock. She moaned as she cleaned him. She finished Hayden as Alyssa lingered over the last drops of cum on Paige's pussy.

She moved her chest to Paige as the waitress sat up. "Clean me too."

Paige licked the cum off her tits, then sucked both nipples. She slipped a finger between Alyssa's lower lips and sucked it clean. "For good measure."

Alyssa kissed Paige. "Are you okay with what happened?"

Paige looked at both faces, then down at her sweaty body. The corners of her mouth gave the hint of a smile while her eyes drooped enough to show that a part of her regretted what had happened. "Yes. I'd never been with a woman, had a threesome, or had such a big cock. Now I have, and I won't be curious about it any longer. I won't do this again, but I'm glad I did it once."

Alyssa lifted Paige's chin. "Are you worried you will stray again, now that you did the first time?"

"No. Look at this body. My self-discipline made it this way. My self-discipline will keep me from cheating again."

Hayden chuckled. "I guess we weren't as good as we thought we were, Alyssa."

Paige shook her head, laughing. "Oh, you were good. Better than advertised." She looked at Alyssa. "And you were even better than him. If my husband wanted to, I would try another woman with him."

"I'm glad we could broaden your horizons." Alyssa patted Paige's belly.

Hayden palmed Paige's pussy. "You know I frequent the restaurant, if you change your mind about me broadening something more intimate than your horizons."

Alyssa moved by the window to dress. She waved to the neighbor before he returned to his yard.

21

MONDAY, MAY 24, HOME

"Nancy says your afternoon is clear. Come home now. It's an emergency." Alyssa hung up, then texted her husband to check his messages.

Twenty minutes later, Robert burst through the laundry room door into the great room. "Alyssa, what's wrong that you need me to—" He stopped and stared at her lying on the kitchen table, her head propped on her hand and her leg cocked up. With no clothes, she was showing him everything. Even after the day's sex, she felt her pussy moisten and her lips bloom open under his hungry gaze.

"That's the reaction I wanted. I'll tell you about my day while you strip. Then you can reclaim me."

"You didn't call."

"I knew I couldn't lose it because we were pressed for time. I was safe."

"While you were building a charity house? They might frown on that. Hayden has you keyed up for anything. What the hell, Alyssa?"

"Not just Hayden. A female bodybuilder too. And we didn't get caught, well, except by the neighbor, so nobody is upset."

"A female bodybuilder? You're making this up to distract me."

"I'm naked, offering myself for you to feast upon to distract you. The bodybuilder part is true. Stand closer and I'll get that gorgeous cock even harder while I tell you about it." Alyssa stroked and fondled Robert's cock while she described Paige's hard breasts, muscular legs, ripped tummy. She squeezed and rolled his testicles while she described the threesome, the way Hayden's dick had made Paige bulge while he fucked her and Alyssa rode her face. She jacked the head when she described the neighbor watching Hayden come on their tits.

"That was my adventure for the day." She waved her hand along her body like a model displaying a prize. "Will you reclaim me and make me yours again? I'm clean but would love you to make me dirty again." She sucked his hard cock into her mouth.

"That's a hot story. Let me show you what I think of it."

Robert climbed onto the table and pushed Alyssa onto her back. He nestled his cock into her wet opening and nudged forward.

"No foreplay, Babe?"

"Your lunchtime sex was the foreplay. This is the main event, Baby."

"Perfect."

He pulled back and wedged in farther, spreading her walls as she gripped him. He repeated the move twice more before he pressed his pubic bone against hers, compressing her clit. "You're soaked. You didn't bring me his cum, did you? You know I don't allow that."

Not this time. "No, Babe. I'm dripping. I've been daydreaming about this all afternoon. Give it to me."

He did. He filled her pussy with his cock, pressing beside her cervix when he was seated against her and dragging across her G-spot when he pulled back. The stretching pulled at her lips and electrified her clit. Tingles radiated out from her pussy to her nipples and her ass.

What felt best was watching his eyes. They locked onto hers. The softness around them even as he pounded into her body reminded her why she loved to come home to him. He wanted her to feel every bit of sexual excitement he could fuck into her while he loved her, and wanted her to feel all the soft warmth he could blanket over her. The sparks knotting behind her clit were nothing compared to the inferno in her chest that he fanned with every glance.

Alyssa's pussy contracted around Robert's cock, and her first orgasm started building in the depths of her belly, growing with each thrust, each tweak of her breast. *Give me more. I want to come so hard. Keep hitting those spots.*

Robert sped up, then stopped. He lifted her legs up and back across her elbows, opening her up. Alyssa clenched her ass, knowing he was going to plunge deeper, and anticipating the stretch that would pull at her cervix and set her body alight. He leaned back, maximizing the pressure his cockhead placed on her G-spot when he pulled back and the top when he bottomed out. He pinched her clit, making her squeal with the pain she loved.

"Play with your breasts."

I love when he takes charge. He loves me so much.

Alyssa pulled her breasts up and pinched the nipples, the pinch and the stretch pushing her orgasm to the tipping point. The orgasm in her belly grew and pressed against its limits, ready to explode.

Robert's cock swelled inside her, spreading her walls, making them ache. In two more thrusts, he lunged deep inside. The hot cum splashed in her. The warmth spread across the top and sides. She felt it coating her, and Alyssa's orgasm erupted. She pulled her nipples and tightened her legs around her husband. Her head pressed against the table, and the warmth of his cum spread from her womb out into her body.

Alyssa pulled him down to kiss her. "Thank you, Babe. I am yours and always will be. I love you."

Robert remained atop her, tracing the lines of her face with his fingers. He kissed her eyelids, then spoke. "The bodybuilder decided out of the blue to join you in your tryst?"

"I offered. I think she was intrigued with trying a woman. This afternoon she became quiet, like she regretted it. She said she would play with me again if her husband approved, but I don't think she'd take a man again."

"Bringing in a married woman is dangerous, Alyssa. What if the husband finds out and wants to blame you? That's beyond my reservations about Hayden."

"The way I see it, she is responsible for her own marriage. If she is willing to cheat, that's up to her."

"It is her decision, but you pitched her on it."

Alyssa sighed. "True. I thought it would be fun. Her body was so strong. It was different from being with a man, but her body wasn't soft like a woman's either. Despite her reservations, she had a great time." *She liked being the center of a threesome. Just like I liked giving it to Hayden.* "And I know how to handle Hayden. Please don't worry."

"Don't forget who loves you."

22
FRIDAY, MAY 28, HOME

ALYSSA SANK INTO Robert's lap when she walked out to the back patio. She kissed his cheek and enjoyed his arms around her waist while they watched the sun sink into the trees. *I love this.*

"Do you think you can handle a day without visiting your new house?" Robert held Alyssa in his lap as she squirmed to face him.

"Robert, what do you mean? We fly to Houston tomorrow to bring Susan home. What does that have to do with the house?"

"Come on, Alyssa. You have spent exactly eighteen forty-six at the grocery store near that house every afternoon for the past two weeks, and our cooler is in your trunk. That's odd, don't you think?"

"I've just been taking the workers some Gatorade when I check on it."

Robert laughed. "I figured you would. The credit card charges just confirmed it. I'm glad. I didn't have to go by there myself."

"How long have you known?"

"Since last Wednesday. You know I check the credit card every few days. You had stopped three times by then."

"Why didn't you ask me about it?"

"What is there to ask? This was your idea, investing your raise. We are on the papers together, but this is your project. You don't need me pestering you for updates looking like I'm monitoring your every move. Since you won't be able to swing by over the weekend, I wondered if you need some extra TLC."

"Extra TLC is always good." She caressed his cheek. "But this feels like you're watching me. Don't you trust me?"

"Absolutely I trust you, but you know how often our credit cards have been compromised. I check for unusual items every couple of days. Three days of the same charge at a grocery store we don't use was unusual, but when I noted where it was, I put two and two together. Like I said, I'm glad you're so involved."

"So you weren't watching me?"

"Alyssa, Baby. No. Is there some reason I should? Do you have anything to tell me?"

You mean other than the fact that, in those two weeks, I fucked Hayden three times more than the two I told you? Including today? And we have lunch every Wednesday? And we text several times a day, including when you are sitting a few feet away? And I'm intentionally keeping those secrets because I know you are upset that I'm seeing him so much? And I'm going to lie to you again right now? Her stomach filled with lead. "No, Babe. Nothing to tell you except that the new porch is coming along fine. We should be able to list it in a couple of weeks." She placed a peck on his forehead. "Then we can buy the regular rentals. Thank you for helping me with this."

"This has been all you. I just signed the papers."

"You made me earn the funds for it. Don't forget that."

Her phone dinged. She looked at the screen, then at Robert. "Let me answer this real quick. Amelia has a question."

Robert nodded. Trying to look natural as she angled the screen away from Robert's view, she opened Hayden's text: "Meet me tomorrow."

"I can't. We are flying to Houston to bring Susan home."

"Meet me early. I need to see you."

Her chest filled with heat. He really wanted her. She didn't understand why her instead of the other women he could have, but she decided to enjoy it. *I wish I could.*

"Can't, early flight. Be back Wednesday. See you then?"

"Sure. See you then."

Alyssa reread the exchange before closing her phone. *He really likes me.* She smiled and caressed Robert's chest. *So does he. I remember I'm yours first. Let me prove it. Let's play.*

Alyssa stood and stripped off her clothes. "Now you. Let's go pack naked. First one finished gets to be on top."

"Deal."

23

SATURDAY, MAY 29, HOUSTON HOTEL

ALYSSA DOWNED HER drink in a gulp and held the glass up to the waiter for a refill. The hotel staff cleaned around Robert and Alyssa, who sat in the restaurant, waiting on their food. They had arrived late and didn't have the energy to leave to hunt supper.

Alyssa leaned toward Robert, patted his hand, and smiled. "That was the best flight I've been on in years."

"You must be kidding. We spent the last two hours circling in the turbulence, waiting to land. I couldn't even sleep."

"Yes, but the young pilot sitting beside me kept me calm, telling me how they handle things in the cockpit."

"He would have told you anything to keep watching your boobs bounce in that top."

Alyssa frowned at her husband and sat back in her chair. "Robert, he kept me calm. You know how I hate rough flights."

"Was it what he told you or how he looked that kept you calm?"

She chuckled. "He was cute."

"Cute? As stuffy as it was in the plane, your nipples weren't hard because of the cold."

"You saw them?"

"You're wearing a satiny halter with no bra. Everyone saw them, including your pilot friend."

"Okay, I enjoyed how he looked at me, and his forearm was so firm and strong. But I really appreciated how calm he was."

"You don't think the guy eating a chicken biscuit out of his hat while we boarded would have kept you as calm? I mean, he was polite enough to put the hat back on his head when he finished."

She chuckled. "I know. That was, well, not really gross, just very bizarre. He made me worry a little. But they moved him to balance the load. The stewardess said so."

"Babe, that plane probably weighs a hundred tons when it takes off. You think swapping one one-hundred-and-fifty-pound man for a two-hundred-pound man a few rows away balances the load? Flight attendants say that when they want to make someone's flight more comfortable without embarrassing anyone. That pilot probably wanted to sit next to you and asked the crew to make the switch."

Alyssa couldn't believe what he said. She hadn't thought about the change of seats, but it made sense, and a glow of pride and lust began to warm her inside her chest. "I didn't know that. I'm more turned on now than I was when we landed. If it bothered you that I talked with him, you could have stayed awake."

"No, Baby. He made you comfortable and excited. I got some

sleep. Besides, I am well past getting jealous when you talk with another man. Or sleep with them, for that matter."

Alyssa leaned to him and placed her hand on his again. "You say that, but I know you worry about me despite claiming to be fine with our arrangement. And I love you for it."

"I'm fine with our arrangement. I only worry when we stretch the rules."

"You mean when I stretch the rules."

"Only because I haven't stretched them yet."

"And you won't. That isn't your style."

The waiter set their food in front of them, then refilled their drinks.

"You're probably right. I'm not a rule stretcher." He looked beyond Alyssa to the bar as the bar-height eight-top behind her emptied with a flurry of noise. "Well, speak of the devil."

"What?" Alyssa turned, then jerked her head back to Robert as she recognized her seatmate eating alone at the bar. "My goodness. What's he doing here?"

Robert laughed. "Staying here? If you want to know, go ask him. In fact, would you like him to join us? He might want a little company."

Alyssa's stomach flipped as the warm glow in her chest tickled her nipples. "What are you saying?"

"Invite him to sit with us at dinner rather than alone at the bar, if he would like some company."

"I thought you meant something more...intimate."

"I meant dinner conversation. If you want intimate, you know our rules."

"I wouldn't kick him out of bed, but I'm getting intimate with you tonight."

"That's music to my ears. If you want to invite him to our table, go ahead. He'll remember you more than he will me."

"He seems lost in his thoughts. I'll offer, but I won't push."

Alyssa walked to the young man at the bar. "Hello again, Sean. Remember me?"

His eyes lost their glassy stare as he turned his head. They traced over Alyssa's face, up to her eyes, and he smiled. "Of course, Alyssa. Talking with you was the best four hours of my day."

"Would you like some company?"

He backed up an inch or two. "Whoa. Aren't you with your husband?"

Alyssa shook her head. "Not what I meant. I am indeed with my husband. We're eating right over there." She pointed to Robert, who waved. "We thought you might enjoy some dinner conversation. If you'd rather stay here, we won't be offended."

"Really? You aren't just being polite?"

"I could have been polite by waving if we made eye contact. If you'd like to join us, please do."

"I will. Thank you." He followed her to the table and shook Robert's hand as he sat. "Thank you for inviting me over. I grow weary of solo nights in hotels."

Robert smirked. "The glamorous pilot's life, jetting around the globe, a different woman in each city, is a myth?"

"For me, at least. Some of the older guys talk about the good old days and layovers with flight attendants, but my experience says that hot, sexy layovers are few and far between."

Robert nodded. "That's probably their experience too. They have conglomerated stories from all their buddies. A friend of mine is a pilot, and he writes books in hotel rooms. No hot stewardesses for him either."

Alyssa wagged her finger at Sean. "You told me you had a girlfriend. Your disappointment at not having hot, sexy layovers in every city might not meet her approval."

"Um, yeah. She believes the myth. But she's not my girlfriend."

"She was this afternoon. What happened?"

"Because of our late arrival, I was swapped with another pilot. He piloted my flight today, and I will pilot his flight tomorrow. When I texted her that, she texted me to fuck off. Oops. Sorry about the language."

Alyssa shook her head. "Ouch. Sorry about that. Had you been together long?"

"Only a few months." Sean's phone rang. "That's her. Excuse me a minute." He walked out of the restaurant to talk.

Alyssa took a swig of wine. "Too bad. He seems like a nice guy."

"One that can make your nipples hard just by talking."

"Oh, Robert, you make my nipples hard just by talking. See?" She pulled the sides of her top, tightening the silky fabric over her breasts, accentuating the hard points capping each one.

Robert raised his eyebrows. "Those have been that way since I suggested you invite him over."

Alyssa felt her face flash hot. Her pussy tingled too. "You can't blame me. He's hot and available." She winked at Robert, who laughed.

"Available? You want a piece of him? Make him feel better about being dumped?"

"I told you, I'm getting a piece of you tonight. But under different circumstances, I could make him feel better. And he could do the same for me."

"You bad girl."

She smirked through her wine glass. "Be nice. Here he comes."

Sean sat down and downed the remnants of his drink before speaking. "That didn't take long. She yelled at me for cheating on her a while, then told me she put my stuff from her apartment on the table with her key to my place. She didn't even let me talk before hanging up."

Alyssa rested her hand on his forearm. "I'm sorry. Having that happen while traveling must be rough."

Robert nodded. "Yeah. That's too bad. Let me buy you a drink to wash her away."

"No, thank you. One is my limit. Alone on the road is an easy place to drink too much."

Alyssa stood. "I'll have another, Babe. Would you get it while I powder my nose?"

⧽

"Sure." Robert waved at the waiter as Alyssa walked toward the restroom. "Sean, this may surprise you, but hear me out. Would you like to start forgetting your girlfriend tonight?"

"Of course. This pleasant conversation with you two is a start. Do you know any tricks other than booze?"

"I do. I think you do too. You see, I noticed the way you touched my wife's arm when we flew through turbulence. And I noticed your watching her ass as she led you to our table."

"Look, I don't mean to offend—"

Robert raised his hand to calm the young man. "Easy. We're not offended if she is starring in your MILF fantasy."

"She is a beautiful and sexy woman."

"More than you know. Plus, I think you are starring in her hunky pilot fantasy." Robert looked around and lowered his voice. "Would you like to focus on a woman other than your girlfriend tonight?"

"What do you mean, exactly? I don't want to assume any-thing about your wife. Nothing like this has happened to me before."

"She sometimes enjoys two men. I am inviting you to join

us tonight for whatever sex the three of us want. Is that exact enough?"

"All three of us? I'm not into guys."

Robert smiled as he shook his head. "Me either. I am into giving my wife pleasure, and she likes the rare treat of being double-teamed. I'm asking you to help me do that, any way she likes. Would you care to join us?"

Sean ate the last bite of his steak. "That's the best offer I've had in a long time. If you are serious, I'm in. Does she want this?"

"She hasn't said so specifically, but I know my wife, and I'm certain she does. When we head to the elevator in a few minutes, hang back a bit so I can talk with her alone. I'll wave you over if she says yes."

◈

Alyssa let her hand linger on Sean's muscular shoulder. "I hope you feel better. You'll find another girl in no time."

"I'm sure I will. Thank you for the kind words, and for letting me share your table tonight."

Alyssa leaned her head on Robert's shoulder as they moved toward the elevator. "That's too bad for him, but if she's so jealous, he can do better."

"Do you want to show him how much better?"

"What do you mean?"

"I mean, if you want two men tonight, I'm willing to share."

A tremble shook Alyssa's knees, then ran up her hamstrings. She could not believe what he had said. This had to be some kind of test. She wanted to pass it, but her pussy throbbed, offering its opinion of the delectable pilot at their table. "You said you didn't want to see that again."

"I don't want to see. I'm willing to participate. And control, if I need to. I know you like more than one man inside you. Do you want it tonight, with Sean?"

Alyssa crossed her arms to control her trembling hands. What had been a fantasy only ten seconds ago could happen. Her pussy throbbed and ached to be filled. *Holy shit. Too good to be true. Careful. He's still uneasy about all this. At least about Hayden, but he's a thousand miles away and hasn't texted today. Don't seem too eager.* "You would do that for me?"

"I would. I love when you are happy, as long as you remember who's number one."

Yes. Heat rose from her crotch to her neck. She grinned up at him and moved her hand to his arm. "You're always my number one. Let's do it."

Robert turned to nod at Sean, who was staring at the two only a few feet away. He joined them as the elevator doors opened.

Alyssa punched Robert's shoulder. "You already set this up."

"I needed to know if Sean was interested."

Alyssa moved against Sean as the car began to rise. "Are you interested, Sean?" She pulled his head down to kiss him and rubbed his cock through his pants.

"Mm-hmm" was all he could manage before he opened his mouth to accept her tongue. One hand lifted her ass cheek, and the other rubbed the satiny top over her nipple. The doors opened, and the three headed down the hall, Alyssa with a man on each arm.

"If you didn't leave any men in the bar, can I have the one you aren't using, honey?" a fiftyish-year-old woman in a slinky blue dress asked as she approached from down the hall.

Alyssa glared at the woman, then softened to a smile and leaned her head onto Robert's shoulder. "Nope. He's giving me a regal gift tonight. I get two magnificent stallions, and I intend to savor every second."

"I wish I were you. Enjoy, sweetie. If you change your mind, I'm in 14038. It's never too late to knock."

Alyssa cackled. "We're in 14040, neighbor. I'd say we will try to keep it down, but I'm holding nothing back tonight. Sorry."

"I'll be listening, and jealous. Have fun." She passed them, continuing toward the elevator.

Alyssa snuggled against Sean while Robert opened the door. She nudged Sean toward the bed. "Wait over there a minute."

She turned and gave her husband a slow kiss. She put her hands on his cheeks to hold his gaze. He needed to know he had her attention. The horny tingling in her breasts had not overwhelmed the uncertain flopping of her stomach. She thought about the implications of what was about to happen, of what Robert was about to see and do. This was not getting revenge on three assholes. This was him bringing someone in because she wanted someone to join them. She wanted to enjoy a wild night and had no intention of feeling guilty later. Because she knew her husband, she needed to confirm his feelings.

She forced her smallest smile and relaxed the muscles around her eyes, going for pleased but concerned, knowing it understated thrilled and terrified grappling inside her chest. "Are you sure you want to do this? You want me to fuck both of you? Here? Together? You want to see me enjoying the next few hours without any ulterior motive like we had before?"

"I plan on participating, not watching, so yes. I want to give you this. You would never ask to bring another man into our bed, but I know you want it sometimes. Let me give you a fantastic night. Let us thrill you in every way you like and perhaps some ways you haven't tried. Turn loose. Surrender to your lust. Scream, moan, wail, and trust me to keep you safe. Make that woman get carpal tunnel listening to us. Enjoy it without any hesitation."

"I love you." She kissed him again, letting her lips linger on his without trying to nibble or open, letting him feel the calm love of a wife for her husband. The love she had always had for him. When she pulled back, she let her hands drop along with her nerves. Her pussy pulsed with her heartbeat. The love in her chest warmed her like coffee on a cold day. As it spread, her body quivered in anticipation of what they would do to her.

She made a show of looking Robert up and down. "You are a big part of this, so get those clothes off. You too, Sean."

The men disrobed without further delay. Alyssa stood at the door, still and watching. *Ah, a young hardbody. Not too many muscles, and little hair. I'm going to enjoy this.* Sean finished first and moved toward the bed. "Not yet. You two come here and get me naked."

Alyssa gave each one a kiss when they reached her. "Take your time, boys. Make me quiver."

Robert laughed at Sean's bewildered look. "Give her a kiss, remove an article of clothing, and show her how much you like what you uncover." Robert kissed Alyssa again, then knelt in front of her with one hand at the top of each of her butt cheeks. He trailed his hands down the thin pants, pressing hard enough only for the fabric to ripple along Alyssa's skin more like a wispy memory than a touch. He teased her ass, then caressed down the backs of her legs, creating a trail of static tingles wherever his fingers touched.

Alyssa held Sean's bicep when Robert removed her sandal and rubbed her instep with a firm grip, the contrast and pressure on her tired foot sending wide, slow, warm snakes coiling up her calf. The other foot felt even better. She gripped Sean as her legs slackened. *They're so strong. They are going to make me feel so good.*

Sean stepped in front of Alyssa as Robert stepped back. He kissed her and ran his hands down her bare back to her ass, cupping the cheeks. Then he knelt, letting his hands glide along the outsides of her legs to her ankles, gripping her tighter, like he wanted to feel what she looked like under the slacks.

His hands eased up the insides of her legs, softer this time. *Tease me. Make me wetter.*

When his fingers reached her crotch, they rubbed over her pussy lips, firm enough to bounce over the folds, soft enough to tease. Eight little shocks crossed Alyssa's clit, making her shudder. When his hands reached the waistband, Sean opened her slacks, wriggled them down her hips, and dropped them into a pool at her feet.

Robert kissed her mound through her panties. He traced the leg holes and waistband of her panties with his fingertips before moving over her cheeks and pussy, pressing the fabric into her wet, opening slit. He slid a finger inside the leg of her panties and then between her lips, giving them something to grip and drawing a moan. He pulled his finger out, leaving her empty, and made a show of sucking her juices off it. "You are so ready, Baby. Do you want to come?" He pulled her panties down. She held the hard muscles between his neck and shoulders to balance as she stepped out of them.

Sean kissed Alyssa as Robert stepped back. His firm fingers traced the hollows in the sides of her ass cheeks. Alyssa's skin bristled in goose bumps at the chill that raced up her spine. As his fingers climbed the edge of her halter, her ribs and the sides of her breasts crackled where his fingers grazed her skin. Sean stopped there, pinched the fabric on both sides, and pulled the sides tight, accentuating her protruding nipples, then raised and lowered it, rubbing them with the shiny fabric.

"Yes. That feels so silky," Alyssa whispered as she let her head fall back and closed her eyes to savor the sensations on her skin. She placed her hands on top of her head and swayed her hips, trying to rub her lips together, aching for some friction between them.

Sean released her halter, moving his hands to her upper chest and upper back. He caressed south slowly, using small circles on the skin of her back and the satin on her chest. He skirted around the edges of her breasts. The frustration made her whimper when he dropped his hand to slide her top across her flat tummy instead of pinching her straining nipples.

Sean's fingers teased into her navel, then drifted to her hip bones beneath the hem of the halter. As they slid up her sides, they inched the halter up until it caught the lower swell of her breasts. Even as it caught under her breasts, he kept raising it. With the flick of a wrist, Sean let her breasts flop down, flicking her nipples on the tight satin with an electric pulse through her chest.

"Oh yes. Touch my arms as you go." *I'm so ready.*

Sean extended his fingertips to trace her armpits and the insides of her biceps while lifting the halter up and off. He kissed her again as his fingers traced back down. He pinched her nipple with increasing pressure.

That hurts. Damn. Ropes of pain fired from her nipple, connecting with its twin to the left before coiling around her pussy from the inside, where it became pleasure. She moaned, and he pinched even harder and pulled, multiplying the pain.

Alyssa's knees buckled when Sean slapped his free hand down across his hand and the distended breast he was pinching, yanking her nipple like it had been pulled off. The explosion of pain ached, stung, and throbbed in turn, each feeling shoving a different pain through her chest into her gut.

Sean caught Alyssa before she fell, clutching her against him as she trembled. Alyssa bit Sean's chest as she came with a long, tortured scream.

"No hitting!" Robert yelled as he lunged toward Sean, gripping his shoulder.

"Sorry. Some women like it. It won't happen again."

Alyssa let Sean hold her as the waves coursed up and down her body, her legs weak and her body quivering. Robert's hand on her back quelled the waves, and they gathered under his palm, transforming into a warmth that spread within her until it seeped out her pores.

God, that made me come. Alyssa stiffened her legs and took her own weight, then nodded over his shoulder at Robert. "I'm not into pain, but let him do the other one. The shock devastated me."

"Are you sure?"

Alyssa nodded, unable to say the words again.

Sean released her and stood back. "You want me to pinch your nipple hard, like this?"

Alyssa moaned as he pinched her right nipple even harder than he had the left. She felt like razor wire was being stretched between her nipples and down to her clit. She fought to stay upright as her knees buckled. "Yes."

"And you want me to slap your tit like I did the other one?"

He released her nipple. The blood rushed back into the sensitive nub, actually increasing the pain. And the pleasure.

Alyssa's legs quivered. The place atop her vagina was rumbling with another orgasm ready to burst, and they had barely touched her there. *I'm going to come again. I'm close right now.* "Yes."

"Tell your husband that you want me to slap you. He's a good man, and he won't let me hurt you unless you tell him you want it."

He pinched her nipple again, squeezing tighter than he had a moment ago. Electric shocks stiffened her body, and she stood on her toes as he pulled up, stretching her breast farther than he had the first one. If he pulled any farther, pinched any harder, her nipple might simply detach. She both dreaded and wanted that.

God, this hurts. But just one more. Alyssa panted and grunted as she struggled to speak. "Babe, I want him to slap my tit. It's okay. I'm asking him to. Let him do it, please."

Robert released Sean's shoulder. "Once."

Before Robert had finished his answer, Sean's hand came down on Alyssa's breast. Again he knocked his fingers down, pulling her nipple with them until it reached its limit and snapped back into shape.

Alyssa screamed again as the massive orgasm rolled through her, buckling her knees and igniting flames inside her that licked at her skin, pain becoming pleasure as it wound through her body, deep beside her pussy, where the pleasure launched another wave.

Caught by both men, she spasmed between them while they held her up. Tears ran down her cheeks as she clutched at their shoulders. She buried her face in Sean's chest. Robert wrapped both arms around her waist, her pain gathering under his hands and morphing into the warm afterglow that slowly drained out her skin.

When Alyssa stood on her own, she spun to reach for Robert's cheek. "Too intense for every day, but my nipples are ready to make me come again. Thank you, Babe, for letting me have it, and for protecting me from it."

He broke their eye contact to look at Sean. "No more. Understood?"

"No more. I'm glad she liked it though."

Alyssa squealed and cackled when Robert and Sean picked her up and tossed her onto the bed. *Tossed me like a rag doll. So strong. Next round.*

Robert pointed to Sean while they stood at the foot of the bed. "Let us, both of us, please you. Lie back, Baby."

She shuffled up onto the pillows. Sean and Robert knelt on either side of her. She switched her head between the men, kissing one and then the other. She reached to grasp both cocks, stroking them while four strong hands shifted from caressing her to rubbing and squeezing. First one finger, then a second finger entered her pussy, spreading her open folds, sliding along her inner lips.

They each have a finger in me. Dirty.

Robert caressed and rubbed her angry breasts, avoiding her nipples even as she squirmed to force contact with her sensitive buttons.

Sean traced his fingers along her hairline, down by her ear and jaw, to her chin, then moved his thumb along and over her lips. He urged her chin down and pressed his thumb into her mouth. *Yes, take what you want.* Alyssa sucked the thick digit in and swirled it with her tongue like it was a cock. She bobbed her head on it, slurping and drooling over it.

When Robert pinched her left nipple, electricity surged from it to its partner and deeper into her, finding the remnants of her earlier explosions, reanimating them.

More shocks. I like that it lingers. "Keep going, Babe. Make me feel good." She tugged on Sean's cock. "Bring that up here, unless you only want me to suck your thumb."

Sean scurried beside her head. Alyssa held his cock in her hand, admiring it. *It's pretty. Good size, smooth, straight. I'll like this.* She pulled it to her mouth, sucking the head as she pumped the shaft. She opened her mouth to drool and lubricate, then used the liquid to enhance the sound of her slurping.

She took more of him with each bob, but her neck tired and her abs ached from holding herself up. She pulled off Sean's cock and flopped her head to the pillow. "Babe, let me ride your face a minute while I suck Sean, then I want both of you inside me."

Robert sucked her right nipple, pressing it against the roof of his mouth with his tongue and sending more electricity coursing through her as he mashed the inflamed button.

"Ooh, maybe just one more of those first." She held her other breast, offering the nipple to his mouth. Robert sucked it in, compressing it, giving her delectable pleasure and pain. "Thank you, Babe. Now on your back."

Robert lay on his back. Alyssa straddled his head and lowered her wet pussy to his face. His tongue penetrated her slit, and her clit found his hard septum. She ground against it as Sean stood on the bed and returned his cock to her mouth.

With the better angle, Alyssa sucked all of him in, the tip entering her throat as she swallowed to avoid gagging. In only a moment, they found a rhythm between rubbing her clit on Robert's nose and sucking Sean's cock into her throat. As she moved, the men's hands roamed her body: Robert's cupping her ass cheeks and teasing her anus with his fingers; Sean's on her head and neck, moving with her as she swallowed him. She stroked across her nipples, finally pinching and pulling them, driving her orgasm to the edge of breaking through.

She pressed harder against Robert's face, mashing her clit and letting his tongue dive between her slippery lips, occasionally withdrawing so he could suck one or both, stretching them. When his tongue entered her again, she pulled her nipples until they hurt and tensed her thighs. Her movements stopped as her climax rolled through her. Sean remained buried in her throat until she had to pull off, gasping for breath.

"Oh yeah. Now I want both of you in me." She crawled backward over Robert, who looked up at Sean.

"Get the bottle of lube off the dresser over there." Robert pointed toward the end of the bed.

As Sean found the lube, Alyssa slid her husband's cock inside her pussy and slid all the way onto it, bottoming out. When he tapped her cervix, she kissed him. "You feel so good."

"It's about to feel better, Baby." He looked past her shoulder. "Go slow. Get her ass ready."

The bed moved as Sean climbed on. The cold lube surprised her anus, sending a chill through her pelvis and drawing a yelp. She hummed as he rubbed it onto her pucker with firm pressure. Another cold dollop hit, and his finger pressed inside. She adjusted while he stilled, nodded, and Sean used his finger to pull the sides of her opening, easing it open. Alyssa relaxed and looked over her shoulder. "I'm ready. Put your dick in my ass."

Alyssa arched her back as the second cock entered her. "That's it. Keep going."

Robert cradled her tits as she pressed backward. "Mmm" was all she said as Sean's hips met her ass cheeks. All three remained motionless, savoring the moment.

Alyssa smiled and restarted the proceedings. "Now, fuck me good. Make me come."

Sean pulled back and plunged back into her. Robert, more restricted, thrust up and down, bouncing his wife to get some movement. They established a pattern in just a few strokes. *Yes, one in, one out. I'm always full. So good.*

Sean jerked her head back by a handful of her hair. Alyssa wailed as every follicle on her scalp prickled.

"No pain," Robert admonished before Alyssa could complain.

"After she liked being slapped, I thought she would like it."

Alyssa looked over her shoulder. "Just give me pleasure. Make me full." She squeezed her sphincter around his cock. "Come on now, back to the good fucking. Fill me up, you two."

They reestablished their pace, and soon Alyssa was building to another orgasm. "Pinch my nipples, Babe. I'm close." *Make the pain feel so good. I want to be stuffed when I come.* "Sean, match up with Robert so you're both inside me at the same time."

Sean matched Robert on the next thrust. Both men were pounding into her, spurred on by her louder grunts. Her head hung forward and bounced with each plunge. Her sweaty hair clung to her face.

Here it comes.

Alyssa raised her head, arched her back, and squeezed every muscle in her pelvis, pushing both cocks deep into her and gripping both glorious cocks as her fourth orgasm of the night cascaded out of its bounds within her belly. Her thighs clamped against Robert's sides, and her neck muscles strained against the skin. As her wail quieted, she remained frozen in place, her orgasm outlasting her breath. A few seconds later, she fell forward, panting.

Beside her head, she heard Robert say to Sean, "Keep going. She'll have a bunch of those." Both men resumed their movements, driving hard into her as one, then alternating, then together again. Alyssa closed her eyes and let the unpredictable fucking surprise her with heightened sensitivity, the shocks flying from her overflowing holes.

She felt Robert swell inside her. She braced for a hot shot of cum on her cervix, delivered at the point-blank range he did so well, but he stopped moving. Alyssa groaned and gripped at him, trying to coax his load to set her off. "No, don't stop."

Her ass must have clenched at the same time. Sean warned, "I'm coming." He gripped her shoulders beside her neck and held her in place as he drove into her.

"Fill my ass. Come in me."

He groaned as his spunk shot into her ass. The heat filled her and expanded outward as her ass spasmed around his smooth shaft. He pushed in one last time, staying still a moment before pulling out and dropping to the bed beside the couple.

Alyssa looked at him. "Go wash. You fuck my pussy next." She leaned down to her husband's face. "Fuck me right, Babe. Make me come again."

As Sean got off the bed, Alyssa rolled onto her back, opening her legs for her husband and holding her arms wide in invitation. Robert knelt between his wife's legs, eased his cock between her lips, and drove all the way in. She raised her ankles to his shoulders, lifting her hips so he could fill the deepest parts of her. He fucked down into her, tapping her cervix and letting the curve of his cock drag the head along her G-spot with every stroke. Alyssa's orgasm was nearing the bursting point.

"Oh yes. Fuck me hard. I'm so close. Make me come again. Fuck me, Babe. Give me that big cock. Come in me." With that last announcement, Alyssa grabbed her knees and pulled, thrusting her hips against him, taking him deep. Her guttural moan filled the room as she flushed hot and clenched again on his cock.

The extra squeeze and the dirty talk must have set Robert off, because he buried himself in Alyssa, spraying his cum directly on her cervix, expanding her orgasm. They both froze, pressing themselves against each other with every ounce of energy they had, letting their bodies share fluids where they joined.

Robert used his hands to lower Alyssa's legs to the bed, where they splayed out, exhausted. Alyssa closed her eyes and whispered, "More."

"You have to be kidding. After that, she wants more?"

Robert turned toward Sean. "How long have you been watching?"

"Long enough to get hard again. She really wants more? She can't even open her eyes."

"More. Fuck me."

"You heard her. Get in here and give her what she wants." Robert kissed his wife and climbed off her, letting Sean fill his spot without delay.

"This won't hurt her?"

"Not if you fuck her normally. I was a little surprised my first time with her like this as well. She likes it, so go ahead. Remember, no pain."

Sean lined his cock up in her oozing slit and eased in. He moved slowly, and her lips stretched, enhancing the full feeling. He caressed her breast, side, and hip with one hand, supporting himself with the other. He felt good, but Alyssa wanted to get fucked hard tonight. *Give me more.*

She tightened her pussy around him and whispered, "Harder."

He lifted her hips off the bed with both hands to meet his thrusts. Alyssa felt her body being moved by the hips instead of using her body to move her hips. She liked it. He was taking what he wanted from her.

"So strong. Harder."

He picked up his pace enough that Alyssa's breathing quickened, punctuated by louder huffs pounded out by each collision. A few more strokes and she squeezed his cock with her pussy. Sean sped up, and swelled inside her, spreading her walls from opening to cervix, giving them a smooth hardness to grip and try to catch.

"I'm going to come."

Alyssa opened her eyes. "Come on my tits. Paint me."

Sean dropped her hips and jacked his cock above her. The first spurt flew to her chin, leaving a trail down her neck and between her breasts. The next three fell onto her breasts, as he aimed from one to the other. The rest of his load fell onto her belly, with the last dribbles falling on her gaping pussy.

Alyssa looked at her husband through half-open lids. "More, Babe. More."

Sean climbed off Alyssa, and Robert replaced him, sliding into her with one stroke. Alyssa loved when his familiar breath tickled her neck, and she sighed at his return. He began slowly. She felt his love for her, knowing he moved his cock inside her the way she liked, teasing her pleasure spots.

She lay still, lying just as she had moments earlier, but her body spasmed as orgasms lined up within her under Robert's practiced hand. When he bit her nipple with his teeth, the first one flowed, making her purr deep in her chest and find the will to squeeze her lifeless thighs against his hips one more time.

Oh god. This is what more is like with him. I'll never be the same. Please keep going.

Robert's even pace hit the spots that electrified the storming orgasm looking for a way to escape over and over. Her body was exhausted and limp, but he continued, and she found the strength to flex her abs as she neared another release, forcing her pussy as far onto his cock as she could get until she came and collapsed again, completely spent.

"Look, this has been great, but it's two in the morning, and I have to fly tomorrow. Thank you for all this. I'll let myself out."

Robert turned to Sean. "Your hard-on says you want to stay just a little longer."

"This is the sexiest thing that's ever happened to me. I've been hard the entire time."

Robert cupped Alyssa's cheek, but she kept her eyes closed. "Baby, do you want one last time with two?"

She nodded.

Robert looked at the young man. "You could probably bust one more nut. To help you sleep, of course, right?"

"Sure. I'm close watching her keep coming like that. It won't take me long."

Robert rolled Alyssa on her side, presenting her ass to Sean by bending her legs.

She roused. "No. On my back. Edge of the bed."

Robert and Sean helped her move so her head hung over the edge of the bed. She opened her legs and said to Robert, "Get back inside me. Sean, fuck my mouth, all the way into my throat."

She leaned her head back as he dropped his pants to his ankles and placed the tip of his hard cock on her lips. She pulled him forward by his balls until they touched her eyes. She pulled his balls back, then forward again in time with Robert's thrusts in her pussy. *He tastes like me. I'm coming again. So dirty. So good.*

Sean and Robert matched pace, Alyssa swallowing when Robert's thrusts nudged her onto Sean's cock. He held a breast in each hand, pulling them as he drove into her face, stretching and making them ache where they attached to her chest. *This is how my tits feel when I have a gang bang.*

She clenched her pussy around Robert, trying to hold his tip against her cervix, trying to prolong the stretching he gave her with every lunge inside. Sean entered her throat and blocked her breath before pulling back, the briefest sense of panic tightening Alyssa's chest every time.

She pulled Sean forward with one hand on his ass, and pulled Robert in deeper with her other hand on his arm as she came. Her groans escaped around Sean's cock, and he swelled against her tongue. Her hand fell limp as she came down from her orgasm, and Sean pulled out and sprayed Alyssa's face with a large load, hot cum landing on her chin, lips, nose, and eyes as she giggled.

Alyssa felt Robert swell, but instead of filling her again, he pulled out to shoot his cum along her body, mingling it with Sean's.

God, the cum. Love the cum. "More. Come on me. Paint me."

Alyssa rubbed the cum into her tits and scooped the cum from her face into her mouth, making a show of swallowing it as she watched Sean watch her. "Mm, that's so good. I'm glad you came, Sean. And that you came."

"Um, yeah. This has been amazing. Thank you. I'll remember this for a long time."

Robert laughed. "Now you have a story to tell the old-timers."

Alyssa repositioned as Robert locked the door behind Sean. "Thank you, Babe. That was wonderful. Do you think you can reclaim me now? I'd love one more load all over me."

Robert wagged his semierect dick at her. "See what you can do with this."

"Mm. More." She pulled his hardening cock to her mouth.

24

SUNDAY, MAY 30, BREAKFAST RESTAURANT, HOUSTON

"Tell me, what inspired you to ask Sean to join us last night?" Alyssa looked over her coffee cup in the packed restaurant.

"You want to talk about that now?"

"Sure. It's so loud, nobody will hear. Why did you invite him?"

Robert looked around. "I thought you would like it. I know you enjoyed what happened in the Embassy Suites. I didn't expect the slapping, but I thought I could let you feel good. Did you enjoy it?"

"I did. Thank you, Babe." Alyssa plastered on a smile.

"But not as much as you hoped."

Alyssa's stomach fell, and she wished she had not broached the subject. She had wanted to see if she could expand on what

243

they had done, but instead he read her every expression, the way he always did. *Bad move, Alyssa. You keep screwing this open marriage thing up by hurting him.* "I didn't say that."

"Your eyes did. I've known you for over half your life. I know when you aren't saying everything."

"It isn't that. I loved it. I felt so good, and you made me orgasm so much. It was just different from what I expected."

"What did you expect?"

Alyssa looked around for eavesdroppers this time. "I expected to be used. I thought I'd be treated like a whore: left exhausted, addled, and sore at the end of the night. Maybe that's why I came so hard when he slapped my tits. It's why I hung my head over the edge of the bed and let him fuck my mouth."

"Treated like a whore. Like the three men who abused you did?"

Alyssa hung her head. *He knows I liked it. I didn't hide that I liked the sex. He can't understand why.* "Yes. I know you didn't like when that happened, but it is so different. It's intoxicating, exhilarating. I hoped to get that with someone who wouldn't hurt me like they did. I hoped to have that with you."

"Oh."

This is a truth that won't hurt. "Not that what you did wasn't exceptional. It was. I knew when you stripped me that it would be a great night, and having you inside me, hitting all the spots only you know, I was over the moon. It was just different from what I envisioned when you offered."

"I'm not sure I can do that to you. Certainly not the way they did. Probably not the way Sean did either. I can't bring myself to hurt you."

And that's why I love you so much. I wish I could explain it better. "I understand and appreciate that you love me too much to see me hurt. And I understand and appreciate how far you stretched to have Sean there in the first place. I loved what you did, and I love you for doing it. Honestly, I had so many climaxes, and except for my bruised boobs, I'm not beaten up today. I can't wait for you to feel this generous again."

She squeezed his hand on the table, locked eyes with him, and smiled. This one wasn't forced. "It wasn't what I expected, but it was new and wonderful. It was a gift from my loving husband, and I loved it and I love you. Thank you again, Babe."

"I'm glad you enjoyed it. Maybe next time, I'll give you a little more excitement."

"Don't change a thing. If I have one man in my ass and one in my pussy, I'm over the moon."

The pitcher bounced off the table, splashing orange juice onto Alyssa. Alyssa shrieked as the cold liquid soaked her shirt, and Robert moved aside as some crossed the table to spill onto his lap.

The waitress scrambled with the napkins on their table and a rag in her apron to contain the spill. "I'm so sorry. Let me get some towels."

She ran to the kitchen, returning with a handful of kitchen towels. She wiped up the table and began wiping Alyssa's shirt, jerking her hand back when she touched Alyssa's breast. "I'm sorry. I should give you this." Blushing, she handed the towel to Alyssa and another to Robert for his pants.

While Robert and Alyssa both said the obligatory "It's all right," the waitress put her face in her hands. When she looked again, her eyes got wide. "I'll be right back, ma'am."

Robert looked at Alyssa and shook his head. "Had you known you'd be getting soaked, I bet you would have worn a bra."

Alyssa looked down at her nipples, apparent in the thin white top, now see-through with the addition of the juice. She put her arm across her chest, aware that the entire restaurant was watching. She laughed when she saw one woman bop her husband's shoulder as he stared. "Probably so, but not wearing one seems to have made me popular."

The waitress returned with a blue shirt in her hand. "Ma'am, I am so sorry. This is my extra staff shirt from my locker. I promise it is clean. We look about the same size. Please take it. You should at least have a dry shirt."

"You don't need to give me your shirt."

"No, ma'am. I spilled the juice, and you are wet and a bit… exposed. You need a fresh shirt, and it's what we have available. Please, take it. I'll show you to the restroom." She handed Alyssa the shirt. When Alyssa stood, the waitress walked across the dining room toward the restroom, Alyssa behind her, noting the men shamelessly ogling her chest.

In the restroom, Alyssa pulled the fitted shirt over her head and stretched it over her breasts, having to pull it down to meet her shorts. She checked the mirror in the tiny room. *We aren't quite the same size everywhere, my dear.* The pressure awakened the ache in her breasts, and the memory hardened her nipples, which poked against the fabric, hurting more, reminding her, and continuing the mental and physical cycle of pleasure and pain. *I should pull a shift; I'd make a ton with my tits bulging out like this. Stop, Alyssa. The girl did the best she could for you.*

The waitress handed Alyssa a plastic to-go bag when she came out of the restroom. "For your wet clothes."

"Thank you. You are too kind. I'm sorry you spilled. You must be embarrassed."

"Oh no, ma'am. You ended up covered in juice, not me, and my shirt is a bit tight on you." Her eyes rose from Alyssa's breasts to her face, and she flushed. "Can I ask you a question? I dropped that pitcher because I heard you tell your husband that you had one man in your pussy and one in your ass. Does he accept that, and is it that good?"

The conversations I have with waitresses. "We have a special relationship, and we are very open with each other. And yes, it is exquisite." Alyssa looked down the hall and leaned to the waitress. "You know how full the biggest, fattest cock you have ever had made you feel?" She placed her hand on the waitress's waist and leaned closer. "Double it."

"Oh god."

"It's not for every day, but it's a good treat. The orgasms roll one right after the other." Alyssa rubbed her hip as she slid by to return to the table.

"Paulie's most effective ad ever is that shirt," Robert chuckled to his wife as she sat down. "Every man in the place knows where you eat, and wants to eat there too. Or maybe wants to eat you."

"Stop. She literally gave me her own shirt. It's better than my winning the wet T-shirt contest. Let's go back to the hotel and change. I'd like to be able to breathe."

25

SUNDAY, MAY 30, HOUSTON HOTEL

ALYSSA WAITED BY the hotel door while Robert tipped the valet. As he caught up to her, a familiar face came out the door pulling a carry-on. She waved and stepped in close to whisper to them.

"Thank you for last night. The man I picked up didn't have the stamina of you three, but your screaming and moaning woke him up to give me rounds two and three. I got the feeling that's unusual for him."

Alyssa laughed with the woman. "I'm glad our noise worked out for you. The last time I stayed here I had similar neighbors, but I only had my fingers as a partner."

"Oh, my fingers were busy too. They were knuckle-deep and fidgeting while my lothario recharged." She looked at Robert. "It sounded like you are much better than average. If I weren't leaving for Phoenix, I would invite your wife to give you a two-on-one like you gave her last night." They all laughed. She looked back at Alyssa. "You are lucky. Keep him around."

"I intend to. Enjoy your flight. Phoenix, you say? Our partner last night is piloting a flight to Phoenix today. If you are on the same flight, maybe he will give you a tour of the plane." Alyssa leaned in. "And if he offers, let him slap your tits."

"Maybe so. I'll ask, even if it isn't the same pilot."

The lady got in her Uber, and Robert and Alyssa entered the lobby.

"Mrs. Alyssa Davis!"

Alyssa turned to see the person calling her name. She smiled, recognizing the tall dark-haired beauty walking toward her. "Sonia!" The two trotted and met in a hug. "I hoped I would see you."

"You did? What did you have in mind?" She eyed Robert with one raised eyebrow.

"He knows, Sonia. Robert and I have a strong marriage. Robert, this is Sonia, one of the ladies I told you about."

They shook hands. "It is a pleasure to meet you. If you don't mind my saying, Alyssa's stories don't do justice to how beautiful—no…how regal…you are."

"You flatter me, Mr. Robert Davis. Similarly, her tales of you undersell your visible qualities. Your qualities are on display for all, Alyssa. You have amended your style of dress since we last met."

"Not typical for me, though I have loosened up. There was an accident at the restaurant. I need to change before we head to the museum."

Sonia again raised one eyebrow. "You traveled to Houston to attend a museum? Did a special exhibit entice you?"

Alyssa chuckled. "We are meeting our daughter to drive home with her. She has an exam this evening, and we will leave tomorrow morning. We planned to kill some time in the natural history museum."

"Alyssa, Michael would have remained in town had he expected your arrival. Is the reservation in your name, Robert?"

"Yes."

"Will your daughter be staying with you tonight?"

Alyssa shrugged and nodded. "Probably."

"Please come with me." She strode to an empty station at the end of the reservation desk. "Here. You are in a regular room. I will upgrade you to our executive suite."

"Oh, our room is just fine. We don't need a suite."

"Robert, upgrading special guests to unoccupied suites is my privilege. I am pleased to give you a separate bedroom, in the instance you and Mrs. Davis would like to express your love for each other while your daughter sleeps in her own bedroom. Do not worry, your rate will remain unchanged."

"That is very kind of you." He turned to Alyssa. "Are you sure you told me everything you did while you were here? You made quite an impression."

Alyssa felt like she had been punched in the stomach. Her hand covered her belly, and she gasped in a breath. After all they had done to recover after her trip here, she felt his lack of trust physically. *He didn't mean it as an accusation. He was joking because Sonia is happy I'm here. He trusts me. I hope.* She thought of Hayden. *Even if I don't deserve it lately.*

She looked him in the eye. "I told you everything. You didn't want me to omit anything, and I didn't. It hurt both of us, but you know everything, I promise."

"I remember, and I believe you. I was joking because we are getting the royal treatment." He cupped her shoulder the way he always did when he wanted to reassure her. Like always, his touch settled her.

"She did not tell you everything, Robert. She could not, for she is unaware of how much impact she had on my husband and me. We still speak of her, and it strengthens our bond each time. Come with me. I will show you."

Sonia opened the door into the back hallway and beckoned them to follow. After a few yards, she stopped between a window and a bench and looked at Alyssa. "You told him everything?"

"Everything. Even about this place."

"Then you know that your wife and I shared passion against that window, first between each other, then with one of our staff. The incident was one of the most erotic events in my entire life. This bench is here so Michael and I can make love when we want to relive that night."

"I see."

"You do not, yet. Look at the window. Do you see the outline of a woman's breasts and face? It is not as clear as it once was."

Robert moved to his right two steps. "I see it now, in this light."

"That is the image of your wife, orgasming on my tongue. Do you see the rings around her nipples? Her nipples were hard enough to depress the skin surrounding them so it did not touch the glass. I have tried to replicate such a hardness with Michael against other windows but have been unable to. The rings reveal how much pleasure I provided her then. Thus, when Michael or I want to rekindle the passion of that night, we come here, and let her image watch us."

"Amazing. Does your staff not clean the windows?"

"They do. They are forbidden from cleaning this one. They call it 'the sacred lady.' Only one of them knows the story."

Robert nodded. "The man who walked in on you."

"Richard. He and I share a smile when we pass in this hallway, but we say nothing."

"Please thank him on my behalf for his discretion."

"You do not understand. All staff who met your wife that week hold her in the highest regard. She provided calm and kindness in a time when the other guests spread anger and frustration. They would find it most unseemly to speak poorly of Alyssa."

Alyssa blushed. "That is kind to say, Sonia. Thank you. I'm sure there were others."

"There is your modesty again. It is why you are remembered here, and why I upgraded your room. I will have a bellman bring your bags up."

"We'll bring them, Sonia. We will need to pack up first."

"Very well. We will meet in the elevator lobby on twenty-four in twenty minutes. I will show you the suite."

⬦

"God, I couldn't wait to get that off," Alyssa said as she peeled the tight shirt over her head.

"I bet. The seams left red marks on your sides. I notice that it didn't constrain your hard nipples." Robert cupped a breast and thumbed the hard nub. "They must be your superpower."

"I couldn't believe Sonia showed you that and said those things. I'm so embarrassed."

"Don't be. That window print is super sexy, even, what, three months later? Clearly, she thinks very highly of you. I think in that regard, you are on a short list."

"Even if she thinks highly of me for fucking her? And her husband?"

"Baby, given how our own sex life has changed, I'd say *especially* because you fucked her and her husband so well. She seems to be an expert in fucking."

"Are you sure you are fine with what she showed you in the hallway? That was before our arrangement."

"It was, but we sorted through all that. And that image of you is arousing. Speaking of which, you want to fuck your husband well before we head up? You already have your shirt off."

Alyssa pulled his hand off her tit to slip a T-shirt over her head. "Fucking you well takes more than the ten minutes we have left. Maybe I'll show you in the new suite. Come on. She'll be waiting."

When the elevator doors opened, Robert stood back to let Alyssa exit first. Sonia stood by one of the three doors in the landing. There was no hallway. He stood back to admire the two women as Sonia explained the exclusive floor to his wife.

Sonia stood a bit taller than Alyssa. Where Alyssa had fuller breasts and hips, Sonia was lithe, with definition in her face that hinted at the athletic body her slacks did nothing to hide. He envisioned the two of them in the hallway downstairs—Alyssa's chest and face pressed against the window, Sonia's face pressed into Alyssa's ass—and he envied the worker who happened into the hallway at the magical moment three months ago.

Sonia entered the suite first and opened the blinds. The floor-to-ceiling windows flooded the sitting room with light, silhouetting her as she turned.

Alyssa stopped in front of him. "Wow. This is some suite. Thank you, Sonia."

Sonia laughed. "Yes. Its grandeur has transfixed you. Come in so Robert can see as well."

He patted Alyssa's ass. "Thank you, Sonia. I have a great view from right here."

"Try the view from here." Sonia walked to the head of an eight-person conference table beside the window. "There are only a few buildings in this direction as tall as this one."

Alyssa and Robert stood beside her to look out over the city. Robert pointed to the buildings nearby. "You are right, Sonia, this is a great view. We can see for miles."

"I revealed something quite personal downstairs. I would ask you two something personal in return."

They nodded.

"Your joint presence indicates you resolved your marriage issues. What did you decide?"

Alyssa looked up at him with a tiny smile and took his hand in hers. Her nipples poked out the thin T-shirt. Robert wondered if she was remembering or anticipating. "I made amends with Robert. Then we decided to open our marriage."

"That sounds quite simple. Would you agree, Robert?"

He chuckled, and squeezed Alyssa's hand to let her know he loved her. "Simple? No. We have tried a lot, and enjoyed a lot, but some things have been terrible."

"Yeah. We had a couple of rough spots. Why do you ask?"

"You know me to be direct in my speech, Alyssa; I do not fear offending you. Robert, you do not know me. If your wife has described our encounter, then you will understand that I am not shy in pursuing my desires, and offense is not my intent." She turned to face them. "If your marriage is open, I propose that an afternoon of passion between we three is preferable to a museum, should you be so inclined."

"Wow. That is very direct." He turned to Alyssa. "You almost ruined our marriage when you were here last, but you sure made friends. I wish I had been here to see it."

Something—anger? Hurt? Regret?—flashed across Alyssa's face too quickly for him to identify it before she smiled at him and traced a finger along his bicep. "I wish you had been here, too, but if you had been, I wouldn't know how impressive Sonia is."

"It is you two who are impressive. I would not have chosen to seduce you in my favorite place in the hotel otherwise."

Robert laughed. "I'm used to seductions moving a little slower, but if you want to call it a seduction, I'll go along." He turned to his wife. "She's asking you, Baby. Would you rather go to the museum?"

Alyssa didn't look away from Sonia, who was unbuttoning her blouse. "Yes," she whispered.

"I think she meant no, Sonia, but kiss her to make sure."

Sonia dropped her blouse to the floor and wrapped her arms around Alyssa, pulling her head close for a long kiss. Alyssa moaned and hugged Sonia. Sonia feathered her fingers up and down Alyssa's back, slowly increasing the contact with every pass until she gripped an ass cheek with one hand and a shoulder with the other, the impressions in Alyssa's clothes revealing her strength.

Sonia broke their kiss and extended her hand to Robert. "Join us." She kissed him as he leaned in, and Alyssa pulled his ass, pressing the three of them together, their sides touching his. He alternated kissing Sonia and Alyssa and letting them kiss each other.

Robert gripped Alyssa's ass cheek and lifted it, knowing she liked feeling his strength and drawing a hum from her kiss with Sonia. In the other hand, he caressed Sonia's hard ass, letting his fingers slide along the cleft between her cheeks.

Alyssa kissed Robert and pulled her body away from his. He heard the clinking of a belt and the purr of a zipper as she unbuckled Sonia's slacks by touch alone. When he broke their kiss, Robert looked down at Alyssa rubbing Sonia's pussy over her panties.

Alyssa shook her head. "Panties? How proper of you."

"Had I anticipated an interlude this afternoon, I would have dressed appropriately. The panties obscured my wetness when we were downstairs."

"You are soaked. You got wet downstairs?"

"From the moment I saw you across the lobby." Sonia pulled Alyssa's shirt over her head, then removed her shorts. "You wore panties as well." She rubbed Alyssa's pussy over the cotton material. "And you are moist."

"I got turned on at breakfast, but I've been dripping since you called my name." Alyssa kissed her husband. "Let's get you ready."

Alyssa unbuckled his belt and dropped his shorts while Sonia kissed him. He pulled away only long enough for Sonia to pull his shirt off. Hot wetness engulfed his cock as soon as his shorts were clear of it.

"That's been ready," Robert said as he worked Sonia's panties down over the width of her slim hips, sucking the hard nipples topping her small breasts as he did.

Alyssa winked up at him. "I know. I wanted to do a taste test."

"A taste test?"

"Before you fuck Sonia, and after." Alyssa stood and positioned Sonia against the conference table before pushing between her breasts, having her lie on it. She lifted Sonia's legs up and out, then kissed up the inside of her left thigh before taking a long lick of her pussy. "And before Robert fucks you, and after."

Alyssa turned, offering Sonia's ankles to him. "Show her why I was desperate to come home in February, Babe. Let me show you off."

Robert chuckled. "No pressure."

He kissed Alyssa as he took Sonia's legs. He spread them only wide enough to kiss the insides of her ankles. He kissed up her legs, alternating from side to side, keeping her legs up, straight, and close to his head as he kissed his way down, spreading them like a wedge as he neared her cunt.

As he reached Sonia's knees, Alyssa gasped. He looked up to see her leaned against the window, rubbing her clit with one hand and pulling a nipple with the other.

She made eye contact. "The glass is cold. Keep going. Watching you is so hot."

"Yes, please, Robert, resume kissing my legs. My anticipation grows."

Robert continued his trek up Sonia's thighs, smiling and nodding at him the two times he paused to look at her. He hesitated at Sonia's pussy, instead nibbling the tight tendons straining to hold her legs still. As he lowered his head to introduce his mouth to Sonia's lips, he heard another moan from Alyssa but didn't look up. He licked along the outer edge of Sonia's lips, circling her four times before dipping his tongue between her slit from the top to brush her clit.

Sonia shuddered and bent her legs at the knees, catching his hands between her thighs and calves. He pressed against them, and she resisted, pushing back as if she wanted her legs on his back, but that was not his plan. After a brief battle of wills, he pushed her legs out and up, opening her for his exploration.

Sonia jerked when Robert sucked her clit from beneath its hood by trapping it against his top teeth, then flicking it against them while sucking. Her hips rose, pressing against him as she gasped. He released her clit, shifting to suck her inner lips one at a time into his mouth and stretching them apart. He pulled a hand from beneath her knee to sink two fingers into her, bearing down on the back wall of her tunnel.

Robert pulled his head back, watching as he fingered her. A single drop of juice spilled out and ran over her anus. Wanting to increase her sensations, he smeared the drop across her pucker with a finger and returned his mouth to sucking her clit. Not letting up, he inserted his finger into her ass and pinched against his fingers in her pussy when he bit gently on her clit with his teeth.

Sonia's hips arched off the table against his face. Her thighs clamped around his head, but that did nothing to slow the ministrations of his fingers or his nipping on her clit. She yelped and writhed, her hips humping forward and back.

Her spasms slowed. Her legs released Robert's head. Her breathing became more even. Robert raised his head and smiled at his wife. "Is that what you wanted me to do?"

"It's a start."

"Please continue. Alyssa, please join us."

Alyssa pulled off the window with a squeak, leaving a sweaty print of her back. She put a knee on the table and swung her other leg over Sonia's face as if she were mounting a horse, facing Robert.

"Bring yourself to me." Sonia gripped Alyssa's thighs and pulled her pussy down to her mouth. She noisily slurped the juices there before raising her hand to slip a finger inside.

Alyssa gasped, "Yes," and leaned forward to lick Sonia's clit, making Sonia's hips jerk again. Alyssa smiled at Robert. "One more taste test, then fuck her good." She opened her mouth.

Robert dipped his cock between his wife's lips and pushed forward until he felt the tip hit the back of her throat. She pulled her head back, then bobbed forward a couple of times before pulling off and sitting up straighter on Sonia's face. "Show her how good you are, Babe."

Robert dropped his cock to Sonia's open slit and shoved about halfway inside. He rotated his hips a bit, feeling parts of her insides with the head of his cock. He pulled back, reinserted a little deeper, and explored again. The third time he pulled back, he plunged forward, her slippery channel open and wet for him.

His balls bumped her ass, and as he wiggled his hips again, he felt the hard nub of her cervix and heard her groan into Alyssa's pussy.

Alyssa pulled a hand off her own breast to grab Robert's hair. "Do that again. Make her moan. It feels great on my pussy." She pulled him close for a kiss, then pushed him back. She settled lower on Sonia's face and held still as he drove in and wiggled. "Oh yeah, Babe. Make her moan."

Robert pulled Alyssa's head forward until she rested her hands on the table beside Sonia's waist. He lifted one of Sonia's legs, raising and replacing Alyssa's arm so it held the leg between it and her body. He repeated the process on the other side so that Alyssa's arms were holding Sonia's legs back, lifting her hips so Robert could get the deepest penetration. "Keep your weight on your hands to hold her legs back for me."

He reached under Alyssa to cup her breasts, rolling the nipples a bit and drawing a purr as he plunged his cock into Sonia. Robert probed, then stilled as he found the sensitive spot beside Sonia's cervix.

He smiled at his wife. "Hang on, Baby."

He leaned back and fucked Sonia with a steady rhythm, tapping beside her cervix with every downstroke and rubbing her G-spot with every backstroke. He dropped one hand from his wife's breast to circle Sonia's clit in time with his thrusts and watched as sweat beaded on the tan skin of her legs and belly. Sonia moved her hips against Robert's hand and hips as much as Alyssa would let her, moaning and jerking every few thrusts.

Alyssa humped forward and back, rubbing her lips and clit on Sonia's face. Robert watched his wife's eyes narrow and her brow furrow, knowing an orgasm was building within her. He sped up, hoping to make Sonia hum and buzz Alyssa's clit.

The pale skin around Sonia's pussy flushed pink as Robert continued to fuck her. Her legs quivered against the backs of

Alyssa's arms. Her grunts from beneath Alyssa's pussy became more frequent and louder. Her hips bucked against him in the rhythm that Robert was using to make her come. Her defined abs tensed and her pussy squeezed on Robert's cock.

The pressure on his cock and the sight of the two beauties entangled in front of him made Robert erupt. He drove fully into Sonia, spraying his seed deep inside her. Each spasm swelling his cock met one from her walls trying to constrict it. He stayed buried inside her as their climaxes and breathing slowed.

Alyssa watched the abdominal muscles of both partners flex and strain as they came. She held her hips still, rising enough for Sonia to breathe but not enough to relinquish the vibrations of her orgasmic groans. Alyssa felt her own orgasm near the edge, then subside as Sonia couldn't continue eating pussy while her climax crested. As Sonia's tan lines lost their pink tinge, Alyssa pressed down onto Sonia's mouth, seeking release.

Sonia resumed licking and sucking Alyssa's clit, and she added a finger to Alyssa's ass, pressing against the two in her pussy. Her ass clung to Sonia's finger, stretching around the knuckles and closing around the narrower finger as it moved in and out. Sonia sped up and pinched the fingers from both hands together inside Alyssa, pulling and compressing the tissue there and shooting sparks inside her body, pushing her orgasm closer to eruption.

Robert returned both hands to her tits, pulling them, the stretch aching against her chest as she writhed. *So close.*

She looked at her own ass print on the window, then at Sonia's pussy. Robert's cock remained buried inside. Some of the combined cum smeared their junction. *He really filled her. This is so fucking sexy.* Alyssa arched her back, pinning Sonia's head to the table and pulling her breasts from Robert's grasp as she came.

A groan originated deep in her chest and expanded her throat so that the veins, muscles, and windpipe felt like they would burst the skin. When the sound stopped, her mouth remained open, her face hot, and her throat tight for another few seconds. With a gasp, she filled her lungs and rolled beside Sonia on the table.

Robert moved to pull out of Sonia, but she wrapped her legs around his hips. "Not yet. Remain inside me for a moment."

Sonia pulled Allyssa's hand to her abs. "The best sex I ever had on this table was with the president of Honduras. You have eclipsed that. Michael will labor to reclaim me after this afternoon."

"You said he's out of town?" Alyssa raised her head to make eye contact.

"Yes."

Alyssa squeezed Sonia's hand. "In that case, he can't reclaim you yet. I'd like another round, if you can stay."

"You did indicate the desire for a taste test."

Alyssa rolled onto her elbows and brought her face above Sonia's pussy. "I did indeed."

Sonia unwrapped her legs from around Robert's hips. "Robert, withdraw slowly. Do not let me spill. I have something planned for your wife. Alyssa, clean your husband's cock with your mouth. Perform your taste test, then wait for us in the bed."

Alyssa put her mouth at the entrance of Sonia's pussy. She licked along the top of Robert's cock as he withdrew from the long-legged beauty. When the tip emerged, she lifted the shaft with her hand and took as much of it into her mouth as the odd angle would allow. She slurped and swallowed noisily, looking into Robert's eyes and making a show of cleaning him.

When the end of his shaft was clean, she pulled it out of her mouth and grabbed his hips. "Come here. Let me get the rest."

Alyssa licked the base of his shaft, moving it and her head to get all the parts she could reach without climbing off the table. She caressed his cock until it began to harden, then dipped her lips to give Sonia's clit a peck before climbing off the table and walking to the bedroom. She winked over her shoulder. "Don't make me wait."

Robert looked down at Sonia, who had held her legs up near her shoulders the entire time Alyssa had cleaned him. "Robert, help me from the table." He lifted her off the table, and she glided to the bedroom. Not being a fool, he followed.

Robert reached full hardness at the sight before him. Sonia was propped against the headboard, caressing her small breasts, while his wife lapped at the cum that had dripped down the long, outstretched legs. As she reached Sonia's pussy, Alyssa pressed her chest into the bedspread, bending her neck to lap at Sonia's pussy while arching her back. Robert admired the view of his wife's open pussy before moving forward to use the access her position provided him.

He kissed his wife's pussy and dug his tongue between her folds before lining his cock up with her soaked opening. He drove into her with one stroke, not stopping until he felt the hard nub of her cervix touch the underside of his head. Alyssa's walls clenched around him, and she moaned. Robert let her relax, then backed up and rammed home again.

Robert's thrusts drove Alyssa against the bedspread and Sonia's pussy, jostling both beautiful bodies, almost like fucking both of them at once.

Sonia rolled her head back as Alyssa ate her. She pinched and pulled her nipples farther than should be possible for such small tits. The light-brown nipples and the pale skin around them showed bright-pink marks from the abuse.

Robert rubbed his thumb across Alyssa's asshole, mesmerized by her perfect ass cheeks rippling as he slammed into them. The sweat on her back glistened and defined her muscles as they strained to keep her hips up and her face down. He felt the tip of his cock dragging along her back wall, all the way from her opening, until he bottomed out beside her cervix. She pushed back against him, fucking him just as much as he was fucking her. Even having come a few minutes before, he knew he would not last long with this stimulation.

"Robert Davis, look at me." Sonia made eye contact. "Do you find me beautiful?"

"Yes. Beyond beautiful." He looked back down at Alyssa's ass.

"Do you like my firm breasts? My flat stomach? My long legs?"

"Yes. All of them. They are beautiful and sexy." He looked at Alyssa's back and her hair.

"Look at your wife perform cunnilingus. Is that beautiful and sexy?" Sonia's breathing stuttered, and her tits flushed bright red.

"Yes."

"Why, Robert?" Sonia clamped her thighs onto Alyssa's ears as her neck strained and her abs rippled, revealing her orgasm as much as the low groan coming from her mouth. Her head pressed against the headboard and her breasts pointed toward Robert as her back arched.

"Because Alyssa is smiling."

Sonia's moans took Robert to the point of orgasm, and he shoved deep into Alyssa and filled her, the sensation setting off another round of gripping waves clutching his cock. Robert held her hips up as she bucked against him, her head still clamped between Sonia's thighs. As she stilled, Sonia relaxed her legs, and Alyssa slid forward until her head rested on Sonia's belly a moment before she rolled to the right.

Robert let Alyssa slide off his cock, then lay down on the other side of Sonia. Sonia stroked their heads as Robert's eyes closed. As he drifted off to sleep, he heard Sonia say, "Let him sleep. Come with me."

✍

Alyssa ran a hot bath in the large tub, pouring in some crystals to create some lavender-scented foam while Sonia retrieved some chardonnay and two glasses from the extensive wet bar.

"Come, Alyssa. We will soak together." They sat at opposite ends, letting Sonia's legs drape over Alyssa's in the middle of the large oval.

"I am glad you saw me."

"I am pleased as well. Your husband is an impressive lover, with a quintessential cock. The two of you together become an event unto itself. I look forward to Michael's return. His reclaiming may require an entire day. He will be jealous."

"You were the dynamo in bed. And on the table. We just rose to your occasion. This was so much better than a museum." Alyssa lifted her glass to her friend.

"Indeed, though with imagination and effort, the museum can be interesting as well. The gemstone exhibit has some dark corners."

Alyssa giggled. "You haven't."

Sonia gave a wry half smile. "One of the former security personnel and I knew each other." She sipped her wine.

"Surely there are cameras."

"Of course. I have a copy of the security footage."

"Sonia, every time we talk, I learn something." She took a gulp of wine. "Can I learn something else from you?"

"I will answer what questions you have, Alyssa. Whether that enlightens you, I cannot promise."

"When we talked before, you mentioned that you and Mike have regular partners, the ones you visit more than anyone else, that you even care for."

"Yes. Beth and Ramon."

"Right. How do you keep Mike as your priority when you see Ramon?"

"It is simple. I love Michael. I enjoy Ramon. Upon any choice regarding whom to accompany, whom to follow, whom to consider, I choose Michael without hesitation or reservation. My love guides me."

"I see." Alyssa looked at the wall, unable to meet Sonia's hard gaze. *I go the other way too often.*

"You are not asking for my experience, Alyssa. You seek advice. What have you done?"

"I have a partner I see a lot. He is smart, funny, well liked, and kind to everyone. I really like him. And if you can believe it, his cock is perfectly shaped, just like Robert's but a little bigger."

"You are infatuated, but that is not all."

She has great knowledge, and she sees through every question I ask. She's a tough adviser. "Robert was getting upset because I saw Hayden too frequently, so I withheld telling him every time I saw Hayden. I haven't even told him when we met and didn't have sex."

"You have met your lover and not had sex? Why?"

"He's great to talk to, and he has helped me with a few things when even Robert couldn't. I don't know why he wants to spend time with me, but I look forward to our lunches together."

"Is that within your open marriage agreement?"

Alyssa finished her wine with another gulp to settle her rolling stomach. *That's the real question.* "No. We agreed to tell each other every time, no overnights, no emotional attachments, and I call before I play."

Sonia raised an eyebrow. "Only you call?"

"I had a bad experience. I'm letting Robert know where I am if I lose my mind again, not getting permission."

"You have not called in advance of all your dalliances with your lover."

Alyssa shook her head. "No. Seeing Hayden this much would upset Robert."

"Therefore you dishonor your marriage? This is the second time you and I have spoken of your dishonesty. I cannot help you with that."

She's scolding me like a child. Why do I feel worse for disappointing her than I do for lying to Robert? God, I'm a mess.

"Are you afraid of Robert? What he might do?"

"No. Yes. Sort of."

"He does not appear violent. Will he hurt you?"

She waved her hands in front of her face. "Oh no. No. He wouldn't become violent. Never."

"Then what do you fear that you lie about this lover?"

"I'm afraid he will tell me not to see Hayden again."

"Is that one of your rules, that you can stop the other from seeing someone?"

"No. But he could point out the emotional attachment."

"It is already there. Does it grow?"

"I don't know. I like him, and everything I learn of him makes him more appealing, not less. And —" She looked away from Sonia's withering gaze. She wiped her eyes with a towel while she fought back the sob that impeded her ability to speak. "I think I am developing feelings for him. A friend warned me that having repeated sex with someone eventually makes it mean something more. I feel like a high school girl with a crush."

"A crush can be dangerous, or it can pass. I do not believe you have endured the changes you have to damage your marriage over a mere infatuation. There is more?"

"We have had some tense conversations about it. I have let texts from Hayden interrupt arguments with Robert about seeing Hayden so much, and lied about who it is. Plus, sex with Robert isn't as good after I've been with Hayden. He doesn't hit all the spots like normal when he reclaims me. I've faked some orgasms, and I haven't had to do that in a long time. It's still good, but it doesn't make me explode like it used to. It doesn't wipe Hayden from my mind; it makes me want him more." She dropped her face into her hands to weep silently.

When Alyssa raised her head, Sonia had refilled their glasses with the bottle sitting by the tub. "Have a sip to settle yourself."

Alyssa drank half her glass. "I didn't mean for all of that to come out. I never even considered those thoughts before, consciously. The dam just broke."

"Your situation will not easily be resolved. You must think about what you desire most. You must be honest with your husband and yourself."

"That's your advice?" She had wanted Sonia to tell her what to decide, not that she needed to decide for herself. *I need to know what to do.*

"Yes, though you knew all of this when you began talking. There is good news that you have not considered."

"What could possibly be good about this?"

"Two items of truth. First, until you have found undesirable qualities in this man, you do not love him. Love only comes when you perceive the good and the bad and still feel love. Until then, you are only infatuated, and infatuations can be overcome."

"If I see the bad and still feel this way, then that's bad, not good." *I'm afraid that is how I will feel, and that it will break me. And Robert.*

"Perhaps, but you can decide like a woman instead of like a flighty schoolgirl."

Alyssa nodded, swallowing the flicker of angry pride that flashed in her chest. "And the second truth?"

Sonia nodded toward the bedroom door. "The man asleep in there already knows your struggle, and he loves you still."

"How does he know? And how do you know that?"

"I noted how he watched you today. He anticipates your needs and wants. He acts for your pleasure and your happiness. When you can't see him, he still acts only for you. That man already knows your mind and heart."

"That can't be true. He certainly has enjoyed our open marriage, just like I have."

"You would know better than I, though I watched him orgasm today. I am a beautiful, sexy woman, and unfamiliar to your husband. Most men would watch me fondle my own breasts even if I were not a novel experience. I could not hold his gaze, even when I orgasmed on your face. He watched you. Let that factor in your thoughts."

Alyssa's chest emptied, leaving an ache that prevented her from breathing. She counted to ten and tried to inhale, finally forcing a bite of air that reset her system with a shudder. *She sees that, but I don't? God.* "No other advice?"

"You must choose your own path. However you proceed, I urge you to be honest with all involved starting now."

"Thank you, Sonia." Alyssa moved across the tub to hug and kiss her friend's cheek before settling back and finishing her wine. "One more please."

Sonia smiled and poured the last of the chardonnay into Alyssa's glass.

Alyssa drank half of it and grinned. She reached under the water to massage Sonia's feet. "The president of Honduras gave you the best sex you've had? I'll rub your feet if you tell me."

Sonia found Alyssa's feet by her hips. "I will tell you and reciprocate. Not the best I've ever had, merely the best I've had here."

"Tell me anyway."

"Powerful men, in whatever way they are powerful, excite me. The president was visiting the consulate, and he stayed here. We met briefly in the lobby, but I thought nothing more of it. One of his security detail approached me to tell me the president wanted me to join him for a drink in his suite."

"Just a drink?"

"I am not naive. I understood what was asked before I let the guard escort me up the elevator and frisk me."

"He frisked you?"

"In part for security, in part so he could feel my body. I expected that as well."

"And then?"

"We had a drink. He was quite direct that he wanted to fuck me. I was to speak only English with him, because he had Spanish-speaking women all the time."

"Did he know you were married?"

"Yes. He did not care."

"So what made it the best?"

"The power. He ordered me to strip while he and his guards watched."

"They were in the room?"

"Yes. Four of them, wearing suits."

"Oh my. What happened when you were naked?"

"He told the guards to hold my legs and arms and spread me across the table. Two held my arms out wide, and two held my legs wide and back, opening me for him to step between my legs to fuck me."

"Just like that? No foreplay?"

"The command to join him was sufficient foreplay. I had lubricated from the time I entered the elevator. His cock was large, but it slid completely in. He fucked me until I was close to orgasm, then he told the guards to roll me over on my chest and pull my feet to the floor so he could enter me from behind. They did, and he continued to take me, also opening my anus with his fingers and using my own fluids to lubricate it. Again, as I neared orgasm, he ordered the guards to roll me over, and to suspend me in the air by the window. He stepped between my legs and impaled my ass with his cock. This time, he did not stop, but he ordered the men to move me as he stood still. They masturbated him with my body. I was helpless and aroused. I orgasmed three times before he filled me with his semen."

"Oh my god. That must have been amazing."

"It was, but I was not done. The guards laid me on the table. Their erections stretched their trousers. They removed their clothes. They were sweaty and panting from the exertion. The president sat in the chair between my legs, watching. He told them I had only spoken English, so they could not fuck me."

"Did you know that would happen?"

"I anticipated it. Many important people visit the hotel. I see many unusual things. I did not want them, but I would have fucked them to extend my time with El Presidente." She smiled. "He told them to masturbate onto me. They knelt on the table and doused my face and body with large loads of cum. When they finished, I took each of them into my mouth for a moment or two. They helped me stand, handed me my clothes, and ushered me to the hallway, naked and covered."

"What did you do?"

"I paraded to Michael's office and had him reclaim me on the desk."

"Did anyone see you?"

"It was the dinner hour. Many people saw. Some took pictures. None said a word."

"How on earth did today's everyday threesome top that?" Alyssa rolled her eyes at her own joke.

"That was an exercise in power. He commanded, we obeyed, and the eroticism overpowered me. Today was an exercise in love. Robert was masterful, as you were, but your love for each other compounded my pleasure because you shared it with me. Your feelings overpowered me today."

"Wow. I love Robert, but five men at once? That's a lot to top." *How can our lovemaking be better than that?*

"Perhaps. I do not know, as only one had me that night." She shook her head. "You will find your own path, Alyssa. I hope you flourish along it."

26

SUNDAY, MAY 30, HOUSTON STEAK HOUSE

ROBERT WATCHED ALYSSA walk from their table toward the restroom, but leaned close to his daughter when she gripped his arm.

"Dad, I can't believe you are staying at that hotel."

"Susan, your mom and I talked about it, and we are both fine with what happened there in February. We are still together, and our marriage is different but strong. The hotel is still a fantastic hotel."

"There are lots of good hotels in Houston, Dad. You could stay at another one and not have to relive that week when she cheated on you."

The softness around Susan's eyes showed her concern for him

even as her steel grip on his forearm revealed her anger at the situation.

"Are you still upset by that, sweetie? What Mom did?"

"Yes and no. It's between you two, and I hear that everything is fine. Plus, you even have some interesting guests sometimes, but it still feels weird."

"You have been talking with Clay."

"Of course."

"That was only one time, and he wasn't supposed to see her that morning."

Susan rolled her eyes. "She probably should have left before the eighteen-year-old boy got hungry."

He smiled at her sarcasm, yet another sign she was truly his daughter. "Okay. Back to the point. Mom and I have changed our marriage a bit, and we are happy with the changes. I hope you are happy that we are happy."

"I am. I can't forget hearing her have sex with someone else that morning, and how much it hurt me. It hurt me for you."

He patted her hand on his arm as he looked around for eavesdroppers. "Oh, sweetie. Thank you for that. Please remember Mom and I agree that having sex is just that, nothing more. We both always enjoyed it; we now enjoy it with other people as well as each other. You know it hasn't changed our love for each other or our love for you."

"I know. I'm getting used to it."

"Keep talking to Clay. He's getting used to it too."

"I hear he's really happy with Sawyer."

Robert smiled, relieved that they finished the difficult portion of the conversation. "It appears so. According to the alarm system, he took her to the house last night and earlier today."

"How do you know he took her there?"

"Can you think of another reason he would need to visit the

house for a couple of hours while he's staying with Grandma and Grandpa?"

Susan laughed. "Fair point. I'm glad they are having fun."

"What about you? Are you having fun, sweetie?" Alyssa patted her daughter on the shoulder as she returned to her seat.

"Yeah, I am. In fact, can I beg off staying with you guys tonight? After the orgo exam today, I want to blow off a little steam. Would you be upset if I went back to school tonight?"

"No, sweetie, of course not." Alyssa patted her daughter's hand. "Are you blowing off steam with anyone in particular?"

"Yeah. A guy named Josh. I like him."

Alyssa beamed. "Great. When do we meet him?"

"Maybe later, Mom. For now, we are just hanging out."

Alyssa nodded. "Okay, go back to school and blow off some steam. Pick us up in the morning. Not too late; we have a long way to drive."

"All right. Do we need to call an Uber or can you give us a ride back to the hotel?"

"Dad! I want to go back to school, but I'll always take care of my family. I'll drive you back, then go hang out. You guys come first."

27

SUNDAY, MAY 30, HOUSTON HOTEL

ALYSSA CLOSED HER phone. *No texts from Hayden since Friday.* Her stomach tightened only enough to feel a little empty. *He can't be mad that I came to get my daughter. I hope. Maybe not understanding family is his flaw. He doesn't care about marriages, maybe not kids either.*

She replayed her conversation with Sonia. She needed to be more honest with Robert. *But when I am, he will insist I stop. Am I ready for that? Am I even willing to stop seeing Hayden? Am I willing to fight with Robert to keep seeing Hayden? I feel so good with him.*

She needed to decide what she wanted. Hayden gave her excitement. Her body tingled in anticipation when she knew she would see him, and it trembled for hours after he finished with her. He showed her new positions and had promised to set up a threesome for her. And he'd gotten a hotel room Robert

275

wouldn't even try for. *He gets better and better the more I know. And the sex breaks me.*

Then there was Robert. For twenty-three years, he had been her rock, the reason she could feel safe at home, the best part of her life. He loved her, and she loved him. She couldn't imagine life without him beside her. And every time they made love... *What a connection. Nobody has ever made me feel that way, and Hayden never will either. His love fills me. No, completes me. I could never relinquish him.*

So why am I upset that Hayden hasn't texted me? Why am I hiding him from Robert? Why can't I have both?

Because our open marriage allows sex, not attachment.

A knock at the door broke her train of thought. "Who could that be?" Alyssa said to the empty room as she stood to open the door. Before it opened halfway, a mass of blonde curls burst into the room, gripping Alyssa in a giggling hug.

"You're back!"

The girl looked up, and Alyssa squealed and hugged her back, thrilled to see her friend and intrigued to see her lover.

"Beth! It's so good to see you! Come in. Have a seat. How did you know we were here?"

"Sonia texted me. I came as soon as I could drop Carly at Mom's. Have time for a visit?"

"We're in for the night. Susan is picking us up in the morning."

Beth winced and hissed in a breath through her teeth. "She's not still mad, is she?"

Probably, but she hasn't said that to me. "Not overtly. She said she hasn't totally accepted our open marriage, but other than that, we're on solid ground. She's very protective of her dad."

"Where is Robert? I'd like to meet him."

"Taking a shower. We can catch up a bit before he comes out."

"How is the open marriage going?"

"Good, I think." She glanced at the bedroom door, relieved to hear the shower still running. "It has been more good than bad, and I have found a guy."

"Is he hot?"

Alyssa grinned. "Mm-hmm. Young, well liked, smart, kind, and a great lover. He's helped me when nobody else did. Everything I know of him is impressive, and everything I learn about him is good. He's too good to be true, and he's become a regular partner."

"Perfect in every way?"

"So it appears. That's what worries me."

"Falling for him?"

The giddy excitement of describing Hayden to Beth gave way to the heavy dread of having to choose between dropping one man and hurting the other. Her stomach knotted. "I didn't think so, but I've been secretive about my visits with him, and I don't stop thinking about him after Robert reclaims me. I didn't realize the problem with all that until earlier today."

"Sonia is good for that, isn't she? Be careful. Having a lot of sex with someone, even with no strings attached, eventually means something. I mean, look at us."

Alyssa felt like she had been punched in the gut. Too many people were independently giving the same warning for her to ignore it. *But I'm different. I can keep them separate.* "One of my other friends told me the same thing. You and I have a different relationship. We have sex because we care about each other, not the other way around." She smirked. "You are looking for sex tonight, right?"

Beth cackled. "Only if you can. You aren't alone. I don't want to intrude." She gave an exaggerated look around the room and leaned to kiss Alyssa, holding her face between her hands.

"Mm. You might be able to intrude with kisses like that. It's only Robert and me, so if you want the full experience, I bet we can talk him into it."

"I know how much you missed him when you were here before, even with everything you experienced. If you will share, I'd love to see what makes him so special."

"Baby, who are you talking to? Is Susan here?"

Both women turned to see a shorts-clad Robert holding a towel in the doorway.

"Babe, this is Beth. She's the one who helped me with the police, among other things to help get me through that week. Beth, this is my husband, Robert."

He smiled. "Alyssa always smiles when she speaks of you. I can't repay you for getting her out of danger. Thank you. It's nice to put a face with a name. A very pretty face, if you don't mind my saying so."

She smiled at him. "Thank you. She spoke highly of you as well. From what I can see, she undersold, if you don't mind my saying so."

"You are too kind. I'll leave you two to catch up."

"Babe, just slip on a shirt and join us. Oh, open a bottle of that chardonnay and bring some glasses."

"I don't want to intrude."

Beth beckoned with her hand. "Please. As much as I want to visit with Alyssa, I'd like to get to know you at the same time, to judge for myself if you are as great as Alyssa made you out to be."

"Robert, be polite to our guest and sit with us."

"All right. You don't have to force me to sit with two beautiful women."

"You two have to be the hottest parents at your kids' school," Beth said to Alyssa as Robert headed into the bedroom.

A couple of glasses later, Alyssa needed to address the tingling nipples and low-grade heat between her legs that had tormented her since Beth arrived. She leaned over to Robert.

"Babe, last night you shared me with our young pilot friend. Tonight, would you like me to share you with Beth? It seems like a fair trade, doesn't it?"

Robert leaned back, and his eyebrows rose. "You know we don't keep score like that, Baby. Don't feel like you have to share to keep us even. After all, we were with Sonia this afternoon. Have you even asked Beth if she would like that?"

"Oh, I'd like it," Beth interjected before Alyssa could respond. "I apologize for interrupting, but I'm in."

Alyssa laughed. "You had her when you walked out shirtless."

"Flatterer. You two don't want some girl time?"

"Don't worry, Babe. There will be plenty of girl time while you recover. Show her how you keep me so satisfied. Please? For me?" *I need to see if what Sonia said is true.*

"Baby, you know I'd be perfectly happy making love with you right here on the couch. Beth could watch. But that would be rude, wouldn't it?"

"Very rude. Oh, sorry. I interrupted again. Like I said, I'm in." Beth grinned at the couple.

Alyssa patted Robert's thigh. "Come on, Babe. You showed me off last night. Let me show you off tonight."

Robert stiffened and gritted his teeth.

Alyssa gripped both his hands. "I shouldn't have said it that way. I want Beth to experience how wonderful a lover you are, because I care for her. And I want you to experience how wonderful a lover Beth is, because I love you more than anything in the world. Will you do that? I promise you will have pleasure you don't normally get."

He pursed his lips. Alyssa worried he would turn her down for the first time since she had thought about a threesome.

"And you just want us to pleasure each other? Nothing for yourself?" Robert asked.

"Like you, Babe, I intend to share. I get both of you as well."

Robert laughed and turned to Beth. "Are you up for both of us?"

Beth yanked her silky top over her head, revealing her full breasts and hard nipples. As she stood to remove her miniskirt, she winked at Alyssa and looked Robert in the eye. "When Sonia described the afternoon, I didn't even bother with underwear. Did you?"

Robert stood and dropped his shorts, letting his hard cock pop up to point at the petite blonde. "Never do." He pulled off his shirt and eyed her up and down. "You are even more beautiful naked. Not many women can pull that off, but you do."

She blushed. "Thank you. You look amazing too. Nice cock." She closed the distance between them and circled his cock with her small hand, not quite touching her fingers and thumb. "Your wife is beautiful naked too. Alyssa, why are you still wearing clothes?"

Alyssa shook her head. "I was mesmerized by you two. Keep going. I'll join in a minute."

"Baby, Beth is right. You are more beautiful naked than clothed. Strip for us, then sit and watch while we discover each other. Touch yourself, but don't come. We will make you explode soon enough." He palmed Beth's ass and kissed her, keeping his eyes on Alyssa.

I get so wet when he takes charge. Alyssa stood and swayed in front of Beth and Robert. She pulled the hem of her shirt up to the bottoms of her breasts before dropping it and pulling the waistband of her workout shorts away from her hips and lowering one side, then the other to just above her mound. She lifted the hem of her shirt again, catching the undersides of her breasts to pull them up, then letting them jiggle back into place as she lifted it over her head. She presented her breasts in her hands, pinching the nipples. *As if they could get any harder.*

Alyssa turned away from Robert and Beth, then stared at them over her shoulder as she hooked the waistband of her shorts with her thumbs and wiggled it down. She stopped just as it reached the peak of her ass to watch Beth gasp as Robert rubbed a finger along her slit. Alyssa smirked and lowered her shorts farther. She kept her legs straight, bending at the waist to bring the shorts all the way to her feet, revealing more of her own pussy to Robert and Beth as she descended. She put her hands flat on the floor and stepped one foot, then the other out of the shorts, looking between her spread legs at the others. *I'm not waiting long to join in.*

She traced her right index finger up her right leg from the ankle to the knee in small circles, then added her middle finger to continue her circular trip up the inside of her thigh. She placed one finger on either side of her pussy and spread it, displaying her wetness before dipping both fingers inside.

She stood, turning to face Robert and Beth while dragging the wet fingertips up her abdomen to her breast, leaving a glistening trail to her nipple. Abruptly, Alyssa dropped her hand, plopped back onto the couch, and hooked one knee over the armrest. "I'm waiting." She returned her fingers to her pussy, rubbing along her blossomed lips. "But not for long."

Robert pulled Beth in for a kiss. His hands stroked up and down her back from shoulders to ass cheeks. On the second pass down, he gripped both cheeks and lifted. Beth wrapped her legs around Robert's hips, hanging on him until he laid her on the couch. His lips dipped to her neck, then lower. Robert held himself up with one hand and rubbed the other along Beth's leg from her foot to her hip as she curled it beside him.

Beth held Robert's head with both hands as he kissed down toward her breasts. She guided his face to the undersides of her breasts and the outer edges, letting him work his way toward her erect nipples. When he sucked her left nipple into his mouth, Beth gasped, and she pressed Robert's head into her chest.

Robert nibbled his way down her flat belly.

"No. Come up here. I need your cock in me." She pulled his head toward hers.

Robert nodded to Alyssa. "She wants you to have the full experience."

"Give it to me later. I need a cock in me now."

Robert made eye contact with Alyssa and grinned. "Not yet, you don't."

He kissed down Beth's stomach, working over her sides and the junctions between the abs and obliques. His fingers feathered along the side he wasn't nibbling while Beth squirmed. His mouth stopped just above her mound. Her abs fluttered, and her pussy lips bloomed open as she held her hips still, watching his head hover above her sex.

When Robert maneuvered to kiss the inside of her knee, Beth arched her back and pounded her fists into the couch cushions. "Tell him to hurry," she wailed at Alyssa. "I need to come."

Alyssa smiled at her friend and winked at Robert, who was tracing up Beth's thigh with his tongue. "Oh, you will, Beth. You wanted to know why I missed him? Now you find out."

As Robert neared the top of Beth's thighs with his lips, his hands shifted from holding her legs up to skimming them from the back of her knee to the curve of her ass. Alyssa knew he was not touching the skin but stimulating the fine hairs, delivering chills and building delicious anticipation of a firmer touch.

On the second pass down from her knees toward her pussy, his thumbs grazed her lips, and Beth shuddered. Two more identical passes with his hands and his lips hovered just above her slit, close but still not touching.

Beth wove her hands into Robert's hair. "Not again. Finish me, please." The last word retreated back into her throat as Robert placed his lips around as much of her pussy as he could to create a vacuum around her slit. His hands held her thighs wide and high, opening her to his mouth. He licked again, parting her outer lips from the inner ones and tracing the canal between them with the tip of his tongue. As he reached the top of her pussy, he pressed hard against the shaft of her clit, running over it from side to side like a speed bump.

Beth pressed her cunt into his mouth as her breathing grew ragged. She gripped Robert's hair with her hands but didn't control where he moved.

Robert slid a finger inside her pussy and rubbed against the ridges of her G-spot before adding a finger, rotating them to press down against the back wall of her vagina, and fucking her with them. He pulled her clit into his mouth, peeling the hood back by trapping it against his teeth, then stroked its underside with his tongue. As he fingered her, he extended his thumb to press against her asshole.

Beth clamped her thighs on Robert's ears. Her butt clenched and relaxed, humping her pussy against his sucking mouth and plunging fingers. Robert continued his stimulation, pleasuring her through her climax until she pushed his head back. "Please, so sensitive."

Robert withdrew his fingers, then kissed Beth's belly and nipples as he rose along her body. He raised his eyebrows at Alyssa, who had the neck of the empty wine bottle inside her pussy, rubbing fingers over her clit as she stroked it in and out of herself, stopping about halfway down the expanding shoulders.

Alyssa smirked at him, then rolled her head back and closed her eyes, stilling her hand.

Robert kissed Beth's mouth when he reached it. Her breathing hissed as he lined up his cock with her open pussy. He inched inside, pushing forward until he was about halfway in, then stopping. Breaking their kiss, Robert raised his body to look in her eyes and cup her breast with his hand. Her tongue snaked over her upper lip as she panted.

Robert pulled back until just the head remained lodged inside her, then pushed forward, reaching a couple of inches deeper than his first thrust. He stayed inside long enough to pinch her erect nipple at the base, limiting its blood flow. He held it and slid his cock backward at the same pace he had entered, again stopping when only the head parted her lips. He waited, watching her.

Beth stopped breathing, clearly waiting for Robert to fill her again. He remained still, knowing she wanted to be filled and knowing the anticipation would make it more powerful when it came.

Robert watched her inhale. He released her nipple, letting the blood return to the purple nub, and drove his cock inside the small blonde beneath him, thumping the sensitive spot beside her cervix as his balls tapped her asshole. Beth's wail continued as Robert sped through several deep thrusts, rubbing her G-spot and buffeting the top of her canal with every stroke.

Beth's spasms returned from their short break. She pulled Robert's back with her hands and his hips with her calves. Robert continued his thrusts as she flexed, not letting her rest from the storm inside her body. Her face reddened while she couldn't breathe. The neck muscles and veins rose against the skin until a small grunt and a large gasp relaxed them.

Robert felt Beth's tendons resist his body each time his hips pushed her legs apart and back. He looked down to marvel at her flat belly creased in two lines where she folded upon herself, her sweat pooling in them. Her full breasts rolled in circles in time with the pounding he gave her.

Robert looked at Alyssa's slack face and focused eyes. His gaze wandered down to where her hand pulled her nipple, then down her stomach as it rose and fell with her breath, to her hand stroking the bottle into and out of her pussy. He looked farther down the leg she had closest to Beth, past the wetness she had smeared on her thigh, all the way to the foot she pointed and relaxed in time with her masturbation.

Robert rose to press his cock against the front wall of Beth's pussy to increase her pleasure by mashing his cock against her G-spot as he moved. He forced his head against the sensitive spot beside her cervix when he bottomed out, making her grunt on every stroke. She arched her back and wailed as her body twitched, her pussy muscles squeezing Robert's cock in waves before sagging into the couch. He reached his boiling point and pulled out of the young blonde to shoot his cum across her tits and belly. When the last few drops dribbled onto her open pussy, he looked at Alyssa.

"Was that what you wanted?"

"Yes, Babe, it was. Now let me in there."

Alyssa dropped the bottle on the floor and crawled over Beth's head to lick her breasts, slurping the cum off them as Robert lowered her legs and backed away to sit in a chair. Alyssa licked and slurped her way down Beth's stomach, finally reaching her mound and licking the cum deposited there. *Time to wake up, Beth.* Alyssa sucked Beth's clit and plugged her opening with two fingers at the same time as she lowered her soaking pussy onto Beth's mouth.

With a muffled grunt, Beth curled her hips forward toward Alyssa's face and lapped at the wet slit on her mouth. She drove two fingers into Alyssa, then pulled those fingers out and worked one into Alyssa's ass while replacing the two in her pussy with fingers from the other hand.

Fuck, I'm so hot right now. She's making me come. Alyssa pressed her pussy onto Beth's face, writhing to grind the fingers inside her for maximum effect. She pulled her head back from the delicious blonde pussy below her and made eye contact with Robert. Her ass clenched around Beth's finger, and a small gush of fluid flowed down her lips.

Robert cupped Alyssa's cheek. "That was beautiful, Babe. Now finish her."

Alyssa dove back into Beth's pussy, fucking her with her fingers harder than before. Beth's legs had been quivering before Alyssa pulled up, and the brief interruption did little to delay Beth's climax. In just moments, her thighs clamped on Alyssa's head. Her fingers pressed into Alyssa as she spasmed. Alyssa stayed in place until Beth's breathing returned and her muscles gave out. Alyssa crawled off Beth to the end of the couch and sat, panting. Beth rested her feet in Alyssa's lap, and Alyssa caressed them absent-mindedly.

Beth propped herself up on her elbows and looked at Robert. "You fuck her like that all the time?"

He laughed. "No, sometimes we go slower."

She looked at Alyssa. "If I got that every day, I'd never get out of bed. Except to fuck in the kitchen. Or the garage. You need to keep him close."

Alyssa laughed. "I wouldn't trade Robert for the world. He's the best husband in and out of bed."

Beth turned to Robert. "You were magnificent. Thank you for not listening to me. That buildup made the sex so much better." She pulled her feet back and curled against Alyssa. "It's been good to see you. I should go."

Alyssa stroked Beth's sweaty hair. "You don't have to go, does she, Robert?"

"Baby, that is a question for our young mother here, not me."

"I don't want to be in the way. It's late."

Alyssa squeezed Beth's shoulders. "It is late to disturb your mom. Is Carly staying with her?"

"Yes."

"Then you stay here. Because it isn't too late for round two, if Robert is up for it."

Robert harrumphed. "You girls talk about me like I'm not even here. If I'm going to get up for round two, the two of you will have to get me up, if you know what I mean."

Alyssa pushed Beth back, stood, and offered her hand to the petite blonde. Beth smiled, took her hand, and followed her to kneel in front of Robert. Alyssa guided Robert's half-hard cock into her mouth before pulling off and holding it for Beth to do the same. "You taste good on his cock. But then, everything tastes better with cock."

Beth laughed and lowered her mouth over the head, letting some drool run down the shaft, then turned to kiss Alyssa, sucking her lips one at a time. "I taste good on your mouth, too, but I guess everything does." She pushed Robert's hardening shaft to Alyssa.

Alyssa stood and lifted Beth with her. "Babe, now that you

are getting hard, let's move this to the bed." She held Beth's waist, and the two naked beauties made their way across the floor toward the bedroom. They looked over their shoulders when they reached the door to see Robert walking behind them, his hard cock bobbing with every step.

28

MONDAY, MAY 21, HOUSTON HOTEL

Alyssa looked over her coffee cup at Beth. "Are you doing well?"

"I am. I don't have a regular man, but other than that, everything is good." Beth sipped her coffee. "Look, it isn't my business, but be careful of this guy you are seeing. I watched your face when you talked about him, even when you said you were keeping secrets about him and not reconnecting with Robert afterward. You could mess up your marriage with what is going on in your head, and after having a sample of Robert, I don't think you want to do that."

"I won't mess up my marriage. Did that once. Never again. I'll stay in control of my head and my heart."

"Please do. If he's the man he appears to be, Robert won't

tolerate being fooled twice. I don't want either of you hurt." She put her hand on Alyssa's knee and leaned in. "I want to have nights like last night for years to come." She kissed Alyssa, who kissed her back.

"You two warming up for round four? I thought when we had round three in the wee hours, you might be done."

They allowed their kiss to run its course before turning to Robert. Alyssa smiled at him. "Beth was just telling me that she would like more rounds with us for years to come. What do you think, Babe?"

Robert crossed the room to kiss Beth. "I look forward to it as well, young lady. We'll coordinate for the next time we are in town."

Beth beamed. "I can't wait." She glared at Alyssa. "I expect to see both of you the next time you are in Houston."

"Oh, you will." Alyssa looked at her watch. "We'd better get moving so we will be ready when Susan gets here." She stood and extended her hand to Beth, helping her up. They hugged and kissed, each patting the other's ass before releasing. "I'm so glad we saw you."

Robert hugged and kissed Beth as well, also cupping her ass. "I loved meeting you, and I look forward to seeing you again. Thank you again for helping Alyssa a few months ago. If you ever get up our way, please let us know."

Alyssa patted Beth's ass toward the door and shrugged her robe off her shoulders, leaving her naked. "Robert, come make me yours again, and hurry."

She stepped to him, kissed him, and untied his robe. She slid it off his shoulders and steered him to sit on the couch. She straddled his knees and turned to Beth.

"You can go or you can watch, but this time is just the two of us."

She winked at the young blonde, who waved at the couple and slipped out the door as Alyssa lowered herself onto Robert's cock with a groan. "So much better than a bottle, Babe."

❧

"You again? Every damn time I come here, I find you in my mother's room." Susan could not believe who she saw as she approached her parents' room.

Beth turned from Alyssa's door and glanced across the elevator lobby at the beautiful brunette striding toward her. "Hey, Susan. Um, look. You may not want to go in there right now. Your mom and dad are…engaged?" She smiled. "Can I buy you a cup of coffee while you wait? I would love to talk with you."

Susan felt a flush fill her cheeks and stopped walking. "Engaged? Is that a euphemism like 'getting some Mommy and Daddy time'?"

"Let's just say that most children don't want to visualize their own conception. Come on. You have at least half an hour." She linked her arm in Susan's and headed to the elevator.

Coffees and muffins in front of them, Susan and Beth sat away from most of the patrons. Beth took a bite before speaking. "You were surprised to see me this morning."

"Yeah. I was going to help my parents pack before we head back. Why, exactly, were you there?"

"Your mother and I became very close in February. You know that. I'm sorry you found out the way you did, and I'm sorry that it hurt you and your family. I'm not sorry that we are friends, and I very much enjoyed meeting your dad last night."

She gripped Susan's hand and smiled. "Your mom and dad have moved past your mom's infidelity in February, and they seem happy with how things turned out. I wouldn't have visited and they wouldn't have invited me to stay if that weren't the case."

Susan winced, conversing with her parents' lover suddenly uncomfortable. She told herself to act like an adult. "So you, ahem, engaged with them too?"

Beth giggled. "Mm, delightfully." She cut off her giggle. "Sorry if that is too much information."

Susan shook her head.

"You have great parents, you know."

"I do know. I will protect them if I need to."

"I know you will. So will I. You remember when we first met? After your mom told you about Lieutenant Frazier? You were glad that I had helped her then."

"I was. I still am."

"I promise, I care just as much for her now as I did then, and I love your dad too."

"You love him?"

"Whoa. Slang meaning only. I mean I love him like a close friend. Because of that, I will do everything I can to support them whenever they need it." She took a sip of coffee. "That's why I think you and I can be friends too."

Susan tensed her abs. This was unexpected. "You want to 'engage' with me too?"

"Oh, if you wanted to, I would. You are as beautiful as your mother, and I hear your father's iron in your voice. We could have a great time…engaging." She held up her hands. "But what I meant is that we both care for your parents. We are on the same side, and we can work together if we need to. We could even be friends on our own."

"I'm not into girls."

"I mean friends." She took a bite and washed it down. "I want to tell you something as a friend. Your mom is seeing a guy she really likes."

"Shit." Susan held her hands together to stop them from

trembling. She couldn't believe her mother would be so stupid again.

"She didn't say who he is, but your dad knows she is seeing him as part of their open marriage."

"You are bringing this up for a reason. What is it?"

"Maybe nothing. Your mom seems pretty taken with the guy. If she misplaces her priorities, she may need your help."

Susan stood up. "If she misplaces her priorities? Is she leaving my dad? After everything?"

"No, no. Not that. Nothing may happen at all." Beth held Susan's hand, gently tugging her back into her seat. "We talked frankly about it. She's infatuated but knows she hasn't seen his bad side yet. When she does, things will balance out. However, if something does happen, she may need you."

"If something happens, I'll help my dad."

"I know you will. Your mom will need help too. They will need help together. And you will need help. I'm offering to be your friend when you need me."

"Thank you. If you can be half the friend to me that you were to my mom—"

Susan glared at a portly, balding man leering at them from across the room. When he looked away, she turned back to Beth. "Do you ever get used to it? The staring? I'm asking as a friend." She smiled.

Beth smiled back. "Well, as a friend, I'm not used to it, but I work in a hotel. It happens a lot. As long as they keep their distance, I try to take it as a compliment. Yes, he was fantasizing about two young, beautiful women. He wasn't staring at her." She nodded at an elderly woman pushing a purple sweatsuit to its fashionable limits. "He was staring at us. Today, at least, we are the best-looking women in the coffee shop. Yes, it's creepy, but I try to take it as affirmation that I look good today."

"I'd just as soon not star in his fantasies."

"Me too." She winked. "But we are so hot together in his fantasies." She held up her hands again. "Only kidding."

"I know. But we would be so hot together." Susan cackled and slapped Beth's shoulder. "Seriously, thanks for telling me about my mom. And thanks for being her friend. I look forward to us being friends too."

Susan looked up. "Are you two satisfied? It's a long way home, and fooling around in my car like a couple of teenagers is prohibited."

Alyssa blatantly tugged her skirt hem lower while wiggling her hips. "I'm never satisfied, but we can keep things calm until we get home."

Robert patted his wife's ass. "Maybe."

Alyssa kissed Susan on the head. "Besides, daughter of mine, weren't you the one who blew off some steam last night?"

29

MONDAY, MAY 31, I-10 EAST

ALYSSA CLOSED HER phone after confirming Hayden still had not texted her. *Maybe he got tired of me. Maybe that saves me from myself.*

Looking forward, she watched the speedometer climb as Robert accelerated away from the congestion coming off the bridge. "Robert, don't get a ticket."

"No worries. We should be good for the next few hours to Montgomery. I'll be safe and get us there fast."

Susan turned in her seat and muted the radio. "Mom, Dad, since we're past the traffic, can we talk a bit?"

Alyssa leaned forward in the back seat to be able to hear the two in front. "Sure, Sweetie. Always. What's on your mind? Is everything okay at school?"

"Yes. School's fine. I'm fine." She made eye contact with

Alyssa. "I'm worried about you two. Your marriage arrangement. Can you tell me about it?"

Not what I expected. She's smart. She has us captive for almost a thousand miles. And she doesn't want to talk to Robert. She's grilling me. Alyssa put her hand on Susan's shoulder. "Sweetie, our marriage is good. It's strong. We love each other very much and are happy together. Why do you ask?"

"Because I don't understand why, if you love each other and are happy together, you allow each other to have sex with other people. Isn't exclusive sex one of the basics of marriage?"

Alyssa's lunch rose in her throat. She anticipated and dreaded this conversation. *Get this right. We still have more than twelve hours to drive.* "For most people, yes. It was for us for twenty-two years. We…well, I…discovered that many people don't have exclusive marriages. They view sex as separate from the making love that occurs between husband and wife. They view sex as a pleasure, an entertainment, as opposed to something to be hoarded and used as a test, if you will, of how much the couple love each other."

"But if making love is only sex, only entertainment, then what does a couple keep only between themselves? What makes them a family?"

Robert is staying quiet. He'll step in if he needs to, just like always, but he is very interested in my answers. "That's the right question, sweetie. The answer is love. Your dad and I have opened our marriage to sex with other people, but we haven't opened it to loving other people. We only love each other." *Can I swear to that?*

"But how? How can you have sex with other people without falling in love with at least some of them?"

"Susan, without getting into details, have you had sex with boys you've dated?"

"Mother."

"Sorry, sweetie, but you opened this can of worms. You wanted a serious conversation about our marriage, specifically our sex life. Your own experience may help you understand. I'm not deflecting. Humor me a minute. Have you had sex with boys you've dated?"

"Yes. Not all of them. Only a few."

Alyssa smiled. "That's good, honey. Now the next question. Have you had sex with boys you haven't dated? Or girls you haven't dated?"

"Mom, really? No girls. But yes, a couple of guys." She looked down.

Alyssa raised Susan's chin. "That's nothing to be ashamed of. We learn from experience, good lessons and bad. You are learning right now. Did you feel differently when you had sex with the boys you dated versus the one-night stands?"

"I didn't say they were one-night stands, but yes. It felt different, especially the next day."

"You didn't care for the boys you didn't date, right? If a boy you dated needed you with him, and a boy you didn't date needed you with him, whom would you choose?"

"The one I dated."

"Would you even think about it?"

"No."

"Even if the boy you didn't date was better at sex?"

"Maybe. It depends on the date." Susan laughed. "No, I understand what you are saying, and even great sex wouldn't override love."

"Now imagine that instead of a boy you dated, the person who needed you was your husband of more than twenty years, the father of your children, the man you celebrated successes with and cried about failures with, the one who will always be there when you need him with you. If you had to choose between what that man needed, and what a man who was just a sex partner needed, which would you choose?"

"My husband."

Alyssa's confidence built as they talked. She was giving the right advice to her daughter and the right answers to Robert. Maybe everything she had worried about would fade away. *If I can follow my own advice and keep things separated in my head and my heart.*

"Right. And it isn't just about what he needs. It's about what you share, what you do together, how you trust, all those things. It's about who I want to spend time with when I'm not having sex, which is most of the time, contrary to what you may think. Does that make sense?"

"Yes, but still, how can you be intimate with someone multiple times and not develop feelings for them?"

There it is again. I can't escape it. But I'm different. I'm in control. "The feelings happen, but they aren't love. I have this…um, I mean…like Beth, for example. I have feelings for her, and she has feelings for me." *That was close. I don't want to ponder feelings for Hayden right now.* "She can't replace my family. Right, Robert? You have been quiet."

"I've been listening. These are good questions, and we haven't directly addressed them ourselves."

Alyssa's stomach tightened further. She was glad her trembling foot was hidden by the seat. "Wait, you have been wondering these things? Why didn't you say something, Babe?"

"Because we haven't needed to yet. Our rules protect us from those complications. Sounds like you have been thinking though."

"Well, you're right, we haven't had enough time to have any serious partners, so feelings aren't an issue. I talked with Sonia about it, and I have thought some this weekend."

"No serious partners? Not even Hayden?"

What I didn't want to discuss. Or think about. "He's not serious." *Maybe a little serious.* "Yes, he's a repeat partner, just like Jessica is for you. But there is no feeling there. He can't replace you, not if I bed him a thousand times. A million of him can't replace you in my heart. You never have to worry about him. You will always be first for me, whatever the situation." *I'm almost certain that's true.*

"Well, Jessica isn't exactly a repeat partner for me. The two times I've been with her over three months aren't quite the same as the several times you have been with him over the past couple of weeks. Nonetheless, I appreciate what you are saying, and that you have thought through it."

She relaxed the knot in her stomach a little, knowing he still trusted her to do the right thing. "I have. And I mean it. It bothers me that you were worried." *And that I'm a little worried.*

"Baby, I wasn't worried. I noticed your frequency. I knew we'd talk when you were ready. Or when Susan was ready."

Alyssa leaned closer to her daughter. "See, sweetie? We are working through your questions right in front of you, and we both hold our marriage more important than anything else."

"I want to make sure that you both feel that way, Mom. The thought of our family coming apart is horrifying. Dad, is that what you think too?"

He nodded. "Susan, all the sex in the world isn't worth hurting the family. The family is absolutely my first priority."

Alyssa put one hand on Robert's shoulder and the other under Susan's chin. "Oh, sweetie. Our family is strong, and it is our number one priority. Numbers two and three, also. Don't you worry." *But sometimes, it is so good to go outside the family.*

30

WEDNESDAY, JUNE 2, CUPOLA HOUSE

ALYSSA STARED OVER the woods from the glass cupola. Her pride had faltered earlier, and she had texted Hayden after lunch, inviting him to meet her here. She needed to see him more than she needed to avoid bending to his silent power over her. More than her body needed him to shatter her with orgasms, her heart craved the flutter that followed his soft smiles and sweet whispers.

She turned to overlook the empty driveway below. She looked at her phone that showed no missed calls. She looked at her desperate text, lonely at the bottom of the strand.

She turned again, the woods between her and the house behind providing a sense of isolation from the outside. The conversation from the drive from Houston replayed in her mind for the hundredth time.

Susan and Robert asked about protecting the family. I said whatever I thought would allow me to keep seeing Hayden. What is wrong with you? Do you really want him more than your family?

I know I don't. I only like being with him. He makes me feel desired. Adventurous. Young. That's all.

That isn't all. Look at the facts. I have only used our open marriage with him and while sharing with Hayden or Robert since we met. I look forward to the lunches and the texts as much as the sex. Well, almost. Anyway, I'll be done with him when we finish our business with the houses.

Is business why you texted him today? Why are you disappointed that he didn't reply and didn't show up?

Because he makes me feel the way Robert used to make me feel.

Shit. That's the truth. I love Robert. I love my family. And I love the feeling I get with Hayden.

That's risky and destructive.

And exciting.

Her phone dinged. Her heart leaped to her throat as she opened the messages app.

"Everything okay?"

Robert is my protector, the one who misses me when I'm gone. He's rare and precious. Don't blow up your family for some excitement.

"Yes. Checking the house. On my way home now."

But I need excitement. If only Hayden would respond.

31

FRIDAY, JUNE 4, CUPOLA HOUSE

Robert approached the gray-haired man standing beside the stack of wood strips. "Are you Joey?"

"Yes, sir, I am. And who am I speaking with?"

"Robert Davis. I own this house."

Joey shook Robert's hand. "Your wife checks in almost every day. It's nice to meet you. What can I do for you?"

"Just checking on the progress. I'm surprised to see you here late on a Friday.

"The guys left an hour ago. I like to wrap up the week on my own."

"Sounds like you're a good boss. What is left to be done?"

"We need to run the wiring and lights, put up the ceiling, paint, and stain. Should be done by the end of next week or early the following week, depending on weather."

"Sounds great. Thank you for the good work."

"Are you really going to sell this? Alyssa, I mean, your wife, really seems to like it." Joey pointed to the cupola above them. "Every day, she stands up in that cupola, smiling and admiring the view. Hayden told me it's the reason she bought the house. She may not want to part with it."

"She says she wants to sell it, so I believe her. How do you get up there? He didn't show us when we walked through."

"The plans show a false panel in the master bathroom wall, just inside the door. I haven't used it. We only go inside when we work there."

"I see. I'll check it out. Thanks again for the great work."

Robert went inside the house and found the false panel. It opened under his push, and he climbed up. He looked out the windows, noting that half the roof was glass as well. "I see why you like it, Baby," he said to the empty room. He texted his wife. "Come straight home from work. We have a date tonight. Love you." As he descended the steps, he received a thumbs-up and a kiss emoji from Alyssa. He smiled and pulled back the covers on the bed.

Alyssa pretended not to notice that Robert wasn't taking the usual route home, but her familiarity with these roads unsettled her stomach as he drove.

Despite resisting Hayden's demand that the house be for him only, she wanted that too. Her legs weakened every time she drove near the house. Pulling into the driveway quickened her breath and made her mouth dry. The feel of the doorknob in her hand hardened her nipples, making them tingle, begging to be touched. By the time she walked up the cupola stairs, she fought to keep her hands away from her throbbing pussy.

Was that the house, or the things Hayden had done to her

there? He played her body like a master: new positions, new sensations, new risks every time they met. He did things for her, like she was special. His words melted her even when they kept their clothes on. She never considered declining his invitations. He was too glorious…addictive…necessary. She wanted everything he could make her feel, and more.

But every meeting created new secrets. She couldn't repeat Hayden's inventiveness in her own bedroom any more than she could tell Robert every time she met Hayden. He'd see her lies. He would hear the excitement in her voice if she asked him to tease her with ice, or fuck her against the window, or bend her backward over the couch to the limits of her flexibility before filling her contorted pussy. He would know she had seen Hayden again.

He would make her stop.

If I haven't stopped already. It's been a week. No texts. No Wednesday lunch. No reply at all. Maybe he's done.

But I still need him.

Robert would say she was becoming attached.

I'm not attached, just maximizing the enjoyment in our brief time together. I want more rapturous sensations to become indelible memories. Memories of the best I've ever had. Memories of him.

All those memories were tied to the cupola house. She wanted to protect them from her real life, like a book to be reread when she needed to escape. Those memories could reemerge every clit-tingling time she drove by on the street.

Her heart pulsed in her throat as they neared what had to be their destination. She turned toward Robert and talked about the two young guys who almost came to blows at the bar they had just left, rather than beg him to go straight home. Maybe she could get by with a quick tour before leaving. As nervous as she was, her body had been conditioned, and it needed sex. She prayed she could do it at home and not here.

"What are we doing here, Babe?" Alyssa asked as Robert turned into the cupola house driveway. "We've already had a great dinner, and that band at the bar was a lot of fun. I want to get you home and have the big finish to our date." She leaned across the console to nibble his cheek.

"I thought we could finish here. After all, we have made love in every other house we ever owned."

"True, though we lived in those." *I told him this might happen. It will be okay if we are not in the cupola.* She smiled at him. "But I'm game if you are. Let's go."

She waited for Robert to come to her door before getting out. *Dark, tipsy, gravel, and heels don't mix well.* She snuggled into his arm with both hands as he turned on the flashlight on his phone. "It's chilly."

"It is supposed to get cold tonight, and you just have that thin blouse. Come here."

He wrapped his arm around her waist, steadying her as she stumbled through the gravel.

She wasn't here to meet Hayden, but her body responded. Her nipples hardened, and her pussy ached to be filled.

Inside, Robert steered her into the kitchen, where he opened a bottle of wine and picked up two glasses. He kissed Alyssa. "Let's go upstairs."

Robert set down the wine and lit some candles when they entered the bedroom.

Her chest relaxed, secure that Robert had not discovered the secret stairwell. *Okay. We're staying in here. He did it up right. It's no wonder I love him so much.* The tightness in her chest relaxed, replaced by the familiar warmth his romantic gestures always kindled. *I'll love this memory too.*

"Robert, you prepared this. When?"

"This afternoon. Amazing what's included when you buy something fully furnished. Sit on the bed a minute while I finish."

She sat on the bed. He went to the bathroom and closed the door. Candlelight flickered beneath it. Her pussy tingled as she thought of showering together by candlelight. Maybe Robert would press her body against the glass and fuck her from behind. *Please do it with the windows clear. Even if nobody's outside, take the chance to make me come for the world to see.*

She smiled and wrapped her arms behind Robert's head as he returned to her from across the room. "Come here, you beautiful man. Show me how much you love me."

"Oh, I'll show you, you beautiful woman."

His fingers scratched along her scalp as they kissed, sending chills down her spine. With his other hand, he cupped her ass and pulled her hips against his, intensifying her own grinding.

Alyssa ran her hands along Robert's shoulders and back. She compressed her breasts against his hard chest, the pressure sparking in her nipples. *God, he's still so strong.*

She ground her belly against him, letting the hardness in his pants rub across her own hardening clit. *I've been waiting for this since dinner.* She ran her hands between them, under the opening of his jacket, and pushed it open and off his shoulders.

Robert released his grip on her head and body. As the jacket fell, he kissed her neck while both hands circled along the waistband of her skirt until they met at the clasp in the back. Alyssa shuddered as the cool air chilled her skin, only to be warmed by Robert's hands sliding inside it and squeezing.

Seconds later, the skirt puddled around her feet, Alyssa stepped out of her heels while she tugged Robert's tie off his neck. She opened the buttons of his shirt with skill and patience mastered over years of undressing each other for sex. When she reached his belt, she unbuckled it and opened his pants, working the loose slacks over his ass, dropping them to pile atop his shoes.

Alyssa's pussy throbbed when his hands moved from her hips to the hem of her blouse. She raised her arms to let him lift the blouse off, leaving her in only the small, lacy bra and panties she had worn to work. She knew her white tan lines created a pale underline to the gauzy beige material, and she felt her hard nipples stretching the fabric.

"Those look so sexy on you. No, you look so sexy. Those show you off. Take them off."

Foreplay is almost over. The hint of a smile teased his lips as she dropped her bra and panties.

"I love when you wear this shirt. It really shows off your chest. But it looks better off." Alyssa unbuttoned the bottom button, then took Robert's cock in her mouth as she knelt to remove his shoes and socks.

With gentle fingers under her jaw, he urged her to stand. "Come with me."

He led her by the hand into the bathroom. Their reflection in the windows let her know he had unfrosted them. Anyone outside would be able to see in. Her pussy throbbed as she gazed at all the glass.

The rectangle of light beside her reflection made her turn. The cupola stairwell was open and lit with candles. Robert smiled at her and guided her toward it.

"Do you know what this is, Baby?"

"I've never seen this." Her stomach tightened like a belt cinched two notches too far. *Why did you lie, Alyssa? There is no reason to.* She knew. *Because Hayden wants you to.*

"Come see." Robert led her up the stairwell. At the top, a single candle flickered atop the half wall beside the stairs. He guided her in front of him.

"What a view. It's so dark outside." Alyssa looked around at the windows, toward the houses she knew were in the distance. *I haven't seen it in the dark before.*

Robert wrapped his arms around Alyssa's stomach. "Look straight ahead."

Alyssa gasped, then leaned back against Robert as she stared at their faint reflection. In the candlelight, dark hair framed her blurry face. Her body showed clearer, with the shadow of her left side obscuring her right. The shadows on Robert's arms defined his muscles like black paint. His head reached above hers, and his shoulders framed her more petite shape, with his right side also in shadow. Between the strength in his arms around her and the vision of his size enveloping her, she relaxed, feeling safe and loved. "I wish I had a picture. We look beautiful like this."

"We do." He kissed her ear and squeezed her waist.

Neither one moved or spoke while they watched the shadows flicker across their bodies.

His cock stirred against the cleft of her ass.

"Mm. I like what you are thinking."

"How do you know what I'm thinking?"

"If your dick is getting hard for any reason other than me right now, we need to talk."

Robert brushed his fingers across her hard nipple. "The same goes for you, then."

She turned to face him. "Make love to me, Robert. Right here, in this beautiful place. I want to feel our love together."

Robert sat on the chaise beside them. She straddled him, taking all of him inside her slick pussy. She wrapped both arms around his neck; he wrapped his around her waist. Not moving, they kissed. The touch of his skin on her chest, her lips, the insides of her thighs, the same touch she had felt thousands of times, somehow felt warmer, softer, closer. She fell into her own thoughts, meditating on the sensual pleasure of their touch.

Robert kept one arm across her back, but the other slid up to her shoulder and down to her ass, then back again. Alyssa ran one hand through his hair and down his back, hoping the love from her caresses nourished the same warm glow in his chest as his caresses did in hers.

Robert's cock twitched inside her, breaking her reverie. She ground her hips in small circles, just enough to let his cock stretch her walls and her juices coat his shaft. She wanted to savor this one.

A little more. She rose an inch or two, then lowered, beginning a slow ride that massaged his cock against the best parts of her pussy like waves on a calm sea.

The hair on his chest brushed her nipples as she moved. *Just rough enough.* They stopped kissing as Alyssa rose and fell with longer, but still leisurely, moves.

His hands on her ass moved with her, Robert clearly letting her set the pace even as he kept her body pressed against his. When Alyssa rose until his cock barely spread her lips, Robert feathered his hand from her back to her breast and nudged her to stay upright as he lay back on the chaise.

"Ride me, Baby. Show me your body."

"Enjoy the show, Babe." With both hands on top of her head, she rode his cock. She shifted from a fast bounce when she felt fresh to a slow grind when her thighs burned. She flipped her hair with her hands, sometimes letting it fall across her face, sometimes holding it back to make eye contact with Robert. Even as she tired, she moved until Robert gripped her hips and held her still.

"Look up, Baby."

Alyssa turned her head. "The stars. The roof is glass too."

"Yes, Baby. You always wanted to make love under the stars. Turn around and lean back. We can watch them together a while."

Without pulling off his cock, Alyssa spun around and leaned back, reaching her hands backward to Robert's shoulders. "This is perfect," she whispered.

Alyssa gazed at the stars, oblivious to everything else, until Robert started easing in and out of her. His hands floated to her hips, holding her still as he accelerated his thrusts. Returned to the moment, Alyssa resumed moving her hips. Still slow, she raked the front wall of her pussy across the underside of his cock, keeping pressure on her G-spot and building the orgasm to come, even though he couldn't reach as deep inside her. They moved together, keeping the pace slow. Robert thrust in and out while she ground in circles.

Alyssa stared at her own reflection, moving, grinding, her tan lines accentuating the movement against the dark sky. Under Alyssa and shaded, Robert's reflection in the ceiling glass was only a shadow. Where they joined was the only exception, well lit and exposed by her spread legs, his cock hard and wide and dark. *Anyone could be beneath me. Robert, Hayden, anyone. This is so sexy to watch. And I get to see the stars.*

Alyssa jumped at a streak in the sky behind her reflection. "Did you see that? The shooting star?"

"No. I was watching your gorgeous back as you rode me. I'm sure I got the better view."

"Thank you, Babe. Are you getting close?"

"I feel good, though at this pace, we could go all night. You?"

"I was just enjoying it, but the shooting star has revved me up. A little harder?"

Robert sped up. Alyssa stared at the ceiling and ground her hips in time with his thrusts. Her hands slipped on his shoulders, now sweaty in the warm room. Her legs ached from stretching her toes for purchase on the floor around his flexing thighs. Alyssa lurched forward, driving Robert's cock deep to stretch her pulsing channel. She pulled one nipple and strummed her clit while grinding on Robert, reveling as his cock pressed around her cervix. With a grunt, he came, splashing her insides and setting off her release.

When her spasms stopped, Alyssa lay beside her husband. "I love you. Thank you for making love to me under the stars. It was as wonderful as I'd imagined. This was a perfect date."

"Yes it was. I'm glad we came up here."

"Me too. What a beautiful place to make love. Our private place." *Why did I say that? I've had Hayden here too.*

"Yes. Our private place. It is our house, after all."

"It is." Alyssa laid her head on Robert's chest and twirled her fingers in his chest hair until they went down to bed.

32

SATURDAY, JUNE 5, CUPOLA HOUSE

ROBERT TOOK HIS cup of coffee up to the cupola after pausing to look at Alyssa still sleeping in bed. He settled into the chaise for the sunrise. He sipped his coffee and watched the eastern sky lighten. He looked up at the glass ceiling and paused, watching the condensation inside the window glisten as the sun reached those windows first. As the sun rose, the sparkles spread down the windows. As the sun rose over the horizon, the rays hit Robert's eyes, and he turned to the side.

Robert hung his head. The window to the right of the sun revealed the image of a woman in the condensation, her hands raised, the side of her face, shoulders, and chest pressed against it. On each breast, there were thin rings around the nipples, just like its twin on a window in Houston.

Alyssa woke to the sun warming her face. With her having only been here in the afternoons, the unfamiliar shadows bewildered her. She sat up and reached toward Robert's side of the bed. Feeling the empty bed, she turned and saw the sunlit bathroom beyond. Knowing now where she was, she settled back into the bed, rolling toward Robert's side, figuring he was probably on his second cup of coffee.

Last night had been marvelous. In the cupola and again in the bed, she and Robert had connected. Physically, they hadn't had a better session in weeks. Emotionally, she had put aside the guilt of lying to him—*not lying, sparing his feelings*—in lieu of simply loving him for the first time in a month.

She had buried thoughts of Hayden under her love for Robert when they came to bed. She'd focused on every point where their bodies touched, cherishing the tiny nuances she usually took for granted. She'd watched his eyes. She'd never known he watched her face when he touched her body and her body when she reacted to his efforts. When she came, their eyes had locked. When she'd pulled his body onto hers, wanting to luxuriate under his bulk afterward, the hint of a self-assured smile curled his mouth. *That's a memory of this place worth keeping.*

Making love under the stars had been even better. Watching their ghostly reflection while the entire universe watched them had made her orgasm bigger than any she had shared with Robert in weeks. *Was that because I couldn't see his face? Was it because I could imagine Hayden beneath me? Surely not.*

But she imagined his face clearly in the reflection, seeing his perfect cock fill her in the candlelight, spreading her wider and deeper than Robert had done. She imagined her hands slipping off his sweaty shoulders, only for him to catch her and push her harder onto him, not letting her rest as he thrilled her body.

Her thoughts scrambled from one to the next: Robert in the

bed, Hayden against the window, Robert under the stars, Hayden against the pole, Hayden on the kitchen floor, Hayden in the mirror, Hayden on the couch, Hayden over the deck railing, Hayden, Hayden, Hayden.

Robert walking away, shaking his head.

Alyssa froze. She was imagining her lover when her husband was here in the house. *Hayden's house. It will always be Hayden's house in my mind, even now that I've been with Robert here too.*

As if she summoned him, Robert stepped from the bathroom toward the bed.

"Good you're awake. Come up to the cupola. There is something you must see."

❧

Alyssa stepped into the cupola ahead of Robert, dazzled by the sparkling condensation on the windows. "It's a house of diamonds. It's beautiful."

"It is. I guess the humid air inside and the chill last night created condensation. The sun is catching the droplets perfectly. Look to your left."

Alyssa never knew her stomach could feel completely empty and knotted tight at the same time until this instant. She saw her image framed by tiny prisms. She remembered Hayden driving her against that window the first time she'd seen it. *Shit. Cover this.* She forced a chuckle. "It looks like the owners used this room happily before getting divorced."

"That was my first thought, but recent events suggest another explanation."

"Really? What's that, Babe?"

"I saw your imprint in Houston. Sonia was quite specific that the rings around the nipples were impossible to replicate. Do you see the rings on this one?"

That damn window. So sexy at the time, both places. I didn't realize my nipples were like fingerprints. "Babe, maybe Sonia couldn't get her nipples that hard, but plenty of women probably can."

Robert nodded. "I considered that. Then I thought that given how clean the rest of the house is, they probably cleaned these windows before closing. So that imprint must be recent."

"Do you think someone broke in?"

"When I met Joey yesterday, he said a woman comes up here every afternoon."

The weight of his coming accusation gripped her heart, but she completed the dance they had begun. "Who?"

Robert sighed and shook his head. "The same woman who told me last night she had never seen this. What exactly are you lying to me about, Alyssa, and why?"

Alyssa slumped against the window and locked her knees to remain standing when the strength left her legs. Her chest ached now that she knew the damage she had inflicted on her marriage. *Everybody warned me.*

"Yes, that's me. When Hayden and I first viewed this house, we had sex. He pushed me against the window and fucked me while saying the neighbors could see. I knew they couldn't, but the thought ramped up the excitement. That's the only thing I haven't told you." *Another lie, but Hayden hasn't contacted me in days. We may be done anyway.*

"Why didn't you tell me, and why didn't you show me the cupola when we toured the house?"

"I don't know why I didn't tell you that day. I told you everything else. Maybe it just slipped my mind. When we toured the house, I remembered you hadn't seen it, and I didn't want to take you up there with Hayden. That way, when I did eventually tell you, you wouldn't feel like he was mocking you." *Not quite true, but I will protect his feelings. More lying.*

"What else have you not told me?"

Most of the times I've seen him. That everything about him impresses me. That he makes me feel wanted and special. She sighed. *That I miss him.*

"I have met him here. I come to this room every day. I love looking over the woods to the neighbors far away." An ache filled her chest as she realized she had hidden more than her time with Hayden from Robert. "I'm sorry, Robert. I should have shared this with you. We could have enjoyed it together. I messed up."

"I understand. This place has memories only with him. I apologize for tainting your memories last night. It won't happen again."

"Babe, wait. That's not what I meant. Last night was one of the most beautiful memories I have with you."

"Just in the wrong place. I didn't know I was intruding."

"Robert—"

"Come on. Let's go. This place makes you lie to me, and I won't stay any longer. Let's go home and wash away the stench of this place before we talk further."

He lumbered down the stairs.

33

SATURDAY, JUNE 5, HOME

ALYSSA TUCKED HER bare feet inside the long fuzzy robe when she sat on the couch with Robert. Sunlight streamed through the big windows, making the room warm, but her feet had chilled from walking on the hardwood. Somewhere inside she probably knew that folding her feet into the seat and covering them created a psychological barrier, a layer of protection she needed for this conversation, but the move was unconscious, like the slight calm that settled her belly when she did it. Hiding her skin protected her ego…and her heart.

Robert laid his phone on the end table beside him and turned to Alyssa. "You could have dried your hair. I'm not going anywhere."

"No. I waited too long to talk with you. I don't want to delay any longer."

"Good enough. Go ahead."

"I haven't been honest with you."

"I know."

Her breath caught, and her stomach knotted. She had been so careful. *Shit.* "What do you know?"

"Nope. I won't make this easy for you. Talk."

She inhaled and sighed, then her breath hitched as she inhaled again. Settling her stomach became impossible, and it roiled inside her. She focused on breathing, fighting the sob that lurked in her throat, threatening her ability to speak.

"Start at the beginning, when you first broke our agreement."

Alyssa wrapped her arms over her stomach, sighed, and began to talk. Starting with the first day she'd viewed houses with Hayden, she laid out every secret meeting with Hayden. She admitted hiding the cupola from Robert. Tears stopped her twice.

Robert remained still except to hand her a box of tissues from the end table beside him.

Across half an hour, her body tingled when reliving the exciting parts, and her chest became an empty cavern when she admitted putting their marriage behind meeting Hayden. She described the thrill of meeting secretly, the wonder of inventive sex, and the guilt of lying about it. The roller coaster of emotions left her sweaty under her robe, but she kept it tight, hiding from Robert's scorn behind its terry-cloth barrier. She closed her eyes and sighed, clutching her stomach in fear of his response.

"Why didn't you tell me all this when it was happening? Why break our agreement?"

She'd known he would cut to the heart of the matter, but she struggled to answer. She wanted to be honest, but she wasn't sure herself. There was no answer that wouldn't hurt him, nor was there one that wouldn't hurt her.

"I don't know."

Robert stared without moving.

"The first time was so spontaneous. I didn't intend to withhold anything, then I was ashamed that I had, so I moved on. After that, you became annoyed with how often I saw him. When I told you about it, it hurt you. I didn't want to hurt you, so I didn't tell you all the time."

"You knew that meeting him upset me, and your solution was to hide it?"

The question hit her like a punch. When he phrased it that way, the hurt she wanted to avoid couldn't be hidden. Her behavior was what hurt, not his knowledge of it.

"It was stupid. I see that now. I thought it would pass, and we would be okay. At least, that's what I told myself."

"What else?"

"That's all of it. I am sorry I didn't tell you before, but I've told you everything I remember."

"That isn't what I mean. Who do you text when you smile and play with your hair? That used to be me, but it isn't now."

The blood must have physically stretched her neck as it emptied from her head. Vertigo rocked her, and she gripped the back of the couch to prevent falling forward. She hadn't considered how her feelings might change how she treated everyone, including Robert. Had Hayden infiltrated her mind so deeply that he affected how she texted? Surely not. This had to be a test. After a few deep breaths, the dizziness passed, and she looked at him.

"I don't know what you are talking about."

"No, you probably don't. Your face doesn't hide much, especially when you use your phone. It used to be cute. I'd text you when I could see you without you knowing. It was usually nothing, just to let you know I was thinking about you. I loved watching you smile and twirl your hair with your right hand when you read those texts. I knew that hearing from me made you happy."

"I do that?"

"Yes. I still see you when we are watching TV, or at one of Clay's events, or when you are getting ready for bed. That text dings, you smile, open it, and twirl your hair while you read it. But those aren't my texts. Are those Hayden's texts? Or is it someone else?"

Alyssa shook her head. "I don't know. I didn't know I did that until you just mentioned it."

"Come on. After all the chances I've given you, you're finally being honest. Don't blow it."

Alyssa looked down. "Probably. I like when he texts. I feel desired."

"That's more than liking it. Do you have feelings for him? Do you love him?"

Her head jerked up. *No. He can't think that. But he does, and he isn't wrong.*

The empty cavern in her chest enveloped her entire body. Her thoughts stopped. Her emotions stopped. This conversation should have been a confession followed by a reconciliation. It had become a fork in the road of their marriage, and she didn't know what to say.

She inhaled to speak but let her mouth open silently. On her second try, she said, "No. I only love you."

Robert's head flushed red. "That's what I thought." He stood. "Alyssa, I warned you about too many times with this guy. Jessica warned you. Sonia warned you. Now you have put us in a spot."

"How do you know all that?"

"You think they are only your friends?"

"Those bitches."

He held up his hand. "Don't say any more. I'm going to get groceries for supper. You stay here on the couch and figure out what you want. We can talk more when I return." He left.

Alyssa pulled her knees up and sobbed into them.

❧

Alyssa wiped her eyes on her cuff. Her vision cleared as the robe soaked up the tears.

She loved this room. The big windows made the room bright enough to see every corner without turning on the lights. When Alyssa needed a boost, she came here. The rest of the house was decorated with prints and art; this was all family. The walls hung thick with framed photos. Every horizontal surface held mementos. This bright, airy room encapsulated most of her life.

"You're a smart one, Robert, still speaking to me from far away." She picked up their wedding photo from the table beside her. *We were so young, so happy.* She scanned the room. Returning the photo to the table, she stood to tour the walls.

God, they were so little, but I remember like it was yesterday.

Yes. Foot surgery. Four weeks in bed. Robert handled everything. Took care of the kids. Meals in bed. Carried me to the bathroom. Bathed me. Nursed me through physical therapy. Held me when I cried from the pain.

That one year with matching Christmas pajamas. Glad Susan grew out of that phase.

She stopped at the wall across from the bay window, the brightest in the room.

Anniversaries. A picture from all twenty-two trips. Even pregnant in a bikini. Both times. "What a whale I was." She put her hand to her lips. *Robert has those two in his home office. Says they show me more beautifully than any of the others. Never understood that.*

Ugh. Camping last year. Damn COVID lockdowns. Broadway the year before. That was fun.

She leaned over the framed school photos of Susan and Clay

to peer at the last two photos. *Why do I look happier in front of that musty tent than I do in New York?*

Alyssa heard the door to the garage shut followed by footsteps and giggling. Alyssa turned, knocking the picture of Susan to the floor.

"Mom? Dad?"

"In here, Clay." Alyssa turned toward the door to her right, stepping on one of the shards of glass. "Ah! Damn it!" Her foot jerked back reflexively, keeping the cut ball of her foot up, but landing the heel on yet another shard. "Ow!" She jerked it up and balanced herself with a hand on the table.

Clay rushed in and scooped her up in his arms. "Let's get you out of this glass."

Alyssa wrapped her arms around his neck. Sawyer stood watching from the doorway. Clay spoke to her as they edged past.

"This may take a while. Can I catch up with you later?"

"Sure. But you owe me."

He smiled at her. "I do. I'll text you."

Another way I've hurt my family with this. She buried her face in his shoulder to sob.

Clay sat Alyssa on her bathroom counter. She clung to him when he tried to pull back, and he leaned in to hold the hug.

Clay patted her back and kissed the top of her head. "Let's see that foot." He pulled the first aid kit from under the sink and crouched to examine her. He tweezed the two pieces of glass from her foot. The brief sting coursed up through her ankle, but she remained still.

"Ouch. Are they deep?"

Clay used a towel to blot the blood. "Not too bad." He folded four large gauze pads.

"Four pads? You said not too bad."

"Not bad at all. The extra cushion will let you walk more

comfortably after the bleeding stops. My mom taught me that extra softness make it better."

Alyssa choked back a sob. "Sounds like you had a pretty good mom."

"The best." He taped the bandages in place. "There." He put away the kit and scooped her up again. "You want to go back to the family room?"

"Yes, please. I have a mess to clean up."

Back on the couch, Alyssa watched Clay sweep up the shattered picture frame. She fought the sadness that quivered her chin and threatened to make her cry again. "I ruined it."

Clay put down the broom and sat beside her. "No, Mom. You broke a fragile glass frame. The important part inside is fine."

A warm calm settled in the pit of her stomach for the first time in an hour. "The important part is fine. It hurt though."

"You will heal in no time."

She patted his knee. "Thanks to you. You are a great son."

"I'm taking care of the important stuff the way you and Dad taught me."

"Yes, you are."

"I'm going to buy a new frame. Everything will be good as new in no time. Do you need anything?"

"Could you get my phone from my nightstand, please?"

He's becoming quite a young man, Alyssa. He did what Robert would have done. He turned down his horny girlfriend because you needed his help. Could you have done that?

I haven't.

Do you think Clay believes you were crying over a picture frame? Or did he help you because he understood there was a deeper issue?

He's so perceptive. He knows what to do every time.

Someone to emulate. Can you do what he would? Can you give up the best sex you've ever had? Can you stop loving Hayden?

She thought. Hayden was like a drug. Every time he contacted her, she needed the fix, the high. Seeing him less may not help. Stopping cold turkey might be her only hope.

I must. I can't resist him. But my family is more important.

Will you restore your monogamous marriage?

She pondered the thrill of slipping away with other men over the last few months, and the delight when she returned to Robert. She wanted the excitement of behaving what society would call badly. And she wanted the love and stability of returning to Robert, especially when he reclaimed her so hard she was sore the next day. He liked that too. Keeping their marriage open should work if she obeyed the rules.

I'll just get rid of the danger, not the excitement. There are other men than Hayden. I'll get my thrills there.

Will that be enough? Will I miss the connection?

We'll see.

Alyssa opened her phone to text. "Getting involved with you was a mistake. I won't see you anymore. Don't call. Don't text. We are over." She hit send and powered it off.

"I'm still in here, Babe."

"I know."

Alyssa watched an old couple walk two dogs in front of their house while listening to Robert put away the groceries. She was ready to talk. The last hour, she had waited in this room, phone off, thinking. She knew what she had to do, but every second she waited to communicate it to Robert increased the chance she would change her mind and equivocate his concern away. She needed to tell him before she lost her nerve.

Just put away the ice cream and come to me.

Robert handed her a glass of water and sat at the other end of the couch. "You okay?"

She nodded.

"Clay said you hurt yourself."

"It was an accident. I broke Susan's picture frame and stepped on the glass."

"He said you were more upset than hurt."

"He's perceptive. And a sweetheart."

"He gets that from you."

Alyssa shook her head and looked at the floor. "You mean he took it from me. I haven't been much of a sweetheart lately."

"Not with me, in any event. What have you decided to do about it?"

Alyssa turned on her phone, dings echoing in the room as it received multiple texts. The icons at the bottom showed that she had missed six texts and four calls.

"Well?"

She opened the texts. Robert was at the top. ("Do you need anything?") She tapped her strand with Hayden right below and handed the phone to Robert. "You may have to scroll up. Some texts came in. Calls too. I wrote what you wanted me to, I think."

"No texts on this strand. Yours is the last message. Is this what you want, or what you think I want?"

"Let me see." She took the phone back from Robert. Even after the last week, silence was not the reaction she expected from Hayden. A dull ache settled in her chest.

She opened the strand from Robert and scrolled up, reading his messages:

"Clay said you are hurt. What happened?"

"Are you okay?"

"Why aren't you answering?"

"I'm not angry right now, just concerned. Are you okay?"

"Please don't hurt yourself."

"Leaving the store now. Do you need anything?"

He had been worried, and she had not responded. She had hurt him again, just like Hayden had hurt her by not responding. Hurting Robert was a thousand times worse. The ache in her chest intensified. *Blew that part too.*

She looked at Robert, then opened the phone app. Two calls and two voice mails from Robert. She played the first one on speaker. "Baby, Clay called and said that you cut yourself. He said it looked like an accident but you were more upset than you should have been. Look, if you broke something in that room, even by accident, I'm worried about you. Please call me and let me know that you are okay. Please don't hurt yourself. Please call."

Alyssa looked at Robert but couldn't speak. She looked away while her guilt grew.

Robert broke the silence. "The next one is more of the same."

After a couple of long blinks to fight back tears, she faced him. "You were worried?"

"Of course."

"Even after what I've done?"

"What you have done would be irrelevant if I didn't love you. I'm angry and sad, but I still worry when I hear you are hurt. Especially when you don't answer your phone."

Alyssa stared at her phone. "I turned it off so I wouldn't hear from Hayden."

"It worked. You didn't."

The lingering disappointment that Hayden hadn't responded burst into flame with the gasoline Robert tossed on it so callously. Fire rose in her throat, and she leaned forward, her angry voice rising in her chest but not yet past her throat.

He held up his hand in apology. "Sorry. I didn't intend for that to sound so mean."

He looked in her eyes, clearly waiting for them to indicate she was ready to continue. She stared back, the hurt that had her ready to yell at her husband subsiding while her brain reminded her that she had almost yelled at Robert because Hayden hadn't texted her. She closed her eyes and took a deep breath. *Easy, Alyssa. He's trying to fix this.* She nodded for him to continue.

"Tell me, did you write what you wanted, or what you think I wanted?"

The fire erupted up her throat again, this time escaping her lips. "Does it matter?"

Robert's head flushed red.

It was her turn to raise her hand in apology. She held her breath and counted to three. "I didn't mean that so harshly. I mean, like when we are correcting the kids, we want the right behavior first, and we can work on the motivations afterward. Isn't that what you are doing here?"

"It isn't what I'm doing. I said when I left that you should decide what you want. You. Not me. We would talk when I got back. I'm back. So, again, what do you want, Alyssa?"

I wish I knew for sure. She nodded.

"You know how I broke the picture? I had leaned close to our anniversary trip wall. I wondered why I looked happier in the picture from last year's muddy, hot, buggy camping trip than in the picture from New York the year before."

She waited, but he sat impassive. She shook her head.

"I figured it out as Clay and Sawyer stumbled in. New York was the perfect vacation. Beautiful weather, nice dinners, Broadway plays, even a trendy dance club. We did so many fun things. Camping last year was the opposite. Hot and humid, rain at night meant cold dinners and muddy hikes, two days without showers. It was as uncomfortable as any anniversary trip we ever took, even that first one when we suspected somebody in the attic of that fleabag motel was videotaping us."

She sipped her water, relieved that the corners of Robert's mouth hinted at a smile from the memory.

"I was not happy about that trip, but I was happy when we took that picture. We had ridden out a storm. We had made love, then we had talked and caressed while the storm raged outside the tent. We focused on each other. No activities or plans interrupted that. We focused on us for two days, and I was so happy."

"And?"

"And I turned when I heard Sawyer and Clay come in. My robe caught Susan's picture and knocked it off the table. I turned to look into the great room and stepped on the glass."

"I'm glad it wasn't intentional."

"That's what upset me though. Clay rushed in to lift me out of the glass, and I realized that I shattered everything. That, too, was unintentional, but I still broke everything. Our family. Our trust. Our love. All over feelings I shouldn't have and don't want. After Clay fixed my foot, I sent the text."

She crawled across the couch to Robert. She leaned close to his face and locked her eyes on his. "I'm sorry I hurt you. I'm sorry I lied to you. I'll never see him again. Can you forgive me?"

"I can, if that is what you want. You still haven't said what you want."

She felt for his hand and gripped it in both of hers. "I want us to stay married."

"What exactly does that mean to you?"

"It means I'll never see Hayden again."

Robert opened his mouth, shut it, then spoke. "Does that mean you still want an open marriage?"

She held his gaze so he would understand her sincerity. *We can do this. We will get it right this time.* "Yes."

"You know that's how this problem started."

"Yes."

He shook his head and sighed. "So that's it? You won't see Hayden again, but you want to keep playing with others, opening us up to the next Hayden?"

"Yes and no. Yes, I will never see Hayden again. Yes, I still want the excitement of playing with others. No, I refuse to open us up to the next Hayden."

"How will you do that?"

He didn't say no. She controlled the excitement fluttering in her belly. This was working out. "I don't know, but I have a temporary solution. Can we stay open but pause actually being open until we figure out how to be safe?"

"The best way to be safe is to return to a monogamous marriage. We agreed that is what we would do if this didn't work out."

"I know. And I know it's me who keeps screwing it up. And I know only I want this." She smiled at him. "Sonia is quite perceptive. Plus, I watch you when we play with other people."

"I want you to be happy."

"I know. You deserve to be happy too. I think you have been happy when you were between the legs of"—she counted on her fingers—"Jessica, Summer, Keegan, Sonia, and Beth. Is there anyone I'm forgetting?"

He nodded. "Carol and Dawn. Except the first time with Summer, all those were with you, which is my favorite way to experience them. I enjoyed those women, but I have no desire to sleep with them again if it harms our marriage."

He gripped her hand this time. "I like exciting sex just as much as you do. I think about the consequences ahead of time.

You deal with them when they arrive. That's why it hurts when you don't keep our agreement. Our rules protect us from those consequences."

"I know."

"One of those rules is no emotional attachments. You won't see Hayden. Fine. What about your feelings for him?"

Alyssa limped to the wall of anniversary photos. She ran her finger along a couple before replying.

"That's a hard question, Robert. I don't want these feelings. I've buried them, fought them as best I can, but they grow inside me and fester in our marriage." She turned and looked him in the eyes as best she could through her tears.

"I'm forced to admit to myself and to you that I care for him. Not like I love you, but not some schoolgirl crush either. I don't know how to make it go away, but if I never see him or talk to him again, maybe those feelings fade."

She turned back to the wall, scanning the photos hung since the children were born. They had decided back then to focus on their marriage to keep it strong. Even the children needed to be second sometimes. She had forgotten that recently, but she remembered it now. Hayden had to go.

"One thing I know. Whether my feelings for him fade or not, I love you. There is nothing I want more than to keep putting pictures on this wall. Pictures of us living a happy life together."

"That's a better answer than 'I don't care about him.' Your answer still sucks though."

"Like you said, it's honest. Sometimes the truth sucks."

"If you had been honest earlier, the truth wouldn't suck so much now."

Alyssa choked back a sob.

Robert continued. "You want time away from him to let your feelings die, fine. Here's what I will agree to. You have zero interaction with him. If he texts, or calls, or stops to help you with a flat tire, you don't respond. You walk away. And you let me know immediately."

She nodded but didn't turn. "What about the house?"

"Oh, the deal on the reduced commission? I stopped caring about that deal when he tried to steal my wife. I'll let Rosalyn know we need someone else. If she asks why, I'll tell her. That commission deal will disappear like beer at a frat party."

"Okay."

"Alyssa, I mean it. This is our last chance. You have feelings for another man, which I cannot abide. Our marriage teeters on a razor's edge. If you make a mistake, in action or communication, it's over."

"I understand."

She heard Robert's footsteps as he walked toward the door.

"Robert?"

"Uh-huh."

"Why are these two pictures of me pregnant the only ones in your office?"

"I've told you. You are more beautiful in those than all the others."

"How? I'm huge."

"Exactly. You are objectively a beautiful woman. You were when we met, and you still are today. But when you were pregnant, you let babies cause you pain and wreak havoc on your body to grow our family, literally growing our love. There are no pictures in the world that show your inner beauty better than those two. That's why they hang alone in my office. None of the others measure up."

Alyssa smiled. "I never thought of that. Which picture of you shows the same thing, for my nightstand?"

He picked up her phone and took a selfie, then handed it back. "This one."

⁕

Alyssa watched Robert reading in a chair as she finished cleaning up after supper. They had skipped doing dishes together tonight, each preferring to be alone with their thoughts. She missed him beside her but said nothing, knowing the uncomfortable silence was part of her price to pay.

She knew the night would only get worse, and she knew he would let it. He wasn't vindictive, but he would view it as fair to wait for her to make a peace offering. *It's on me to make this better.*

She looked out the window. It was dark outside. *It's time to start healing.*

She stepped beside his chair and placed her hand on his arm, ready to ask her question and afraid he would decline. "It's dark outside, so the mosquitos should be in. Want to take a walk?"

He lowered his book to his lap and looked up away from her, letting her know he was considering it.

Come on. Please say yes. I want to hold your hand and walk, even in silence. Please show me I haven't ruined everything beyond repair.

"Okay. It should be a pretty night. Let's walk."

For the first time today, her chest lightened as she pulled him from his chair.

They had passed several houses in silence before she took his hand. Their fingers fit together as if they hadn't considered ending their marriage today. His firm grip had never comforted her in their entire relationship more than at this moment.

"I'm sorry, Robert. I don't know how I became so oblivious to what is important to me, but it won't happen again. You are everything to me, and I can't believe I ever thought otherwise."

"So you think everything is all right now?"

"No. I have hurt us. But I am glad to have a chance to recover. I hope you see what I'm willing to do."

"It wasn't easy to give you another chance, but here we are. I love you too much for my own good."

The silence shifted as they walked, becoming the peacefulness they had enjoyed for years, and she lifted his hand to kiss his fingers as they neared the lake at the bottom of the hill. They stopped, and she faced him, staring into his eyes before gripping him in a tight hug. After a moment, he squeezed her tight and kissed the top of her head.

We will be okay.

When his grip relaxed, she squeezed him tighter, refusing to let him go. He held on to her, and she memorized the feeling of every inch pressed against her, never wanting to let go. A tingle started buzzing between her legs. *Yes. We need to heal. Let him take me back as his wife.* After what could have been five minutes, she relaxed her grip enough to stare into his eyes.

"I love you, Robert."

"You could show it better."

She looked away to settle her sharp response, knowing he was right. They needed more quality time together to soothe his pain. The line of parked cars gave her an idea. She nodded and smiled up at him.

"I haven't thanked you yet." *This is just what the doctor ordered.*

"Nope."

Alyssa looked around. "Nobody's around. Come with me."

She scurried down the street, pulling her husband by the hand past the parked cars, hoping he would play along. They reached the stub end, where trees surrounded the lone streetlight on three sides. At the trunk of the last car on the street, she pulled Robert into a passionate kiss and rubbed his back and shoulders.

She unbuttoned her blouse and pressed her bare breasts against the rough fabric of his polo.

"No bra. Did you plan this?"

"I skipped the bra because it was hot. This is me spontaneously thanking you for another chance." She kissed him again.

She broke the kiss again to strip off her shorts and panties, then kissed him again, this time squeezing his hard cock. Her pussy throbbed, anticipating him filling her.

He pointed up. "We are right under the light."

"Everyone is at home, not walking down this dead end." *It would be so hot if someone saw.* She hopped up onto the trunk lid, leaning back with her weight on her hands and spreading her legs. "Come here, Robert. Let me thank you the way a wife should."

He opened his shorts and stepped between her legs, his erection leading the way.

He never wore underwear, but she decided to play with him by using his own words. "No underwear. Did you plan this?"

He smiled, then rubbed his cockhead up and down her slit a few times, wetting it and spreading her wider. He tapped her clit twice, firing sparks through her body.

So good. Straight to my nipples and back. She pulled his wrist, sliding his cock inside where she wanted it. "Oh yes, Babe. Come inside where it's warm for you."

She raised her knees and rolled her back down to lie on the trunk lid. When her head touched, she lifted her legs up and wide, holding them with her hands as he slid in and out. "Touch me, Babe. Make me feel good." *There it is. Hit my cervix every time. Thumb my clit. Squeeze my tits.* "Just like that."

Robert leaned back, pressing the head of his cock harder against her G-spot as he moved. His changing pace and roaming hands didn't let her body adjust to the sparks of pleasure; they rolled from one sensitive spot to the next. A hot flush sprouted in her chest and spread to her neck and tits.

She squeezed around the hard tube inside her, letting each ridge and vein massage her flaming nerves. "Here I come. You close?"

"Almost there."

"Come with me, Babe. Fill me up when I come."

She raised her head to look him in the eye. They stared at each other as he stroked. Her abs tightened. She held her breath. His cock swelled, and she let the breath in her lungs flow out in a rush as the orgasm overflowed from deep in her belly. "Babe. Now."

He shoved into her just as her pussy clamped down on his cock. Cum splashed on her cervix, inflating her orgasm. Her body curled up, pressing her legs against him and flexing her arms and abs, but not breaking her eye contact. *Yes. Look at me as you fill me.*

Her body relaxed until her head rested on the trunk lid again. Robert held her legs in his elbows as his cock softened inside her. As he slipped out, the head and a dollop of their cum ran down across her pucker, sending one last spasm through her body. Alyssa moaned. "I love that. Thank you for waiting, Babe."

She gripped his arm and pulled up to sit. "Most of all, I love you, Robert Davis." She hugged him.

"I love you, too, Alyssa." He rubbed her back. "Um, Baby? I don't think this is a brown car."

"Huh?"

"Your back. It's all dirty." He lifted her off the car. "See?"

She turned to see a black silhouette of her back and ass in the dust-covered car. Their cum rested in the crotch. Alyssa laughed. "Somebody gets to make up a good story about tonight. Wipe my back with my panties."

"Really?"

"I can't wear this white shirt with dirt all over me. Wipe me off."

Robert wiped her back, ruining the white panties. She dropped them in a trash can as they strolled up the street, arm in arm. She pulled his arm against her side. "Be ready for more when we get home."

Alyssa's adventures continue at
www.SageMallory.com/books.
Go there now.

ACKNOWLEDGMENTS

Many thanks to Tim, who helped me understand the Hayden character. Wherever you are now, may you reap your just rewards.

I must again and always thank Lyss, who pushes me down the hard road to better storytelling. I will get there one day. If there are errors or shortcomings, they are mine, not hers.

ABOUT THE AUTHOR

Sage Mallory lives near the water, working by day and creating adventures for sexy, determined, evolving women by night. Sage enjoys cooking, hiking the mountains, deep discussions, and escaping the hectic pace of life inside a great story.